VIENNA
a Novel

Eva Menasse

*Translated from the German
by Anthea Bell*

PHOENIX

A PHOENIX PAPERBACK

First published in Great Britain in 2006
by Weidenfeld & Nicolson
This paperback edition published in 2007
by Phoenix,
an imprint of Orion Books Ltd,
Orion House, 5 Upper St Martin's Lane,
London WC2H 9EA

An Hachette Livre UK company

1 3 5 7 9 10 8 6 4 2

First published in Germany in 2005
by Kiepenheuer & Witsch

A CIP catalogue record for this book
is available from the British Library.

ISBN 978-0-7538-2171-8

Typeset at The Spartan Press Ltd,
Lymington, Hants

Printed and bound in Great Britain by
Clays Ltd, St Ives plc

The Orion Publishing Group's policy is to use papers that
are natural, renewable and recyclable products and
made from wood grown in sustainable forests. The logging
and manufacturing processes are expected to conform to
the environmental regulations of the country of origin.

www.orionbooks.co.uk

EVA MENASSE was born in 1970 in Vienna, and read history and German studies. She had a successful career as a journalist, writing for the *Frankfurter Allgemeine Zeitung* in Frankfurt and as a correspondent from Prague and Berlin. She left the paper to write her first novel, *Vienna*, and now lives and works in Berlin as a freelance author.

ANTHEA BELL was educated at Somerville College, Oxford, and translates primarily from German and French. Her translations include works of non-fiction, literary and popular fiction, and books for young people including (with Derek Hockridge) the *Asterix the Gaul* saga by Goscinny and Uderzo. Recent translations include E.T.A. Hoffmann's *The Life and Opinions of the Tomcat Murr* (Penguin Classics, 1999), W. G. Sebald's *Austerlitz* (Hamish Hamilton, 2001) and Sigmund Freud's *The Psychopathology of Everyday Life* (Penguin, 2002). She has received a number of translation awards, including the 2002 Schlegel-Tieck award (UK), Independent Foreign Fiction Prize (UK) and Helen and Kurt Wollf prize (USA), all three for the translation of W. G. Sebald's *Austerlitz*; the 2003 Schlegel-Tieck award for the translation of Karen Duve's *Rain* (Bloomsbury); and the 2003 Austrian State Prize for Literary Translation.

The Beginning

My father's birth was a precipitate delivery. He and a fur coat were sacrificed to my grandmother's passion for bridge, since although her labour pains were beginning she insisted on finishing the game. Except for a single dramatic occasion, my grandmother had finished every game she ever played in her life; breaking off in the middle of a game was unthinkable. Consequently she almost missed my father's birth as she sat playing cards. Or rather, that was why my father almost came into the world under a green baize card table, which would in fact have suited his character and way of life pretty well.

Bridge was my grandmother's sole pleasure in life. She was sitting in the Café Bauernfeind with her friends playing bridge, as she had done almost daily since marrying my grandfather and moving from a small Moravian village to Vienna. It was her way of coping with a world which she very seldom liked. She shut her eyes to it, went to the coffee-house and played bridge.

On the day when my father was born the game went on a long time. More coffee was ordered. The pains didn't seem to be getting any stronger, and the ladies playing bridge with my grandmother weren't bothered about them anyway. When it came to settling up, the ritual argument between the players broke out. One of them never paid her gambling debts straight away but always asked for more time, thus creating confusion. Yet the money amounted to only a few groschen. Sometimes one of the players might win a whole schilling, but she was sure to lose it again next day. All things considered, the outcome was never of any significance, but none the less the ladies argued shrilly and were cross with each other. Two of them were not particularly good at arithmetic, and the other two, one of them being my grandmother, had poor eyesight but wouldn't admit it.

The lady who always totted up the winnings was one of the two who were poor at arithmetic. She often mixed up the columns, whether from lack of concentration or dishonesty no one now knows, for she got the sums wrong to her own disadvantage too. In addition, she had very crabbed, ornate writing, particularly with figures.

The third lady, the one who always wanted credit, was prepared to pay only her debts of two days ago. She had lost money the day before too, but she lost more then. And she lost most of all on the day of my father's birth, so she wanted to pay that day's debts least. I don't know anything about the fourth lady.

The head waiter in the Café Bauernfeind was a long time coming to be paid for the coffee. He was a good-looking man known all over town, and the ladies, with the exception of my grandmother, used to conduct childish flirtations with him. My grandmother never flirted. Something in her had frozen over early; she was a pale, sandy-haired beauty who never showed the world a face of anything but stern irony. She ranted and raged only at home. Her bosom was fabulous. The head waiter at the Café Bauernfeind treated her with particular courtesy. He was at least ten years her junior, and as for what the bridge-playing ladies imagined him and my grandmother doing, they wouldn't for the life of them have said it out loud, not even in private to each other. Yet the head waiter at the Café Bauernfeind probably felt nothing but respect for my grandmother's unapproachability, and she may never even really have noticed him. All she did notice, with annoyance, on the day of my father's birth was that the waiter was slow in arriving with the bill. The ladies rummaged in their purses and fidgeted on the plush seats. My grandmother was jittery. It was getting dark, and her pains were growing stronger.

My uncle, who was seven years old at the time, woke up when the light came on. He slept on a narrow sofa placed crosswise at the foot of his parents' double bed. He woke up because it was suddenly bright in the room and because his mother was shouting. She was lying across the matrimonial bed in her fur coat, a black Persian lamb. My grandfather was shouting too, but from the doorway. In addition my father was shouting, having just slipped out and ruined the fur coat, as the story always went later.

My father was shouting because that's normal for a new-born baby. All his life my father would conscientiously try to act in what he considered the normal way, even if his efforts were seldom in point of fact successful. Indeed, my grandmother's attitude to this last pregnancy of hers, and the birth itself, called for conduct as normal as possible on his part. For my grandmother, already over forty, had not wanted a third child, and had tried to get rid of it by means of knitting needles, hot hip-baths and jumping off the table. She liked to tell this story later.

But my father had avoided the knitting needles, and clung on tight when she jumped off the table; that's how it must have been, my family always said later, nodding. No one mentioned the hot baths. Then my father tried to please her by slipping out quickly and painlessly, but it was rare for anyone to be able to please my grandmother at all. My father had ruined first the bridge party and now the black Persian lamb, one of the generous gifts with which my grandfather tried to atone for his countless infidelities. My grandmother deigned to accept these gifts without a word, and went to the coffee-house to play bridge.

My grandmother was shouting because the midwife

wasn't there yet. Because the baby was still attached by the umbilical cord and there was blood everywhere. And because my grandfather seemed unable either to get the older child, my uncle, out of the room as my grandmother thought proper, or to put on his outdoor clothes and go to fetch a doctor or the midwife.

My grandfather, whose preferred tone of voice was in fact a low-voiced, morose mumble, was shouting because my grandmother was shouting. Otherwise he would hardly have made himself heard. In addition his own nerves were all on edge. The picture presented to him on his matrimonial bed was both grotesque and fascinating. It must have been slightly reminiscent of Greek mythology, not that my grandfather was familiar with the subject: a creature that was half human, half a black sheep seemed to have been born. For from a sense of modesty in front of her husband and her son, my grandmother was holding her fur coat firmly together over the lower part of her body. She lay half curled up on her side, her body around my father, whose head was all that emerged from the coat. He looked particularly blood-stained and new-born against that black, furry background.

'It's all your fault,' shouted my grandmother, 'you fetched me too late!'

'Where's my scarf?' shouted my grandfather from the doorway. 'You should have come home sooner!'

'You landed me with this baby!' shouted my grandmother. 'In the cupboard by the door.'

'I suppose you absolutely had to get to the end of the game,' shouted my grandfather. 'Which cupboard?'

'What shiksa were you gadding about with?' shouted my grandmother. 'Are you blind? The cupboard beside the door, I said.'

'Oh, give it a rest,' said my grandfather in a tone of resignation, having found his scarf and preparing to go out. For, as everyone who knew him even slightly was aware, his mistresses were invariably Jewish and most of them were married into the bargain. He was intimately acquainted with only a single shiksa – the woman he had married.

It was in these circumstances that my father came into the world, the son of a Jewish commercial traveller in wines and spirits and a Catholic Sudeten German woman who had left the Church.

A few weeks later Aunt Gustl, one of my grandfather's sisters, came to take a look at the baby. Aunt Gustl had married a rich Christian, and thereafter acted the great lady. Her father, my great-grandfather, had already kicked up a tremendous family row about his son my grandfather's decision to marry out. Although my grandmother came from near Freudenthal and not Bratislava, whenever the conversation came around to her he would begin to declaim, disapprovingly, the old rhyming couplet: 'A goy for Vesuvius left Bratislava, she was planning for free to get hold of some lava.' Only the most essential contact was maintained. My grandfather's parents, who came from Tarnów, had stayed where immigration had washed them up: 'Matzos Island', the Leopoldstadt area close to the Augarten park, in one of those grey streets where it's chilly and damp even in summer, and the stairwells smell of mould and cabbage. 'Fishmongers and pious folk,' said my grandfather scornfully, 'tasteless, cheap and vulgar.' He moved to Döbling, the district favoured by doctors and lawyers, notaries and opera divas, property owners and silk manufacturers. The fact that he could afford only the outskirts of Döbling, near the Gürtel, made no difference. It was Döbling all the same.

When Aunt Gustl told her father about her forthcoming marriage she felt confident that the loud and terrifying rages of the old days would by now have died down to a small, depressed residue, for Aunt Gustl had been an extremely tough character from her youth. 'Is he a Jew?' her father asked, and at that moment he must have appeared to Aunt Gustl delightfully weak and helpless. She was wearing around her shoulders her new fox stole with its shiny little eyes, a recent present from her wildly enamoured fiancé, and she was both inwardly and outwardly triumphant. 'He is not a Jew, he's a bank manager,' she replied, a saying that became proverbial in my family and has been used ever since for those regarded as harmless fools. For such, it soon turned out, was kind-hearted Adolf 'Dolly' Königsberger, also known to us as 'Königsbee', who died young.

After their wedding Aunt Gustl's hubris came into full and succulent bloom. As her first and unequivocal step, Bank Manager Königsberger's wife changed the coffee-house where she played cards, for there were class differences between coffee-houses. She was no longer to be seen in either the Bauernfeind or the Zögernitz, but was said to sit at the card tables in the Ringstrasse, where the good life had swollen the wives of senior civil servants and the widows of manufacturers to such corpulence that their pearl necklaces rested horizontally, in several strands, on their white-powdered décolletés. Aunt Gustl was not quite so opulent yet, but she was tending that way.

She seldom went to see her parents in the little street near the Augarten either. Instead, she attended the opera and the theatre on smart, dim Dolly's arm, and she went to Baden to take the waters. She aimed to join the upper middle class, she played rummy and dice poker with impoverished baronesses, and for tactical reasons she sometimes curbed her ambition and let the baronesses win. She was employing both cunning and brute force in an attempt to move up two classes at once, instead of accepting, as my grandfather did, that to climb one step, from Matzos Island to Döbling, from immigrant book-keeper (the father) to Vienna-born commercial traveller in wines and spirits (the son) was the maximum humanly possible. But what infuriated my grandfather most was the showy crucifix set with precious stones

6

that she now wore around her neck, 'that sanctified mill-stone', as he called it. She really had worn it from the day she married Königsberger the bank manager and not just, as ill-intentioned members of the family said later, after the Nazis marched in.

So Aunt Gustl bent over my father to deliver her opinion, coming so close that her crucifix dangled just above his little nose, and said, 'Looks like the head waiter from the Bauernfeind.' My father gazed at her with his baby-blue eyes, which were to stay that colour all his life, grabbed the crucifix and tore it off.

Then my grandfather refused to pay for the broken chain, because he thought it impossible for a baby to tear apart a chain which didn't have at least one defective link already. She should be glad the child had torn it off and she hadn't lost the millstone in the coffee-house, he told his sister, because how did she know how honest her Christian friends were? On the other hand, he said with derision, she'd probably have heard the clunk of such a great lump of metal falling anywhere.

Later, when the conversation came around to Aunt Gustl, he always said, 'Yes, well, a chain is only as strong as its weakest link.' Judged by my grandfather's usual stand-ards, this was almost shockingly close to cliché. He said no more, because he didn't like to talk about Aunt Gustl, not after she passed him by without a word once during the Nazi period. And the gold crucifix on her bosom had been clearly in view, so my family always said.

My father's first years of life were fairly ordinary. He went to the coffee-house every day, holding his stern and beauti-ful mother's hand, was made to sit down with my grand-mother's bridge partners, who noticed nothing anyway except their hands of cards – and out of the corners of their eyes, the head waiter – and was told off for swinging his legs. In between games, when the attention of two of the players could be temporarily devoted entirely to the head waiter as he skipped around the café, while the lady totting up the winnings was writing her tiny little figures without concentrating properly, my grandmother would sometimes hiss, 'Sit up straight.'

My father was a quiet, friendly child. He could play bridge before he could talk. According to family legend, his first word was 'rubber'. The extremely un-childlike concentration with which my father followed the fortunes of the cards for hours on end was extraordinary, and would have attracted attention in any other family. In ours, however, anything else would have been considered disastrous.

At the age of four my father had his own pack of cards. A year later, when he made his first attempts to give my grandmother's bridge partners tips on the sly, by rolling his eyes when they played certain cards, his brother was forced to look after the smaller child in the afternoons. So my uncle reluctantly took my father to the nearby little park and its small, untidy stretches of green turf. While my uncle and his friends went off to play with a home-made football, my father sat on the ground dealing out games of patience. Sometimes he managed to interest another child in his cards, and then they played snap together. Of course there was always some small prize at stake. With his charming, baby-blue smile my father, who always won, ended the game by raking in marbles, groschen and Manner-brand toffees. At the age of six he began organising snap matches in the park. Girls a year or two older than he was particularly liked to play. My father could never understand why girls were strictly excluded from all the boys' games in the park. He liked girls from the first, and was both patient and friendly with those whom he taught to play cards. He didn't even seem to notice that this made him look ridiculous to the other boys. Beaming, he would invite anyone who was interested to join in his card games, asking them to put their stakes down first. The older boys, my uncle's friends, just laughed at him and his cards. But once he was rather well off for childish treasures, his pocket bulging with marbles, they tried to win something back from him. When they couldn't, they almost admired him for a brief while, but in the end, and in a higher sense probably correctly, they decided that he was a scamp. They beat him up soundly and took his winnings away by force.

When my father and my uncle went home after a day of this kind they feared the fuss my grandmother kicked up. She would blame my uncle for not looking after his brother well enough, calling him a 'useless good-for-nothing' and a 'dangerous ne'er-do-well', and she would seize my father by the shoulders and shake him roughly because he had got dirty. She would tell him he was 'filthy as a guttersnipe'. She would take my grandfather to task for 'landing her with these two little pests'. My grandmother was very creative in her domestic tirades. Right at the end of her life, when she could barely tell her children and grandchildren apart, let alone the countless different tablets she had to take, when she was kept alive only by her rage against the world she was preparing to leave – and she held even that against it – her art in delivering inventive insults attained its height. She reserved her harshest words for the nursing nun, who in spite of all her cutting and nasty remarks looked after her in the most exemplary way, fed her, washed her and put the bedpan under her. My father, whose natural desire for harmony assumed exaggerated dimensions as he grew older, took the nun out of the room with a murmured apology. Outside the door he spoke to her imploringly, fiddling with one hand at a hangnail on the other and looking at the ground like a schoolboy; in short, he was the picture of misery and embarrassment. Back in my grandmother's room he said reproachfully, 'Oh, Mother, and with all she does for you!'

'What does she do for me?' snarled my grandmother.

'She washes you, she looks after you, she's very good to

you,' said my embarrassed father, who found my grandmother's spiteful treatment of the nun just as unpleasant as
having to remind his mother of her physical fragility.

'Good, is she? What do you know about it?' snarled my
grandmother. 'She's a snake in wolf's clothing!'

These were the prospects facing the two boys as they made
their way home. My father was crying, because he hated
physical tussles more than anything else in the world. He
didn't like coming close to other boys or men at all, a
characteristic later deplored by some people and severely
criticised by others, because this aversion represented the
only but considerable obstacle to the development of his
astonishing talent for football. As he walked along beside my
uncle, who was silently cursing him – my uncle never said
much, often not even when he was asked a question – he
kept his head bent and looked down at his feet. At every
step he took, a strap torn loose from his sandal flapped on
the cobblestones. His ankle was scratched. The hem of his
trousers was torn. His right knee was bleeding and his left
knee was bruised. But worst of all was that he had lost his
cards, all but one. The boys beating him up had demon-
stratively torn most of them to pieces, less out of sadism than
to add the last emphatic touch to their grim determination
that no more cards should be played in the little park. When
he finally managed to tear himself free and run away he had
been obliged to abandon the rest of them, including the
pretty snap cards showing acorns and bells. It must be said,
to my uncle's credit, that he had defended his little brother
as heroically as was in his power. But even as a child my
uncle was particularly small and slight, and he stayed that
way. In his wedding picture he still looks more like a
twelve-year-old Frank Sinatra than the much-decorated
jungle fighter that, remarkably, he really was at the time.

My father had only one card left. He had clutched it tight
in panic and without thinking, and even during all the

kicking and punching he hadn't let it go. By the time he opened up his clenched fist on the way home, it was little more than a small dumpling sodden with fear. Once he unfolded it, however, it turned out that he had managed to save the Queen of Hearts. He took that as a good omen, for up to that year of his life, his eighth, my father was an optimist.

When they got home nothing was the same as usual. Fiery-eyed Aunt Gustl, a rare visitor, passed them on the stairs. Without a word of greeting she hurried down to the front door of the building, wafted along on a cloud of perfume, but from the doorway she gave them a last glance that was almost human. Their mother was sitting in the kitchen, and looked as if she had finally frozen solid. She stared at the two of them for a little while, and only then, automatically, did she begin to tell them off. But somehow she didn't have the strength for it, it was as if she were telling them off out of a sense of duty, to keep a tradition going although for the last half-hour it hadn't existed. Even on that day she was telling people off, my family said later, both appreciatively and with a slight shudder, and then they would smile and nod.

My grandfather was at home too, pacing nervously up and down with his order book under his arm, for no real reason and solely out of habit, that suddenly superfluous book which until a few days ago he had been carrying around from coffee-house to coffee-house, from corner shop to corner shop, from inn to inn, in order to take down orders for wines and spirits. Outwardly he was the same as ever, well groomed, his hair combed while it was damp, in a freshly ironed made-to-measure shirt with a monogram, always with something of the look of a dandy, a playboy about him. But his nervous restlessness was far greater than usual.

From that day on my uncle, who until now had wanted nothing to do with my little father, assumed responsibility for him entirely of his own accord. He took off his brother's ruined shoes, washed his knees and put him to bed.

They had to move in two days' time, they hadn't been given long. Herr Hermann, who lived on the ground floor with his wife and son, had delivered the message in courteous and correct tones. Herr Hermann had once been a footballer. My grandfather, one of the most fervent football fans ever born, had seen many of his games. Josef Hermann, known as Pepi, had played in the 'Wunderteam', admittedly only as a defender, but still he had been in it. In the sports papers that my grandfather read avidly at the coffee-house, they used to say things at the time like: 'Pepi Hermann has always been considered a useful, good, honest and fair player, but in Sunday's match he showed yet again that he is one of the ablest tacticians we have.' However, it was not so much these comments as Pepi Hermann's rock-like invincibility in his own penalty area that, in my grandfather's knowledgeable eyes, placed him somewhere in the middle ranks of footballing gods.

After the end of his playing career Herr Hermann lived quietly. Unlike my grandfather, who travelled to the Hohe Warte by tram to see the match every weekend, he went to the stadium only rarely and on special occasions, usually when the functionaries of the First Vienna Football Club obsequiously invited him to sit in the VIP grandstand. Herr Hermann probably required some financial inducement. His wife was in poor health and his son had no talent for football. 'Does he play?' he had replied indignantly on the stairs when my grandfather asked that question. 'He most certainly plays! But guess what, he plays the violin!' It was this Hermann-Pepi, to give him his name turned back to front in the Viennese manner, who had brought them the news, and on the same day he also brought them Herr Eisenstein, who ran his leather goods business in a basement a few buildings away. Herr Eisenstein was very old, at least in the eyes of my eight-year-old father, but very amusing. It wasn't just that you could always borrow money from him in the last resort when it had run out at home and all other resources failed; Herr Eisenstein had long been both an ardent and a hopeless admirer of my beautiful but cool grandmother. It was claimed that he was the only person who could sometimes make her laugh. No, what my father never forgot about Herr Eisenstein was that he had once shown him, at least in theory and with the aid of a few patches of leather, how to stitch a football together.

All at once the world had become an adventure, a game of chance that he didn't yet know how to play. Lost in reverie, my father sat high up on the van taking the family's furniture and a few crates through the city, far away from the little local park on the Gürtel and to a district where there were wonderful big green spaces but the narrow streets smelled of mould and cabbage. He had already forgotten the expression on the face of Hermann's non-sporting son when he suddenly turned up in the apartment with his violin case, looking embarrassed and yet showing a touch of wounding self-confidence that was visible for the first time that day. And he would soon forget those few dismal months with his grandmother in her apartment near the Augarten too, the lack of space, the lamentations of the old lady, who had only recently been widowed – 'A bit of luck for Grandfather anyway,' the family used to say later – he forgot the unpleasant smell emanating from her many black skirts, and how he couldn't help wanting to laugh when he thought that, fat, black-clad and asthmatic as she was, she could hardly climb the five floors up and down and thus couldn't leave the apartment any more. He was allowed to go to the Augarten now and then, closely guarded by his brother. Soon it got too cold for that. He forgot the evening whisperings of his parents, who no longer went to the coffee-house, and the tearful visits of his big sister Katzi, who had always seemed to him less like a sister than a beautiful, far-away, affectionate goddess. But he never forgot that his brother, my uncle, was always making him approach Katzi's stout fiancé to beg for pocket money for both boys. Most of it, however, he forgot for decades, and some of it for ever, since my father used to forget the less pleasing aspects of life very quickly, or alternatively he made an amusing joke of them.

On the day before her two sons left, my grandmother had them photographed at the Purr & Kubla studio. In the photo, she was as cool and straight-backed as ever. The children wore suits and perfectly knotted ties, and my grandfather had secretly had monograms embroidered on their shirts, an unauthorised and completely unnecessary expense, and my grandmother had made him pay for it with her usual reproaches. Unfortunately there was nothing to be done about my father's jug-ears, and my uncle, whose ears were set neatly beside his head, as my grandmother noted with satisfaction, looked hardly any older than his brother, although he was already fifteen. The photographer treated my grandmother with deference. Her clear, correct manner of speech, without a trace of dialect, made him take her for a German, as many others would too, which was an advantage at the time. It was the only reason why she had been able to make an appointment at all, that and the fact that the wife of Königsberger the bank manager was a regular customer, or it would hardly have been possible so soon before Christmas.

Purr & Kubla was a well-known studio and produced handsome, stiff-looking pictures. So it must have been the haste and the way the appointment had been quickly fitted in, or perhaps the master's mind was not entirely on the job because of either my grandmother's majestic appearance or the turbulent times, but whatever the reason, the photographs show the two boys looking scared to death. These last pictures are a little blurred around the edges too.

Next day they went to the railway station, the

Westbahnhof. They took a taxi, yet another entirely un-necessary expense, these days too, but this time my grand-mother had opposed it only as an automatic reaction. My father immediately and for ever forgot the moment when he said goodbye to his parents in the station concourse, because crowds of other children were already waiting on the platform, apparently just for him. He began playing with them at once, with a wide and confiding smile on his face. Suddenly some of them turned rough and pulled at the tassel on his warm, pointed cap – 'They wanted to pull off the woolly ball on the end of it,' he said later – he defended himself, he wept, then he uttered a piercing yell, and finally my uncle forced the worst of his tormentors to go away. In the end, when they got into the train the tassel had some-how disappeared anyway, pulled off and left behind some-where on the Westbahnhof platform. My father was soon laughing again. The train hissed. He was sitting in a com-partment next to a pretty little tear-stained girl, and he enticingly took the cards with the pictures of bells and acorns out of his pocket. The little girl had never played snap before. She had nothing to bet on the game either, no marbles, no buttons, no Manner toffees. After a brief pause for reflection, my father played with her all the same. She was pretty enough. It was true that he won game after game – 'Well, what would you expect?' he used to say later in comparable cases, when he had preferred beauty to brains – but in the end he even gave her a Manner toffee, as a kind of comfort. Outside, Austria passed by. The people looking after them were solicitous, the older children, including my uncle, were upset and depressed. My father noticed none of that. In a station far from home, improbably kindly women handed fruit and chocolate in through the windows for the children. The German they spoke sounded funny. My father was enjoying himself, and waved like mad. The women smiled back.

★

My father woke up in a hospital, burning with fever. Nurses in tall white caps spoke to him, shook him, shouted at him, but he couldn't understand a word they said. All the children had disappeared, including his brother my uncle, and so had his cards. For the first time in his life my father was alone, and desperate. He shed baby-blue tears. He bit his lips nervously. When one of the nurses saw him doing that she slapped his mouth with the palm of her hand in passing, and when he anxiously asked about a little need of his, she didn't understand and turned away. So my father wet the bed. That was not to be the worst of it. The nurse soon detected the worst because of the smell. Then, at the age of eight, there he was sitting on a toddler's potty among all those tall beds. The cross nurse's wooden clogs clattered up and down on the stone floor between the long rows of beds. She left him sitting on the potty as a punishment. His bare feet were icy cold. A hundred years later, when darkness had fallen, he was found by a nurse on night duty doing her rounds. She shook her head, made some noises that sounded kind, and put him back to bed. She even warmed his little feet with her hands for a moment.

My father had unusually small feet, even when he grew up. 'The best footballers have small feet,' he liked to say, and we children would always take our shoes off and compare our feet with his. Even at the age of ten my brother had bigger feet than my father, and that was the start of one of the many childhood traumas he allegedly suffered. When he was a student, and for his first philosophy class wrote an essay on the relationship between utility and beauty, my brother managed to work in a paragraph about the mutilation of Asian women by foot-binding. 'Anyone who has ever seen the severely crippled feet of high-class Chinese women will realise that the attempt to impose ideals of beauty by force leads straight to totalitarianism,' the nine-teen-year-old wrote fervently. 'We human beings are all equal, but we do not look the same. We all serve society in our own way. The foot is for walking and running, and if it can no longer do those things it is useless. Furthermore, its size and shape say nothing at all about the worth of a human being.' 'Very good,' his professor wrote in the margin of the essay; he knew nothing about football, and was one of the few who didn't ask my brother questions about his name and the family relationship that therefore sprang to mind.

My sister had medium-sized feet and claimed, on those grounds, that she would be a medium-good footballer. 'Girls don't play football,' said my father, baffled and shaking his head, 'better take your tennis racket and knock up against the wall.'

As my father found out, the kind nurse, a young Indian girl, worked only at night. Next day the cross nurse was back. The clatter of her wooden clogs announced her arrival from afar. She brought food that my father didn't want. He turned his head away. She held his chin in one hand, forced his mouth open with the other and pushed the food, a brown mush, into it. My father retched. She pushed the food down with the fork as if force-feeding a goose. He swallowed. At the fifth forkful he threw up. She asked him, 'Did you like the food?' He stared at her, not understanding. She asked, 'How are you, you little brat?' Then she asked, 'How are you doing?' She said, 'Say: Very well, thank you.' He stared at her. She shouted, 'Say it! Say: Very well, thank you!' My father looked at the brown mush on the bedspread in front of him, and he looked at her fork. He felt ill. Any moment now he would start crying again. He said quietly, 'Very well, thank you.'

Next day the doctors did their rounds, a great many of them, with glasses and friendly faces, accompanied by a murmuring white troop of nurses. One doctor bent over my father, felt his forehead and his cheeks, and asked, 'How are you doing?' 'His' nurse, the cross one, was standing in the background. My father could feel her looking at him. 'Very well, thank you,' he whispered.

'Scarlet fever,' said the doctor to one of his companions, 'look at him. No doubt about it. Scarlet fever,' he told my father in friendly tones, 'that's what you've caught.'

'Very well, thank you,' whispered my father. The doctor smiled and patted his head. 'Good boy,' he said.

The phrase became symptomatic of his life. He used it to his foster-parents when he was exhausted after standing for hours in the same place with a great many other children, waiting for someone to take him home too. My uncle described the whole process later as a sale of children – 'No offence meant,' he said, 'but that's what it was.' However, it was my uncle himself who had drawn it out at length for my little father, because at first he absolutely refused to let him go on his own. Most of the couples who came wanted just one child, preferably a little girl. In fact many of them would have taken the little boy with the baby-blue eyes, but no one wanted two boys at once, particularly when the other was already fifteen and past school age. There was a Jewish tailor who was looking for an apprentice and spoke a bit of Yiddish German, and he finally won my uncle round. The tailor, who was reminded by my uncle's almost transparently slight figure and thin fingers of his own early days as an apprentice, and who urgently needed help, pointed out that his little brother would be better off with a family out in the country. He offered to wait around and be interpreter until a suitable family was found.

The suitable man was warm-hearted but awkward. He was 'very rustic', as my father would probably have said of anyone else, but he never uttered the slightest derogatory word about his foster-father. The suitable woman was tougher than her husband, with the snippy self-confidence that comes from resentment of one's own insecurity. The husband, on the other hand, was easy-going and kindly; the points on which nothing could move him showed up only later. He bent down to my father, who was tired to death and had only just recovered from the scarlet fever, and asked if he would like to say goodbye to his brother now, and then go to Stopsley with them. 'Very well, thank you,' said my father.

My father entirely lost any sense of the general application of this remark, and could no longer say when he really meant it and when it was a lie. In cases of doubt he would always have assumed that the remark and he himself were truthful. To admit that it was often a lie would have meant recognising the frequent incongruity between facts and what was said about them, the inner truth and the outward appearance. However, all his life my father loved congruity and harmony, so he used the remark to mollify not just a challenging environment but most of all himself. Nine years later, after his return home and when he was taking lessons from a sick old woman teacher to revive his German, he tried hard to find the right, the perfect translation for it in the patient monotone of her didactic utterances. If it was to be perfect it couldn't be literal; he was seeking the parallel German term for his real or apparent well-being. During his German lesson one day, the old lady's neighbour brought in some ration coupons as payment to the retired teacher for coaching her daughter. The woman rang the bell, the tired old teacher opened the door, took the coupons, my father pricked up his ears as they exchanged words. '*Und sonst?*' asked the neighbour. How was she otherwise? '*Alles bestens, danke,*' replied the old teacher – everything was fine, thank you, she said – and she closed the door. So my father had found the turn of phrase he needed, and it proved much more adaptable than the original English. In good and bad times alike, he was now always anxious to show that 'everything was fine'. He learned to put it as a question ('Well? Everything fine?') in such a way that any other answer was practically impossible. When he hurried to hospital to visit my brother, who had broken his leg during a school skiing expedition, he found him weeping bitterly in his hospital bed. Still weeping bitterly, my brother pointed to his leg in plaster, stretched upright and hanging in traction. My father nodded sympathetically, glanced at the strapping Salzburg nurses, at the remains of a golden-yellow schnitzel still standing on the bedside locker. 'But otherwise,' he asked, 'everything fine?'

Chutzpah

Nothing had been heard of Aunt Gustl for years when she phoned one day, announcing in accusing tones that she was on her deathbed. 'I don't ask anything,' she said imperiously, 'I don't need anything. I just want to see you once again.'

'For heaven's sake,' said my father in alarm, 'I'll come at once. Can I bring you something? Is there anything you'd like?'

'I told you, I don't need anything. It's a long time since I wanted anything. Just come and see me,' commanded Aunt Gustl.

'Some little thing,' begged my father, who on principle never went to see anyone empty-handed, but at the same time was always terrified of bringing the wrong thing. 'Something sweet?'

'Do you want to kill me?' inquired Aunt Gustl indignantly. 'I'm nothing but skin and bone!'

'All the same,' cried my father, 'you have to eat!'

'Why would I need to eat when I'm dying?' Aunt Gustl contradicted him, and then graciously relented. 'Well, an apple strudel, if you'd be so kind.'

As it turned out, my father's cousin Ferdinand, known as Nandl, Aunt Gustl's total failure of a son, was in prison yet again. This time, much to the amusement of the local papers, he had been caught shoplifting with twenty metres of insulated cord and two pieces of cheesecake in his trouser pockets. 'Why Did Thief Take Insulated Cord?' the *Kurier* asked itself, smirking, and went on to describe in detail the greasy marks left by the cheesecake on Nandl's trousers to right and left of the upper thigh area. However, the suggestion that Nandl was frisked at the supermarket checkout because of those greasy marks is a malicious rumour, remembered in my family merely as proof that his native stupidity was oozing its way out, so to speak. No, Nandl was picked up because he already had form.

His many previous convictions meant that the case of the insulated cord and the cheesecake instantly earned him six months. According to my father, Nandl was the dimmest criminal in the country. He specialised in cheque fraud, a craft he practised so clumsily that he was usually arrested within days. My father claimed that whenever a forged cheque turned up, or cheques were reported stolen, the first thing anyone did was to find out whether Ferdinand K. was currently in prison or 'on the outside'. That, claimed my father, was the way every investigation of cheque fraud, without exception, began in Austria – they checked to see whether Nandl could or could not be the fraudster.

A typical way of putting it in my family was to call Nandl's trouble congenital, for he was undoubtedly the victim of a disastrous inheritance. Although he was as tall and good-looking as his father Dolly, and could be as charming and seductive as his mother when she wanted something (as she usually did), he had inherited Dolly's limited intelligence in fatal combination with Gustl's criminal energy. 'To look at him, you'd think he could make a living conning girls into getting engaged to him,' my grandmother had remarked in Nandl's youth, before he committed his first offence, 'but he's too stupid even for that.' The 'even' derived from the fact that my grandmother had a still lower opinion of women in general than she did of men.

'Criminal energy?' asked my sister, painting her nails. 'Would you actually call Aunt Gustl criminal?' But just at this moment the subject was changed, because my brother, who had turned right against all the family's traditions and rituals when he began studying at university, and particularly against its articles of faith – that is to say, its basic stock of anecdotes – launched into a speech for the defence on behalf of Dolly Königsbee. Dolly, he said, hadn't been a fool; on the contrary, he'd been brilliant. 'He wasn't dim-witted,' my brother informed us, 'it's just that his brilliance was impaired in a single area, the use of language.' He rested his chin on his hand, with his cigarette almost setting fire to the locks of hair above his ear.

'Sit up straight,' my father told him, 'and you shouldn't smoke so much.' My uncle just shook his head. He thought my brother was 'going through an awkward phrase', but had never said so straight out. 'How can anyone who's too stupid even to get the hang of ordinary expressions be brilliant?' my grandfather always asked, baffled. 'But Grandpa,' my brother would say condescendingly, 'you don't think he made those mistakes by accident, do you?'

Dolly Königsbee had entered my family's treasury of anecdotes because there was hardly an idiomatic expression or foreign word that he hadn't twisted and distorted. It was his undoing to love foreign words but at the same time to have a truly terrible memory. He loved his *Dictionary of Principal Idioms*, his *Manual of Polished Language*, his *Quotations From Antiquity*. Unlike his wife, he was not in the least vain, but he believed that it suited the dignity of a bank manager to introduce the occasional classical quotation into his remarks when he was talking to his staff. He thought it was cultured, and his example would inspire the employees to improve their own education. 'Pater semper imperfectus,' he used to advise them with a kindly smile. 'We never stop learning.'

As a result Dolly Königsbee was a popular character in my family. Dozens of his grotesque verbal distortions were in circulation among us, and new ones were invented; when a politician or a footballer perpetrated a howler, and it was mentioned in those newspaper columns entitled 'Gleanings' or 'Quotes', my family rejoiced. 'That could have been a real Dollyism!' When they spoke of him as Nandl's amiable but helpless father, he was 'Dolly'; when they spoke of him as Aunt Gustl's henpecked husband, he was 'poor Dolly', but at the same time he was venerated for those Dollyisms.

The older generation, who had known the bank manager personally before his early death, even tried to assume his own touchingly self-satisfied smile when they began a sentence by saying, 'as Königsbee would have said'; the younger generation had to struggle with the fact that after a while this introduction came to be omitted, because the origin of such phrases seemed sufficiently well known. So in her childhood my sister was found to be using phrases such as 'we could waggle about the price' or 'they went ground and ground the houses', or crossly calling her fellow pupils 'blighted sepulchres', expressions common in the family. My brother, in fact, actually benefited from Dolly later; he gave his famous essay on the sports administrator Felix Popelnik, whose past as a concentration camp guard he uncovered, the title of 'Like Felix from the Ashes?', a classic Dollyism.

As soon as a certain amount of Dollyisms that happened to suit a subject had been uttered, or if there was an outsider present to whom we could explain the Dolly phenomenon all over again, my family automatically embarked on a kind of competition to find the best. 'I've been rioting for three weeks and I still haven't lost an ounce,' chuckled my father. 'Mind you don't duck things up,' my mother would promptly reply. 'It's his evil freeman,' my uncle went on. 'Yes, but he uses it as a walking-horse,' his wife Aunt Ka would say. 'You're recriminating against him,' my brother would complain histrionically. 'And you're all snakes in wolf's clothing,' my sister would add, wrinkling her brow with concentration, but then my mother would kick her under the table.

'Dolly was a genius,' my brother happily concluded yet another of these well-rehearsed family performances, 'I always said so, and in the last dessert anything else is only primary.'

Aunt Gustl sat enthroned in bed, propped on her pillows, her hair done and her face made up, greedily forking apple strudel into herself. The food in the Sisters of Mercy Nursing Home has never had a very good reputation. All the same, at the first mouthful she froze expressively. '*What* is this?' she asked with revulsion.

'Apple strudel,' replied my father apprehensively.

'Where did you get it?'

'The Aida,' said my father.

'How could you?' she said scornfully, shook her head and slowly went on eating. No one knows to this day why, among all the torments Aunt Gustl thought up for him later, this was what most infuriated my father. 'Oh, I don't want anything, I never ask for anything,' he would still mimic her grimly, years after she had died, 'but an apple strudel must come from Demel's even if I'm on my deathbed.'

Aunt Gustl was planning to do something for her son 'for absolutely the very last time'. And my father was called in to help her, because for the moment she couldn't even get up and dressed. She needed a pair of tights ('from Palmers, of course, where else? Those Gazelle tights pinch you in the crotch!'), she needed a new blouse, she needed someone to take her dark suit to the cleaners and collect it again, she needed someone to take her pearls to the jeweller's because the catch was broken, and most of all she needed an appointment with Dr Schneuzl. Dr Schneuzl was a departmental head in the Justice Ministry, and Dolly, God rest his soul, had played tennis with his father about a hundred years ago. Dolly gave Dr Schneuzl credit to start up the tennis club near the Prater, remember? . . . Dr Schneuzl would be able to do something, maybe anyway, we'd see, we must try it anyway.

My father objected. He knew nothing at all about tights. He'd have to ask my mother. My mother would ask him furiously if his 'family mania', as she called it, went so far that he and his 'excessive solicitude' didn't even stop short at 'that old shitface', dying or not. 'Oh please, the children!' my father would say, horrified, as soon as my mother had uttered the words 'old shitface'. 'Oh, please!' she would mimic him. 'Whereas you couldn't care less that your father is turning in his grave!' With advancing age my grandfather, who had previously shown his dislike of other people by ignoring them or at the most making sharp remarks, had developed an obsessive hatred for his sister Gustl which culminated in the repeated use of the expression 'old shit-face'. In the end he never called her Gustl in conversation any more, he no longer employed his old, ironic appellation of 'Madam the Doctor Doctor Bank Manager's wife', referring to the two doctoral degrees earned by poor Dolly who had died young. He had called him, affectionately, Doctor Dolly-Dolly, because he liked Dolly – 'he was a decent human being, unlike some,' my grandfather had said at the time, but that was as far as he would go with a side-swipe at Gustl before the war. Later he never described his sister as anything but 'that old shitface'. We thought it was senile dementia, particularly when he refused to give any reason for it. 'I shall take the reason to my grave, and it will lie easy with me there,' he is said to have told my brother once, but unfortunately my brother mentioned that only long after our grandfather's death, so some of my family doubted the authenticity of this statement.

My father had reached this point in his reflections when Gustl's hand with its brown liver spots crept over the bedspread towards him, took hold of his own hand and rubbed a little apple from the strudel over the back of it in a mollifying gesture. 'Look, my dear,' she cooed, 'I know I'm putting you to a lot of trouble, but after all he's my only child and you're my favourite nephew, and if you'll help me just this once, I'll leave everything to you.'

'God forbid!' cried my father, raising his hands in protest, and if he didn't in fact cry out in protest and raise his hands, then at least his physical attitude and his face conveyed shock and rejection. All his life my father had a very disturbed idea of the causal connection between giving and taking. It made him feel quite sick to suppose that he might be thought calculating. So he was happy to do most of his friends and relations any favour (my mother being the exception), but refused all small tokens of appreciation with a horrified, 'But that's not why I did it!' At the same time he was almost beside himself with gratitude if anyone did something for him (my mother again being the exception). He preferred to receive no thanks at all for his labours, because then he could still respect himself and other people. He didn't like giving presents either, or anyway not generous ones, in case it might be thought that he wanted something back. No, he was happiest to watch other people giving and taking from a safe distance. The least little thing would make him see morally coercive relations of dependency looming, he detected nepotism where it didn't exist, and he derived deep satisfaction from not being a part of such systems but prudently giving them a wide berth. It never struck him that in this crucial point he disastrously failed to achieve his lifetime aim of being a good, genuine, typical Austrian.

Aunt Gustl's disgraceful lure of a legacy – 'and what does she have to leave anyone?' my mother would scornfully and predictably say – had at least got Aunt Gustl what she wanted. My father couldn't refuse to do a service for which a legacy was offered, for that meant it must be a considerable service, one that really mattered to the person offering the bribe. However, he absolutely had to turn down the reward of the alleged inheritance itself, for if he accepted he would be thought calculating in general. Such was the simple way my father's mind often worked. 'Just as you like,' purred Aunt Gustl happily. As I have said, she was tough from her youth. 'But I'm sure you'd like to pick some little thing. Think of your children.'

The first and until now the only time that Aunt Gustl had tried helping her useless son was in the early fifties. Nandl had been henchman to a famous gang of fraudulent textiles salesmen who met at the Weisskopf. This establishment belonged to Vickerl Weisskopf, an excellent cook and a terrible businessman, who had survived the war in some way that was never explained. Some people said he had been freed by the Russians from a small camp somewhere, others that he had been their prisoner. To be taken prisoner by the Russians, he would have had to be in the German Wehrmacht in the first place, but no one had time for these niceties in the post-war years. However, the Russians must have had something to do with it, for they still came to his restaurant, he never had any trouble getting vodka deliveries, and he obviously understood the language a little. Vickerl Weisskopf was considered a good fellow, not least because he played down his wartime experiences. He was so fond of cooking and tipping back the vodka with his friends that he entirely forgot about business, and that, at least according to my father, was why the Weisskopf, a dark, wood-panelled restaurant with smoked glass mirrors and yellowish crystal chandeliers, made so little money even though it was always crowded. 'You know what people are like,' my father would always say later, reproachfully. 'They come in, they guzzle the chicken liver and chopped egg that Vickerl automatically puts on the table, they have a vodka or so on the house, and off they go without paying for anything.'

'The decent thing to do,' my father continued in the same vein, 'would have been to order a main dish at least. Paprika chicken, for instance, Vickerl did a really good paprika chicken!'

'But even then,' pointed out my uncle, modifying this statement, 'he usually forgot to take the money.'

The Weisskopf was where all the good guys went. Here, for instance, usually alone and wearing a blissful smile, sat Heinrich H., who dealt in something described in the Weisskopf, with a grin, as 'fake icons'. Heinrich H. had been liberated from Dachau. Sometimes, when he was very drunk, he would tell the company wild stories of the lists of men to be shot on which he had found himself, and the hair-raising coincidences whereby he had survived again and again. 'Go on with you, don't be such an idiot!' people would tell him with distaste, moving away. 'It was God that saved me!' H. would cry, his voice breaking, and he would clumsily open his commercial traveller's case, take out one of the tastelessly painted Madonnas, and kiss her theatrically. Then he would chuckle and sink back as if in his death throes.

Heinrich H. was successful. Sometimes he was away for weeks on end, always wearing a suit and tie as he made his way from Vienna to Semmering, into the Wechsel area and far on into Styria, palming off his cheap Hungarian figures of saints on the local population sometimes as valuable antiques, sometimes as miracle-working relics. There seems to have been a great need for Christian cult objects after the end of the war. H. also had crucifixes of different sizes with him, 'to suit any nook or cranny'. He was good at dialects and talking to the people known in the Weisskopf only, and dismissively, as 'country bumpkins'. He got on particularly well with farmers' wives. He could see the religious mania in their eyes, and the greed in the eyes of the farmers, many of whom had never been able to forgive themselves for turning away desperate Jews during 'those terrible times'. On their remote farms, they hadn't been sure whether buying Jewish valuables at a shamelessly low price might not be some new kind of criminal offence, and so they had refrained.

The Weisskopf wasn't a restaurant exclusively frequented by shady characters, but the fact was that in the first post-war years when, so my father said, no one had anything to eat, most people followed a very strange assortment of professions out of sheer necessity. After Nandl Königs-berger's arrest, however, it cost Vickerl Weisskopf large quantities of vodka and other so-called Russian methods of persuasion to ensure that the image of his restaurant wasn't too badly damaged – for there was no denying that the con men who did a fraudulent trade in textiles frequented the place. In fact the con men, brothers called Karli and Joschi and a third man nicknamed 'the assistant sheriff', were not really gangsters, but more like the spaghetti Western heroes of their time, harmless would-be Viennese Al Capones, three good-looking young men who were perhaps just a little too polished, trying to make up for their humble origins with plenty of cheek, posturing and hair cream. They were smooth operators who enjoyed not only their undemanding job but also the excitement of the chase. The idea of a fraudulent trade in textiles seems in fact to have sprung more from a lavish meal at the Weisskopf than from any calculating criminal brain. Anyway, they used to travel around to the most remote country farms with several bales of suiting fabric. Joschi, Karli and the 'assistant sheriff' used a Chevrolet for this purpose, a circumstance that in itself won them not a little admiration in this still largely car-free period. The car wasn't theirs, of course; they borrowed it from a girlfriend of Karli's, who for her part is said to have been very well acquainted with several high-ranking Allied army officers, as my grandfather used to say, eyebrows raised with a wealth of meaning.

Two of them would drive to an isolated farmhouse in the

undulating hills of the Bucklige Welt, the Schneeberg area or the Traisen valley, and stage an emergency. They would claim to have run out of money and petrol, so now the farmer had a once-in-a-lifetime chance to acquire a bale of top-quality fabric at a ridiculous price. 'You won't get another offer like this,' they would say, smooth-talking the farmer's wife, urging her to go over to the boot of the car, thrusting the fabric between her thumb and forefinger so that she could feel it. Their suiting always at least *looked* top quality, deceptively like what they themselves were wearing with such inimitable elegance. Once the farmer had agreed, and the farmer's wife had taken the money out of the old stocking where she kept it, they would thank the good folk effusively. They pocketed the small sum of money with expressions of mingled relief and rueful regret, got into the car, started the engine, waved, stopped, switched the engine off and climbed out once more. Did the farmer and his wife know a suitable tailor? Maybe such excellent fabric ought not to be put in the hands of the first clumsy fellow to come along from Kirchschlag or Türnitz! As it happened, they still had business to transact in these parts, they'd come back tomorrow with a tailor whom they personally trusted – no, really, don't mention it, the least they could do in return for services rendered just in the nick of time!

Next morning all three turned up. It seems that the 'assistant sheriff' had a remarkable talent for taking professional-looking measurements, he had a pincushion which he could clamp to his wrist, an awe-inspiring pair of tailor's shears, and he had picked up some of those pre-war forms for entering measurements from the famous menswear store Knize am Graben. He politely asked the customer's name, wrote that down first, 'Herr Oberhuber' or 'Herr Unterberger, yes, yes, just so,' and added his measurements – 'and the right sleeve a little wider, right.' The pre-printed forms bore a dashingly sketched drawing of a slender, elegant man in a suit. If the 'assistant sheriff' was in a particularly good mood, or if there were children watching, he sometimes even drew the pattern on the back of the fabric with tailor's chalk. A made-to-measure suit doesn't come cheap, of course, the farmer and his wife realised that. But all the 'assistant sheriff' wanted was a deposit on the extremely high price named – 'we know each other now,' the ever-smiling Joschi liked to add. Thereupon the three skilful city gentlemen pocketed the deposit, put the fabric back in the car and drove away. Later, in the Weisskopf, they would be laughing fit to spill their vodka as they repeatedly described how the farmer had awkwardly removed his working clothes to be measured for a suit between the dunghill and the haystack.

Nandl joined the con men because he looked so smart. Once, during one of the famous parties held in mid-October allegedly in memory of the Russian Revolution, a couple of drunks made Nandl change clothes with the head waiter some time in the small hours. The result was astonishing. The head waiter went pale. Vickerl Weisskopf had some difficulty in assuring him that he could keep his job – Nandl would never be able to carry plates without upsetting everything, nor could cashing up be seriously entrusted to him. Nandl Königsberger in tails looked like a star of silent movies. And then there was his smile, in between shy and impudent and thus in general somehow obsequious, with the result that Joschi and Karli, fatally, decided to take him on as their chauffeur. They didn't really need him, but they wanted to polish up their act as a service to the audience sitting in the Weisskopf keen to hear their stories. 'A good bit of slander and you're half-way there,' said the clientèle of the Weisskopf. Business was going well too – of course they didn't live by fraudulent operations with suiting fabric alone, now and then they smuggled cigarettes and nylon tights to Hungary, and could be engaged as a team for various semi-legal jobs – and when your business is doing well you get yourself a status symbol. Nandl was provided with a suit, a side parting to his Brylcreemed hair and a peaked cap, and was taught to drive the Chevrolet. It could have gone along like that for years. All Nandl had to do was open and close the car doors, touch his cap with his hand, drive, keep quiet, and now and then collect or deliver bales of fabric or smuggled goods in the city centre. He had no cash and no responsibility entrusted to him. So all might have been well if Nandl, brainless as he was, hadn't invited a girl out into the country one summer weekend, and with the usual ulterior motives, and because he vaguely remembered a nice view and a good supper, took her to a country inn at the foot of the Rax mountain range, where the landlord was still waiting for his made-to-measure suit.

When my mother brought the first tights back from Palmers they were too dark. Aunt Gustl, groaning, rolled them over her insteps and heels, pulled them half-way up her calves, and then complained reproachfully, 'You think I'm dead already?' My mother, who was afraid of Aunt Gustl and well aware of her own cowardice, which she tried to forget by making particularly furious remarks at home ('what on earth does the colour matter, no one's going to see them under her skirt!'), packed the tights up again in silence and took them back to change them. In Palmers they asked her not to return worn tights in future – for in trying them on, Aunt Gustl had pulled small threads here and there. My mother couldn't manage to prevent her from trying the tights on; if she even tried it, she did so rather feebly. It took my mother weeks to solve the tights problem. Once the toes weren't reinforced, another time Aunt Gustl wanted a different kind of gusset, once the waistband was too wide, another time too narrow, then she thought she would prefer 'Champagne' to 'Cognac' ('but never "Mocha" again, do you hear?'), and finally she insisted on seams up the backs of the legs, 'the way we wore them when I was young'. There followed a drama in several acts. It seemed to do Aunt Gustl a great deal of good. From her bed, she easily managed to send my mother chasing all over town, bringing to bear a well-judged admixture of blame, reproaches, promises and the desperation of a dying woman 'who'll never be wearing tights in this world again'. A page had been torn out of the telephone book at home listing all the Palmers branches in Vienna, for even then you could in practice exchange Palmers products in almost every branch, not just the one where you bought them.

Meanwhile my father had managed, by means which he would never disclose, to get an appointment with Dr Schneuzl. Making a date with the head of a ministerial department to play tennis or golf or have lunch is no problem, but an official appointment during working hours, when the outcome might commit him to something, represents a not inconsiderable challenge to the pulling of all available strings. Back on the first occasion a few years after the end of the war, it seems to have been my grandfather who got in touch with old Councillor Schneuzl, Dr Schneuzl's father. There are some indications that Aunt Gustl forced her brother, my grandfather, to escort her to the Justice Ministry, just as she was now trying to force my father to perform the same embarrassing service.

If she really wanted Aunt Gustl could be an impressive sight at any age, even now that she was well over eighty and claimed to have 'risen from her deathbed'. She was wearing her pearls, which she had preserved all through the war – 'don't ask me how' – her hair was elegantly done, and of course she wore a tailored suit that set off her physical assets to good effect and flatteringly hid her less advantageous areas. Aunt Gustl's problem was unusually well-rounded feminine curves – above all a voluptuous bosom and a pertly protuberant bottom that took up a lot of room – oddly combined with particularly slender, almost spindly extremities. In old age the women of my family often look like pretty dumplings on stilts; Aunt Gustl was a fine example of the type. Her strong point in tactical negotiations also arose from a rather unlikely mixture: she could combine humility with breathtaking chutzpah. She had brought along a box of chocolates tied with ribbon, and offered it with such a guilty smile that refusing was impossible. The recipient of this gift had no option but to get over the awkward situation as quickly as possible, without any polite havering. In Vienna more than anywhere else, corruption is quite often the result of extreme embarrassment, an inability to reject encroaching advances well enough.

Even as Schneuzl tried to stuff the monstrosity of a box in a desk drawer, Aunt Gustl was reminding him of the old days, when he or his father before him used to play tennis with her poor Dolly, God rest his soul, on those beautiful courts in the green spaces of the Prater meadows, 'and I hear the club is doing as well as ever?' she asked, sweet as sugar, her eyes flashing. 'Oh, you made your investment at the right time, it's certainly paying off now.' She made herself even clearer. Back in the early thirties it had been far from easy to get hold of sufficient funds, she remembered that very well; in his responsible position her husband, poor Dolly, had to reject so many other applications for credit. Those were difficult times, as Dr Schneuzl knew; people were poor, oh, how quickly we forget. 'But we're straying from the subject,' she said, even before Schneuzl, steamrollered by her flow of talk, had found the courage or opportunity to make any rejoinder, and she launched straight into a distraught mother's dramatic monologue.

Here again, with sure instinct, she found the right mixture of all the requisite overtones and undertones, simulating an entire chorus with her solo voice alone. She sang of bad times, under-nourishment, the impossibility of giving children all they really needed in the twenties; oh, she blamed herself, but in such a way that any right-minded man would have wanted to kiss her hand, murmuring, 'No, no, oh no, dear lady.' She supposed she had been too strict, too ambitious, she hadn't thought enough about what was due to children; people saw all that rather differently today, didn't they? But then her Ferdinand had never given her a moment's anxiety, such a good boy he was, and so very affectionate too – not that that had anything to do with it – but anyway he was attentive, courteous, endearing – 'Isn't that so?' she said, ramming her elbow into the ribs of my grandfather on the first occasion and my father on the second. 'You've known him from a boy, isn't that so?'

My father nodded awkwardly, whereas my grandfather, decades before, may well have grimaced. Both would have been reminded of the scene in the Bauernfeind in the early autumn of 1937, when just for once Bank Manager Königsberger's wife condescended to play bridge with my grandparents as she used to. Suddenly Nandl had turned up with a group of adolescents, all in white socks and white shirts, with red, black and white armbands clearly visible around their upper arms. Nandl was laughing and smirking all over his face; he wasn't yet fifteen, but tall and strong already, and he had the right kind of friends. They pushed in through the swing doors, all eight or ten of them, heels clicking, hands shooting up high, yelling 'Heil Hitler' in unison, making the card players at the green baize tables jump while the waiters took refuge behind the bar. My grandfather put down his cards, stood up very slowly and went over to Nandl. No one stopped him, least of all Nandl's smart friends. Then he slapped Nandl's face with meticulous precision and told him, 'Get out of here, you stupid boy, and don't you ever do that again.'

Grandpa was not acting the hero but simply infuriated, so my family said later, and everyone nodded. A good thing too, that was always the ritual response, because heroes get to die. All the same, there were whispered tales in my family of what he had been doing in the war, and we shook our heads portentously. 'So what about it?' my sister would ask, bored, as she leafed through a fashion magazine. That usually led my mother to say sharply, 'Well, it left Granny a nervous wreck, anyway,' and introduce a change of subject.

Aunt Gustl was far from grateful to my grandfather for stepping in, although what Nandl had done was still forbidden at the time. After a split second of horror she snatched up her coat, leaped to her feet, and ran after her son and his friends. As she ran she spat back over her shoulder, 'Look after your own brood, why don't you?'

'. . . Isn't that so? Come on!' she now continued to badger her escort, employing the persuasions of her foot as well as her elbow. With great presence of mind, Councillor Schneuzl forced himself into this tiny gap in the conversation. Placing his fingertips together and beginning, 'My dear, my very dear lady,' he embarked upon a monologue, the answer that might have been expected of an understanding family friend into whose jurisdiction this case most, most unfortunately did not fall. He spoke unctuously of 'a not inconsiderable offence', and of the necessity to bear in mind 'the force of example', which was why even apparently slight criminal offences had to be sternly punished. He mentioned the 'unusual amount of public attention' that had been paid to this crime, 'not the kind we see every day . . . very well,' Councillor Schneuzl had concluded, 'yes, so it was the first time, but just think: what a terrible idea, shamelessly duping the credulous, uneducated rural population, devising such a wicked plan, and then coldly putting it into practice on his own initiative alone.' For Karli, Joschi and the assistant sheriff had made a good job of bringing pressure to bear on the witnesses, while Nandl had declined to make any statement at all, and indeed tactically that was his best course of action anyway.

'Well and good, so this time it was only a matter of comparatively insignificant theft,' concluded Dr Schneuzl, 'but what about all those previous convictions? What about his lifelong criminal career?'

Here Aunt Gustl collapsed. According to my father, 'she wept like an old crocodile.' A glass of water had to be fetched, and later a small mocha coffee, she had to be moved from the hard visitor's chair in front of the desk to the usual Biedermeier sofa dating from former Imperial Austrian days to be found in the offices of departmental heads, and there she clung, trembling, to the head of department's arm and suddenly announced, her breath coming alarmingly short once again after a brief period of calm, that she wanted to tell 'the whole truth', however dreadful, however really unspeakable it might be.

'I'm Jewish, you see,' she whimpered for the benefit of the interested Councillor Schneuzl, and we are told that the golden crucifix was clearly visible on her still attractive bosom as she spoke. 'I don't know if a great gentleman like you has any idea what *that* meant only a little while ago.' There followed a heart-rending tale of the will to survive at any price, of being thrown out of her own apartment, of forced labour, fear, hunger ('not so much as a little bit of butter in all those years'), of neighbouring Jews who disappeared overnight, there were fewer and fewer of them, it was the same in Nandl's class at school, think of it, even children weren't safe any more – without embarrassment she recounted everything she vaguely knew about the wartime experiences of my grandfather, who was sitting right there beside her. 'As a decent human being you won't know about all that, you wouldn't have known it at the time,' she sobbed, but for months she hadn't been able to let Nandl out on the streets, oh, the informers, the persecutors, the people who would betray you, it had done dreadful damage to his tender childish soul, and then there was his old grandmother, he'd loved her so much, she was taken away from the Augarten apartment on Transport Römisch four stroke nine, they'd found out only recently, she went to Theresienstadt, oh, I tell you it's only too easy to understand that he doesn't know good from bad, how could he, so much to make up for, all those lost years, she'd do anything, everything to get him back on the strait and narrow, tears, hoarse sobs, the marks of fingernails digging into the departmental head's forearm, and so on and so forth.

'You see, his father was in the Party,' she wailed to the astonished Dr Schneuzl, 'and Ferdinand has only just found out!' Her walking stick slipped off her lap, starting a ladder in her tights ('Champagne with back seam'), and fell on the wooden floor. 'You yourself know what it means today, when every brave soldier is branded a war criminal, when our own Federal President is treated like Stalin in person.' And then came a heart-rending tale of how Nandl had grown up without a father, was simply unable to satisfy the alleged high moral demands of the bank–manager father he had hardly known, that was how he took a wrong turning, and now, now of all times when his mother, a broken woman on the brink of death, had believed for the first time that he was a truly reformed character, he had sworn to her on his soul there'd never be another forged cheque, it was now of all times that he had found out about it, you yourself know, all that unhealthy delving about in the past, it must end some time, just think, last time she visited her Nandl in prison he had jeered, 'Like father, like son,' that was what he said. 'And to think of my Dolly, he must be turning in his grave, the best man ever to face his God.'

Shortly after Gustl's second visit to the Justice Ministry Nandl, now over sixty, had married while in jail. What no one knew was that he had a bad heart. The whole family was sent a wedding picture taken by the prison photographer, the last word in sad absurdity. Only those who had known him before could still guess at Nandl's former good looks; he now walked with a stoop, he wore thick medical-insurance glasses, and he had 'put on a fair bit of weight', as we used to say in my family when we wanted to be polite about it. His bride, an unhappy monster of a woman, sat with a meagre bunch of roses on her lap in one of the artificial leather chairs trimmed up to look historical, wearing what my uncle described as a flowered tent big enough to take three, and looking, so my brother remarked, 'as if her four thousandth lonely-hearts ad had surprisingly won her twenty schillings'.

The news of Nandl's death in prison came not long after the wedding announcement. He had not wanted to be buried beside his father in the Central Cemetery, said the prison governor over the phone, not at any price, but in his wife's native village in the Weinviertel, the wine-growing district north of Vienna, near the Czech border. 'It's all the same to me,' grumbled Aunt Gustl, when my father had to go to the nursing home bearing the sad news of her son's death. She didn't say much else. Only when my father turned to go did she repeat, without any direct relevance, the sentence with which my father had vented all his rage and shame in the street outside the Palace of Justice after that visit to Dr Schneuzl. 'I never doubted our chancelessness.' It was a classic Dollyism.

A few years later, when Aunt Gustl too had finally died, Nandl's widow turned up at our apartment unannounced, asking for the rug and the TV set which Gustl, on her deathbed, had apparently promised her daughter-in-law. With malice aforethought my mother gave her our old set, which really differed from Gustl's only in having no remote control. She didn't give her the rug. The rug – and this is one of the few things of which we can be certain in our family – the rug was one of the items that Aunt Gustl had taken from my grandparents 'for safe keeping', and then 'forgot' to give back after the war.

Nandl's widow stood in the stairwell panting and trying to carry the TV set away. Just as my mother was about to close the door she asked, eyes downcast, if we happened to need a cleaning lady. There were patches of sweat on the tent that would take three. She was a good cleaner, she said. My mother gently closed the door. We never heard any more of Nandl's widow.

Good and Bad Luck

My father's chief problem during the war was Mr Bulldog. Mr Bulldog, whose appearance, needless to say, did justice to his name, was one of the wealthy men in Stopsley and owned the pharmacy. Mr Bulldog's pharmacy had two branches, one on each side of the little town. He had several employees. He sold medicaments and cosmetics, newspapers and magazines, sweets, cold drinks and savoury snacks. Mr Bulldog also sat on the town council and captained the darts team, of which Uncle Tom, my father's foster-father, was an enthusiastic member. Mr Bulldog was also instrumental in running the project to build a public open-air swimming pool in the impoverished little town, which was full of factory workers. 'We must make Stopsley more attractive,' said Mr Bulldog at every opportunity, and it was also on his initiative, of course, that the rather grand Victorian town hall in the High Street was demolished and replaced by a faceless modern building. But that was much later, long after my father had gone home. All the same, it bothered him every time he came back to visit Stopsley.

Mr Bulldog did not like 'Jew-boys', and announced the fact everywhere. To establish his position as a local worthy, Mr Bulldog regularly drank in all five of the pubs in the small town and did not, like Uncle Tom and most of the men, patronise one as a regular. He would have a couple of half pints in the Red Lion, eat a snack at the Wheatsheaf, chat in a friendly if condescending way, his voice already slightly slurred, with the landlord of the Dog and Duck, go on drinking steadily in the Old Dr Butler's Head, and finally be carried home roaring drunk from Dirty Dick's. Or in the opposite order. When he had to go to Luton he made himself out, to his business acquaintances, to be a man who was extremely sensitive to public opinion. For as soon as he left Stopsley, Mr Bulldog's self-confidence sank to zero. Even in Luton he felt like the village idiot. That was why, when he went to the county town, he spoke in inflated terms of 'the mood among the common people' and thus attracted a certain amount of attention, particularly after the beginning of the war. It need hardly be said that at home Mr Bulldog posed as very much a man of the world. In the pubs, working-class men listened patiently as he gave them the benefit of his political views, and no one contradicted him when he expressed his 'firm conviction' that there must be good reasons for the 'campaign' against the Jews now going on in Germany. Not that he was any friend to the Germans, by no means. The fact was that at first he had great difficulty, like many other English people, in distinguishing those German-speaking Jews who had suddenly arrived in their country in large numbers from the hated war enemy. One day Mr Bulldog almost came to blows with an American over the question. No one now remembered just what had brought the well-dressed American to Stopsley in the first place, but he happened to be sitting in the Dog and Duck having a beer when Mr Bulldog launched into one of his speeches. 'Lock them all up!' demanded Bulldog vociferously of his pint, just as if he were prime minister. Then he looked challengingly around and asked, 'Well, can any of you tell me why there are so many Krauts around these days?' The men – most of them employed in Waterlow's printing works, and some in the firm of T.C. Smith, car-parts supplier, although the T.C. Smith men traditionally favoured the Red Lion – looked straight ahead and did not take sides. Bulldog was in full flow now. Carried away by his own eloquence, and believing himself on safe ground, he spoke at length, once again, on the sensational subject of the fifth column. Next thing we knew, its friends would be landing in Ireland, Bulldog fantasised, and those 'cowardly Irish sods' would do nothing but drink and make children instead of keeping an eye on their bloody coastline. One day the rooster would crow, Bulldog prophesied, Londoners would wake up, and only then would they discover that their cheap cooks and gardeners had cut their throats!

'Absolute nonsense! You should be ashamed of yourself!' said the foreign businessman suddenly, and the working men didn't move, only their eyes looking his way with interest. Instead of locking up the German Jews, the stranger went on quietly but in cutting tones, they should be given as many guns as they could carry. They'd take much more satisfaction in teaching those darn Nazis a lesson than the Brits, whose great idea had been appeasement!

Bulldog rose to his feet, jaw dropping. Here the landlord of the Dog and Duck, carrying a freshly drawn pint, got between him and the stranger's table. 'That'll do now, Bill,' he murmured, putting the beer in front of him, and Bulldog sat down again. While he was still thinking, red-faced, of some clever rejoinder to make, while the workmen stared into their beers and the stranger sat biding his time, the only 'Jew-boy' in the whole of Stopsley entered the pub. The skinny salesgirls of the pharmacy in the north of town had told him he could find their boss there.

'Good afternoon, Mr Bulldog,' he said shyly. 'I've come about the ad. I'd like the paper-delivery job.'

'What the hell!' swore Bulldog. 'You mean you can ride a bike?' My father nodded. At the age of ten, he had shot up, but he was thin as a rake.

The situation at home was difficult. Uncle Tom was out of work, sacked yet again for arriving at the factory late because of a hangover, Auntie Annie was thinking of taking

44

a part-time job as a school cook because she couldn't make the money stretch, even with what she got for the board of her three foster-children, and my father badly needed the price of a fare to London. My uncle had written to say that he was probably going to be interned soon, and meanwhile Katzi was hoping to stop off in London on her way to Canada, so there wasn't much time left for him to see them both.

'The Jew-boy, eh?' asked Bulldog, although he was not quite sure of himself here. With the unpredictable stranger watching, he tried to control himself. Some of the workmen, however, were looking a little concerned. They knew my father, who was often sent to fetch his foster-father home from the pub before he had drunk the last of the family's money. Annie always sent my father. It was the only thing to do. Uncle Tom was in the habit, and not just when he was drunk, of taking my father by the shoulders, giving him a hug, and murmuring in sentimental tones, 'He's a good lad, my son is, right?'

He never said the same of the other two boys, brothers called Norm and Pete, who were also in his and Annie's care. They were English boys evacuated to the country because of the war, like so many London schoolchildren. So after nine months as the only foster-child, my father suddenly had two foster-brothers whose parents visited them at intervals. My father, on the other hand, the youngest of the three, had received his last postcard from Vienna two months before war broke out. That was almost a year ago now, and sometimes he thought, fleetingly and with a guilty conscience, that he could hardly remember his parents' faces any more.

'I'm from Austria,' said my father politely.

'Austria, oh yes?' said Bulldog derisively. 'No such place now, isn't that so?' Then he asked, 'How old are you, Jew-boy?'

'Nearly thirteen,' my father lied, adding with what for

him was unusual courage, 'But I'm Austrian.' At that the workmen suddenly laughed, and the American said, 'Hear, hear!' just as if he were British.

When they came to arrest my uncle he was sewing a pair of pyjama trousers. Talking about the war later, he sometimes said, with a cheerless smile, that he spent the first half of it at a sewing machine and the second half on the wrong front. The Jewish tailor from Soho had not been wrong: my uncle's delicate little fingers quickly learned to manipulate the fabric and the machines, although he was not in the least interested in the tailoring trade. The tailor was sorry about that. He couldn't leave the business to his daughters; they were childish and frivolous, and would soon, he hoped, find reasonably acceptable husbands and leave home. And to the tailor's great grief, his only son was a Zionist. The one person who made ironic comments on the son's heroic plans, and could give the good tailor any reason to hope he might change his mind, was my uncle. 'Wants to go off to the desert!' jeered my uncle, who couldn't stand hot weather, shaking his head. 'Mind you get a solar topee in good time.' Josh, the tailor's son, had a few arguments with him, but at heart they liked each other. They were about the same age. 'You ought to know better than anyone that our sort can't stay on in Europe,' Josh usually told him. 'What I do know is, those barbarians will stop at nothing,' my uncle usually replied, 'and then it'll be up to us to put things right. Each in his own place.'

It wasn't long before my uncle found himself mingling with communists. Refugees from Austria met at the Austrian Centre near Paddington Station. All the homeless young Austrians now living in London as household helps, cooks, nursemaids, gardeners and unskilled labourers came here for discussions, to stage plays and plan outings, and much of all this was organised and ideologically supervised by the communists of the Young Austria movement. My uncle spent every free moment he had in the house in Westbourne Terrace, although not everything was to his taste. For instance, Austrian Jews danced in dirndls and lederhosen in London at the time, when Jews at home were forbidden not only to wear national costume but to show any sign of life at all beyond mere breathing, on pain of severe penalties.

And although it was the communists who kept Austrian traditions going, with a view to stressing the independence of a country that politically no longer existed, such practices were deeply abhorrent to my uncle. He disliked taking part, for the sake of propaganda, in something that he had despised at home as being reactionary and Catholic. He was equally adamant in rejecting the tailor's efforts to drag him off to synagogue now and then. As a child, my uncle said later, he used to go to synagogue only on the days when there were presents for children there, 'but don't ask me if that was for Purim, Christmas, or the festival with that ugly house made of branches.' My uncle was a cool, dry free-thinker all his life, and neither symbols nor rituals, nor even the people closest to him, could ever really touch his heart.

What mainly attracted him to Young Austria, besides the fighting spirit of the political lectures promising a world-wide alliance against Fascism and the prospect of news from home, which was both sparse and contradictory, was a group of young men who began doing their utmost to enlist in the British army. They all had English papers stamped 'Refugee from Nazi oppression', so from the British point of view they were politically impeccable, if still a little too young. My uncle had already gone off to take a medical examination for training as a fighter pilot. Either no one there noticed that he was a foreigner, or it made no difference at the time. However, they did soon realise that my uncle was practically blind in his left eye. He hadn't known it himself, but so ended his first dream.

Because of that near-blind eye he was still sitting in the

gloomy basement in Dean Street, wasting his time sewing, as he saw it. Then two uniformed men came to the tailor's workshop one morning. It was very early, and the tailor himself wasn't awake yet, although my uncle, an early riser all his life, was wearing a checked pyjama jacket over his trousers only to make sure of its fit – unnecessarily, of course, for the English pyjamas made with bored precision by the former star pupil of Döbling Grammar School had never yet had anything wrong with them.

One of the uniformed men looked down at him, looked at his papers, read out under his breath 'Refugee from Nazi oppression', looked at the pyjama jacket again, and then said, 'We'll be back in two hours' time. I don't suppose you'll run away from us.' When they had left, my uncle finished dressing, wrote a few matter-of-fact lines to Stopsley, said goodbye to the horrified tailor, who began saying at the top of his voice how ashamed he was of his country ('We can none of us choose our country,' my uncle heartlessly told him), and went off to report to the tribunal of his own accord. He hated nothing so much as wasting time. If they were going to lock him up they had better do it at once, 'and then I'll get out sooner too,' he later explained his own thinking to us, always with that typically cheerless smile.

My father enjoyed his paper round. It was true that Bulldog harassed him whenever he could, but the bicycle provided for his work and the sports news on the back pages of the papers made it all worthwhile. My father fetched the papers from the pharmacy on the south side of Stopsley early in the morning, at Bulldog's insistence cycled straight into the middle of the village to throw the first newspapers of the day over the mayor's garden fence and Bulldog's own, and then worked his way back south again. He delivered news-papers to the northern part of Stopsley last, just before school began. The north side of the village was inhabited mainly by working people who lived in small, modest terraced houses. Because of Mr Bulldog's uneconomic demands (although, with a nasty grin, he described giving rich newspaper readers precedence over the poor as 'service to the customer'), my father cycled almost twice as far every day as was really necessary, but Stopsley was not and still isn't a large place.

At first, when my father got the job Uncle Tom let him off going to pick dandelions early in the morning, but this dispensation lasted only a short time. After a few weeks during which Uncle Tom had done the tiring and tedious work alone, dandelion-picking was back on the agenda for Wednesday evenings and the weekend. My father had to come home early from the Boys' Club specially for the purpose, and then they would each take a large hessian bag and go out into the gently undulating meadows. 'Come on, Sunny,' Uncle Tom would say encouragingly, 'it's really not that bad.' But my father hated it. He hated all the bending, he hated the dandelions that grew with such self-confident luxuriance in the meadows, just as if there were no war, no Bulldog and no absence of postcards, and for that reason he even hated rabbit stew, the one real meat dish that Auntie Annie made once a month, thanks entirely to the trials and tribulations of dandelion-picking. He would say later that only picking those dandelions had been as bad as Mr Bulldog's malice. Mr Bulldog and the dandelions were what really soured his life during the war.

My uncle was regarded with disfavour by the tribunal for his fervent wish to join the British army. The tribunal chairman didn't think it was normal. While many English boys were doing their best to get out of it – 'last week another of them broke his own arm,' said the chairman gloomily – this one was running around like a man possessed from one recruiting office to the next: not eighteen yet, a foreigner, and half blind. He had a good job as a tailor, another member of the tribunal pointed out, 'with good folk in Soho, but no, he's always hanging around with the other Germans.' My uncle said nothing. He had already explained that he had taken refuge in England as an Austrian and a Jew, and as an Austrian and a Jew he wanted a military training and a gun so that he could go back to the Continent, fight the German Nazis, and help to liberate those Austrians and Jews who had stayed at home. The tribunal had laughed awkwardly, and showed no sympathy or even understanding. They were a bunch of well-meaning aristocrats with strong teeth whose military careers so far had led them not to the general staff, but only to administrative jobs of secondary importance. Suddenly, however, they felt needed and responsible. They had political factors to take into account. There had been certain incidents since the Germans started their air raids. A couple of families showed their German Jewish employees the door, allegedly for stealing or hitting the children, or something else of that kind. The families who had vouched for refugees coming into the country were now firing them. These were isolated cases, but the press took a lively interest in them. No one now knew what to do with a couple of young housemaids, a pair of middle-aged chauffeurs, two or three elderly housekeepers, and the old gardener of German descent in Ipswich who was said to slink around the houses at night, pressing his wrinkled face to windows. Two men had been beaten up in a London suburb; their own fault, they must surely all know by now that it was better not to speak German in the street. 'You see,' the chairman told my uncle, 'you may perhaps find it difficult to understand us, but we have your own safety in mind by classifying you as Category B.' My uncle shrugged. He hadn't really hoped for anything. If you were Category A, you were interned at once. A Category B man was interned later. Those classified as C remained unaffected in principle, but were told not to attract attention, to observe the evening curfew for foreigners (from midnight to six a.m.), and in all cases to report any change of residence to the police. If they transgressed against these rules, the consequence was classification as Category B at the very least.

My uncle went back to the tailor in Dean Street. He wilfully stayed away from Young Austria for a week, but then he realised that it made no difference to his B classification. He wrote to Stopsley again in a mixture of English and German. 'Next week would be a good idea. Katzi is coming. Staying for two days, then going on to Liverpool & Canada. She's staying at 39, Christchurch Ave., Kilburn. Meet us there.'

Uncle Tom was far from sober when my father put the problem to him. That, as my father had calculated, was both his chance and a risk, because he didn't have much time to make his little speech. The way home from the Dog and Duck was 'too short for me to find it first go off every time,' as Uncle Tom liked to murmur with a shamefaced grin when he stumbled past Annie and in through the door. Uncle Tom was not by any means an alcoholic. He didn't have the money for that. But once or twice a month, no one ever knew when in advance or why, he was overcome by some kind of melancholy, failed to come home at the usual time, and my father had to go and fetch him. Next day 'all four of us lads', as Uncle Tom jokingly liked to call the three boys and himself, had to put up with the expression on Auntie Annie's face. It was true that these occasions had been more frequent since the beginning of the war. Uncle Tom would get into the company of a few old Waterlow workers who feared for their sons' safety, and drink with them. If he and Annie had had children of their own, they would have been about my father's age, too young to fight in the war.

It seemed to Uncle Tom, in his bemused condition, 'clear as day' why my father absolutely had to go to London for a day. And in spite of the number of pints he had drunk, he was still aware that it was not sensible to let a boy of under eleven travel to the big city alone ('although you look like a big boy now,' he said proudly, holding my father by the shoulders). But he also knew that Annie would make life hell for him if she knew he had been in on the plan. 'Right, then,' he muttered, concentrating, 'you get on the bus, you change in Luton, then you go to King's Cross, or is it Paddington? And from there . . .'

'Yes, I know all that,' my father interrupted in a whisper. They were outside the cottage now, and any moment Auntie Annie would see them from the living-room window. 'It's about the money,' my father whispered. 'Can you lend me ten shillings until next week?'

'Ten shillings,' murmured Uncle Tom, propping himself on the garden fence. It turned out that he had paid only today for the darts club outing. Stopsley was playing Dunstable in the county championship on Friday. Stopsley pennants and badges would have to be bought. The money was gone. He had paid it to Bulldog. My father knew better than anyone that Uncle Tom, one of the best players in the darts team, couldn't back out now.

Uncle Tom was in favour of going straight back to the Dog and Duck to wheedle the money out of the landlord. With some difficulty, my father kept him from doing so. They agreed in whispers that my father would ask Bulldog for an advance on next week's paper round. Uncle Tom was sceptical. He feared Bulldog almost more than my father did, and at every opportunity, particularly when picking dandelions, he told 'character-building' tales in which Bulldog played a leading part as a very bad example. In anything and everything, so Uncle Tom informed my father, who agreed anyway, a 'decent man' must do his best to be the complete opposite of Mr Bulldog. Beginning with the fact, Uncle Tom preached, that every decent man patronises only one regular pub.

★

Katzi arrived at Victoria Station in the evening. She was very beautiful and pale as a ghost. When she hugged my uncle she wept a little. 'How grown-up you look,' she told him. After that they said only the minimum, for my uncle had immediately explained about the dangers of speaking German in public. Perhaps I'm being over-cautious, he thought. But he didn't want to run any risks with Katzi, who was as tall and blonde and striking as her mother, Katzi in her chic Viennese dove-grey suit. Katzi didn't know any English yet. She would soon learn to speak it in Canada, but at the moment she knew only a few words. She could speak a little Czech, she said, giggling, and nudged my uncle. 'Ahoj, jak se máš?' And Italian. 'We have so much still to learn, who'd ever have thought it?'

She had no news of their parents. She had left Czecho-slovakia at the last minute, had then spent months in Italy battling with her tuberculosis, and was cured at last. Her stout husband had been in Toronto for some time. Her ship would leave three days later. It was called the SS *Penelope*. Katzi thought that was a lovely name. She had always taken an interest in ancient Greece, but it was unusual for girls to go to grammar school in her time, apart from the fact that it was expensive, and even my uncle was able to go only because he had the maximum reduction in fees. Katzi had sometimes read my uncle's books. She had been a shoe salesgirl in Vienna, and right at the end had helped Herr Eisenstein in his leather goods shop. Her papers described her as 'office worker'.

At the time of the Anschluss, she happened to be on a family visit to Freudenthal. My grandmother, usually quicker than her light-minded husband to recognise a crisis when she saw one, had immediately telephoned Haas the jeweller.

Salomon Haas was married to Ilse, a friend of my grand-mother's youth. She had caused a family scandal just as my grandmother did. For a long time after that, my great-grandmother and Ilse's mother looked at each other with pursed lips if they met while out shopping. Why us, those pursed lips seemed to be asking. When there are so many nice, upstanding young fellows about, they seemed to be saying. My great-grandmother and Ilse's mother never said anything when they met out shopping. They glanced briefly at each other, and then looked away again.

Their daughters' marriages, as they saw it, were not pleasing in the eyes of God. The people of those little villages were all Catholics, and inter-married among themselves. So the weddings of their renegade daughters had to be celebrated on the most modest scale possible, somewhere neutral too, in a distant city. Ilse and Salomon Haas were witnesses at my grandparents' wedding and vice versa. The idea of refusing the two young women who had left the fold a proper wedding, with friends and family there, was supposed to make the gravity of their misdemeanour doubly clear to them. My grandmother never mentioned the subject. Only in great old age, when she was ill and bad-tempered all round the clock, did her feelings once, surprisingly, come out: she hadn't been in the least sorry for any of it. All the fuss when her sisters and cousins got married, all those peasant rituals, she hissed, it was simply ludicrous, ridiculous. While he still had the strength to do it, my grandfather would try to defend his good Moravian sisters-in-law and cousins by marriage in a rather unexpected way. 'Think of the camps,' he reminded her. 'They paid for it bitterly later.'

For my grandfather was convinced that my grandmother had been better off with him and her move to Vienna when she married. She had been spared the resettlement camp, the violence of the angry Czechs, all the horrors of setting off with fifty kilos of baggage in stamped bags. 'Well, that's all I was spared, then,' spat my grandmother, who always had the last word.

In the eyes of my grandmother's family and Ilse's, their

daughters' husbands did at least have two advantages worth mentioning: they were not Czechs and they were not Protestant. A Czech or Protestant husband would have been a disaster. A Jew, however, was still grounds for considerable family displeasure. The displeasure died down almost entirely in the years just after they married, a certain part being played by the way the sons-in-law prospered in business, and the fur coats worn by the daughters when they sometimes honoured their little home villages with a visit. Then, in the years before the war, the displeasure surfaced strongly again.

Salomon Haas hurried off to my grandmother's relations with the telegram. They didn't ask the goldsmith in these days, and only when Katzi came to the door was he able to tell her the news sent by her mother, which was more of a direct order. So Katzi stayed in Freudenthal until she had a Czech passport. She stayed on with her uncles and aunts and cousins, who were rejoicing at the Anschluss and hoisting banners, fervently hoping that the Führer would soon liberate them too.

Katzi told my uncle none of this, for as soon as they were in the Tube there was an air-raid warning. The Londoners streamed into the underground stations. Katzi hung on to her suitcase in spite of all the pushing and shoving. My uncle carried her other case. There was an unpleasant smell down there. My uncle tried not to be parted from Katzi, so they kept looking at each other in all the confusion. Sometimes my uncle tried to give an encouraging smile, but suddenly he felt afraid of the people around them. The people around them were afraid of the bombs. What a lovely girl she is, thought my uncle. I hope no one speaks to her. 'People get talkative when they're afraid,' my uncle would say later, in connection with his experiences at the siege of Meiktila, which went on for weeks. He could not keep a certain note of contempt out of his voice as he told these stories. Later on my brother, undoubtedly inspired by my uncle, wrote a much-praised essay entitled, 'On the Connection between Fear and Loquacity'. The fact that this essay was both extensive and equipped with a proliferation of footnotes caused a certain amount of adverse comment in the Viennese coffee-houses that my brother frequented, but of course only when he had left again.

Katzi smiled faintly. People spoke to her, one man clung on to her briefly and then said something. Katzi smiled, nodded, shook her head reassuringly, spoke with her eyebrows, her nostrils, the corners of her mouth and her chin, saying by these means: it doesn't matter, don't worry, everything's all right, I quite agree with you. By now she was sitting on the floor of the station platform, right on the edge, with her suitcase beside her. I hope they won't push us on to the rails, she thought in alarm. Suddenly an official made his way through the crowd, shooing everyone back closer to the wall. Katzi realised that space had to be left for people to pass down the platform. She panicked. She had to get away from the edge of the platform, but there was no room behind her. She looked around in alarm for her brother. But hands were already picking up her case, and space was made for her. A woman spoke to her soothingly, and didn't seem to expect an answer. 'Thank you,' Katzi whispered in English.

How boring it is here, how stressful, she thought later, after the lights had been out for some time. She thought of the SS *Penelope* and what the ship would look like. She thought of the sea and the milky place where it merges with the sky. She didn't think of her stout husband. Suddenly everything inside her head was very peaceful, bright and still.

Mr Bulldog had merely laughed nastily. 'Advance?' he jeered. 'And then you won't turn up at all next week, I suppose?' My father was in despair. He pointed out that he had never made a mistake yet, had always been punctual and, as Mr Bulldog must know, he needed the job. Bulldog was not to be moved. It suddenly appeared to my father very tempting to fling the bike down at his feet and tell Mr Bulldog that only an idiot like him could even think anyone would cheat him out of such a tiny sum. 'There'd be some point if it was a week's takings from both pharmacies, yes,' my father would shout, trampling hysterically on the spokes of his beloved bicycle, 'but no one's going to get his hands dirty for a few shillings!' And later Uncle Tom (even though he'd have to pay for the wrecked bike in endless monthly instalments that would almost ruin him) would reassure my devastated father by saying that at some moments in life, when all diplomatic measures were exhausted, you just had to shout, curse and break things, 'but only then, Sunny, only when there's really no alternative, and only when the cause of it is Bulldog.'

My father woke from this daydream when Bulldog called him back with an almost friendly, 'Hey there, Jew-boy!' The bicycle, intact, was leaning against the wall of the pharmacy, and Bulldog was standing in the sun outside the door. If he cycled round for two afternoons next week delivering medicines, he could have his advance. The two afternoons of work would of course be unpaid. 'Interest,' grinned Bulldog. 'As I'm sure you know, nothing in life comes free.'

'Very well, thank you,' said my father.

Since doing the deal with Bulldog had taken some time, he missed the bus which he had meant to catch. Later, my father never stopped to think whether missing it had changed anything; might that first bus have got through? The mere question confused him. The idea that everything could have worked out differently, the game of 'If . . . then', was not something that my father indulged in.

So he waited patiently outside Stopsley town hall. There

was still plenty of time. A couple of boys were kicking a ball about in the road. My father joined them. The next bus left punctually two hours later, but only reached the outskirts of London, where it came up against a roadblock erected by the fire brigade. First the bus driver got out and spoke to two ARP wardens, then the passengers gradually gave up hope and climbed out too, my father last of all. Somewhere beyond the roadblock, several bombs had dropped. A little smoke was visible in the distance. The streets were impassable, and there was still no clear information about an official route diversion. The passengers sat down by the roadside, one woman handed round biscuits, the sun came out from behind the clouds. So they waited. Two hours later the next bus arrived from Luton. Anyone who wanted could go back on the first bus. My father, without hesitation, decided not to. He hung around for a while watching two men play cards, but they were playing by rules he didn't know, and very badly too. When there was a shower of rain everyone got back in the bus until it was over; the driver raised no objection. When the sun came out they sat down by the roadside again.

My father thought of Mr Bulldog and the two afternoons delivering medicines next week. Two afternoons fewer at the Boys' Club. He didn't want to miss the weekly film. He shrugged his shoulders; worse things happened. If the advance had depended on extra dandelion-picking he would have turned it down. Or would he? He wasn't sure. He tried to conjure up a picture of his sister. He saw her with fair hair (smooth and shiny, not curly like his own), a very girlish laugh, and a particular fragrance. Remembering smells is so difficult until you smell them again . . . it must have been some kind of scent or *eau de parfum*. He had picked some flowers for Katzi behind the house near the rabbit hutch, but now he wasn't sure if that had been a very good idea. The flowers were already looking rather limp. He thought briefly of his big brother. He was proud of him.

The word 'internment' didn't mean much to him, and he imagined his brother wearing a splendid uniform. He wasn't to know that, on the contrary, my uncle would be kept busy for months repairing uniforms for other people. Uncle Tom had said that internment was a crying shame, and a crack-brained idea too. But his big brother, my uncle, had written to say he would be on an island. My little father thought an island sounded interesting. Dandelions? The sea? He fell asleep.

When asked later what he remembered of his last day with Katzi, my uncle always said, 'Not much.' They had been forced to stay down in the Underground the evening before until the all-clear sounded, so long that when they finally reached Katzi's lodgings he couldn't go home any more, so he slept on the sofa there. Next day they stayed in Kilburn, strolled up and down quiet, tree-lined Christchurch Avenue, and once went all the way down to the busy street at the junction. What was then the biggest cinema in Europe stood there, and they even thought of going to see the film now showing. It was *The Great Dictator*. My uncle, who had seen the film already, thought it would be ideal: first, Katzi would easily be able to understand it, and, second, it would cheer her up. But Katzi didn't want to stay out so long. On the way back, although my uncle no longer remembered that, Katzi instinctively quickened her pace. But 'our little one', as Katzi lovingly called him, still hadn't arrived. They drank tea. They ate sandwiches. They waited. For the umpteenth time, Katzi looked through all her papers and travel documents. She made plans for getting her parents out of Austria. Once she was in Canada she would see to everything. They'd all come, first the two boys from England; her stout husband would fix it. Her parents-in-law were rich.

'Guess what, they already have a big house with a garden,' said Katzi, 'even though they paid a fortune just to emigrate.'

'We'll all stay there at first, but not for ever,' said Katzi, 'that wouldn't be a good idea.'

'Although,' said Katzi, 'my mother-in-law cooks lovely Viennese dishes.'

'So does our mama,' said my uncle. He wasn't committing himself to the subject of Canada, which he thought an impossible idea. He had visas in his passport for Shanghai, Panama and Tangiers. That was all he had been able to get. If they let him stay on in England that would be good luck enough.

'If you really are interned, and God forbid,' Katzi told him, 'the first thing you must do is send me your address. Don't forget! Remember, I can't do anything for you without an address!' My uncle nodded. Next moment he had forgotten his promise, and soon afterwards he forgot the whole conversation.

Katzi talked about children. She very much wanted to have a baby, now that she was married and would soon be in safety.

'A little Canadian,' she smiled, nudging my uncle. 'A John or Jim or Jack.'

'There wouldn't be any point in it here,' she said later. Her 'here' sounded very vague. My uncle did not reply. Nothing was further from his mind. Katzi had immediately noticed that there were no children to be seen anywhere outside. On their short walks, they had passed five schools, and although it might be the holidays the buildings looked as if the children had been evacuated. Why they looked like that my uncle couldn't explain later. Nor could he explain his dogged insistence that my grandparents had only ever played cards with Jews in the coffee-house before the war, only with Jews, never with Christians. 'You just somehow knew it,' he used to say, with more than a touch of impatience, 'believe you me, that's how it was.'

★

A football hit my father on the head. A boy was standing in front of him staring at him, and instead of apologising he finally asked if my father would like to play too. The bus was still standing there. The bus driver glanced apologetically at the passengers and shrugged. They were right beside a football field – 'There are football fields for boys on every street corner in England,' my father was still saying reproachfully decades later, 'and here at home they wonder why there's no new talent coming along.' The bus driver promised my anxious father to hoot when the bus was ready to drive on again. So my father joined the football game. There were ten of them, five a side. The pitch was reduced in size by half; they had put a little goal inside one of the big ones and another little goal on the half-way line. The little goals had no nets, but consisted of proper goalposts. At the Boys' Club my father was already one of the football aces, as he always proudly told us later. He also played excellent table tennis in his youth, in middle age he learned to play a respectable game of tennis, and only when his friends took up golf between the age of fifty and sixty did he opt out. 'Call that a ball?' he said scornfully. He did not recognise balls that didn't fly through the air as balls at all.

His great love was football. Football was the opposite of dandelion-picking: running instead of slow strolling; leaping instead of bending; looking at the goal in the distance instead of looking down and thinking of hungry rabbits. And even if the ball has to go into the goal (and all his life, even back in Austria, my father used the English word 'goal'), like dandelions into the sack, then it comes out again at once and the game goes on.

By now it was hot again. A few raindrops were still glittering in a theatrical way, but next moment they had dried up. The clouds were fat and fluffy. At certain times in England the sky seems to be both wide and high. In Austria it's usually high. In Moravia and Italy it's usually wide. Only

61

in England, in a certain early-autumn atmosphere that may come at almost any time of year, can it be both at once.

Those passengers who still hadn't given up waiting gathered around the playing field out of sheer boredom. My father got possession of the ball. One of the opposing team, an older boy, ran to tackle him. At first my father was alarmed, because he hated collisions; he hated being touched, jostled, maybe kicked. But out of the corner of his eye he saw which foot the big boy would be putting his weight on next moment. It was, of course, the wrong one. My father waited a minute, then elegantly dribbled the ball around the other boy's undefended free leg, and while the boy was still swaying, trying to stop and turn, he was long gone. The ball did everything my father wanted. It stayed with him, it stuck to his foot, he could even, teasingly, let it run a little way off; he knew that he and the ball were, in a real sense, inseparable. 'The ball is round,' my father used to say later, with his mischievous smile, and we children knew that he meant far more by that than the obvious fact. He meant himself, life, his attitude to life. We never entirely understood it, but we guessed at the philosophy indicated by his remark. A ball was much more reliable than anything else in the world, he used to say, if you only know how to treat it, 'but most people don't.' My father liked to act as if being good at playing football were just a matter of intelligence, humility and love of the ball.

As if in a trance, he saw that someone else was trying to get the ball away from him. Come on then, thought my father happily, it's yours if you can get it, and smiling he passed the ball right between the other boy's legs, swerved sideways, and retrieved his ball. Finally he centred the ball, a move which was already his speciality. Another boy shot the goal, but everyone came over to clap my father on the back. The stranded bus passengers at the side of the field whistled and applauded.

So he spent an afternoon aglow with happiness, pride and

triumph somewhere on the outskirts of London. When he boarded the bus back to Luton in the evening, drenched with sweat, he had not only forgotten the squashed flowers by the side of the road, he had almost forgotten why he came in the first place. He was thinking mainly of Dinger, Dinger Brown, the boy who invited him to play and had been a congenial partner. He and Dinger played and passed and attacked as if the two of them were alone in the world. And whenever my father, like a sleepwalker, brought Dinger's centre down with his chest and straight on to his right foot, or whenever he had dribbled past everyone else, deceiving them, like a thin, lanky champion fallen from the skies, he made for the goal, worked out what the goalie was planning to do, and as soon as he thought he knew he just said to himself, 'Bulldog!' Then, confident of victory, he breathed out and shot. And scored.

Heaven knows where Katzi got the idea of presents, or the money and opportunity to buy them, but anyway, when she said goodbye she left my uncle a drawing set to give my father, consisting of three hard pencils, a pair of compasses, and the kind of complex ruler in several parts with a protractor that technical draughtsmen use. My father was delighted with it, used it for a while, and then treasured it for sentimental reasons: apart from a couple of photos, it was all he had left of Katzi. She gave my uncle a book. Literature of some kind, he would mutter discontentedly later, he didn't know where the book was now, couldn't remember its title, thought vaguely that Katzi had written something in it. Trakl? Could have been Trakl, said my taciturn uncle decades later, looking unhappy. When questions got on his nerves he would change his strategy. From then on he claimed to have lent the book to some communist from the Ruhr in the internment camp who was keen on literature, and it must have been lost there. My family for some time held it 'ursus' him (as Königsbee might have said)

Fading It Out

For over half his life my grandfather was a gambler, a passionate, uninhibited gambler magically attracted by any kind of risk. In terms of his life as a whole that's a good deal of it, the rather longer first part. Perhaps, given the choice, he would have liked to be a gambler in the second half of his life too, but he wasn't allowed the option.

My grandfather gambled at cards and gambled for money, but most of all he gambled with opportunities, customers, business deals, delivery dates and commissions, with women, with hints and with dreams. He realised that you can't always win. That was the very reason why, like every true gambler, he loved it, loved the bitter-sweet alternation of winning and losing. And there was nothing he liked better than standing on the edge, betting for high stakes at high risk, seeing the abyss race towards him and then rising to triumphant heights. Yet he was not crazy, as my over-cautious father called all unreasonable people who risked more than they were likely to win. To sum up, my grandfather tried to balance risk, loss and profit in a relationship slightly favouring the last of the three. But there were games and games. There were some where the risk in itself wasn't really enjoyable enough for him to want to take it. His love affairs worked on this principle. A woman is just a woman; that may have been his fundamental idea although, famous charmer that he was, he would never have put it so crudely, even in his cups. But there were other games too. For instance, he could quite easily manage to think temporarily of the payments in his wallet at the end of the week as his own property, and take them into a provincial casino or a dimly lit back room in Praterstrasse, where his week's gross takings were just enough for a night spent drinking and playing poker, an expensive bunch of roses for a pretty girl, and sometimes a sentimental little present of a ring for her next morning. Only then did the real game begin: with the exciting sensation of imminent social and financial disaster. With the hectic invention of creative strategies allowing him to avoid that disaster just in time. With the flowery eloquence he would use in talking round suspicious suppliers, with insane projects for opening up brand-new markets for his wines and spirits, anything that would work when he was up to his neck in trouble. You might have considered my grandfather a small-time con man. But there is something sad and desperate about small-time con men, an air of failure clings to them, an aura of incorrigible stupidity, as with Nandl Königsberger and his forged cheques. No, my grandfather was not a small-time con man, but an elegant and successful juggler, constantly improving his performance, a businessman of the kind we like to see today, always courageously keeping the cash-flow going. He was good-looking, wore monogrammed made-to-measure shirts, and parted his hair carefully while it was still damp. He smelled of the *eau de lavande* still made at the time by a very old-established Viennese firm. And he didn't really cheat, he gambled.

His very special ventures usually worked out, although the amount of the sums outstanding, the new debts he would incur to satisfy a couple of creditors, not to mention the amount of money he needed in bribes to keep judicial proceedings at bay, might have made anyone feel dizzy. My grandfather never felt dizzy. It was his firm conviction that the most important thing in gambling was to have iron nerves. But you could have iron nerves only if you didn't keep thinking of the danger. Let the danger tickle your fancy, yes. But let it paralyse you? Out of the question! In this way my grandfather became a mental acrobat, without noticing that the technique was becoming second nature to him. There were certain dangers, hanging over him like rock-falls, that he could fade out of his mind completely, leaving all his mental powers at his command for the part of the game that he could influence, or at least so he claimed in his younger years. 'First the stakes, then the game,' he would probably have said in those younger years, when only my grandmother had really known him. 'Never confuse the two!' Later, in the second half of his life, he stopped saying so, but then he kept away from risks later.

His strange gift really did have some similarity with what we usually mean by acrobatics. A circus acrobat who has just tossed his enchanting partner up into the airy expanses of the big top can't hang around fearing that she will fall to her death. He uses every moment of the time left to him before she drops safely to get himself into the right, perfect position. Then he catches her, everyone applauds, and my grandfather's theory is confirmed yet again. Occasionally, however, something falls through the acrobat's fingers into the sand of the arena, and it was the same with my grandfather. The thing was to ensure that it happened only in rehearsal, when the ropes and safety nets were in place, not during the brilliant performance when everything really *was* at stake.

My grandfather kept the falls during rehearsal secret as far as he could. 'Business is bad,' was all he used to say when he came back from a long trip with no money worth mentioning for the rent or to feed his family of five. My grandmother noted this fact with an icy expression – she would never have ranted and raged about such things, she ranted and raged only for much less important reasons – and sent my uncle off to the corner shop.

There are few embarrassments in life that my uncle had not already suffered at a tender age; perhaps that was what made him so unapproachable later. As a child he had several times protested and wept, shouted and refused to go when he was sent off to the corner shop or the baker's once again. But he soon learned that there was no point in it. Once or twice, when my grandfather was away travelling, my grandmother pretended to give in instead of simply pushing my little uncle out of the door. Later, they would all sit around the table with empty plates in front of them, my tiny father howling somewhere, my grandmother staring at the wall and clattering her cutlery, Katzi carefully nibbling her cuticles, finger after finger, and then my uncle went out after all. If he knew there was nothing to be had anywhere else, he went to see Herr Eisenstein. These measures of self-discipline in early youth left their mark on him for life. For of course my uncle would always rather have gone to Herr Eisenstein, whose tender heart and soft spot for my grandmother meant that he had some little thing to give him every time, in as matter-of-fact a way as possible. But even as a small boy my uncle had learned to be careful and have an eye to the future. Eisenstein once, Eisenstein three times, Eisenstein five times – a time would come when even Eisenstein's patience would be exhausted. And that would be disastrous. So he preferred to go three times to the unfriendly proprietor of the corner shop who hated socialists, and three times to the unfriendly baker who hated Jews, alternating between them. Now and then, in a real emergency, he would go to Herr Eisenstein. He never went to Aunt Gustl any more – he had tried it just once, and he never said a word, all his life, about what happened. As things stood, however, it might be that his father would soon come home with a new coat and money in his pockets, would give the baker's wife a red carnation and pay the owner of the corner shop not only what he owed but an 'advance' on next month. Such things had been known.

My uncle was never happy. Once his father gave him a

new dark green fountain pen, another time he was told that the whole family was going to spend several weeks on holiday in the summer at Bad Vöslau, where his father had rented an expensive apartment near the swimming pool, the medicinal baths and the thermal baths. But my uncle was never happy. He was aware that this state of affairs would not last. 'I knew there was a snag in it—' that, later, was his favourite expression. He was a pessimist who could be grimly happy only when, once again, his prognosis of misfortune had proved right.

His parents' financial circumstances hadn't always been so bad. Indeed, for a long time they had been very good. There was a sturdy Moravian nursemaid to look after my uncle when he was a baby, Katzi wore silk ribbons and pleated skirts, my grandfather atoned for his extramarital adventures with furs and jewellery, my grandmother took refuge in the coffee-house day after day to play bridge when she felt it was all getting too much for her. And much later, in the short period just before my uncle and my father left, everything became easier again. That was when Katzi began going out with stout Herbert, whose parents were rich, and who even, with a twinkle in his eye, gave her two little brothers 'pocket money' whenever he visited. But in between, for a few years, my grandfather seems somehow to have gone out of control, and it was mainly my uncle, between the ages of eight and thirteen, who paid for it.

You might wonder if my grandfather ever felt guilty about that, for instance in the late autumn of 1941 when he was sitting in the Café Johann Strauss on a damp, cold day of drizzling rain, playing bridge. For at the time he often and nostalgically thought of the very risky deals he had done in the past (my grandfather sometimes used the word *machloikes* for them), he thought back to his brilliant *machloikes* of the past while he waited for his partner to play a card at last. His partner, a kindly but unattractive lady, was shockingly lacking in any talent for the game. But he couldn't pick and choose. Not much bridge was played these days, and he was only standing in for someone else. While she still thought he was joking when he said he was going to play bridge in the Johann Strauss, my grandmother had told him he was 'totally crazy', but in the end she positively begged him, with tears in her eyes, to stay at home. 'The Johann Strauss is still open,' said my grandfather, impatiently dismissing her objections, and he turned to the door. 'So why not kill yourself right away? It comes to the same thing!' my grandmother had hissed after him as he left, in a choked voice. She had then taken refuge in bed, fully clothed, and huddled there whimpering so as not to hear the door slam.

My grandfather waited for his bridge partner to lead and hoped in passing that she would lead with spades (she must still be holding spades, but unfortunately she understood nothing about the game), added up deliveries and commissions in his head, compared times, probabilities, the patience of suppliers, and his own moments of glory, and finally boiled it all down to a single date: the early summer of 1935. He could have made it in the early summer of 1935. At that time he was representing the profitable Kratky range of spirits; the red Burgundy vintage was a good one too, and people were happy to order it. Moreover, he had been commissioned to sell a few furs by his Galician cousin, furs which it turned out he could sell very profitably to the bloated manufacturers' wives and councillors' widows with whom his sister Gustl mixed. Although the family later denied it, my grandfather definitely had contact with his sister before the war. Mainly of a business nature, of course, since Gustl always had an eye to her own advantage.

The early summer of 1935, then. If he had known what was going to happen, then in a short time and with a certain amount of juggling skill he could have borrowed, obtained payment in advance and evaded enough tax to emigrate overnight with the whole family, leaving everything behind and travelling to a destination where there would be time and sufficient money left for a new start. Instead, they hired an apartment in Bad Vöslau for six long weeks and enjoyed a holiday instead of getting out of the country. That was because he hadn't foreseen what would happen some years later, and because his financial transactions had never aimed at genuine deception. Perhaps they wouldn't have worked as genuine, deliberate deception either. Stakes for gambling: that was what he had needed like a drug, the uplifting sense now and then of being a rich man with thousands of opportunities, hundreds of businesses, and a handful of girlfriends. That was why he always paid everything back in the end.

Well, paid almost everything back. Sometimes I wasn't allowed to, he thought, shaking his head. Then, right on cue, his partner led: diamonds. Really, she was hopeless. But it didn't matter, anyway. This was just a little game of no importance.

Outside, in front of the big glazed façade of the Café Johann Strauss, through which you could have seen the Danube Canal if it hadn't been so misty, a pick-up truck drew up. A few uniformed men jumped out.

My grandfather remembered, with great uneasiness, the two or three times when he had miscalculated in business, getting the equilibrium between his creditors' forbearance and his own ability to obtain twice as many commissions as usual in an emergency wrong, and with the best will in the world he couldn't save the situation. The first time, luckily, it was short and painless, in the sense that what my grandfather had most feared was the embarrassment of the trial. The first time, thanks also to a mild-tempered Jewish judge, he had got off with a suspended sentence.

Inside the Johann Strauss tables were now being overturned, china broke on the floor, the proprietor came out of the kitchen, silently clenching his fists in his trouser pockets, the guests sat as if turned to stone, looking at the floor, and only his ugly bridge partner stared at my grandfather as if he were a ghost. He smiled reassuringly at her. He tried to form the word 'Spades' inconspicuously with his lips. She rolled her eyes in despair, and didn't seem to understand.

The second time, remembered my grandfather, concentrating, he had been unlucky when his precise if frail calculations, which left very little leeway (that was the secret of their charm), had been wrecked by unforeseen outside circumstances. A delivery of wine from Hungary had been held up at Customs, and this delay, although it might have been anticipated, was the last straw: the customer waiting for the delivery, to whom he also owed money, lost his nerve and laid a complaint. An artist's bad luck, thought my grandfather, silently cursing Customs once again. He had never had any trouble with Customs before. All the same, of course it was unpardonable of him not at least to have considered the possibility. On this second occasion he spent three weeks in jail. That wasn't too bad. Three weeks – it was like a trip into the country, the children had noticed nothing wrong; even Katzi, even his beautiful, clever and sometimes very anxious little daughter Katzi hadn't noticed anything.

A heel came down on a pair of glasses, crunching them. A cheerful-looking man in civilian clothes was going from coat-stand to coat-stand, carefully searching pockets. 'Whose is this?' he called suddenly, holding up an ordinary grey gentleman's coat. 'Come forward please, come aboard, please, your tourist group is waiting!' What a sense of humour the man had. Unfortunately he reminded my grandfather of something connected with Nandl. One of his fine friends?

On the third occasion, thought my grandfather, concentrating again as he reached automatically for his glass of red wine, the two previous convictions had been taken into account, which was unfortunate: he got three months, including one day a month of particularly severe incarceration. He and my grandmother had agreed to say he was on an extended trip to make purchases in several countries, finishing with a visit to Semmering for the good of his health. 'Your father needs a rest,' his wife had told the children, her face giving nothing away.

How can anyone say if a marriage is good or bad? My grandparents always agreed with each other on important matters, without any ifs and buts. One of those important matters was keeping up appearances and saying nothing. For the same reason, when they were in want they suffered want in style. It would never have occurred to my grandmother to pawn the good Herend china or her jewellery. They tightened their belts, sent the child round to the corner shop, bought on credit there and waited for better times to come. And in the end, somehow or other they always did come.

Who dares wins, thought my grandfather, with relief. Anything else is suicidal madness in times like these. As the cheerful coat-searching expert left, he jogged my grandfather's arm, making him spill a few drops, and said in a tone designed to give offence, 'Your very good health, and do forgive the disturbance.' Out of the corner of his eye, my grandfather saw Adi Jacoby being led out and climbing into the pick-up truck. Had Adi Jacoby been carrying what my grandfather liked to call 'the German Reich's dog-tag' in his coat pocket? He wouldn't have thought him so stupid. Rule number one: on those occasions when you have a reason not to wear the dog-tag, don't carry it on you. Obvious. Rule number two: don't have your ID on you either. Not having it with you was forbidden, but sitting in the coffee-house playing bridge was even worse. 'Forgetting' your ID delayed things, anyway, and with a bit of boldness and luck you still had a chance. But having the dog-tag or your ID in your pocket instantly answered all their questions, and your game was up. To think some people didn't realise! My grandfather shook his head. The platform truck drove away. November mists merged again outside the Johann Strauss. 'Whose turn to lead?' asked my grandfather.

The playful and cold-blooded elements in his nature were forgotten later, because he changed so much that no one knew about those qualities any more. But long after my grandfather's death his impatience was remembered. His impatience was proverbial. When, for instance, my father once again told the story of their last visit to a football match together, his inborn love of exaggeration was perfectly matched with my grandfather's impatience, which was carried to extremes in his old age. He had to call for my grandfather so early, my father said, that they reached their seats while the under-21s match was still going on. 'Even football's not what it was,' muttered my grandfather, whose eyesight now left something to be desired. 'This is only the boys playing,' my father explained. 'I can see they're only boys, am I blind?' snarled my grandfather, for in his role as an expert on the game he was not taking a lecture from anyone, even his son the former football star. By now my grandfather didn't feel comfortable sitting in the draughty stadium anyway, love of the game or no love of the game. 'I'm old, tired, and miserable,' he muttered in English, using the only three English words he knew. Soon after the second half of the match proper began, said my father, his old father had insisted that it was time to leave. 'No traffic jams, and somewhere to park at home,' was his constant battle cry as he suddenly began making his way to the central aisle, his walking stick thrust out before him like a weapon. And how often, my father complained with the eloquence of the practised storyteller, had the two of them then found themselves on the concrete stairways of the stadium, or in the horrible lavatories, the car park, or already in the car when they heard the mighty roar of many voices, followed by the frenzied rejoicing that told them another goal had been scored. 'The second half of the under-21s, the first half of the real match, that was how he was in the end,' my father summed up with a sigh, and my family laughed and then felt a little sad.

Had he been so impatient when he waited for a whole morning in the draughty corridor of the Victims' Welfare office? It was lucky that he'd arrived early enough to get a chair, for he'd had a bad knee since the war. And if it had only been the knee – but you never really recovered from an operation for gallstones and a broken hip, both in war-time. The queue ahead of him was only very slowly getting shorter. It took them a long time to find out who were victims, what of, and how much they ought to get for it. My grandfather could understand that. He was not a suspicious man. He didn't waste time wondering whether there were any former fellow travellers of the Nazi regime here with intent to deceive, making themselves out poor and persecuted, for he would never have thought it possible for anyone in the world to state his Jewish identity of his own free will – unless, as in his case, his own wife made him do it. However, two old bags who must have got up in the middle of the night, they were so far forward in the queue, were speculating in low voices on that very subject as they accusingly scrutinised all the others waiting. One man lost his temper, an old comrade whom my grandfather knew by sight. He clenched his fist and rolled up his shirt-sleeve. The two old bags fell silent for a while. In the following awkward silence, the pick-up trucks appeared before my grandfather's mind's eye again, driving off day after day, black with people who were leaving Vienna from the Aspangbahnhof and the Westbahnhof. My grandfather could have done without this memory in his present situation as a petitioner, which was deeply repugnant to him. He concentrated. There was a humming sound in his head. He faded the picture out. It was brilliant, the way I organised that truck, he suddenly thought, relaxing. He had never been particularly practical, but once he had taken something into his head he was a good organiser. Above all, he always knew people. Getting hold of a truck two years after the war, who else could have done it? thought my grandfather with satisfaction.

My grandfather had paid for the truck in kind: potatoes, onions, jam, even a bit of bacon fat, anything he had been able to obtain from his many contacts in Kagran. Those contacts were the only good part of what he liked to call doing 'sauced labour'. It was something he wanted to forget as quickly as possible, for after all the war was over and done with, full stop. But arriving at the Westbahnhof in the year 1947 in a pick-up truck with a driver to meet his younger son, that had really meant something to him, he had been happy to give valuable foodstuffs for it. What good was it going to do? my grandmother had nagged. 'Do you know how long the boy's been away?' he had snapped back. 'I know to the day,' my grandmother had spat. 'Well, so what's he going to have now?' my grandfather had asked, rhetorically, immediately answering his own question. 'Plenty, that's what.'

'I'm afraid we can deal with this quickly,' said the woman official when at last she came to my grandfather, who had been waiting in the draughty corridor all morning. She leafed through her file, pretending to study it closely. On top lay the form, signed a long time ago, in which my grandfather declared on oath that he had never belonged to the National Socialist Workers' Party or any of its subsidiary organisations. Next came confirmation that he had worn the 'dog-tag' 'from the day of its introduction to the end of the regime', as my grandfather had declared in his swift handwriting, not quite in accordance with the facts. It was stamped by the Jewish Community office. After that there was the medical officer's certificate of his physical disabilities, a list of the various places where he had done that sauced labour, confirmation by one of the people who had employed sauced labour at the time that my grandfather had received the 'collective legal hourly wage of 0.75 Reich marks an hour', finally a detailed description of everything else, up to and including the story of how he had got into the train with his mother on it and fell out again. Unfortunately there was no bureaucratic proof of the train story – my grandfather had not appeared on any official transport list – but that wasn't the problem. 'The problem, sir,' said the woman official, suddenly looking very stern, 'the problem is your character. The Victims' Associations have dismissed your right to make a claim. Didn't you know that criminal convictions . . .'

Convictions. A criminal, not a victim. Victims' Associations and their officials. Genuine victims, fake victims, pretended victims. Shirt-sleeve rolled up, yes, incontrovertible evidence that you were a victim. But what about him? He'd only worn the dog-tag and done a bit of sauced labour. Nothing by comparison. What could the others say for him? His mother? His mother wasn't saying anything any more.

My grandfather was burning all over. As the Victims' Associations saw it, he was told, it was inadmissible for someone whose character was not spotless . . . Yes, he said, yes, he understood all that. No, he could not produce 'any evidence that his convictions had been declared null and void', no, he stammered, no, he didn't think so, in fact he was sure not, I'm sorry, he said, excuse me, I didn't want to come, I didn't know, it's an oversight, a mistake, I only came because of my wife. In nerve-racking slow motion, the remarks about null and void, proof, convictions had to be entered in his file. The woman official was not very good at typing. She made a great many mistakes, but as she hated mistakes she typed very slowly. He signed the statement, and then the file was closed. The woman official revelled in the knowledge that even at awkward moments she did her job conscientiously and carefully. Most people did get something from her, but not everyone. That was what she was here for. Otherwise they might just as well have a treasurer here paying something out to everyone who applied. But it doesn't work like that, she thought with satisfaction. If it did, then just anyone could come along.

My grandfather took off his hat to her and left as fast as he could. There were still throngs of victims waiting outside, real victims, not greedy pretenders. How many there still were, all the same, a couple of . . . oh, a whole corridor full.

He was hot under the collar, and pulled his hat down further over his face. His walking stick clacked on the floor of the long corridor. There was a buzzing in his head. He concentrated hard on his triumph with the truck only a couple of weeks ago. He nearly didn't manage to do it. He did see trucks in his mind's eye, but not the right one, trucks carrying crowds of people. Adi Jacoby waved from one of them, smiling, the dog-tag in his hand; his mother sat in another, wrapped in her fur coat. She was freezing. He couldn't do anything about it.

There was a buzzing in his head. He tried to picture his son. That would help. Two images overlapped, a little boy with a warm tasselled cap, then a tall stranger. Nothing in between. But how the boy looked! How tall he's grown, thought my grandfather, almost a man. Tall and lanky, like a shy, thin chicken, fresh from England. He had only a seaman's canvas bag with him; he hadn't been able to bring any more, but she entirely forgot to snap at me in her opinionated way, for what must have been the first time in her life she forgot about that, thought my grandfather, relaxing. He himself, on seeing the little seaman's bag, immediately changed his mind about the purpose of the truck, originally a practical one, but now he switched it to a ceremonial function. We brought him home like a king, my younger son, 'just us and the army jeeps on the streets,' murmured my grandfather two or three times in the last days before his death, when presumably he was recapitulating the high points of his life.

And then we all three sat at the back of the truck, he thought, as he made his escape from the Victims' Aid office, sweating and humiliated, I and the boy and the big boy, who by now, surprisingly, was the smaller of the two, wearing his fine uniform. The now smaller big boy interpreted for them occasionally, but there wasn't much to say in those first moments. His wife was beside the driver; it wouldn't be right for her to sit at the back of the truck, she was a lady. 'Still the same old place, you know, near the Augarten,' he had encouragingly told the boy, and the boy had first nodded shyly and then turned inquiringly to his brother, who translated for him in a murmur. Otherwise the boy just looked wide-eyed at the rubble to left and right that had once been Mariahilferstrasse. 'It will soon be back in order,' he had told the boy encouragingly, 'you wait and see, we'll build it all again.'

The very next day he took him for a pedicure. The chiropodist at the Dianabad was back at work already, although the baths themselves were closed until further notice because of war damage. At first my father hadn't the faintest idea what it was all about. His new, old father, that strange, emaciated man, chuckled happily and kept pointing to their feet and talking, making promises, or that was what it sounded like. All this left my father feeling dreadfully uncomfortable. Of course his brother my uncle, who was his only resource, wasn't living with their parents in the musty-smelling apartment any more, he was a much-decorated English soldier and busy interpreting for more important purposes. He was helping the Allies with their denazification. In addition he had a wife and a small son; his wife shopped in the places reserved specially for British soldiers. Sometimes she took her mother-in-law some of the goods from those shops, and wrote down what they were if the contents were not obvious at first glance, for my father, who couldn't remember a word of German, was no help there.

What my grandfather particularly liked about Frau Erna was the way she talked. She was from the country, 'really very rustic,' my father would say later, grinning, and went to great pains to hide her broad dialect when she spoke. She managed after a fashion, but what she had learnt to perfection – and my grandfather could not imagine how she must have worked at it – was how to speak in the third person, using the impersonal pronoun 'one'.

My grandfather and the broadly smiling Frau Erna therefore took my father into the cubby-hole that for now served the chiropodist as her place of work. First the two of them just pointed to the alarming chair, then to my father's shoes. Finally they both bent down at the same time to make it clear to him that he was to take his shoes off. My father hesitated. Finally he got the idea, and sat down in the other chair, amidst much laughter. And then, when Frau Erna, under the amused and moved glance of my grandfather, bent over my father's toes, which had suffered a great deal from too much footballing and were bruised black and blue, she brought out one of those sentences that pleased my grandfather so much: 'May one ask when those feet were last treated?' But hard as she tried to achieve good elocution, her Austrian vowel sounds came through.

To be poorly groomed, to my grandfather, was a disaster. He set almost excessive store by a well-groomed exterior. As I have said, before the war he loved lavender water and made-to-measure monogrammed shirts, even if there were times when he couldn't afford either. He bought them all the same, regarding the money as a good investment. He knew that the baker and the proprietor of the corner shop would never have let his son go on asking for credit so long if his father hadn't always walked through the doorway looking so extremely distinguished, bringing into their small shops the aura of the wide world and the prosperity that must, after all, exist somewhere. Not to speak of impressing his many creditors. Making a good entrance was half the secret, my grandfather firmly believed. And it was here, in discussing personal hygiene and the unspeakable disadvantages entailed by neglect of it, that my grandfather's willingness to say anything about the war began and ended. To be perfectly truthful – which is by no means an established tradition in my family – the only one of us who occasionally showed an interest in the subject was my brother when he went to grammar school.

'Tell us, Grandpa, what was it really like in the war?' was the way he would sometimes try to start a conversation, but all his attempts failed miserably.

'In the war?' my grandfather asked, looking disparagingly at my brother. 'Why, in the war everyone had to smell bad.'

'But,' my brother persisted, although he knew by now that it was hopeless, 'didn't the Jews . . .'

'Stuff and nonsense,' my grandfather interrupted, waving the question away, 'everyone had to smell bad, not just the Jews.' And there was no more to be got out of him.

The chiropodist from the Dianabad is a real artist in her own field, thought my grandfather, as he hurried along Döbling high street after my uncle. It was only three weeks ago that his elder son had suddenly come to the door in British uniform. My grandparents could hardly believe their luck, seeing their firstborn child home again, and in such an awe-inspiring uniform too; one child at least back, perhaps there'll soon be another, we'll wait and see, let's hope so, we'll try everything. But three weeks later, unfortunately, when they still hadn't quite finished celebrating their reunion, hadn't grasped the fact that they were a family again and had a son, a grown-up son who spoke English and was even married, three weeks later this son, who suddenly seemed so grown-up and determined, wanted to go back to

Döbling high street and call on Pepi Hermann. My grandfather didn't even like to think about it. So he thought about
Frau Erna instead, which always worked. A real artist, an
artist with feet, he thought, I ought to take her flowers again
some time, and he walked more and more slowly, being
reluctant to go to Döbling at all, while on the other hand he
didn't want to lose his eldest son, didn't want to leave him
alone, not again, and so he hurried down the street after him
and then stopped once more, was this really necessary?

Frau Erna is no beauty, he thought, quite the opposite.
'Beauty is a woman's undoing,' he murmured, quoting a
proverb current among the misanthropic clientèle of the
Weisskopf. But she was a past mistress of chiropody. Out of
the corner of his eye he noticed the woman in the
tobacconist's come out of her shop and look in amazement
at my uniformed uncle. So she's survived too, thought my
grandfather in annoyance, and turned his mind back to Frau
Erna and her art. In his view, Frau Erna had healing hands.
As he followed my father along the stairway – 'Don't run
like that!' he protested softly – he thought with discomfort
of the septic big toe that had plagued him for weeks towards
the end of the war. Typical, he thought, it was my left
big toe that was septic, while his bad knee was the right
one, everything always turns out the way you can least be
doing with.

My uncle was already ringing the doorbell. My grandfather made out he had to pause on the landing below to get
his breath back. 'I'm not a steam engine,' he hissed up the
stairs. Footsteps were heard.

In the rooms where Frau Erna worked there was a
glockenspiel hanging behind the door. As soon as you
opened that door you heard delicate notes, as delicate as
Frau Erna's hands. Not a loud, angry bell like the one here
in the Döbling apartment. 'However did we stand it?' my
grandfather asked himself in amazement. It had never
occurred to him before. Frau Erna always smiled invitingly

when you came through the door. Pepi Hermann isn't going to like this, my grandfather feared, panting as he stared at my uncle's uniformed back. 'Do come in,' Frau Erna always cried every time with her rosy smile, pointing to the chiropodist's chair.

When Josef 'Pepi' Hermann opened the door, and a second or so later recognised my uncle under his beret, he said nothing at all. History does not relate whether he went pale, as he should have done. 'You lot and your lively imagination,' my uncle always muttered later when asked about it, grumpy as ever. My grandfather kept well behind his son's back and concentrated on thinking about his septic toe towards the end of the war. He couldn't get a shoe on that foot any more; it was terrible because he had to get to the sauced labour, far out of the city, all the way to Kagran. If he just failed to turn up one day . . . well, it didn't bear thinking of. But then, luckily, Frau Erna . . .

My uncle claimed later to have said, in an icy voice, 'Don't worry, we just want to take a look at the apartment.' Then he apparently thrust Pepi Hermann aside with a gesture that he often performed later (it was like opening swing doors). My grandfather grimaced painfully (in his memory, Frau Erna was pulling hard at the nail) and tripped along behind my uncle.

'You can always tell the men of this family by the way they walk,' my mother would say later, pulling a face. She would probably have preferred to say something quite different about 'the men of this family', but she lacked the courage to criticise more than their tripping gait. It was true: all his life my grandfather walked with hasty little steps, and that didn't change even when he got his walking stick, when it was as if he had acquired a third little foot going along in a hurry. My father tripped along too, on feet that were small in pro-portion to the rest of him, and my uncle walked with a tripping step because he was so skinny and weighed so little. Only my brother didn't trip as he walked, and he had two explanations for that, depending on his mood: it was either a deliberate act of defiance, or evidence that he had not inherited every bad quality and ridiculously cranky idea in the family – only most of them, unfortunately.

They walked round the apartment, my uncle very slow and casual in his uniform, my grandfather very fast and nervous behind him. Pepi Hermann staggered along after them. My uncle looked thoughtfully at the white dresser in the kitchen, even opened it and ran his finger over the Herend coffee pot. He thought of Meiktila, where despair had sometimes made it seem a good idea to roar with laughter at a world where craftsmen put loving care into the making of Herend china, which was bought for good money by like-minded people and treasured in bourgeois households, while in other places, like Meiktila, knives and forks hadn't even been invented, but a thousand imaginative ways of dying and killing had been devised.

In the rarely used sitting-room, several football trophies now stood on the old sideboard that my grandmother used to dust and polish so assiduously. My grandfather noticed them. Interested, he was about to emerge from his character as his son's timid shadow and come closer, but a hiss from my uncle stopped him. My grandfather sighed. He had just spotted the championship medal for the year 1931. He remembered every moment of the final. Rain had been pouring down, all the spectators were drenched within a few minutes, but that didn't bother anyone, not in such a world-class match. Pepi Hermann and the other defenders had stood firm as a wall whenever the outside right of the opposing team . . . what was his name, now? He would have liked to ask Pepi Hermann a quick question, but dared not because of my uncle.

'Come on, Father, we're off,' said my uncle icily. He turned once more at the door. 'And how's your son these days?' he asked. This, to his way of thinking, was the nastiest thing he could say, for everyone knew that Pepi Hermann's only son had been killed during an air raid, in the bar where he was playing the violin at the end of the war.

'Listen!' Pepi Hermann burst out. 'I was never a Nazi!'

My grandfather suddenly remembered how Frau Erna sometimes had hot waxing sessions for ladies, using a folding couch behind a specially drawn curtain through which, sad to say, it was absolutely impossible to see a thing. Now and then one of the ladies would utter a little scream, and then he heard Erna blow on the sore place and soothe the ladies like a mother comforting her child. 'There, there, it'll be fine, over soon, won't it, just a little self-control, right? And then madam can go anywhere.'

'Yes,' replied my uncle, 'that's what I thought.' In a perfectly friendly manner he turned to Pepi Hermann again, as if he had something confidential to say. 'Do you know, Herr Hermann,' he said, 'I've been back in Vienna almost a month now, and I still haven't met a single Nazi. Can you explain that?'

'I'm afraid not, Major,' whispered Pepi Hermann, whose nerves were in shreds. The neighbours all seemed to be listening behind their doors.

'Sergeant,' my uncle corrected him, and then they left. My grandfather was thinking that when the hot-waxed ladies came out from behind the curtain to pay, their cheeks all red, they had always looked happy, in spite of the pain they had just suffered; they were hot and flustered but happy all the same. And he too had been very happy when the septic nail was finally off, although his toe still throbbed horribly. He felt consoled. Out in the street he told his son, 'That'll give him something to think about.' My uncle shook his head angrily. 'You don't think he'll have nightmares over that, do you?'

'But I don't understand,' said my sister, carefully disinfecting the assortment of silver earrings that she wore in her pierced ears with a cotton-wool ball. 'It was your apartment.'

My uncle said, sharply, 'We didn't want to be like them.'

My father said, thoughtfully, 'Grandpa admired Pepi Hermann so much – and he really was a fabulous footballer.'

My mother said, understandingly, 'Grandpa didn't know if he could afford the apartment any more.'

'That's right,' my father was quick to agree. 'What's the point in saying you want a place back if you can't afford it?'

'You make me sick, all of you,' said my brother, getting to his feet and putting his half-smoked cigarette in the ashtray, and he marched out of the room making a lot of noise about it.

It's a fact that after the war my grandfather no longer gambled as he once did. He had lost his courage and his cool head. He did spend every spare moment in the coffee-house, playing bridge, but only for the tiny, meticulously calculated sums for which my grandmother played too. He didn't play poker, he didn't play billiards in gloomy Praterstrasse back rooms, he didn't go to the casino any more, he very seldom gave a pretty young lady a rose these days, and when he did the young lady was one of his daughters-in-law. It was at this time that my grandmother began publicly nagging him about his former mistresses, in so far as she knew about them and they had survived the war. These days my grandparents usually sat in the coffee-house together playing bridge at neighbouring tables. My grandmother, pointing her stern chin at another woman playing with them, would suddenly say out loud, 'Looks like a monkey.' 'I pass,' my grandfather would say at the next table, shaking his head gloomily. 'I double,' cried my grandmother triumphantly. 'She doesn't just look like a monkey, she plays like a monkey too.' Apparently no one reacted in any way worth mentioning to these accusations. 'Oh, do lead and stop talking so much,' was the most another lady might say. The last remaining bridge partners, who had all played with each other 'in the old days' and were playing together again, were accustomed to one another, like elderly animals in the zoo. They couldn't be offended by people of their own kind any more, they had simply lost the heart for it. And my grandmother, who had once been known as 'that German woman', had been someone of their own kind of person for a long time now.

My grandfather did not go back into the wines and spirits trade after the war. That was interpreted in the family as a deliberate move, and it was claimed that he had found the perfect way to combine his profession and his hobby when he became a commercial traveller for Arabia Coffee for a while. 'In the coffee-house during working hours, in the coffee-house after working hours too,' said the family, laughing, 'that, as Königsbee would have said, was what he was dated to do.' It's a fact, however, that my grandfather was no longer in any condition to return to his old, gruelling way of life. So he became dogsbody to the coffee importer, who just let him go ahead, as my father guiltily said much later, and the more successful my grandfather was, the more his employer cut his bonuses. For he did know about coffee-houses, whatever his financial difficulties. He went from one establishment to another, taking orders for coffee, asking whether the establishment had enough little sachets of sugar with the Arabia Coffee logo on them, checking up on its stocks of Arabia Coffee paper napkins, Arabia Coffee ashtrays, and those little round paper doilies with pinked edges that are placed between the cup and saucer of every serving of freshly brewed coffee in the best coffee-houses, so that even the most unobservant customer must at least subliminally take note of the brand. But when the coffee importer also expected my grandfather to change the defective neon tubes in the Arabia Coffee advertising signs, my father stepped in, put an end to it, and took my grandfather into business with him instead. It

A New Start

So soon everything was all right again. My father and my uncle married, had children, got divorced and married again. My uncle had had enough children first time around. My father hadn't. In spite of the divorces, family relationships were magically harmonious. It was taken for granted that first wives as well as second wives attended family gatherings, the children of the first and second marriages proudly referred to each other as brothers and sisters, and turned on anyone who ventured to call them merely half-brothers and half-sisters with all the condescension of those who consider themselves to have risen above petty bourgeois thinking. My grandparents never let themselves show any preference for first or second daughters-in-law, acknowledging them all equally. Towards the end of their lives, they did sometimes seem to get the chronological order mixed up, or might assign children to the wrong mothers, but in view of the great old age which they both reached they could hardly be blamed for that. Decades later, our ostentatious family harmony peaked in the appearance of a first wife as a mourner at a second wife's funeral, and it was only at the last minute that the family decided not to have the funeral address for the second wife given by a child of the first marriage in the first wife's presence.

My father had soon learned German again. 'There must still have been something left in there,' he would say, smiling. We children roared with laughter when he said words like 'orange' that sounded all wrong and foreign in his English pronunciation. He got his own back by making fun of our English homework. 'How can anyone not know that?' he jeered if one of us wrote, 'She do not know,' or thought the plural of 'mouse' was 'mouses'. 'You are all my little mouses,' he said, 'but you'll never learn proper English.'

English was like ball games to him. He really seemed to think that you were bound to learn both as automatically as you learned to talk or walk. He was stunned when he realised that his son had no talent for football, but just stumbled short-sightedly about on his big feet. He shook his head in despair when my tiny sister, aged four and delivered up to a terrifying, clattering ball machine armed with nothing more than her cut-down tennis racket, mis-hit many of the balls mercilessly racing towards her. But each of us children had a year's luxury on reaching eight; at the age when my father had once been obliged to leave his parents, we were all lovingly permitted not to be instantly perfect at something. 'I'd have had to send you away at this age,' my father would sometimes say thoughtfully, and in retrospect I see these moments as the first, almost imperceptible harbingers of an emotion that really overcame him only much later, in old age.

In those first decades they none of them complained, they just cracked jokes. The years of post-war recovery were presented to us as a time of unlimited opportunity. My uncle was one of the first in Vienna to own a BMW, a metallic blue-green car of the impeccably cool elegance that suited his style so well. My cousins and my brother later admitted that they began smoking so young only because of him, because no one else held a cigarette so faultlessly and gracefully, yet with such breathtaking virility. Wherever he went he was surrounded by heavy English ashtrays, which at the touch of a button dumped first the ashes, then the filter-tip of a cigarette smoked to the very end into an airtight compartment. From five in the afternoon he ceremonially drank whisky, never with ice – 'Oh, no thank you,' he would say with a touch of disdain if ice was offered. He was very much the cool English gentleman, was sometimes described as the Frank Sinatra of Vienna purely because of his looks, since he had no ear for music at all, and he smoked and smoked, kept his own counsel, and went on doggedly increasing his wealth. Soon he had not only a BMW but the title of company chairman and a weekend bungalow with a garden going down to the water, his second wife wore fashionable hats, read his every wish and the wishes of an overweight rough-haired dachshund in their eyes, and covered up for the gloomy silence of both with a sparkling cascade of chatter.

My father, the shy newspaper boy from Stopsley, became the classic younger son. He seemed the antithesis of his ambitious, hard-working brother in every way. He was a daredevil character who loved women, and although he never had any money he charmed his way unstoppably through Vienna. He wasn't interested in politics, only in the football results. The one thing he took seriously was his training. After training, which meant almost every day, he and his entourage, consisting of a few of his twenty best friends and a changing retinue of girls, would go to the Weisskopf or the wine bar selling the latest local vintage. 'There wasn't anything else to do then,' he said later with a sentimental smile.

As long as he played football everyone knew him anyway. A football star, a forward in the national team, really meant something in confused little Austria, which had never been right up there in the big league but wanted to be important again, particularly in the post-war years. My young father was a hero at just the right time. The little boys who hung around the edge of the field at every training session, prepared to knock each other senseless for the privilege of kicking back a ball that had gone out, called him 'the Englishman'. When my father stood on the pitch for the first time with a bouquet of flowers, hearing the new and still unfamiliar national anthem – all his life he could never remember its words – and seeing the little black dots that were the crowd standing in tiers all the way up to the sky, he was astonished to realise that he had actually made it. To my grandfather, that fanatical football fan, this son of his was like a gift from the gods, coming to him late but as compensation. He might be racing around town with order forms for Arabia Coffee during the day, his hips and knees might keep him awake at night, he might decree hysterically, in a manner not at all typical of him, that Katzi's name was never to be mentioned again, and in that matter he imposed his will – but when he saw his son carried from the pitch on the fans' shoulders at the end of a match, as sometimes happened, nothing could harm my grandfather any more.

The beginning of my father's professional career is itself bathed in the almost improbably rosy glow of that new start. On one hand, the difficulties confronting a seventeen-year-old speaking hardly any German in search of a job were considerable. On the other, even we children instinctively realised that one reason why these difficulties were described to us in such bizarre detail was that the happy ending of the story would be all the more of a triumphant contrast. How to overcome all the odds: that was the covert subject of this classic among our family anecdotes.

At first he was going to be a car mechanic, probably because back in England, and partly thanks to Katzi's drawing set, he had been accepted to train as a technical draughtsman by the development department of the car-parts supplier T.C. Smith. He worked mainly on the design of dashboards.

Something to do with cars, then, that seems to be the message that had reached my grandfather's ears. Communication between parents and son was very difficult at first. My father drew well. A youthful colour-washed drawing that he had done in England hung in a glazed frame in our nursery, the only one he had brought back in his little seaman's bag. It shows a goalkeeper in long shorts, leaning against the goal-post and sobbing desperately into a huge handkerchief, with the black and white ball in the net behind him. It's possible that back in those difficult first weeks, feeling helpless, he had drawn a dashboard for his father, who thereupon took him off to the motor mechanic in the nearest back-yard place. For money was no laughing matter to my grandfather any more. Money and food were both in short supply, so the boy had to find a job as soon as possible.

The motor mechanic took him on. 'He won't need to do any talking,' he assured my grandfather, who was apologising for his boy's poor grasp of German. My father was given two blue overalls, and lay underneath an assortment of cars for a couple of days. His knees hurt, his elbows hurt, black sweat ran down into his burning eyes, and he could hardly bear the smell, but he said not a word, and would probably have become a mediocre car mechanic, resigned to his fate, if his mother hadn't come to the rescue. My grandmother would never have let one of her children leave home looking dirty, so she toiled away at the washboard for hours that first evening to get the oil and grease stains out of his working clothes. When my father came home looking even worse on the second evening, she had had enough. My grandparents quarrelled vociferously. My grandfather protested that a mechanic didn't need to look like a bank clerk when he went to work. The profession of bank clerk seemed to him to promise the maximum possible security, respect, and middle-class prosperity, but unfortunately it was out of the question for his son, not just because of the language problem, but most of all because he didn't have a school-leaving certificate. My grandmother retorted that he didn't have to go about like a bank clerk, but if he went about like a pig it would be only over her dead body.

Probably my father got his second chance only because, with his newly pedicured toes, he had just performed so well in trials for First Vienna Football Club that he was immediately taken on as a regular member of the youth team. My uncle, Allied forces interpreter and denazification officer, was asked for his advice. He phoned around, for phoning had become his chief occupation, and later he made the most of it in his work. If he had to speak at all, then speaking to people without making personal contact suited him best. When he left the British army and embarked on his notable career in the import-export business, he was soon in demand in apparently insoluble cases of emergency. He alone was able to prise free a consignment of cotton stuck in some Far Eastern harbour, or track down a cargo of rice that was said to have disappeared and send it safely on to its intended destination. How he did it no one knew. He sat at the telephone chain-smoking. If you waited outside his office door, all you heard besides his hoarse voice was the regular click of the catch on his ashtrays as he disposed of the ashes and most of their smell by dumping them down to the bottom.

After two or three phone calls my uncle had found his brother a position as trainee in a factory. My father was now to be a lathe operator. He had no idea what a lathe operator did. He wondered if that was a good sign or a bad one. To be honest, he thought, he'd had no idea how horrible working as a motor mechanic was, although he had believed he knew roughly what motor mechanics did. As for lathe operators, he could link no mental associations at all to them. My grandfather shrugged and made a gesture as if he were screwing the top on a bottle.

When they set off first thing in the morning – my grandfather with his head held high, determined not to give way meekly again, however strenuous and dirty life as a lathe operator might be, my father apprehensive, and there-fore indulging for once in homesickness for Uncle Tom, the dandelions, and his pleasant colleagues in the bright offices of T.C. Smith – they met the caretaker.

The caretaker – 'Only just back,' said my uncle. 'What, a Jewish caretaker?' asked my father doubtfully – the caretaker stopped them.

'He was a football fan too,' said my father. 'No, that was his successor,' said my mother. 'How do you know?' asked my father. 'Back from where?' inquired my sister, posing gracefully as she painted her toenails with glitter nail varnish. 'Dachau, probably,' said my uncle's second wife, patting her dog. 'I've heard that the political . . .' Well, anyway, the caretaker stopped my grandfather, they exchanged greetings, the caretaker asked after my grandfather's health, how my father was getting on, where they were going – oh, I don't know just what he said.

'All caretakers are nosy,' sighed my mother pleasurably.

'Most caretakers are Nazis,' muttered my brother.

'This one was a Jew,' my uncle reminded him.

'Not a bank manager,' chuckled my father.

'Go on,' fretted my sister.

Perhaps the caretaker and my grandfather had started by talking about the football results. Perhaps my grandfather had praised the footballing skills of his son, who was following the conversation only with difficulty, before adding the rider that 'the boy has nothing but football on the brain' and didn't even want to work. This legendary caretaker, considered a good fairy in my family, may perhaps then have pointed out that talented footballers would soon be earning a lot of money, enough for them to be able to look down on the kind of work that ordinary people did. 'Oh, go on with you,' said my grandfather with his typical lordly gesture – at this point in the story the entire family party reverently performed it, my sister putting down the nail-varnish brush for the purpose – 'what good is that? It won't do him any good now. We're off to the factory.'

'Factory?' said the caretaker in surprise, propping his

broom against the wall. 'What's he going to do there, then?'

'Where was this factory anyway?' asked my brother sceptically.

'Ssh,' hissed my uncle's second wife, patting the dachshund as she waited in suspense.

'. . . What's he going to do there, then?' the surprised caretaker asked. My grandfather was already turning to walk on as he told the caretaker, 'He's going to be a lathe operator.'

On this cue, my entire family enthusiastically cried, in chorus, 'So where did anyone ever see a Yiddish lathe operator?' For such had been the caretaker's famous question that averted bad luck and changed the course of the story for ever.

We later succeeded in impressing our school friends deeply, the girls anyway, by saying in deliberately vague terms that my father had been 'in films'. The boys, who were all interested in football or at least pretended to be, because of peer pressure, didn't need anything extra to impress them. For during our childhood our surname was still very well known, even though my father's career as a sportsman had just ended. My sister exploited both aspects of it. Even as a little girl, she showed her school friends the photographs featuring my father in the national strip; the one where he was up in the air trying to head a ball, hair flying in the wind, eyes narrowed; and the one where he was being carried from the field on the fans' shoulders. But she liked even better showing the pictures of my radiant young father with Alida Valli, Joseph Cotton and Orson Welles. My father's charm also of course raised my sister in her friends' estimation, for his eyes twinkled while he treated little girls as if they were charming young ladies, not small children in checked knee-length socks.

My brother had suffered the torments of hell in earlier

years for exactly the same reasons that my sister shamelessly used to win herself prestige. In gym lessons his fellow pupils enjoyed tripping up the national footballer's son as they slyly stuck their feet out, the sports master liked to tell him off at every opportunity ('Can't your father do a bit of training with you?'), until he hysterically took refuge in some kind of inflammation of the joints that occurs only in puberty, which liberated him from sports lessons for the rest of his schooldays. All the pleasures of comradeship in sports and games among young men, he used to claim later in eloquent self-pity, were denied him because of his father.

'I *had* to be an intellectual!' he cried, with a mixture of vanity and complaint, and the whole family laughed.

'What an entertainer!' they would say, nodding. 'What a storyteller! Papa all over again.'

When he brought his girlfriends home they acted exactly like my sister's friends at school. They were captivated by my father, thought him witty and charming, admired the pictures of him with the film stars. What with all this, in fact, they more or less forgot my brother himself. He couldn't stand up to the competition, and soon became so touchy that the girls, who had, after all, felt no more than a liking for my father, took flight. For a dark period, as a result, my brother mingled only with the kinds of women described by my father as gun-women, typical seventies feminists, long-haired, domineering, scorning cosmetics. 'They have something inside their heads instead,' my brother said crossly when he came home, exhausted, from the meetings of the Revolutionary Marxists, which were shrouded in mystery. 'But you're only interested in a girl's bum.'

At first my father had been merely an employee of a film company. The caretaker had given him the idea. The caretaker's suggestion that no Yiddish lathe operator was known to have had an illustrious career was not, of course, enough for my grandfather, whose overflowing love for the son he thought he had lost expressed itself, among other ways, in his wish to force him into a good, safe job. 'What did you say again?' he had asked the caretaker, with a menacing undertone in his voice, and the caretaker had immediately realised that only a practical suggestion would improve the situation for which his boldness was to blame. 'You can speak English, can't you?' he said, turning directly to my astonished father, and he told him that only a few days ago an English film distribution company had opened in Neubaugasse, they were sure to need staff.

'And how many people in Vienna speak English?' he asked my grandfather with an ingratiating smile. 'All I picked up in the war was a bit of Spanish. Now listen,' he told my father, and at that moment, according to the stories, he must have shown an impressive authority of the kind not usually found in a caretaker, Jewish or otherwise, 'listen, you go along there, speak nothing but English, understand? Only English, and you ask for the boss, right? Don't talk to anyone else, that's important. And when you get to see the boss, then you say, I want a job!' The caretaker brushed down his trousers with the palms of his hands, touched his forehead, although he wasn't wearing a hat, and picked up his broom, shaking his head as he walked away muttering, 'Lathe operator . . .'

My father was all in favour. Speaking English, English people, bright, clean offices, there was sure to be tea in the afternoon, and no work which might, though God forbid, injure his legs. That was how he saw it, but my grandfather was horrified.

'A secure, honest position as a trainee, all fixed up by your brother,' grumbled my grandfather, 'and what's all this stuff anyway? Just some crazy caretaker's chatter!'

My father promised solemnly to be a lathe operator or a motor mechanic, even hire himself out as a carpenter or a street sweeper, if only he could please, please take this one chance.

So soon afterwards my father was standing at the address he had been given, facing a Viennese porter who knew not a word of English, and wondering whether to go against the caretaker's instructions or stick to them faithfully (he stuck to them), until at last the bad-tempered porter took him to see someone else, who was also at a loss and took him to the boss's secretary's office, where a nice girl sitting with her legs crossed casually uttered the words, 'The boss is away on holiday,' thus shaking my father badly.

On the other hand, he told his parents later, when he came home exhausted, the girl had assured him that they really were looking for staff, and said he should come again as soon as the boss was back from holiday.

'So when will he be back?' my grandfather interrupted him.

'In four weeks' time,' whispered my father.

'Like I said, he just doesn't want to work,' cried my grandfather indignantly, and he rose to his feet and went to the coffee-house. My grandmother said nothing. She took a great deal of trouble to give the impression that, even so, there would always be enough on the table for all three of them. As soon as my grandfather was out of the door she opened one of the English cans her daughter-in-law had given her and gave my father a plate of corned beef, which he began to eat absent-mindedly and gratefully.

Four weeks later my father was hired as a cross between office boy and maid of all work. He fetched the boss rolls with sliced sausage in them, he translated film catalogues, and soon he was being sent two floors up to telephone once or twice a week. Use of the telephone was a mark of trust. Two floors up was the office of a British secret service department, and they had the only telephone anywhere around. My father went up there, was led to the precious apparatus, after a while he was connected to the film distribution company's head office in London, and then he conscientiously reported how many posters and how many copies of a film would be needed in the near future in little Austria.

Now and then my father helped to cut the trailer, and he liked doing that too. The precise nature of the work, the cautious cutting up of frames and then neatly sticking them together again, reminded him pleasantly of his job at T.C. Smith's. He made himself useful about the place as best he could, he was friendly, ready to lend a hand, amusing at the right times, and his boss liked him. Winking, he gave my father time off to train when an important match was coming up, and he was generous about away games and summer tournaments with the team. When help was wanted with a big British production being shot in Vienna, the boss recommended my father, and so he acted as assistant to the assistant director for a few chaotic weeks. In a scene that later became world-famous, my father was the body double. He really wore the shoes to be seen in the entrance of a building by night, although it was Orson Welles who stepped out of the shadows. 'I'd have been much more stylish,' my father always used to say, smiling. 'All the same, it was a real money-spinner, that movie.'

In general my father didn't work too hard in those first years. And then he set up his own business when he came upon a run-down restaurant in a back yard next to a porn cinema. Out of this unattractive site at a hopeless address, he made a flourishing shop selling goods bought in bulk, and my grandfather was soon to go out tirelessly seeking custom for it.

My uncle's career also began with some capricious reversals of fortune. At first he had a good deal of luck; we have forgotten today how quickly attitudes to people of his kind changed. The alarm and respect shown by Herr Hermann and the Döbling tobacconist soon gave way to other ideas. My uncle cut out of the paper stories complaining of

'Emigrants Back in Austria on Looting Spree', as carefully as the small report that a tourist whose skin tone was rather darker than most had been asked in a Salzburg tram at Festival time whether he was one of those whom 'Hitler had failed to polish off'. He also collected all the reports of the case in Vienna in which a man returning from exile accused his landlady of welcoming him back with the words, 'Back again, are you? I thought you were burnt and done with.' The defendant was found not guilty, the judge being unable to detect any threat or insult in her remarks, only at the worst 'stupid insensitivity'. It was claimed in the Weisskopf that the tenant who took her to court hanged himself in the same apartment a few years later by way of punishing her, but my uncle disputed that. If it had been so, he said, he would have cut the report out, but he was firmly convinced it wasn't true. 'You can bet he wasn't going to give her the satisfaction.'

My father had no such memories. No one had ever spoken like that to him, he said, these were isolated cases, there are stupid folk everywhere, he personally couldn't remember any such thing, far from it, only good experiences . . . but when he started talking like that my uncle, uncharacteristically, raised his voice, spoke sharply and forcefully, and then they changed the subject. Once we were alone again my father, his feelings hurt, explained to us children that our uncle, unfortunately, had no sense of humour and was a communist into the bargain, oh well, there was nothing to be done about it.

At first my uncle worked in the trading department of a large bank, on its Eastern desk. The Eastern desk, where he and a colleague were mainly occupied with imports of coal from Poland and natural gas from the Soviet Union on a return basis, was suddenly closed down. My uncle and his colleague, a man called Hals, were not, as they had expected, transferred to the business of the Western desk, which at the same time was being greatly expanded, but were fired instead. The bank was administering considerable amounts of Marshall Aid. When the manager visited the USA it had been hinted to him in passing that, unfortunately, Eastern trade and Marshall Aid transactions could not be handled by one and the same bank; it was out of the question, as he would understand. The decision was up to him, but they were sure he would know what was best for his bank. The bank manager, to whom the bank did not of course belong – it belonged to the state, and thus at the time still to the occupying powers – immediately understood, and was ashamed, even years later, that he had had to be given this warning at all. 'Unpardonable,' he would murmur whenever he thought of the embarrassing situation, 'absolutely unpardonable.'

'I think there could have been all kinds of repercussions,' he said to his wife on his return, and thereafter made known his 'deep conviction, arising from direct experience', that the Americans were generous, understanding international partners, 'the best we have'. My uncle thought him a fool. Once, when my father tried the 'He is not a Jew, he's a bank manager' joke, my uncle simply said, 'He's nothing but a fool.' Many years after his ignominious dismissal my uncle discovered that the same bank manager, a man called Twaroch, played tennis with my father and had become a popular member of the Schneuzl Tennis Club: But he only shook his head, as if he might have expected it.

It was in fact his colleague Fredi Hals, a native Hungarian, who suggested to my uncle that they might set up together on their own account, and provided the necessary capital. For although he could have afforded it, my uncle was determined not to risk his own money on such an insecure enterprise. Good-natured Fredi Hals bore him no grudge, and shouldered all the risk himself. Soon Fredi Hals, who was a good ten years older than my uncle, was playing bridge with my grandparents in the afternoons and drinking at night with my father, of whom he was particularly fond, in the Weisskopf, while my uncle toiled away for sixty hours a week or more in their firm, Hals & Co.

As a businessman, Fredi Hals was indolent but a genius. He was always coming up with tips and ideas, legal, semi-legal and illegal alike, and offering them to half the clientèle of the Weisskopf. Once or twice my father smuggled cigarettes for Fredi's family into Hungary when he travelled there for an away game with the team. This was where Fredi Hals's brilliant idea originated. The footballers, Hals realised, were almost never checked at border crossings, indeed they were kept waiting there only long enough to sign autographs. So Hals recruited them one by one, swore them to silence, and paid good money for their services as couriers. In Budapest the players were discreetly contacted, or handed over their packages and small cases in certain shops or at private addresses. Of course someone would talk now and then, so they soon knew all about each other. And of course Hals did not confine himself to First Vienna Football Club, but recruited his couriers from the entire First Division, which meant all the clubs that would be going to Hungary. When the ring was busted two years later, it unfortunately affected the national team. The goal-keeper was caught with a case full of nylon stockings, the left and right defenders with five ten-packet cartons of cigarettes each, the centre forward with chewing-gum in ten pairs of socks, and the team masseur with dollar bills tucked into his underpants. The others tried to wriggle out of it by denying that they knew anything about the rest of the packages and cases with their illegal contents that were still in the baggage compartment of the bus. The bus driver, shaking with terror, claimed to have no idea how they had got into his vehicle. The players who were undoubtedly guilty were fined large sums, the others got slightly lower fines, but the whole thing was hushed up 'in the national interest'. Not even a shadow of suspicion fell on my father, who was in hospital for the first time with his bad lung. And there were no leads to the man who had been pulling the strings either, for the players kept their mouths shut and preferred to blame each other until the investigators finally gave up.

It was entirely due to my uncle's wholehearted commitment and skill that the firm of Hals & Co. quickly became a flourishing if slightly mysterious business (years later its name came up again in connection with assets held by the recently defunct German Democratic Republic, but Fredi Hals was long dead by then, and fortunately no one thought of questioning my uncle in his old age). It was only a matter of time before his youthful marriage broke up, when it became clear that he was seeing far more of his smart secretary than his little English wife and their two sons. Nor was family harmony fostered by the fact that, on the few occasions when he saw his children while they were awake, they got on his nerves dreadfully, and his wife wouldn't let him smoke in the apartment. After a certain inward struggle (for his usual principle was to see things through, keep quiet and grit his teeth), he gave way to his instincts and moved in with his secretary.

The little Englishwoman was left thunderstruck. He saw his sons at weekends, and came to fetch them in his BMW. His second wife inspected their little hands closely before they were allowed to sit on the white leather upholstery. The older boy always felt car-sick, so they had to keep stopping for him to get out. Unfortunately he couldn't sit in the front of the car because of the second wife's large hats. The younger boy had to hold the dog, which scratched his legs and slobbered all over his trousers every Saturday. 'What a wonderful childhood for them!' the second wife said later, pleased with herself. 'Out in the garden every weekend, and we played such nice card games!'

My cousins rolled their eyes. If my uncle and his wife weren't around, they told funny stories of the way Aunt Ka, as everyone called her (only my uncle called her Kali) was so keen to win that she kept trying to cheat the two little boys. Sometimes the elder boy, motivated by the strong sense of honour that he was developing at this time, threw down his cards and refused to go on playing, while his younger brother took his chance to torment the dachshund under the table.

'Me, cheat?' Aunt Ka would cry shrilly. 'You dreadful boy, how can you accuse me of such a thing?'

'Because it's true,' said my cousin defiantly. Once the situation escalated to the point where my uncle, their father, had to be fetched from the paperwork over which he brooded even at the weekend. 'She changes the rules in the middle of the game,' my cousin said, fearlessly blaming Aunt Ka. He knew very well that an open quarrel did not suit my uncle's idea of a 'quiet weekend' as he liked to spend it. Irritated, my uncle stood there in his shorts, his legs looking improbably white and thin. His eyes went from his two sons, one of them almost hysterical in his childish indignation, the other with a globule of snot and a cheeky smile on his face, to his wife, looking at him with doll-like eyes as pleadingly as a little girl. 'She's grown up,' was his verdict, 'she knows the rules better than you do.'

That night my cousins decided to run away. The idea came from the older one, who even in adult life was quick to feel that he had been humiliated, often for no reason, and liked to respond with some emotionally charged reaction. The smaller boy was tired, and too lazy to run away really, but he scented adventure in the air. When they crept out of the bungalow as quietly as they could, making for the garden gate and, well-trained as they were, avoiding Aunt Ka's rose bushes, the smaller boy trod on the dog. Normally the dachshund slept in a basket with a pretty cushion at the end of the conjugal bed, so his nocturnal presence in the garden was rather puzzling. When my cousin trod on him, the dachshund apparently just grunted in his usual way.

The animal had been almost mute from birth. He neither

yapped nor whined, he just kept quiet. Lifelong experience had shown him that he got the best titbits of the humans' food without having to make any effort at all. He had never stood on his hind legs begging, and soon he was too fat for that anyway. Aunt Ka gave him everything she liked to eat herself, and in addition she had a never-ending supply of every possible kind of dog food, dog biscuits and dog snacks. She carefully kept him away from potential enemies, either animal or human. The dog had no reason to express his attitude to life by doing anything but eat obediently. He was Aunt Ka's best friend. She took him to the hairdresser and the beautician with her, and when she was in shops trying on dresses or hats he sat on a chair with a little blanket to keep him safe and warm, stoically watching. In restaurants she ordered a bowl of water for him even as she was being helped off with her coat, and she twittered happily to him all day long. Many of us in my family are of the opinion that, even if you had successfully escaped her flow of chat – which we were always trying to do – she just went on talking unmoved, and held conversations with herself all day long. On the other hand, she herself always insisted that she told all only to her dog. So she was never really talking to herself but always to that unflagging listener the dachshund.

After treading on the dog, which grunted with pain, my smaller cousin had had enough of this nocturnal expedition. It was too uncomfortable for him. He was freezing cold in his pyjamas, he was tired, and his need to quarrel with his grumpy father had been satisfied. He wailed and wanted to go back to bed. The elder boy feigned anger and disappointment, but secretly he had gone off the whole idea of running away. 'We'll get rid of that dog, though,' he said vengefully, picking up the dachshund, which was incredibly heavy and smelled of expensive baby shampoo. The two boys carried him down to the water together, put him in their rubber dinghy, untied it and pushed it off. For lack of independent witnesses there is no knowing whether the dachshund reacted with his usual stoicism (as my younger cousin said) or, for the first time ever, uttered a sound of alarm which was deeply satisfying to the perpetrators of the crime (as my elder cousin claimed).

Very early next morning, when the sun had only just risen, they were woken by Aunt Ka's cries for help. She was running up and down the landing stage, trying without much success to control herself. The noise she was making brought out several neighbours, and people with gardens going down to the other side of the water came out of their houses too.

My uncle's bungalow lay on the Danube–Oder Canal, one of the most ambitious waterway-building projects in Europe, although unfortunately its degree of realisation was in inverse proportion to its ambition. For six hundred years, supporters of the idea had dreamed of three thousand kilometres of artificial waterways, but only a few kilometres were ever actually built, and that was during the Nazi period by the use of forced labour. My uncle hadn't known about that, his younger son said later, or he would never have bought the bungalow. He didn't *want* to know about it, claimed his elder son, and when the facts became widely known he had already lost it anyway, along with the rest of his large fortune.

'What sort of stories are those?' my father complained despairingly in his old age. 'What does that have to do with it? It doesn't change anything.'

'I bet you think that once the pretty canal and the nice little houses were there people might just as well live in them,' said my brother provocatively. Even as a grown man he couldn't refrain from avenging himself at every opportunity for his childhood unhappiness by making some kind of roundabout political or moral point.

But my father came back surprisingly sharply. 'And they say the Romans who founded Vienna were anti-Semitic too!' Then everyone laughed again.

Once my brother and my elder cousin went too far, though, when they claimed, out of a sheer wish to be quarrelsome, that our grandfather had probably had to work on the same canal where his elder son later enjoyed his best years. My then aged father, as the only survivor of his generation, thought he ought to defend all the dead, and clutched his stomach with an expression of pain before saying slowly and carefully, 'Grandpa was working with a construction firm somewhere in Gross-Enzersdorf.'

'How do you know?' cried various family members in chorus. Even my sister widened her eyes, which were royal blue that evening thanks to coloured contact lenses. For the exact details of my grandfather's 'sauced labour' had always remained unknown; the more decades passed, the more interested we felt in them, and the more the whole thing took on an aura of immense mystery. But my father looked at us all accusingly, as if deeply hurt, and went off to his bedroom saying that his stomach was in a very bad way again.

'He can't take it any more,' said my mother, by way of excuse. She was nicer to him now in his old age. Then my brother and my cousin wormed it out of her that 'a long, long time ago' a man had phoned asking for my grandfather. The unknown man said on the telephone that he had worked with him – 'you know, back in those days.'

'But Grandpa had just died,' said my mother, shrugging apologetically.

'Did you get the name and phone number?' asked my brother expectantly.

'The man would be a hundred and twenty now,' said my father drily from the other side of his door, which was ajar, 'and you'd better all go home.'

In any case, the Danube–Oder Canal is not wide, and since it isn't a real canal but just a long stretch of water going nowhere there are no currents. The dachshund had either not got far on his great voyage, or he had been driven back to his point of departure by chance gusts of wind. The rubber dinghy was lying motionless in the water, almost exactly in the middle of the canal. Aunt Ka was helplessly flapping her arms on the bank. The dachshund had put his nose on the soft side of the dinghy, which wasn't fully inflated, and was gazing fixedly in her direction. Aunt Ka was too far off to be able to see him blinking or breathing, so she must have been afraid he was dead.

But this little expedition had obviously done no more than make his asthma worse. Aunt Ka kept him in his basket for days, treated him with medicaments to combat pneumonia 'to be on the safe side', regularly took his temperature and fed him up on fillet steak and liver. The two sons of my uncle's first marriage were banned from the house until the dog of his second marriage was fully recovered. Instead of taking them to the Danube–Oder Canal, my uncle restricted his paternal duties to awkward Saturday lunches in a restaurant in the city centre, just the three of them. Something about the whole story had infuriated him so much that it was never mentioned again in front of him, not even long after his sons were adults. In his absence, however, we were always bringing it up, and poor Aunt Ka's emotions were painted in the most garish colours. 'Like Niobe, all tears, quite crazy with grief,' one of the cousins would always say with a grin. 'Though she was usually crazy enough in normal life,' the other always maliciously added. Just once, however, and not in the family circle but in a private conversation, my younger cousin mentioned the strange way my uncle suddenly froze when he came running out and took in what was basically a ridiculous situation. Aunt Ka was chasing up and down the bank squealing, her arms spread wide, while her beloved dog drifted, abandoned to the water in a brightly coloured children's boat, gazing ahead in his usual mute way. My uncle stopped abruptly, stood perfectly still as if rooted to

Late Love

The household help whom my sister found for my uncle was called Mimi. It's a strange name for an Asian girl, but at first that was all that struck my family about the whole affair. 'From the Philippines or Thailand,' my sister had said, 'how should I know?' In Mimi's favour was the fact that she was very young, very friendly, and above all amazingly cheap; from all we heard she kept a place sparkling clean, and my family were told that she would be understanding about the fits of bad temper to be expected from my uncle. 'A Polish or Yugoslavian girl won't do,' my mother had said bluntly, 'they know too much about what you can do to them and what you can't.'

After Aunt Ka's sudden death and before Mimi came, my uncle felt he had reached the end. Advanced in years as he now was, he could hardly leave his apartment. He was, he said through gritted teeth, a patient for every branch of medicine: he had skin problems, he was allergic to most foods, the asthma from which he had suffered as a child was back again, his lower legs, elbows and hips had been pinned several times after a number of falls, his sciatic nerve gave him trouble, and he had gallstones. In short, there was hardly a part of his body that didn't hurt. His tiny pension meant that he had to think as hard about his modest income and outgoings as he had once thought about international trade routes, but he absolutely refused to take anything from his sons. A man who has worked and paid his taxes all his life should be able to manage somehow, he argued, 'or there's something wrong.' He was obviously determined to make himself a martyr to the fact that something *was* wrong. He scraped and saved and finally even went short of food to top up his medical insurance. It was easily his largest expense, and was almost breaking him financially. My family politely never reminded him of what had happened to all his wealth, which among other things had accustomed him to always insisting on the best and consulting only the doctors he trusted.

So all we could do to help was give practical presents. The family gave him a microwave for his birthday and a washer–dryer for Christmas – 'You'll be calling me Auntie next,' he grumbled. It was his way of saying thank you.

In the first difficult weeks after Aunt Ka's death he spoke with black humour of hanging himself. The family didn't know what to say. My father just shook his head unhappily, my mother whispered in agitation, 'Oh, please don't talk such nonsense.' My elder cousin said roughly, 'Don't be so sorry for yourself,' my younger cousin kept out of it. Plans were secretly made to house him with people of his own age – 'although there aren't many of those left,' as my incorrigible father rather queasily tried to joke. But all our loving arrangements ended in disaster. The little English-woman, his ex-wife, made a great effort and took him to afternoon tea with a gathering of women who had once emigrated from England and now met regularly. 'People with our own kind of history behind them,' the optimistic little Englishwoman said encouragingly to him on the way there. 'A set of silly old women,' said my uncle crossly on the way back.

My father made an effort too, and invited him to lunch in the attractive garden restaurant of the tennis club one weekend. But my father's friends were hale and hearty suntanned senior citizens who went around in sports clothes all day, and my uncle didn't get on any better with them than with the former lady emigrants from England who exchanged news of their grandchildren and great-grandchildren over tea and biscuits.

So he was soon leading a very quiet life indeed. He kept the television on all the time, to avoid having to listen to himself saying nothing all day. He didn't watch it. He used the TV set only to keep in touch with the world situation, and turned up the volume when the news came on. The other programmes transmitted all day weren't on loud enough for him to hear what was said. 'Such nonsense,' he said scornfully, but he turned the television off only when someone visited. Now and then he watched historical documentaries, and sometimes when they had finished he surprised his sons or his nieces and nephews by phoning to tell them, in aggrieved tones, about the details which he knew from his own knowledge and experience were wrong. 'That's the way people work these days,' he said bitterly, 'no wonder they're dumbing down all the time.' Apart from that he never phoned anyone. He had cared for no one all his life, but now he seemed to expect the whole world to care for him, and was hurt when they didn't. Only my father rang him every day, and my elder cousin dutifully did the same, in a bad temper. My younger cousin rang him at most once a week, but his cheerful nature soon dispelled the reproach in my uncle's voice. Although these conversations were the only bright spots in his daily life, my uncle tried to keep them as short as possible. Even at this stage of his life, he didn't like idle chatter. And he definitely didn't want to give anyone the impression that he had been waiting for a phone call.

But all that changed when Mimi arrived. She was a stroke of luck in every way. At first my uncle had picked her just for the low price she charged per hour, although he didn't really want any stranger at all in the apartment. But soon she became the one thing my uncle liked to talk about. He told us how wonderful everything looked when she had cleaned it, although of course if you inspected it really closely, he added, there were still improvements to be made.

'Cleaning behind the radiators,' he said with a touch of triumph. 'I taught her to do that the very first time.'

'She'd never have thought that books need dusting of her own accord,' he remarked proudly. 'Now she dusts two metres every time, and when she's finished she starts at the beginning again.'

'Apparently there are men who don't mind what their homes look like,' he commented critically, 'but I am not among them.'

Mimi became indispensable to him. She did the shopping, she cooked, she washed and ironed, she even cut his fingernails and toenails for him – he couldn't see very well any more – which his masculine pride had never allowed him to let Aunt Ka do. Apart from this practical support, what he particularly liked was that he could speak English to her – her German was nothing to write home about – and that he could understand her high-pitched voice better than the average European voice. He had worn a hearing aid for a long time. But best of all, according to my uncle, was that 'She sings while she works'. My family exchanged glances. So far my uncle had been famous for disliking song, regarding it as the tool of totalitarianism and religion, or at the very least a reactionary popular phenomenon. No one had forgotten the Christmas Eve when, right in the middle of 'Silent Night' (he wasn't singing it himself, of course, just making faces, and my father had been banned from singing long ago), he suddenly took out his wallet, nudged my father in the ribs with his elbow, and said in an undertone, 'Hey, I still owe you a hundred schillings.' Opinion is divided as to whether that was when Aunt Ka, who always sang along heartily and from the depth of her lungs, gave him the first reproachful glance in their decades of marriage, but it looked rather like it.

Very soon my cousins decided to pay Mimi for overtime on the quiet, because my uncle was beginning to keep her from cleaning and ironing so that he could talk to her. To prevent a new disaster – once my elder cousin found Mimi with tears in her eyes because, chattering away to my uncle, she hadn't been able to finish all the housework, thus earning a reproof from him – to prevent a new disaster my cousins agreed with her that in future she would simply stay longer to get everything done, and charge them for the extra hours. My family watched in suspense to see if my uncle would notice and mention it.

'He's not a fool,' hissed my sister.

'He always got his calculations right,' my brother agreed with her.

'He's repressing the knowledge because he's glad of it,' said my elder cousin.

'He seriously thinks she does it for nothing because it's for him,' chuckled my younger cousin, and he was probably closest to the truth.

But all concerned had their secrets. For of course my uncle had found out at once where Mimi really came from. He would never have let anyone do his housekeeping without having a little basic information about her. He was old-fashioned that way. So he made Mimi write him down her address and phone number. In fact he never checked them – when he wanted to change a time for her to come, he called her on her mobile – but he wanted her to know that he minded about these things.

It was typical of my uncle that he told no one about his discovery. 'Who'd have been interested?' he asked later in genuine surprise, when the Mimi business involved more people. He was probably right. Even if my sister had not said she came 'from the Philippines or Thailand, how should I know?' but had happened to know what Mimi's native land really was, I don't suppose anyone would have thought much of it.

He had been interned on the Isle of Man for nine months. He spent those nine months mending and altering English uniforms – 'they never fit,' as he said later with his typical joyless smile. The internees had been taken out of their camp three times to go to the cinema under supervision, and that was the only change in their routine. All three times *The Great Dictator* was screened, which was well intentioned but entirely superfluous from a didactic point of view. On the contrary, the film led many of the interned Jews to take a great dislike to Charlie Chaplin. Compared with what they had experienced themselves, the picture he painted seemed to them shockingly anodyne. My uncle just shrugged. 'They don't know any better, and it makes no difference,' he told one of his fellow prisoners, whose arms and legs had been broken in the Gestapo prison on Morzin-platz. 'And they declared war on the Nazis, after all.'

The local British inhabitants stood in silence in the streets of Douglas, the island capital, watching the shabby procession of internees being taken to the cinema. The internees were living in the British people's cottages. A whole part of the town of Onchan had been commandeered as housing for them. Strange, short-tempered communities of German-speaking men formed. They had to put up the barbed wire around their own camp, but apart from that they were left alone. As always in the lives of my father and my uncle, the English behaved perfectly. Now and then the internees were counted, 'but you mustn't think it was like a concentration camp,' my uncle assured us. 'We stood around at ease and then, well, they just counted us.'

'It was called a roll call,' said my uncle defensively. 'That kind of thing is called a roll call.'

'And we had the same rations as they did,' said my uncle approvingly, wondering out loud, as if proposing a subject for debate, how the Viennese would react if part of Hietzing was suddenly evacuated to accommodate refugees. 'Okay,' he added, 'perhaps Hietzing and Onchan aren't a good comparison, but you see what I mean, it's the principle of the thing.'

After his release it was another two years before the British army would at last agree to recruit German-speaking foreigners. He applied at once. A photo shows him, the thinnest and smallest of them all, with five or six other applicants who had turned up at the recruiting office in a group to demonstrate their pride and their political commitment. After he had all that behind him, after he had passed and been accepted, after he had been given several weeks of basic training in Glasgow and then a special training course ('all done at the run, even cleaning our teeth'), and now that his ardent wish to go and liberate his parents with a weapon in his hand seemed within reach, my uncle was the only one of his comrades to be given tropical equipment. 'I felt lousy,' he would reply, always in English, if he was asked for his immediate reaction. 'I felt just lousy.'

The uniform was lightweight, airy, and khaki all over. A mosquito net was part of it. As I have said, my uncle hated the heat, but that wasn't what he thought of first. Although he knew quite well that it was not for him to ask or demand anything he did speak to a superior officer. The man said he didn't know exactly where my uncle was being sent, and had no influence in the matter. 'It's secret,' said the superior officer brusquely. 'Maybe the Niger, maybe Egypt – how would I know?'

One day Mimi was helping my uncle to look through his mementoes and old wartime documents. It was a long time since he had taken them out. Even the British army mosquito net was among them, although the alarming khaki uniform had been exchanged for an equally alarming jungle-green one even before he reached his destination. Whether he had simply kept the first mosquito net, or been given a new one with the jungle-green uniform, my uncle couldn't remember, try as he might; all he knew was that in the end everything was jungle-green, 'from your under-pants to your handkerchief to your socks', and beyond that too, from your sleeping-bag all the way to the horizon. What he also still remembered were some absurd details, for instance what fish look like when you have 'caught' them with hand grenades, 'Kind of limp,' he said, laughing, and passed one of those invisible fish from one hand to the other, 'all limp and squashed inside.' He also remembered how to remove leeches with a lighted cigarette, and told Mimi about it, but it seemed that where she had grown up the leech problem was already solved. 'Of course,' laughed my uncle, theatrically striking his brow, 'that's the differ-ence between town and country.' They both knew that what they were talking about was not exactly 'country'. Neither knew what might be lurking in the past of one or the family of the other, and what exactly their respective attitudes were. Mimi suspected that her employer had been through dreadful experiences of some kind, typical wartime experiences, but she guessed that she would never hear about them. It was clear to my uncle that Mimi was very young and didn't know much about history; in any doubtful case she hated her country's present regime more than the old colonial power of Britain or its alleged liberator Japan.

Mimi's real name was Mi Mi Kiang and she came from Burma, that remote land of rushing rivers, gigantic moun-tain ranges, and malaria-ridden forests where my uncle had served as a soldier thirty-five years before she was born, the place that had really made him feel for the first time that he was in exile. Together, they looked at a map that my uncle had kept. He showed her roughly the way his division had gone in the year 1944: across the Irrawaddy, to the north-west and the main road linking Mandalay to Rangoon. She just kept shaking her head and tapping Rangoon, because she had never been anywhere but in the capital. 'I can tell you a story, then,' smiled my uncle, and he described how his whole division, eight thousand men strong, had crossed the Irrawaddy one night in hundreds of collapsible boats, making not a sound. During the day Japanese reconnaissance planes had circled above them. So the Japs knew where they were, and they expected to be fired on and sunk at any moment. 'At first we were afraid of everything, in the end we feared nothing,' he said thoughtfully. Mimi looked inquiringly at him, and then she nodded.

Later they looked at his English ID together. It mentioned everywhere he had been between 1938 and 1947. 'Arrived Dover, Dover Court Camp [where the 'sale of children' had been held]; Dean Street, London; Onchan, Isle of Man; London, Leeds, Glasgow, service in His Majesty's Army, 17th Indian Division, from . . . to . . .' A photo fell out showing my uncle with a dark-skinned soldier, who was holding a dagger and brandishing it alarmingly above their two heads. 'My best friend Abi,' said my uncle. 'A Gurkha.' He was not ashamed to sound emotional in front of Mimi, although he didn't go into detail. It seems that my uncle sometimes tried out a number of roles and emotions on Mimi, who he thought was a normal human being. At other times, to other people, he described the Gurkhas of the time as 'not far from wild beasts', and didn't make an exception of his friend Abi. It was only when the Gurkhas arrived, said my uncle with a shudder, that he saw the Japs run, because otherwise, he said, 'the Japs never turn and run for it.' The Gurkhas shrank from nothing. They knew no hesitation. They even scavenged by night for packets of rations that had dropped between the lines, and they were always ready to begin a fight over one, for instance with an enemy patrol. The Gurkhas could get hold of anything that was in short supply. They went fishing too, and to pass the time they killed creatures which they seasoned, grilled and shared with everyone else in the evening. They were 'children of Nature', as my uncle would say wryly, for my family saw mankind as the exact opposite of Nature. 'A Jew belongs in the coffee-house,' my grandfather used to say when he was told of other people going for walks, even hiking long distances. 'Am I a deer?'

The prelude to the war in Burma, according to my uncle, was 'very simple'. As well as Rangoon and Mandalay, there were a few sizeable towns, a few bridges, and the railway line and main road running parallel with each other from north to south. The rest of the country, 'to right and left of those thoroughfares', said my uncle, was jungle, and everyone knew that you couldn't get through the jungle. Everyone, he said sarcastically, except the Japanese. The Japs suddenly came through the jungle in all directions, and the British, who for decades had been in charge of the cities, the road and the railway line, and thus presumably the country itself, were taken by surprise and put to flight 'with a drubbing', as my uncle put it. In his famous account of this colonial defeat the commander responsible, General Stilwell, said something similar, so it seems likely that when my uncle said, 'We were thrown out of Burma – it was a bloody shame', he was influenced by the British newspapers he had read. Two years later my uncle in his jungle-green uniform took part in the counter-attack that was to get Burma back from the Japanese. They crossed the Irrawaddy by night, they made their way to the principal traffic route, they marched south to Meiktila, all of them, an oddly assorted troop who called themselves His Majesty's 17th Indian Division: Sikhs, Muslims and Gurkhas, Assamese and Madrassis, Narga head-hunters, Hindus and West Africans, along with a few Chinese, Englishmen, Irishmen and Scots, and one small Austrian. Feeding this bunch was notoriously difficult, said my uncle later, because some of them ate no pork, others were vegetarian, a third lot lived mainly on rice, and another group mainly on wheat. 'But we somehow always managed,' said my uncle. 'What they say were the problems are greatly exaggerated.'

'Small skirmishes here and there, nothing too bad,' said my uncle, shrugging his shoulders, of the march to Meiktila. Yes, they expected a major Japanese attack daily, but it never came. Then they were outside Meiktila and spent a couple of days attacking it, suffering heavy losses. 'On the third or the fourth day,' chuckled my uncle, with a shudder, 'they sent in the Gurkhas. That did the trick.'

'Why didn't you send the Gurkhas in right away?' asked my old father, puzzled.

My uncle shrugged. 'Because then we wouldn't have had anyone left,' he said. 'War stories,' added my uncle. 'Not really very interesting.'

In the years after the bungalow by the canal had to be sold, my uncle and Aunt Ka had got into the habit of going for 'outings' at the weekend. That was, of course, in defiance of my uncle's dislike of Nature, but here Aunt Ka's influence had obviously prevailed. It was the thing to do. She would have something to talk about when she went shopping on Monday. The couple's outings with their dog went like this: they got into the car around eleven in the morning, they went to a restaurant in the Vienna Woods – always the same inexpensive restaurant – they parked the car a little way off and walked the last five hundred metres. That was as far as the asthmatic dachshund could go in his condition. Then they sat on the terrace and had lunch, Aunt Ka talked and chattered, made acquaintances and let them offer her a *digestif*, my uncle smoked and said nothing, the dachshund wheezed over his water bowl, and after coffee they went home again. Later in the afternoon my uncle 'just looked in at the office', and didn't come back until supper time. They could do with the overtime pay. It appears that these so-called outings meant much more to my uncle than you might have thought at the time, for when Aunt Ka fell very ill many years later he suddenly regretted not having been back to the Vienna Woods for so long. He had probably liked the routine and predictability of these monotonous outings. 'If you're bored, it means you don't have worse worries,' he said on his better days, when Aunt Ka was dead and many of the family were trying to rouse him from the tedium of his existence between bed, the doctor, and the TV set.

So the first clear indication that the relationship was becoming closer was when my uncle, making quite a fuss of it, began resuming his Sunday outings, this time with Mimi. My cousins, feeling pleased, immediately wanted to pay Mimi a flat-rate fee for the outings, but she acted very properly and did not ask much. These outings were different in almost every detail from those of the past, but to my uncle they must still have represented a kind of triumph over time and death. In contrast to the old days, when he had gallantly helped his fashionably dressed wife, her hats and the dog into the car, he and Mimi had to work out a system of getting him behind the steering wheel. First he clutched her, counted to three, and then let himself drop backwards into the driving seat – the first time he cut the back of his head open because he hadn't folded himself up quickly enough – then Mimi turned him through ninety degrees, lifting his legs in, undid the locking mechanism of the seat adjustment with one hand, and with the other pulled the seat forward until he could reach the pedals with his feet. Getting out was easier.

They didn't sit on the terrace in the restaurant in the Vienna Woods, for in his old age my uncle would have claimed that he couldn't stand the draughts even in a locked strong-room. They sat inside, and he did most of the talking all through the meal. Mimi drank no alcohol, and for all his affectionate attempts to persuade her she wouldn't touch meat, particularly not fried in egg and breadcrumbs; she stuck to soup and salad, sat there smiling, and was always ready to jump up and help my uncle out to the lavatory or into his coat. My uncle could be witty and charming when he liked, it was just that he didn't usually see any reason for it. He laughed at his frailty and his family, he told hair-raising stories of the food in Viennese hospitals and the incompetence of doctors, tales that amazed and amused Mimi; he would devise plans in advance for next weekend. 'How about going to Semmering for a change?' Perhaps it was on one of these peaceful Sundays over tea and cake in the Vienna Woods – Mimi liked Austrian cakes and desserts – that she shyly asked him if he could see his way to adopting her.

The reactions of my family to the adoption idea were mixed. My sister said for some time that she never wanted to set eyes on our uncle again because she felt 'just *sooo* bad' about the cleaning lady whom, after all, she had found for him. But no one took her seriously; her penchant for drama was notorious.

My elder cousin gloomily shrugged his shoulders. 'I don't want anything from him, not that he has anything,' he said, referring to my uncle's estate.

My younger cousin was much impressed, for my uncle, to everyone's surprise, had described his plan as 'giving a young person a start in life'.

My elder cousin made a face when the subject came up, and muttered something to the effect that, 'He wasn't so bothered about our own start in life.'

My father just shook his head, and couldn't get over it. 'A total stranger, from Asia too,' he kept repeating.

My mother said something about 'senile sentimentality', and my father's first wife agreed with her, although my uncle's first wife did not.

My uncle's first wife, the little Englishwoman, was proud of her ex-husband again, fifty years after their divorce.

'Always thinking of politics,' she said, nodding. 'Never his family, I'm afraid, but at least politics.' They had met in the middle of the war among the Young Communists of London, and malicious tongues claimed that at the time of their divorce they had suffered at least as much for political as for emotional reasons. After all, they had not married just because they were in love, but to build a new world together on the ruins of fascism and raise a troop of little anti-fascists. In addition, there was the fact that her rival Aunt Ka's family background was, to put it euphemistically, politically dubious, but that subject was taboo. My elder cousin had once, in his early twenties, taken advantage of one of his usual arguments with his father (it was about long hair and the Vietnam War) to make a nasty remark about 'you and your Nazi bride', whereupon my uncle cut off all contact with his elder son for over a year, and even then grimly insisted on a formal apology. My younger cousin and the little Englishwoman practically had to drag my elder cousin along to offer it.

When it came to Mimi's adoption, my uncle had avoided presenting his sons with a *fait accompli*. On the contrary, and this again shows how important the whole thing was to him, he asked their permission. 'If my sons are against the idea then I can't do it,' he had explained to Mimi from the first, and she, blushing red with embarrassment, had nodded vigorously and in silence. After his sons had agreed, there was an awkward lunch in a city centre café at which they were to get to know their future sister better – for my uncle knew nothing about the secret financial transactions between them all. Mimi, who would rather have been invisible (she was painfully aware of the glances from the other tables, and heartily wished that my uncle would stop patting her reassuringly on the arm the whole time), had bravely prepared a little speech, in which she repeated yet again in her piping voice her assurances of why she had made her request in the first place: she wanted nothing, absolutely nothing, no money, no inheritance, she wouldn't be a burden on anyone, the only thing she wanted was the legal status that would allow her to stay in the country. My elder cousin, whose pedantry on matters of principle was very obviously inherited from his father, explained in friendly tones that when it came to inheritance there was an obligatory share which a child of the deceased could not refuse, but he and his brother, as they had already said, were perfectly happy with the whole idea. My younger cousin asked, sympathetically, whether she had already had problems with the police immigration department. During the dessert course my uncle told Burma stories about wild Gurkhas, catching fish with hand grenades, and the way to remove leeches with a lighted cigarette.

And perhaps everything would have been all right if it could have been done quickly. But since 'adoption is rather more complicated than filling in a car-park ticket,' as my father was soon commenting with some irritation, and although my uncle had firmly made up his mind, his health was as frail as his expectations were unrealistic, the business stretched on for weeks.

He had apparently really believed that he just had to go to a notary and sign a form saying 'I hereby adopt . . .', and he was indignant when he discovered that he had to give the adoption tribunal information about 'his personal relationship' with the adoptive child, and his 'motives for adopting'.

'Is this supposed to be a free country?' he asked in shrill and incredulous tones. 'You mean I can't adopt anyone I like?'

My father, true to his nature, was particularly clumsy in his attempts to soothe my uncle. He had found out, he said in a conspiratorially lowered voice, that there'd been a trade in fake adoptions recently. 'Touts signing up poor old pensioners by the dozen,' whispered my father, 'paying them over the odds to adopt some total stranger.'

'I have not been signed up, and Mimi is not a total stranger,' said my irritated uncle, who had been cut to the quick by the term 'poor old pensioners'. 'And as usual you're arguing the wrong way round.'

'What do you mean, the wrong way round?' asked my father, sounding injured. 'I'm only trying to explain why the authorities . . .'

'The state has to protect itself from abuses,' my uncle lectured, not letting him finish, 'but that doesn't mean it necessarily has to treat its citizens as criminals!'

My younger cousin and his mother, the little English-woman, egged my uncle on. It was positively his political duty to overcome these bureaucratic obstacles, they said. If he had made up his mind to take a legal step that might have serious consequences, he mustn't let anything stop him, certainly not an immigration policy that was clamping down more and more. My uncle himself, from the start, had put forward a second argument, which my father, although for safety's sake only in my uncle's absence, described as simplistic: 'If the English had had rules and regulations like that back in our time, then . . .', the argument began, and it was intended to be left hanging in the air, incomplete but pregnant with meaning.

'Then what?' my undiplomatic father of course had to ask.

'Then we'd probably both of us be dead,' snapped my uncle.

'The English did have rules and regulations exactly like that,' said my elder cousin, getting worked up. As he grew older he was getting increasingly like his father, even to a tendency to be a spoilsport. 'It was only for children that . . .'

But my uncle wasn't going to admit that. No one except him was to speak ill of the English. My uncle did not raise his voice, he just became a little snippy, but he interrupted his elder son in a way that silenced him like a schoolboy who has been given a well-deserved reprimand, and left him licking his emotional wounds for weeks.

His younger son had asked a lawyer friend's advice. Together they explained to my uncle exactly what the judge of the adoption tribunal was and was not able to do. However, my uncle had rejected the idea of taking this lawyer along to the tribunal to support him. He was afraid he couldn't even afford the low fee that, out of friendship for his son, the man would have asked. If there seemed to be any suspicion of fraudulent practice, judges could refer the case to the police immigration department. Adoptions carried out solely with a view to getting a permit to stay in the country, and where there was no genuine personal relationship between the two parties, were regarded as fraudulent practice.

'And what, may I ask, does "genuinely personal" mean?' my uncle had snapped at the friendly lawyer, who was in no way to blame for it, and in fact wrote in all the specialist journals opposing these latest legal developments. The legislature could not forbid the adoption itself, the lawyer continued to explain with unwavering friendliness, that was a matter of 'private autonomy'. But these days the state could refuse a permit to stay because even as the adoptive child of an Austrian, the adopted person would still be a foreigner.

'Blah blah blah,' my uncle had said crossly, and then he lost control of himself, something he never used to do in the past when he was not so old and ill, and prided himself on his ironic reserve. 'I liberated this country, and those Nazi bastards still hold it against me!'

The adoption plan suffered its worst setback when a discordant note crept into my uncle's relationship with Mimi. In itself, that was normal enough: in very new relationships, when enthusiasm is still greater than real knowledge of the other person, small things hurt much more than the cause justifies. But how would my misanthropic uncle, of all people, have known about such human feelings?

He had been wondering for weeks whether to tell Mimi about the business with Josh and Will. He himself couldn't explain where the need to confide in her suddenly sprang from, except that it was to do with Burma, and where Burma was concerned he expected special, indeed boundless understanding from her. He had never told that particular story even to his sons; he did talk to them about Burma from time to time, but only when they asked.

Every day when Mimi came to cook he watched her and wondered if she would understand him, if she would share his grief. The adoption on which he had happily decided meant a good deal to him, for a complicated set of reasons. It seemed to him like coming to terms with himself and his past, and in addition Mimi made him feel a little more human.

'He gave her flowers for her birthday,' chuckled my younger cousin. 'He f-l-i-r-t-s with her,' whispered my father, shaking his head in amazement.

Inwardly, then, my uncle was preparing for a kind of marriage, but outwardly, unfortunately, he didn't let it show. He went on checking up on Mimi, for instance looking for dust left behind radiators, for he thought you ought to keep business separate from your private life. He never asked her about her past and her family either, and it did not strike him as odd that she never said anything about them. But every weekend, when she cheerfully packed him into the car like a frail but cumbersome parcel, when they stood outside the shop window choosing cakes together, when he told his stories and made jokes, and she laughed and twittered in reply, when she wrinkled her brow in concern because he was shaken by an asthma attack, he thought with unaccustomed emotion that she would soon be legally his daughter, and you could tell a daughter anything.

He had told the story only once in his life, and that had been a lesson to him. Never again, he had sworn to himself, as the hysterical laughter of simple, red-faced Englishmen made him look up, to find himself staring straight into their open mouths and at their bad teeth, the result of post-war conditions. Never again.

It was when he came home on leave in 1946. He had taken the first opportunity to leave Burma, firmly resolved not to go back. Somehow or other, he knew, he would find a way in England to avoid being sent back to his unit. He took the London train from Portsmouth, where his ship had docked. He was conspicuous in his jungle-green uniform. Dozens of people spoke to him. 'We clean forgot about you boys,' an old man told him, obviously feeling guilty. 'How are you doing out there?'

'The war in Europe finished so long ago,' said a thin woman apologetically. 'But the war with the Japs is all over now too, right?'

'See anything of that atom bomb?' asked a young man, interested. 'Oh, I see, so it was Burma you were in,' he added.

Even before he went looking for his young wife, the little Englishwoman whom he hadn't seen for almost two years, my uncle wanted to visit his former employer the Soho tailor and tell him all about it. That was his firm intention. He wanted to get it 'over and done with', as we said in my family of unpleasant duties, and at once too, because he dreaded the thought. That seems to have been the only reason why he started talking about it in the crammed train compartment. Instinct probably told him to rehearse the story, have the words ready for the grieving father, who deserved a full account. But he had not expected that his chance-met listeners would laugh. 'Too bad!' cried the strangers first, and then added, 'I'm so sorry,' as they tried to control their facial muscles. 'Really, really bad luck!' squealed one woman, with tears in her eyes. 'Jesus Christ!' gasped a man. 'Peaches!' And then they all roared, because as everyone knows, inappropriate laughter is the most difficult sort to keep back, and because my uncle's stony face made the terrible urge to laugh even stronger.

Josh, the Soho tailor's Zionist son, and Will, a red-headed Scot who had been in their unit since their training course in Glasgow, were killed not in the fighting but by accident. To my uncle, it was a 'pointless, idiotic death', and he found it hard to accept. The distinction that he drew between justified and pointless, acceptable and idiotic death would probably be impossible for modern pacifists and anti-war campaigners to understand, but it was clear as day to my uncle. Of course there had to be wars, in his opinion, because they sometimes couldn't be avoided, they were often just, and of course those who fought in war must reckon with the possibility of dying. Over fifty years later, he was even honest enough to admit that – 'at the time, let me emphasise' – he had been extremely glad the two atomic bombs were dropped, because otherwise the war in the Pacific might have dragged on for ever. 'Just look at the map,' he would say. 'Hundreds of little islands. And blood was shed in fighting over each of those fly-specks.'

But pointless death, accidents and what we now call friendly fire simply didn't fit into his scheme of things. The entire operation was difficult enough without accidents. He and his European comrades had gone thirsty for months, they suffered from the heat, they feared and loathed the scorpions, snakes, and all the different insects, night after night they endured the dreadful racket kicked up by the Japanese in what my uncle would later call 'psychological warfare'. And of course they died; they were wounded and they died. 'I got quick promotion,' said my uncle, laughing scornfully when a later generation naïvely supposed it was as the result of his outstanding courage. 'Look,' he explained once, almost indulgently, 'why does a man get promoted? They were all around at first, corporals, sergeants, sergeant-majors. But if the sergeant-major suddenly wasn't there and never would be again, someone else got to be sergeant-major. And all the others moved up too.' However, the thought that in all that jungle-green madness two men had also died of dropped provisions would give him no peace.

'You see,' said my uncle to Mimi's back, and his voice trembled, 'they were killed by packages full of cans of peaches, and I had to be the one to find them.'

Mimi, who was up a ladder dusting books, slowly turned around. Two young British soldiers, red-haired and good-tempered, had died in the Burmese jungle, killed by packages of canned peaches. And the man whose British medal for gallantry she had recently held in her hand had been hysterically afraid of scorpions. She herself had left the country after her parents, like so many others, disappeared. She would see neither her parents nor her country again, or so she assumed, anyway. But almost sixty years ago, some men who were strangers to her had been killed by canned peaches, and this nice, sick old man still couldn't grasp it. Mimi carefully climbed down from the ladder and sat down in a chair opposite my uncle. Then she buried her face in her hands and laughed until she cried.

My uncle watched her laughing until she stopped. Then he quietly asked her to put the rubbish out when she left. Mimi didn't know how to apologise. She never mentioned her parents, on principle. So she acted as if nothing had happened, sighed quietly once more, 'Peaches,' shook her long hair, dried her last tears of mirth, and fetched the rubbish bag. For the first time they parted at odds with each other. My uncle reacted with a bad attack of flu that kept him in bed for weeks, and put the adoption process on the back burner for a while.

During the weeks in which he was bedridden, Mimi's

loving care was greater than ever. To show him how sorry she was, she made another attempt to buy ham at his favourite stall in the Naschmarkt, the big Viennese food market. So far she had just said 'ten decagrams', showing her fingers, but the salesgirls at the stall discourteously pretended to be stupid. 'You want to learn German first!' they had called after Mimi as she walked away, red in the face, without buying anything. The salesgirls sorely missed talkative Aunt Ka, with whom they had happily gossiped about other people, and they distrusted the young Asian woman. 'A Thai tart?' one had asked. 'Go on with you, she's in it for the money, that's all,' the other had laughed, adding something rude about my uncle's age, frailty, and the very different needs that might be deduced from that.

In spite of his great age, my uncle always recovered quickly from his attacks of illness. His pulmonary consultant once told my father that people were seldom so tough, for 'I've never before seen anything like that lung in my whole career.'

'I suppose some psychological factor always gets him on his feet again,' surmised the doctor, 'but I'm no expert there.'

My uncle acted the part of tough guy to everyone. 'Still alive, thanks,' he replied brusquely if you asked how he was. It was only to my father, and only when they were alone, that he complained and groused, describing his aches and pains down to the smallest detail, to my father's great discomfort. But although he always recovered, there was a little less of him left every time. 'Forty-two kilos,' my father groaned in despair, coming back from visiting him, 'it's crazy!' After the flu, going to the adoption tribunal was out of the question. My uncle had to look after himself and stay at home for some time to come. Only once, on a very sunny Sunday, did he venture on a short outing to the Vienna Woods with Mimi, with my father acting as chauffeur.

For weeks my uncle lived as a borderline basket case, and he set the borderline himself with his own strength of will: anyone would have understood if he had gone to bed and stayed there, but he gritted his teeth, got up, dressed, and made his way around the apartment all day until it was time to go to bed again. Now and then he went the short distance to the Naschmarkt with Mimi. And so, one day, he must have decided to try for Mimi's adoption again, out of obstinacy, defiance, and his secret wish for a resolution. He knew that he wouldn't have much time left.

'What do you mean, the British army?' asked the judge of the tribunal, baffled. My uncle raised his voice and told the judge his personal history. If he ever felt that young Austrians these days were insufficiently acquainted with the Nazi past, my uncle could be very didactic. His account was full of remarks like, 'chased away like a dog' and 'came back gun in hand'.

'And then, suddenly, no one would admit to having been a Nazi any more,' he concluded his short but agitated little lecture. 'I've known that more than once.'

'And where exactly did you meet the young lady, Sergeant?' asked the judge.

'In the Naschmarkt,' replied my uncle. He had told the tribunal about Burma too, only the essentials, of course, but now the memories really took over his head. He couldn't help it. For the judge's benefit, he had slightly distorted his reasons for adopting the young Burmese woman, by claiming with pretended emotion that he had been ashamed all his life for what both warring parties, the British and the Japanese, had done to 'the civilian Burmese population. It wasn't like today, when the fighting spares civilian populations,' he had said, with sarcasm that the judge either overlooked or failed to pick up.

In point of fact my uncle's contact with the 'civilian population' had been minimal. Of course while he and his division were under siege in Meiktila, the local people had been under siege too – for the second time, in their case. But he had hardly seen anything of them at all. His experience of the Burmese was exactly what he had imagined a civil population would be like in war, their attitudes ranging from distrustful to servile, and he treated them with the same caution as they showed to him. It was always the same when two foreign powers clashed on the territory of a third: some of the indigenous inhabitants greeted them as liberators, others would put up ferocious opposition as soon as the opportunity offered. No, it was not 'the suffering of the civilian population' that brought my uncle up short in his mind. His thoughts went to his own phrase, devised out of pure calculation, when he said he 'had been ashamed of it all his life'. Was there anything those words did fit, my uncle suddenly began to wonder, while the judge was questioning Mimi about the circumstances of her first journey to Austria. Out of a distant mist, reason told my uncle not to allow the judge's interrogation of Mimi to go unchallenged, but he felt paralysed. He was prepared for the judge to try making the personal relationship between him and Mimi seem implausible ('What would you expect from a man who asks me why I was in the British army?' my uncle would say later, furiously), and he noticed the slight change in the atmosphere, but at that moment he simply could not find the strength to return to the present and stand by the Burmese civil population in the form of Mimi. My uncle was deep in jungle-green memories. He saw himself and Abi 'fishing' in Meiktila. The relief troops were taking for ever to arrive, provisions were short, and the aim of the pilots supplying Meiktila from the air was, as we have seen, often shockingly erratic. Luckily they had water, the lake in which they sometimes went 'fishing', although that was strictly forbidden, not because of the fish but because of the waste of hand grenades. The Japanese attacked every night, but they had already lost command of air space, so it was enough to set the machine-guns up 'crosswise', as my uncle explained, and not a Jap would get through. 'Totally fearless, were they?' scoffed my uncle when he talked about it, with all the disdain of which he was capable. 'You know what total fearlessness really means? Suicide to order! The obedience of corpses. A monstrous crime.' The Japanese advanced on Meiktila in closed formation, and they were bound to topple over like tin soldiers, like cardboard dummies, like skittles.

He would never have admitted it, but these images haunted my uncle. He reacted to what was demanded of the enemy with unrestrained anger, feeling furious first with the Japanese commanders who gave such pointless orders, then with the Japanese soldiers themselves, who went to their death night after night like lambs to the slaughter. He was never able to grasp what he had seen there fully, and for the whole of his life he suffered from strong feelings of aggression towards all things Japanese. There were few occasions for contact later, of course, but a group of cheerful Japanese tourists enjoying the new vintage in a wine bar was enough to put him in a foul mood and make him contemplate a speedy departure. Towards the end of his life unkind fate allowed the opening of two sushi bars in the building on the Naschmarkt where he lived – 'raw fish and seaweed,' he raged, 'no wonder.' As children, to be sure, we greatly admired the way my uncle could tell Japanese from Chinese and other Asians at a glance. For sometimes cheerful Chinese came into a wine bar to try the local wine too. My family would exchange anxious glances, but if my uncle didn't move a muscle, they must be Chinese.

In spite of all the Japs who were shot down 'crosswise', my uncle's division, which had suffered equally heavy losses, was unable to free itself from Meiktila without reinforcements. They waited weeks for the relief troops to arrive. It nearly sent them crazy. Corned beef and biscuits rained from the skies, biscuits and corned beef. Night after night they killed all the Japanese who approached them, automatically and without much risk. After a while the bodies were left lying where they fell and no longer taken back behind the lines, as they had been at first. They were not a pretty sight. It was hot, it was humid, it was all very uncomfortable. Since my uncle was afraid of being driven distracted by life in camp, he volunteered for reconnaissance patrols. During the day he crawled around outside the fortifications to find out which way the next nocturnal attack would be coming. He kept an anxious eye open for mines, scorpions and snakes, paying so much attention to them that his little troop once ran straight into an enemy scouting party in the green twilight of a little wood. Nothing happened. They all dropped to the ground at the same time, and crawled away from each other in panic without firing a single shot.

When they were finally relieved and could hope never to set eyes on Meiktila again, they felt drunk with happiness. For a few carefree days they didn't mind what lay ahead. They just wanted to get away from there, be on the move, marching towards some destination. The destination to which they were ordered was Rangoon. They were to go even further south to recapture the capital city. In the first days after their release from the scorching prison of Meiktila, the task seemed to them both easy and a long way off. They soon paid for the foolish cheerfulness of those first few days, thought my uncle, while Mimi, who had made herself pretty for the occasion, piped away beside him, and an interpreter murmured. Always expect the worst, then you can't go wrong, he thought. Then you can be glad if something turns out better than expected. Never think the other way round. In his mind he was marching again, with Abi beside him. Now and then their own reconnaissance planes flew overhead, and then there was cheerful whistling and waving. On the way they heard the news that their intended target, Rangoon, had already been taken by the Americans and British, moving in from the coast. Large groups of Japanese were in flight northwards, making straight for the 17th Indian Division. As I said before, there was only one main road for traffic in Burma.

'An acquaintance made in the Naschmarkt,' said the judge. 'Do you often pick up young ladies in the street and take them home, Sergeant?' In his head, my uncle tried out several retorts, ranging from the deep-frozen to the furiously angry, but it took him too long, and he missed his chance to say anything at all. In my condition, he thought, they can do anything they like with me. The judge could ask such impertinent questions, he thought, only because he must have seen that he was too old and weak to resist properly. Back then when I was still in uniform it would have been different, thought my uncle bitterly, but now he sees me as nothing but a sick old fool. The next thing he knew, the man was daring to hold his pension against him, that ridiculous, embarrassingly small sum that he would have spent in a single evening in restaurants and bars in the good old days with his Kali.

'What business of yours is my pension?' spat my uncle. Mimi looked at the floor. The judge suddenly turned very nice, 'nice as pie', as my uncle would say later. He explained that if by any chance 'his new daughter Fräulein Mimi' were to have an accident or be unemployed ('and am I right in thinking that so far the young lady doesn't have a steady job?'), then my uncle, as her legal father, would have to pay for everything. He, the judge, thought it most unlikely that my uncle was in any financial position to do so. 'They deal with these things differently in different provinces of Austria,' smiled the judge comfortably, leafing through his papers. 'But the city of Vienna is very keen on covering its costs. Or were you planning to move away?'

'Keen on covering its costs,' muttered my uncle

thoughtfully, now hopelessly defeated, and he carefully stood up. 'I suppose I've not been nearly as keen on covering my costs as I should have been all my life.' Then he left the district court on Mimi's arm.

'He was a real bastard,' raged my uncle next day hoarsely, lying with a high temperature in bed in the Lainz hospital. 'A Nazi, a snake in legal clothing!' He was lying on pale yellow sheets, his last few tufts of hair standing out from his head like a halo, his blue eyes open wide. He consisted of little more than those big blue eyes. He hadn't really been conscious all day, although my family at last, in desperation, sent for Mimi to sing him something. My younger cousin, who had spent the night at the hospital, fearing the worst, witnessed my uncle's terrible fantasies of Burma during those hours. They were obviously to do with the clash with the fleeing Japanese, fifty kilometres north of Rangoon. 'Very clever,' stammered my uncle in his hospital bed, 'calling the planes to our aid, boom boom, firing right into that marching column, kilometres of men in it, it was kilometres long.'

'Any number of POWs among them,' cried my uncle in his fever, 'our own people, no shoes, no hats, no teeth, still made to carry the baggage for the Japs, many of them sick, beriberi, on crutches, sunstroke, just about made it there and then under fire from us, bombarded.' At three in the morning my younger cousin carefully wiped away his tears. He remembered later that even the fabric handkerchiefs in Lainz were pale yellow. 'All the tears he never shed,' said my younger cousin thoughtfully. 'My God, how emotional you are!' groaned my elder cousin, and my father acted as if he had heard none of this story of the Lainz hospital and Burma. We are deeply ashamed of showing emotion in our family. Perhaps my uncle is mainly to blame, that cool, ironic, almost pathologically reserved man who always

138

seemed so stunningly elegant, and lost a little of his composure only in advanced old age.

When, against all probability, he came round from his delirium again, the first thing he said, in English, was, 'Forgive me, Mimi, but I am too poor to be your Daddy.' Mimi nodded, and swallowed. And the next thing my uncle said to his brother my father, reproachfully, as if it were all his fault, was, 'There, you see? I can't die, even of shame.'

The End of the War

Katzi had entirely the wrong psychological attitude to her illness, a young Canadian doctor explained to her in the spring of 1941. 'The more of a hurry you're in to get better, the longer it will take,' he said, and Katzi nodded only because otherwise she would have sobbed with fury. She lay in her bed by the open window, with her head raised, concentrating on the band forming up in the garden. She imagined being among the musicians, because she would have liked a change of view for once. She wondered whether the musicians, looking at the building from the garden, could see only the patients' heads behind the windows, or the whole beds propped up at the windows and on the terraces: an audience consisting of a single row of bedridden patients spreading across the whole long, glazed façade of the sanatorium. 'Sun, rest and fresh air,' the young doctor reminded her, and Katzi nodded and avoided his eyes. 'If you'd eat good food as readily as you write letters . . .' he said, looked at her briefly, and went away.

Next to Katzi, Marjorie was breathing stertorously. She was a red-haired, earthy woman in her late thirties from Detroit, the mother of four children whom she hadn't seen for a year and a half, though she kept sending them post-cards on which she drew a great many little coloured pictures. Usually all the cards said was, 'Lots of love from Mom', for Marjorie devoted all her efforts to the funny stories that the pictures told. Now and then, when a drawing went wrong, she scribbled a 'Don't forget me, kids!' on the card before tearing it up and throwing it away. Marjorie's husband, a taciturn labourer from Windsor, came to visit only once every few weeks. Then he sat beside her bed, and they both looked at the magazines he had brought with him. Marjorie's good humour seemed unimpaired, although she was in a much worse way than Katzi. She had had two operations, and you could easily see the flat place on the left-hand side of her torso, that dreadful pit under her breast. Katzi often stared at it; she couldn't help it. 'Very chic, right?' Marjorie laughed when she spotted Katzi looking, and then coughed like a rusty trumpet.

Marjorie did Katzi good. Katzi soon adopted her tone, and used expressions which didn't really suit her at all. Marjorie was full of praise for Katzi's stout husband because he came to visit every Sunday, smiling awkwardly, always bringing flowers or a small present. She consoled Katzi, and told her it was perfectly normal that she couldn't think of anything to say to him – 'after all, I'm afraid we're not having a riotous time here, are we, honey?' Marjorie even grimly uttered hissing sounds out of solidarity when on some Sunday afternoons the young doctor threatened not to let Katzi have visitors – that was on those Sundays when an excited Katzi had spent the whole hour talking urgently and in a loud voice to her stout husband, because she had had a letter telling her about some new complication in Europe. After such news, Katzi was distracted and feverish, and the doctor made his threats.

The Canadians thought highly of their sanatoriums. During these years they kept building more and more, it was headline news in the papers when another few dozen beds became available, Canadian doctors travelled the world, teaching new operating techniques. Nursing was a popular profession. Cleanliness and light, fresh air, nourishing food, and above all isolation of the sick – that was their proud slogan. Marjorie just laughed at all this and swore by her bottle of 'Liquid Sunshine'. She consumed amazing quantities of the cod-liver oil that bore this euphemistic name. The doctors patiently explained to her that it was a good means of prevention but useless as a cure; Marjorie could not be prevailed upon to give it up, or smoking either.

Katzi was fighting an absurd battle from her sickbed in the quiet, sunny sanatorium. She bombarded her brother, my uncle, with letters to his constantly changing addresses. She wrote to her parents in Vienna. She sent invitations, confirmations and financial guarantees written in clumsy English and elaborate German out into the world, like magic spells, heading them 'Affidavit'. She corresponded with British and Canadian authorities, with nursemaids and foster-parents, with the Quakers and the International Red Cross. What she wanted more than anything in the world was to have her two younger brothers with her, and she persuaded herself at least, and her parents, my grandparents, with whom she managed to keep in touch for a remarkably long time, that she would do it, she'd save them and get them to safety. She didn't realise that she was dangerously ill. She thought her illness, the warnings, all the weeks she had already spent in the sanatorium were just an annoying obstacle, but one that could be overcome. She thought there was almost nothing wrong with her, and she didn't take her coughing and the black spots on the X-rays seriously. After all, she had suffered this disorder once before, but after a while it had seemed to get better of its own accord. She was secretly angry with the two healthy young honeymooners who had crashed into their car. 'We were both flung out, and the car is wrecked,' she wrote to her brother my uncle in the spring. 'Herbert had a broken rib and water on the knee, and I was just bruised. The other couple were slightly injured, not badly. We spent a couple of days in hospital, they took X-rays of me, and instead of broken ribs they found out that my lung was in rather a bad way again. That's all, nothing to worry about.'

'They won't let our little brother see me when he first arrives,' she wrote to my uncle in the summer, while Marjorie, in bed beside her, did drawings. 'He's still a child, and I have TB. They fear it like the plague here, because of infection. But that doesn't matter, the two of you will be with my parents-in-law to start with, they have a lovely house with a garden in a good part of town. I know you'll be very comfortable there, and I'll be sure to send you enough money to go out or do whatever you like.'

'I hear from you so seldom, it's dreadful,' she wrote only two days later. 'You just can't seem to get used to writing 2 × a week. I'm always so scared when I hear the news on the radio, I'm terribly worried about you both. It's a long time since I had news of our little one, I don't know what's going on. Do please write a letter to our parents and send it to me – why didn't you think of that? Send your letter airmail so I don't have to wait so long for it. No more news today. Now I'll wait for a letter from you.'

The worst of it for her was gathering, from my uncle's few letters, that he thought her efforts were useless. 'I know that the state can't send out any more children now,' she said to Marjorie, agitated, 'but privately it must still be possible!'

'He doesn't want to come,' she wept, while the band played out in the garden and her stout husband, at a loss, held her hand. 'He'd rather fight in the war! But he must at least bring me our little brother!'

But when suddenly, as it happened, Marjorie coughed up more blood and pus one night than ever before, cursing, and just couldn't stop, when she was hastily taken away and didn't come back, when the silent labourer left Marjorie's last drawing with her room-mate as a memento before putting the rest of the things in her bag, Katzi became sensible all at once. She sent Marjorie's last drawing, an amusing conversation between a giraffe and a penguin, to my father in Stopsley, where it never arrived. Then she left most of the rest of the correspondence to her stout husband. She did keep asking to see wallpaper and fabric samples for the wonderful 'young gentlemen's room' that she kept promising in her letters, but now she left its furnishing entirely to her husband. But she stopped getting so excited, she was not in a hurry any more, she was quiet and introverted. She ate well, breathed deeply, and did everything she was told. 'The doctors bother me with treatments that don't do me any good at all,' she dictated to her husband in a letter that he later sent to my uncle, 'but don't let it worry you, my dear. Whenever you feel down just remember: my sister is doing everything she can.'

So the summer passed too. Katzi gradually put on some weight. She didn't cough so much, and 'is looking better already', as her relieved husband wrote to Vienna and England. One sunny day she was even allowed to go out in one of the chairs on wheels that she and Marjorie had laughed at so much. 'I'll walk by myself or not at all,' Marjorie had mocked, drawing deeply on her cigarette, 'not in that coffin.' The walking carriages looked like perambulators for adults, made of wickerwork and complete with a cushion for the head and a blanket. Her husband pushed her. Katzi wanted to be wheeled to the middle of the lawn, the place where the band usually played. Once there, she put her golden-blond head out of the ridiculous vehicle and looked at the bright white sanatorium with its glazed façade for a while. She could see nothing but heads behind the windows and the balustrades of the terraces, heads in front of a white background. 'Can you see the beds too?' she asked, looking up at her husband. 'A bit of them, I think. I'm not sure,' he said, and she made a face, dissatisfied.

Katzi now took a particular interest in the way the war was going. Her husband became her private war reporter, reading the newspapers with care and summing up their comments and analyses for her. 'If only the war would be over at last,' she said in despair, because she thought that would help her efforts. Believing that she could bargain for her family better in peacetime conditions, she even hoped for a while that the Russians would surrender. And at this time that seemed quite likely.

So Katzi waited almost a year for an end – an end to her time in the sanatorium, her separation from her brothers, the danger to her parents, the war. Late autumn was unusually warm and sunny. Katzi watched the leaves falling day by day until all the trees were bare. The medical superintendent cautiously began to hold out the prospect of a discharge; it was only the young doctor, hearing him, who always almost imperceptibly shook his head. 'A few months, perhaps only weeks,' Katzi dictated to her husband in a letter for her brother, 'and with a little luck the worst will soon be over for me.'

Her husband came to visit more often now. He still couldn't kiss her, but at least he didn't have to wear a mask over his mouth any more. To Katzi's great relief, he had found a certain Miss Myers, with whom he negotiated by correspondence for several weeks. Katzi thought Miss Myers was a nursemaid who sometimes looked after my father, so he would know her and trust her, and her husband didn't let her know that this Miss Myers was just an assistant in the Stopsley local authority offices, and had never set eyes on my father. At any rate, Miss Myers said she was prepared to travel to Canada, 'bringing the little boy in on her passport', as Katzi's husband wrote to my uncle. 'That's if I will promise her a job,' Katzi's husband wrote, 'but I can't employ her in the office, so I've offered her a position as housekeeper.'

By now the Germans, almost unchecked, were marching on Moscow. Kiev fell, and the Crimea, and a place that Katzi had never heard of before called Rostov on the Don. Contact with her parents in Vienna broke off. Katzi and her husband couldn't find out if the money they sent was still arriving, so they went on sending it.

During November Katzi had waited for news from Vienna with increasing anxiety. When none came she sent money to Aunt Gustl, asking her to take it to her parents and urging her to send news of them and how they were. No answer came. Instead, the authorities finally gave permission for my father to go to Canada. 'So happy!' scribbled Katzi in the margin of the last letter she sent her brother, my uncle, from the sanatorium. 'He'll soon be here.' But not until decades later did my father find out that such a journey had ever been planned. This last letter to my uncle ends with the words, 'I hope you can soon come too. Lots and lots of kisses, and see you very soon. Love from Katzi.'

On the day when she was to be discharged from the sanatorium she suddenly ran a high temperature. The young doctor came, examined her, and left the room without a word. 'I'm sorry,' he said a few hours later to Katzi's distraught husband, 'tomorrow, perhaps the day after tomorrow. No longer.'

'She slept through the night,' says the black-bordered letter that didn't reach my uncle until weeks later, 'and in the morning she was conscious until the last. She talked to me, even laughed, until at a quarter to ten in the morning she fell asleep, never to wake again. I cannot tell you how it feels to have lost my darling.'

When stout Herbert drove home from the sanatorium for the last time, new posters had just been stuck up everywhere. 'Tuberculosis Is Curable And Preventable,' they said. 'If You Are Run Down Or Have A Cough, Get A Medical Examination.'

So the war soon ended for Katzi after all. She was twenty-one. Next day the Japanese attacked Pearl Harbor, and for my uncle, who wanted to be a soldier more than anything in the world, the war had just begun.

During the last few air raids my grandparents went down to the shelter in the cellar together. Before that my grandmother had always gone alone, because my grandfather wasn't allowed into the shelter. It was the closest one to their apartment, and their neighbour, widowed Frau Jacoby, and a few other women whose husbands had to go elsewhere when the siren went sat in it too. These inseparable married couples, who in spite of ominous threats could not be prised apart, in the last resort probably more out of defiance than love, lived within a radius of a few streets, some of them in the same buildings. They inhabited Schiffamtsgasse, Grosse Schiffgasse, Kleine Sperlgasse, Mazgasse, Castellezgasse. They seemed to have been forgotten there, the last few dozen Jews in Vienna and their Aryan wives. And they tried to stay forgotten, that tiny remnant who were still protected.

The Jews who stayed were housed with their steadfast wives in tiny, dark apartments along the Danube Canal. For months they had seen the pick-up trucks drive towards the Aspangbahnhof, but as long as their wives didn't leave them they could stay on. My grandfather had in fact persuaded himself that right at the end, when almost all of them had to go to the Aspangbahnhof, only a couple of reasons were enough to save anyone: he, for instance, had a Star of David from the First War with the golden profile of Emperor Franz Josef on it, a special distinction. He told himself this story because he wanted to feel that he had contributed a little towards his own survival. But my grandmother's impeccable ancestry protected him far better than golden Franz Josef framed by the Star of David. And by now it was incredibly long ago, over two years, since all those Jews had been driven to the Aspangbahnhof week after week, and my grandfather would have liked to forget all about it if only he could.

The others, the 'normal' women with their children who took refuge in the air-raid shelter with my grandmother, had no men left within reach apart from a couple of old gentlemen. Their husbands were far away, or had fallen fighting, which meant that there was a considerable difference between the two groups of women. At the very end, some of those others suddenly got together and hissed, 'Watch out, here comes the German woman!' when my grandmother came in. As I have said, because of her origins as a Sudeten German my grandmother spoke differently from other Austrians, and in Vienna that was sometimes regarded as typically 'German'.

The tensions in the air-raid shelter finally drove my grandmother to seek the anonymity of the anti-aircraft gun tower in the Augarten a few times. She stood for hours there in the park, with two hardboiled eggs and three cooked potatoes in her handbag, experiencing the panic that broke out when the planes flew over and many people still hadn't got into the tower, because it took such a long time for the crowds to be guided along the winding passageways to the different floors. Once inside they stood shoulder to shoulder, some of them on sloping levels because the stairways hadn't been finished, women screaming as soon as the light went out, while others collapsed and had to be carried away through the crowd. Children cried because they had lost their mothers. People quarrelled over the right to lean against a wall. Every time my grandmother hurried home after the all-clear expecting to find the damp, grey building where she and my grandfather lived gone. It contained all that she still possessed: the photographs of her three children and a few letters. She always left the letters and photographs at home, because she didn't want them buried with her under the rubble in some cellar. Something must stay in its proper place, she may well have thought. Or perhaps she wanted to share those last possessions fairly with my grandfather by letting Fate decide what happened to them, and so the papers had to stay at home when she left early in the morning to queue for rations, and my grandfather, dog-tag on his chest, went off to do his sauced labour.

The grey, damp building still stood, although in the end it had not an intact window pane left. In the middle of March, when the city had been full of rubble and ashes for a long time, my grandfather gave up going to work. You simply couldn't get through. It was presumably at this time that he took off the dog-tag for good too. When an air-raid warning went now, they both just stayed at home. They hardly spoke to each other, they simply sat there listening to the noise outside and waiting. Sometimes they played cards.

When news came that the Russians were close to Baden, my grandparents decided to go down to the air-raid shelter together. Those were the days when you stumbled over dead bodies everywhere you went out of doors. A few 'traitors' dangled from the street lights on the Floridsdorfer Bridge. In the Votivpark, officers stayed sitting quietly on park benches after committing suicide. Nazis who knew what was in store for them and preferred to do the job themselves died at the same time as Resistance workers who had emerged from cover too soon – someone could always be found to string them up. Everything was topsy-turvy.

On one of the last times my grandmother went down to the cellar, a woman was saying that the war was as good as over now. As proof she cited the fact that the Viennese were finally beginning to clear up, because mass graves were being dug in the parks. The woman's old mother tugged desperately at her sleeve, whispering to her for God's sake to keep her mouth shut, but she stuck to her opinion.

The wife of Professor Ruttin, one of the tenants in my grandparents' building, could take no more and died, and suddenly the professor too disappeared without trace. My grandfather suspected that Professor Ruttin had gone underground for safety, because now that he was a widower he was suddenly fair game. The underground was getting larger these days. Out in the country, the last contingents of sixteen-year-old Hitler Youth boys were being brought out as cannon fodder. The Russians overran Baden, and suddenly there they were in the middle of the Vienna Woods.

By now my grandparents were alone in the world, and had been for some time. There had been no more contact with my grandmother's family in Freudenthal since Katzi got her Czech passport there, and spoke her mind to the uncles, aunts and cousins in her own civil way when she said goodbye. Except for Aunt Gustl, all my grandfather's sisters had emigrated, to New York, London and Buenos Aires. My grandfather's mother, the fat old lady with all those black skirts, had not had either the strength to emigrate or any understanding of the problem. She had been taken away two and a half years before from the Aspangbahnhof with a transport of elderly people. On reaching Theresienstadt she hardly even tried to make an effort, for she survived the stress of the train journey by only twenty days. She was eighty-one years old. My grandfather had heard by chance of her planned departure and hurried to the Aspangbahnhof, where she said to him, as she liked to say at the time, 'You might as well come along too, Jewish swine,' so in fact my grandfather actually saw one of those trains from the inside. The mistake was cleared up only at the last minute because the Jewish woman who was an aid worker came along, and my grandfather was thrown out of the train. He had a nasty fall as he reached the platform, and broke his hip, collarbone, nose and a bone in his cheek. My grandmother had to be sent for, or he would have been left lying where he fell, with the people helping the old folk into the train inadvertently treading on him all the time. He never talked about it, or any of the rest of those experiences either ('in the war everyone smelled bad'), but it was noticeable that to the end of his life he never got on a train again. Trams, yes, but not trains.

During the last days of the war my grandparents were back quarrelling in their old way once more. My grandmother had taken out two letters and began studying them closely. My grandfather was ranting. But all his shouting could not make her fold up the two letters and put them away with the others. And he himself didn't want to touch them, so they lay there open on the kitchen table. When my grandmother wasn't reading them she weighted them down with the sugar tin. Outside there was firing, bombed-out buildings collapsed days after they had been hit, people were dug out of the ruins, there were air-raid alarms the whole time, although the fighter planes had long since flown on into the Reich, but my grandmother kept reading those two letters again and again. This was the beginning of April. The two letters had arrived years before, but in the wrong order. First came the letter from Aunt Gustl, who had taken refuge for a while with a friend of hers, a baroness, in the Salzkammergut. 'My dr brother,' Aunt Gustl resumed, after first complaining of her poor health, 'we have all suffered a great misfortune. I have just had a letter from dr Herbert saying that our beloved Katzi died of pneumonia on 6 December. We are all in great distress, and must support each other. I feel great pain, but sad, sad as it is to say, she was very ill and there was nothing anyone could do for her. I beg you to be sensible and composed, none of us will ever forget her.' Dolly too had written a few lines. 'My dearest brother-in-law, I am just back from Vienna and I hear this terrible news! I am too upset to send you any words of comfort; I could do with some myself, for I loved Katzi like a daughter. So please just accept my sincere condolences. I hope to see you both here with us soon. With kind regards, Dolly.'

The other letter, which arrived weeks later, was from Katzi herself. 'Dearest Mama and Papa,' it began, 'I am much better now, they're letting me go home next week.' And it ended, 'But it's so long since I had any news from you, I am quite ill with worry. It's dreadful! I have sent you 5 dollars by Aunt Gustl, so that you can buy shoes for Papa. Did you get them? And what does Gustl think she's doing? She owes me an answer to my last letter. I hope so much that you are well and can write to me again. Please write and say whether Herbert can go on sending you money too! Lots and lots of kisses, hope to see you soon, love from Katzi.'

A few days after my grandmother had spread those letters out on the kitchen table, the front line lay between the Westbahnhof, the General Hospital, and the Franz-Josefs-Bahnhof. On 12 April Roosevelt suffered a stroke. Next day the war in Vienna was over, although a few diehards went on defending a bridgehead on the other side of the Danube for three more days. Soon afterwards, when the situation seemed reasonably safe and after my grandparents had scrubbed the dog-tag symbol off their front door with soap and water, my grandmother, her heart a frozen volcano, set off with the two letters to go and look for Aunt Gustl.

In Stopsley they had been expecting the end of the war for a long time, and were disappointed again and again. VE Day was said to be imminent in the autumn, and people panicked because there weren't enough flags and pennants on sale. Mr Bulldog, who had immediately bought in those items, was annoyed to find that Soviet and American flags were in almost as much demand as the good old Union Jack. However, he didn't have large enough stocks of any of the three flags to supply demand. The High Street shops announced, at ever shorter intervals, that there would be sensational discounts on the joyful day. First to promise free beer for all was the landlord of the Old Dr Butler's Head, to be swiftly followed by the other four pubs, but then the Germans put up such fierce resistance in the Ardennes, and the Russians seemed to be tiring so much on their westward march, that the big party kept having to be postponed. Finally the slow course of the war moved into the background; it was a war that had been won long ago, but it still wouldn't end. Mr Bulldog, sitting over his fourth pint, would inform everyone, 'It's only a matter of time before that bastard bites the dust,' but even he reverted to the subject only when he remembered his self-appointed role as a man of the world.

People had other things to talk about: T.C. Smith, the car-parts supplier, had suddenly expanded enormously, dozens of new white-collar and blue-collar workers were being hired, and the little town was surprised to find several strangers there who either moved straight out again or commuted, but in any case made a noticeable difference to the traditional community where everyone had always known everyone else. The first Indian restaurant opened on the south side of town. It offered two different menus a day at a very good price, but it still struggled for the first few months. The daughter of the landlord of the Dog and Duck fell pregnant at just seventeen and wouldn't name the father. The cinema on the High Street closed temporarily after the proprietor took his own life – the people of Stopsley puzzled over his reason in vain. Mr Bulldog announced a competition for the best-kept garden, which to no one's surprise was won by his bony wife. Uncle Tom won a huge cup in the inter-regional darts championships, and it became the gleaming centrepiece of the little sitting-room. He didn't drink as much as he used to, which improved his skill at darts. Norm had finished school and gone back to his parents in London, his brother Pete was still around and had no more visits, but now he was often able to travel to his family in town for the weekend. My father trained in every spare minute he had. He now played at outside right for the Luton Colts, and on many weekends there were scouts in the grandstand who travelled the country looking out for young talent. The other members of the Luton Colts knew that the scouts didn't come for them, they came to see my father play. Once a scout called Mr Williams, who had a moustache, turned up at Uncle Tom and Auntie Annie's house. 'He's only a child still,' said Uncle Tom, both proud and awkward, and then he let Mr Williams talk to my father in private. 'What did he say?' asked Uncle Tom and Auntie Annie later, at supper. 'He said I'm too thin,' replied my father, shrugging. Maybe next season, Mr Williams had predicted, if he ate properly and put on weight and trained hard, and then he could probably take part in a few trial games for various clubs in London which were looking for promising young players.

Two weeks before this, my father had kissed a girl for the first time. Her name was Peggy and she lived in Dunstable, but for reasons that no one can remember now she went to school in Stopsley. My father walked Peggy to her bus every evening. They stood at the bus stop in the High Street, giggling a little and looking at the ground, and then suddenly talking very seriously about their homework, they let one bus go and then the next, and when the last possible bus came they shook hands and Peggy got in. The kiss happened only because it was pouring with rain one day, and no one else was waiting for the bus. My father held Peggy's umbrella, Peggy clutched his arm, the bus came driving through the rain, and then my father quickly put the umbrella down and drew Peggy towards him. She was small, a little plump, and sandy-haired, and a couple of years later my father had as good as forgotten her face.

My father was still doing his early-morning newspaper round. He began with the mayor and Mr Bulldog, but now he ended the round not on the workers' housing estate but at the factory. Before my father took the last newspaper to the manager's office, he stopped at the factory gates where the workers were waiting to be let in. He got off his bike and carefully unfolded the paper so that the back page was showing. As he did so he was surrounded by workers young and old. My father unfolded the paper, the workers crowded around him and commented excitedly on the sports results. They were interested in everything, rowing and football, boxing, hockey, horse-racing. My father took care not to get the manager's newspaper crumpled in the crush, but because many of the workers had been making bets, and they were all eager to see the results, he had to keep saying, 'Hands off!' and 'Let go!' All things considered, the workers were self-controlled, but sometimes one of them did snatch the newspaper roughly out of my father's hand. Then my father would always threaten to stop the illegal news service at once, but of course he found the ritual flattering. He was the herald of the sporting news, and they waited impatiently for him. Sometimes he was too late, and the workers were already streaming into the factory. Then some of them shook their fists at him in jocular fashion as he cycled up, but he would shout out the most important results to them from afar.

'Hold that paper up higher, laddie,' an old worker called through all the noise one day. My father held the sports page out to him. 'Not that way round,' said the man, slamming the paper flat against my father's chest. 'Hey,' said my father, 'hands off!' But then the workers fell silent one by one and gathered behind the old man. My father carefully turned the paper round so that the sports results were facing the workers again, and saw that the whole front page was given over to a huge picture. It showed a crowd of people at night, thousands of tiny heads around a statue. 'VE DAY,' said the caption, in gigantic letters. 'ITS ALL OVER.'

At the bus stop that evening my father gave Peggy one of the red, white and blue ribbons that were suddenly hanging from every window, and Uncle Tom wanted to take him to the pub 'to celebrate'. Predictably, Auntie Annie uttered loud protests, so Uncle Tom went on his own and got very drunk, until my father went to fetch him at closing time. 'My son,' stammered Uncle Tom on the short way home, leaning heavily on my father, but my father laughed, and thought of Peggy, and put Uncle Tom's tears down to the drink.

For my uncle, the last day began just like all the days and weeks before, so that later he could hardly remember it in any detail. He woke up, and rain was falling on the tent. He put a foot out and it sank a couple of inches into the mud. By the time he reached the canteen hut he was drenched, not a dry stitch on him. The damp got under your skin. It was the most monotonous time in his life, even more monotonous that those months at the sewing machine in Dean Street. In Dean Street, after all, he had been able to leave the basement with its suits and pyjamas and go to enjoy the modest entertainments of Young Austria. However, he ended the war in a rubber plantation twenty kilometres outside Rangoon. There was a curfew, and where could you have gone anyway? It rained almost all the time. And even if the rain did stop for a few hours, and the sun appeared behind the mist like a runny egg yolk, the leaves of the rubber trees kept disgorging the water in regular drops, like natural shower-heads. My uncle wondered how long it would be after the rain actually ended, something that by now seemed unimaginable, before the rubber plantation stopped dripping with water too. He guessed it would take days.

He had applied for leave and got it only once. Then he had gone to Rangoon and looked around the city. He had walked down the streets, past shabby wooden houses, he had stood in the harbour looking at the American warships, he had been to the cinema set up for army personnel in one of the few buildings that were fairly stable, and saw a film of some kind there. Apart from that one day he stayed in the rubber plantation.

Against the background of this wet and endless time, only the drama of young O'Malley's love life and the illness of the popular Tahini stood out. O'Malley's wife had sent him a letter telling him that she was going to divorce him. On the first day O'Malley had collapsed histrionically, with the aid of sufficient quantities of alcohol; on the second day he began a counter-offensive. He wrote dozens of love letters, which he read aloud and corrected in line with his friends' comments. In some of the letters he was angry with his wife, but mostly he flattered her, reminded her of the past, and made poetic protestations of his love. He tried both practical reason and the sentimental notion of a marriage made in heaven. All this was done as publicly as possible, deliberately drawing his comrades into the affair. O'Malley needed solidarity and sympathy in his present situation as he needed air to breathe. At first the others had ridiculed O'Malley and passed smutty remarks about his wife, but his naïve, childlike gravity made most of them concentrate on his problems, if only in the short term. There wasn't much else to do. Intensive discussion of O'Malley's case may have caused some of them to push uneasy thoughts of their own wives to the back of their minds. The men estimated O'Malley's chances of success, citing both hearsay and experiences of their own in support of their theories. For a few days the smut and the snide remarks vanished from their conversation, and they thought about tactics and uttered truisms as if they were in a betting shop. O'Malley wrote and wrote, corrected and improved his letters, thought about it. Only a few of the men, including my uncle, stayed out of this collective marriage guidance bureau. My uncle had letters of his own to write, always short and dry. He asked his wife, the little Englishwoman, to look for his parents through the Red Cross and let him know anything she found out at once. He asked her to go to Stopsley and see his little brother. He tried to get drawn into all the O'Malley business as little as possible.

When a letter finally came from O'Malley's indignant and distressed mother, telling her son that her daughter-in-law had moved out, bag and baggage, and moved in with another man, general attention swiftly turned to Tahini. That day Tahini had been moved from the sick-bay to a tent on his own, and the doctors never went into it without face-masks on. The devastated O'Malley was now told, unsympathetically, that he should be glad he'd just got rid of a slut and was otherwise healthy.

Tahini's case made the soldiers uneasy because the army doctors made no secret of the fact that they didn't know what he had. Everyone guessed that an epidemic threatened, but no one said so out loud. Furthermore, Tahini was regarded as a hero who had saved his men's lives in a tricky situation, and now of all times, when everything was as good as over, it didn't seem right for anyone else to die. So a taciturn waiting period began again as it rained outside, or at least as water dripped off the rubber trees.

Day in, day out the men in my uncle's unit grimly did their best not to lose their way in the rubber plantation. Anyone who did get lost, en route to the canteen or returning from a patrol, was mercilessly mocked and became a laughing-stock, although it was infernally difficult *not* to get lost. The rubber trees were so geometrically planted that from every angle the picture they presented looked the same, lengthwise, crosswise and diagonally. There was nothing to help you get your bearings. Anyone who turned half a step aside, because he was looking back or around him, might suddenly not be sure where to go next or where he had just come from.

So the weeks passed by. Although in retrospect it looks as if events came thick and fast, they really just floated about like three or four grains of sand in a viscous ocean of rain. When the happy news came of the super-bomb that was said to have destroyed an entire city in Japan all on its own, Tahini didn't hear it because he had fallen into a coma. In the days between the first super-bomb and the second, or perhaps between the second super-bomb and the Japanese surrender, O'Malley disappeared. At first people joked that in his grief he too had lost his way, then they began looking for him. Meanwhile Tahini died. It was said that at the end blood was pouring from his mouth, nose and eyes. Tahini was burnt along with his last tent, his bed and all his things, which in all that damp took a great deal of petrol, and the stink was terrible. Soon before or soon after that they found O'Malley, who had shot himself in a remote part of the rubber plantation. Soon before or soon after that the Japanese surrendered, and the war in the Pacific was finally over. Later, however, my uncle could never remember the exact sequence of events, for everything had seemed to him to merge together during those weeks.

Matters of Opinion

Looking back, the way our little business started up seems unreal, like a fairy-tale. But in the fifties my father knew a good opportunity even if it seemed odd at first. My father looked like the daredevil sort, particularly in his youth, or at least the kind of man who doesn't go in for brooding heavily and because of that, or in spite of it, finds that everything falls into his lap. In fact he was much more of a careful bourgeois soul than he seemed, much more anxious, always bent on avoiding risk. However, appearances effectively outweighed reality. What looked like a gambler's crazy venture was actually a tailor-made answer to his and his father's needs and talents.

Originally the idea came from that brilliant businessman Fredi Hals. It must have been in the Weisskopf, when my father either complained that he was having more and more trouble with the film company getting time off for training and away games, or else, in his own version of the story, was worried because his father, my grandfather, had recently fallen off a ladder trying to change defective neon tubes in an Arabia Coffee neon ad.

'You need a business of your own,' murmured Fredi Hals thoughtfully over his vodka, and he soon claimed to have thought up something suitable. Later, my father always chuckled and said he had been horrified when he saw that 'stinking pigsty' for the first time. The premises of a gloomy back-yard restaurant off Mariahilferstrasse, right next to the doors of the porn cinema – 'Who'd go in there?' he asked Fredi. 'You must be off your head!'

'Central situation, no passing trade,' Fredi is said to have replied, 'the very thing for you.' My brother later said, maliciously, that Fredi Hals had badly needed 'one reasonably respectable venture in his entire Mafioso empire', but my father was still sure that Hals had developed the idea mainly out of his fondness for my grandfather.

As I have said, Hals used to play bridge with my grandparents after the war, which gave him plenty of opportunity to observe my grandfather's fanatical enthusiasm for sport. My grandfather craved the sporting papers, and when the evening editions came out he sometimes even jumped up from the card table in the middle of a game, much to my grandmother's annoyance. Every weekend he went to the Hohe Warte or some other football stadium, often with Hals, and he was inconsolable when my father's club was playing too far from Vienna for him to go and watch the match. When my father was playing on the Hohe Warte, his home ground, my grandfather would hurry off to the players' changing rooms directly after the last whistle, put his head round the door, and begin to analyse the game and praise or criticise his son and the other team members. This was extremely embarrassing for my father. 'It's a wonder he didn't follow us into the showers,' he said critically later, but at the time, as a young man, he didn't dare stop his father. His relationship with his parents was marked by a vague mixture of feelings: gratitude and a sense of strangeness, respect and lack of understanding – he had missed out on several crucial years with them, but their silence denied the fact, as if those years hadn't been, or at least as if they had not lived through them.

Fredi Hals also knew that my grandfather had travelled around a great deal during his years as a commercial traveller in wines and spirits, and had learnt to make himself reasonably well understood in the languages of those parts of the former monarchy nearest to Vienna, Hungary and Czecho-slovakia. To prepare him for his new job Fredi began counting in Czech and Hungarian while they played cards, as if it were a game. My grandmother didn't like it, because it painfully stirred up some slight residual Czech identity in her, but everyone knew that my grandfather didn't mind in the least what my grandmother thought if it affected only the peripheral areas of life.

My father always took care to emphasise later that in 'his time' every sportsman had another career too, in glaring contrast to today. 'You didn't get to see someone who'd hardly learnt to read and write just because he had a gift for football,' he sometimes said, shaking his head, when he watched television interviews with Austrian footballers. And he added, 'The Austrians are the worst. You never get Germans who can't even speak properly,' which reinforced our childhood impression that there had been a lot going wrong with Austria for quite some time. 'Why, there were a couple of men with university degrees playing in the national team in my time, they had doctorates,' said my father, and this fact, even though it can be checked, does indeed sound fantastic from today's standpoint.

So it was quite normal for my father to become a businessman at the peak of his footballing career. In the small, damp, back-yard restaurant next to the porn cinema a business was built up on the basis of goods that Hals & Co. could acquire or supply themselves. Taking Fredi Hals's advice, my father concentrated on goods which were difficult to get hold of in the Eastern bloc states. For the first few years that meant disposable razors, nylon stockings, ballpoint pens, Doxa watches and raincoats; then he expanded the range of miscellaneous goods by adding transistor radios and cameras, until much later, towards the end of the sixties, he was dealing mainly in all brands of jeans, including denim jackets, denim skirts, denim boots and bags and anything else that can be made of denim. My brother claimed sarcastically that for a while our father even sold denim loo-roll covers.

The target customers for our business were East European sportsmen. Fredi Hals had elaborated on his old idea, and in his typical farsighted way had linked the shortages of the East, about which he knew a lot, as a native Hungarian, to the fact that only sportsmen were allowed to travel, while the strict Eastern border guards usually turned a blind eye to their sportsmen's travel souvenirs. The trump card that Fredi Hals played in this scenario was my grandfather's encyclopaedic knowledge of sports; he always knew in advance which teams would be coming to compete in Vienna. My father signed for the goods, fixed the prices, and then just had to be there at certain agreed times, when large groups were expected. For the slack periods in between, when there were only occasional unexpected customers, or when passing trade from Mariahilferstrasse, the big shopping street, did find its way into the back yard after all, my grandmother or my father's first or second wife, depending on the date, could mind the shop.

Only my grandfather was kept permanently busy. It was he who drummed up trade. He approached Polish waterpolo players, Romanian track and field athletes, Bulgarian weight-lifters in their inexpensive lodgings or at the sporting events themselves. He handed out business cards, promised discounts, told them how to find us. He met Hungarian swimmers straight off the landing stage where the Danube steamer from Budapest came in, and he went to the bus station when East German ice skaters or Czech cyclists arrived. He knew everything because it was in the newspapers, or because the officials of the various Viennese clubs concerned, all of whom of course he knew, had told him. Most of the East European teams, however, arrived by train at the Ostbahnhof. My father and Fredi Hals thought my grandfather would spare himself a lot of travelling around if he concentrated on the railway station. But at first he stood out firmly against the idea. He wanted nothing to do with trains. At some point he changed his mind, apparently when the Hungarian or Yugoslavian national teams were going to arrive there. Business or no business, my grandfather had wanted to meet them in person for a long time.

But he never set foot in the trains. The sportsmen, who were often still groggily getting their things together in the sleeper cars, had our business cards handed in to them through the window. My grandfather, his suit pockets full of cards, got used to spiking card after card on the tip of his cane at top speed and reaching them up. If someone didn't open a window immediately he would tap the handle of his stick impatiently on the glass. 'Fastest way to work,' said my grandfather proudly. His stick technique was so persuasive that from now on he was never bothered by people asking why he didn't just get on board the trains.

Business went extremely well from the start. 'A goldmine, eh?' cried Fredi Hals enthusiastically. 'What did I tell you?' It seems to have suited the shy East European sports stars that the right shop for them was not in lively, central Mariahilferstrasse, but a little special and set back from the main thoroughfare. The East European sportsmen were not so keen on going into the other shops in Mariahilferstrasse, or the two department stores with their glittering portals, which made them feel conspicuous. And there was hardly anything they could have afforded there. But they felt happy doing business with my father. With him and my grandfather, they were all sporting professionals together, they could exchange platitudes about football and boxing, high jump and long jump. For my father too was interested in almost any sport, apart from figure skating, although he was not as extensively well-informed as my grandfather, who enjoyed predicting the likely winners in all the coming matches, their results, or at least who would ultimately be the finalists.

Everyone came to our little shop: ordinary sportsmen and

players as well as team officials, doctors and trainers. For besides all the advantages I have already enumerated (my grandfather's linguistic talents, the concentrated sporting atmosphere, the range of goods tailored precisely to our customers), in my father's shop they could pay with Eastern currencies, which were very unpopular in Vienna. That had been another idea thought up by Fredi Hals, who knew a lot about the exchange rates. There was a mysterious list of roughly what the current rates were under the counter, but as soon as a whole team came flocking into the shop and piled their purchases up in front of him my father converted the prices with a great deal of charm and laughter, and the customers were left with the impression that they had been given another little discount. It was also the rule never to give change in these obscure currencies, but not, of course, in good Austrian schillings either. Supposing the watch and two nylon raincoats came to eight hundred and fifty – whether the currency was forints or dinars, zlotys or krone – and my father was offered a note for a thousand, he would give change, amidst much chatter and sporting small-talk, in plastic ballpoint pens and disposable cigarette lighters. If the customer seemed dissatisfied, he would throw in three extra pairs of socks. Everyone ended up feeling that he had got a bargain. For where else could the sportsmen have done their shopping? The exchange rates they would have got from Viennese banks or bureaux de change were so bad that it was easy for my father and Fredi Hals to undercut them. What with the converted prices, and discounts that couldn't be traced in detail, and sums rounded up by giving away cheap gewgaws, it all evened out. And then you just had to know where to go afterwards to change all that Eastern money back into good Austrian schillings. But that was Fredi Hals's secret. He came once a week to take all this limp currency, all those levas and leis, away. 'He probably did best out of the deal himself,' my brother surmised later, but my father just shook his head disapprovingly.

A number of people think my brother was always grimly opposed to my father's business, but that's not so. Like all my father's children, he spent a lot of time in the shop, and we all started out by admiring my father, we couldn't help it. Everything he did seemed to come easily to him. He never seemed under any strain or pressure, he never appeared anxious. He acted as if the shop were just his hobby, 'and it wasn't much more than that either,' snapped my mother later. She could have wished for more ambition and higher professional aims in her husband. My father could talk to anyone, even when, as quite often happened in our shop, the people he was talking to spoke only a foreign language. My father managed to make wordplay out of the few scraps of the Slavonic languages that he had acquired over time, although when we children grew older we found it rather embarrassing. '*Dvacetdva* – there we are!' was one of his most banal little rhymes, although it usually amused him most of all.

As a salesman my father cracked jokes and was charming, but he wasn't pushy, and never minded when some of the sportsmen got him to show them everything and work out the prices, and then didn't buy anything after all. 'Albanians,' he would say with dislike, but only when the door had closed behind them, although in fact the Albanians were the only Eastern Europeans whom we never saw in our shop.

As a little boy, my brother noticed just how happy the sportsmen were when my father threw in extra little items with their purchases: ballpoint pens and balloons, chewing-gum and disposable lighters. He was proud when, after a successful match at the weekend, the sportsmen started by congratulating my father, shaking his hand and clapping him on the back, before they began looking round the shop. Once one of the customers, a great tall Czech, kicked a ball about with my brother for almost an hour in the yard outside the shop, and praised his talent. My brother never forgot it. It had been raining, the sun was reflected from the wet paving stones, and he raced through the puddles and even jumped into them until he was all wet and dirty. The grown-ups just laughed. Finally my grandmother hobbled out of the shop and told him off, but for a while my brother had felt like a real footballer. Much later, when he cited the huge Czech's praise as evidence that not all professionals shared my father's hurtful opinion – which was that my brother had, he hoped, a talent for all sorts of things, but football wasn't one of them – my father roared with laughter and said, 'What, him? He was an Olympic swimmer!'

When my brother was a little boy, my father unobtrusively pointed out particular stars among the customers to him, and then he often got an autograph. As a child, he had the autographs of all the major East European footballers, and a considerable number of autographs from swimmers, water-polo players and athletes too. It was a shock to him to find that no one at school thought much of these treasures. 'Oh, that Eastern lot,' said his fellow pupils, dismissing them. They dreamed of Spanish, Italian and English autographs. 'Bet you they're all commies at home.'

My father and his first wife had divorced just before my brother started school, and somehow these two events seem to have coincided traumatically for him. He felt that his father had let him down in every way, and after that he wanted nothing to do with either autographs or sportsmen. At the time, in primary school, he already seems to have made up his mind that the best way to deal with the world was always to do the opposite of what my father thought right.

Professional contact with East European sportsmen had made my father a passionate anti-communist. Never a very politically-minded man, he hated and feared communism in a childlike way. Every time he heard sirens howling somewhere, he gloomily muttered the phrase then very usual in Vienna, 'Here come the Russians.' He would never have travelled privately to any of his customers' native lands, although he received several invitations. It was quite enough for him to go to Hungary and Yugoslavia as a member of the national team, and it gave him great satisfaction that both those matches went unexpectedly well for Austria. For both Yugoslavia and Hungary had world-class teams in the mid fifties, as my father could not but acknowledge. However, going to Yugoslavia on holiday, as the families of many of our fellow pupils at school did, was something my father regarded as so reprehensible that he could barely find words for it, failing to understand that taking a holiday there was a social rather than a political decision. Poorer families went to Yugoslavia, more prosperous families to Italy. We went to Italy every year, always to the same hotel on the Adriatic. 'I'm not letting them have a groschen of mine,' he used to say of the Yugoslavs, generalising, and it was only a question of time before my brother began retorting, 'No, you'd rather exploit their sports stars back home.'

My brother began taking an interest in Marxism. At what became the logical climax of their arguments, he described my father as the prototype of capitalist exploitation. The worst of it was, said my brother angrily, that it was the socialist brethren whom he exploited, thereby trying to weaken the system. My brother enjoyed painting pictures in garish colours of the Eastern sportsmen who had been corrupted by my father taking 'all that trash' home to their families and thus creating a new class-ridden society, because their friends and neighbours would be seduced into thinking that Paradise meant jeans and Doxa watches.

But my father was not to be deterred. With a squirrel's prudent forethought, he stabilised the business even though he still affectionately called the premises a pigsty. When he was doing well he would go to the casino with his friends, only for fun and never losing control of himself, but usually everything just went quietly on. My father had no extravagant needs. What mattered to him was having enough money for our summer holiday beside the Adriatic, regular visits to wine bars and the Weisskopf, and his one hobby, his definitely expensive membership of the Schneuzl Sports Club. With the shop as a predictable and reliable source of income – 'No need for me to work myself to death either' – my father was in the Golden Age of his life. From now on it went on in the same way, and the few small changes and crises were kept to a minimum. To start with he had his first wife and their son, my brother; then he was on his own for a while and enjoyed his bachelor existence to the full; finally he had his second wife and two more children. The children grew up, everything went quietly along, in fact it was a case of 'everything fine', and my father was determined that this state of affairs should continue.

In this cocoon of harmony and small pleasures, modest success, and the consignment of history to oblivion, my brother could not help but rebel and be miserably unhappy.

At school it was a long time before my brother won his fellow pupils' respect. In his first school years, when he was still strikingly small and thin and his mother didn't cut his curly hair because it made him look 'so sweet', he was always being thumped. At primary school he was mainly surrounded by robust working-class children not over-endowed with intelligence, and they hit him because they could almost smell his lack of self-confidence. He couldn't defend himself, because his enemies were first too numerous and second too strong, but his defencelessness gave him a choking sense of failure. 'What's the matter?' my father asked him on the weekends they spent together. 'You have everything you want, don't you?' One day, when my brother began crying and stammered that he wished Mama and Papa were living in the same apartment again, my father shook his head and informed him bluntly that some children had no parents at all. 'They live with foster-parents or in a Home,' said my father. 'You don't know how well off you are.' On the only occasion when my brother tried telling him about school and the way they thumped him there, my father said impatiently, 'So they hit you? Well, go on, hit them back!'

Things did not improve until his last couple of years at school, when my brother shot up in height. He now let his curly hair grow right down to his eyes by choice, and he impressed all the others, not just the girls, with his mingled brilliance and effrontery. He was good at school work but didn't try hard. He made it clear that he could easily have been top of the class any time, if only it wasn't so boring and ordinary to be top of the class. He continued to loathe every form of sport, and following my uncle's example he started smoking at sixteen. Nothing could have infuriated my father more. My father was a militant non-smoker who, long before smoking was frowned on in the Western world, would sometimes speak to total strangers smoking in the street, warning them that they were in the process of killing themselves.

So my brother read, smoked, took no sporting exercise at all, and founded a political debating club. Outwardly, the figure he cut as his father's opposite seemed perfect. My father thought there was nothing wrong with Austria the way it was; my brother and his friends were busy with political ideas which took radical change as their central principle. In his discussion groups he posed, like his friends, as the resistance fighter within his own family. But where the others would begin speaking bitterly of their Nazi fathers, he described his own as a capitalist exploiter. Amazed, the others hung on his every word. Once he was really in full flow, my brother described as 'peculiarly infamous' the fact that my father did not exploit throngs of workers like the fathers of some of the sons of Viennese industrialists, boys who were in their crowd, but was trying to use the Eastern European sportsmen to destabilise the classless society already in existence elsewhere. His audience laughed and marvelled. Part of him knew that he was exaggerating wildly, but another part relished the attention he got, the admiration, the sycophantic laughter. He so desperately needed respect and recognition. And he did, after all, have good reason to feel aggrieved and bitter towards his father.

When he had said at home that he wanted to study history, my father replied that he was going to be a bank clerk. This time my grandfather, who usually acted as a buffer between father and son and smoothed things over, was entirely on my father's side. A bank clerk had a proper, secure, respected profession. No long period of training. You were soon earning your own money and wouldn't be living off your family any more. That was how my father and my grandfather saw it, and nothing could make them change their minds. My brother shouted and yelled, he tried 'reasonable' argument, and next moment he was spitting with rage again. Once, before storming out and slamming the door behind him, he threw a lighted cigarette down on the dining-table, where it left a burn mark. Finally even his class teacher spoke to my father and urged him to let his son study at university. Very few of his year were so well qualified to do so, said the teacher. And my brother's mother, my father's first wife, threw all her weight behind him. But she couldn't finance his studies on her own, and my father remained implacable. 'Look,' said my grand-father, who was suffering almost physically from this family discord, 'who's going to take over the shop some day?' My brother shook his head, amazed by such ignorance. But he loved his grandfather and was very seldom rude to him. My grandmother said nothing at all. It was easy to see that she considered her grandson ungrateful and rebellious, and thought his will should be broken as long as she herself didn't have to do anything about it. My younger cousin tried to make peace, as usual. He was already at university and studying economics. He begged my brother 'in God's name' ('what God?' jeered my brother) to train as a bank clerk, and then he could always study history afterwards. He even hinted to my father that he himself might perhaps take the shop over some day. My younger cousin was a born dealer. He was to start many different businesses later, and most of them were successful.

Only my elder cousin, full of bitterness himself, took my brother's side. Suddenly the two of them were going around together all the time, although until now the age difference of seven years had meant that they were not very close to each other. My elder cousin began going to the discussion groups that my brother organised, but they got together mainly, as it turned out unfortunately much too late, to discuss, at length and just between the two of them, the subject of Unnatural Fathers. 'Never appreciated,' they would tell each other, 'no love, no pride,' nodding with indignation. 'They never even notice us,' they cried, 'never take any interest in us.' And they self-righteously and masochistically dissected all the gruesome details of their childhood skiing holidays with their fathers. My cousin was always saying how Aunt Ka's fat dachshund coughing got more attention than his younger brother's broken toe, and my brother was near tears of rage when he described the way his father had once made him practise parallel swings on the ski slopes, and shook with laughter when my brother kept clumsily falling over.

On the day of the disaster some Bulgarian weight-lifters were expected. My grandfather had set out for the Ostbahnhof early in the morning, for there was a rumour that an advance guard of Yugoslavian athletes would be arriving too, although their events weren't until two days later. My father was meeting Fredi Hals in the Weisskopf that morning, for 'business discussions', as he put it. At midday, after school, my brother was to come to the shop, since he had asked for another discussion of the question of banking versus historical studies. Around eleven, two gloomy-looking young men appeared, stood outside the little shop window for a while smoking, and stared in. When my grandmother went out and asked if they were looking for anyone, one of them spat in front of her feet as if by chance before marching brusquely off.

My grandfather arrived at twelve, in high good humour. He had got rid of all the business cards, and sure enough, he had met the first of the Yugoslavian athletes. The Bulgarian team doctor, who had come with the weight-lifters, was an old acquaintance, and had immediately assured my grandfather that he and some of his sportsmen would drop in later. My grandmother had just finished cleaning the place, and was sitting as usual at the very back of the shop on a director's chair between the two plywood changing cubicles. Then my father and my brother turned up at the same time. They seemed to have met by chance in Mariahilferstrasse, because they were already quarrelling as they came down the dark passage. My father was wearing a kind of trench-coat, he had a tan from all his outdoor exercise, and he looked young and casual, a fine figure of a man. My brother looked as if he had been put together all wrong. He was pale, he was chain-smoking, his eyes were narrowed and he wore a coat too tight and much too short for him. His trousers only came down to his ankles too; in those years he was apparently shooting right up to the sky. He didn't think about his clothes much yet, although that was to change radically. He just wore what his mother thought best. My father noticed, but thought it was too early to buy his son adult clothes in good taste. Or so he persuaded himself, at least. That way he saved money.

Their voices were already raised as they entered the shop. My brother was angrily saying something about 'reactionary

173

pressures', my father was shouting about 'seeing reason' and 'taking responsibility for yourself'. My grandmother immediately used one foot to remove the shoe from her other foot and began massaging the second foot's sole, groaning to herself, which let her out of paying attention to anything else. My grandfather opened his mouth to interrupt several times, but never got a chance. The quarrel rapidly escalated. My father was saying something about 'ingratitude' and 'not normal', and he may have come up with the phrase, 'just like your mother', whereupon my brother obviously mistook his family for his inflamed audience at the debating club, and launched with practised ease on his tirade about the 'peculiar infamy' of the way my father did business. The tirade came to a head with the comment that was always greeted with applause by his admirers because of its uncompromising severity: choosing between a Nazi father or such a non-political, brutal father as his own was like having the choice between the plague and cholera.

At this my father went pale and lowered his voice. 'You just think hard before you start calling me a criminal . . . ,' he was beginning, but at that moment a piece of paving stone came through the display window. My grandmother disappeared into the changing cubicle, leaving her shoes outside. My grandfather began busily searching his pockets for something. A young man jumped through the broken pane, shouting, and tore down the modest window display. My sister, who could walk but was still in nappies, fell over my grandmother's shoes and began yelling blue murder. The bully boys turned and tried to flee, but were hindered by a group of East European weight-lifters and athletes who entered the inner courtyard from Mariahilferstrasse at that moment. The young men almost collided with the first athletes, turned, and fled through the other exit from the yard, making for Windmühlgasse. It all happened so fast and was so difficult to follow that the sportsmen reacted by just standing there with their mouths open. Only when my father rushed out of the shop shouting, 'Stop thief!' although nothing had been stolen, did a couple of weight-lifters and a shot-putter set off in pursuit. But it was too late, and the three men managed to get into the maze of yards, passages and entrances to buildings and 'escape unscathed', as that cheap popular paper the *Groschenzeitung* put it next day. The headline of its medium-length report ran: 'Attack on National Footballer'. The reporter had turned up that same afternoon, only a quarter of an hour after the police.

Even before the police arrived, my father had thrust my white-faced brother out of the back door and sent him home. 'He was never here at all, is that clear?' my father instructed all members of the family present. My grandmother shook her head angrily and bit back a comment. My grandfather nodded in relief. My mother, who had missed the whole incident because she was shopping in Maria-hilferstrasse, had her hands full changing my sister's nappy, and was anyway of the general opinion that it was up to my father to deal with his hapless son by himself, except where money was concerned.

Regrettably but inevitably, during the police inquiries our neighbour came along and had his own shrill-voiced say. Our neighbour was a certain Herr Schidowski who originally came from Galicia, and ran a business importing kosher foods in an even more secluded back yard than ours. His handsome, old-fashioned shop sign called him a Whole-sale Trader, but my father used to joke that Schidowski was 'trading wholesale in a very small way'. My parents thought Schidowski 'a nice fellow, but unfortunately something of a fanatic'. His alleged fanaticism consisted in seeing anti-Semitism behind every least little thing, said my father, shaking his head. Schidowski, who persisted in seeking allies in my family, was therefore a constant source of embarrassment.

'You can understand him,' said my father uncomfortably, 'given his story.' But everyone tried to keep out of Herr

Schidowski's way as far as possible. For reasons over which later generations of the family would still be puzzling, my grandparents in particular avoided him like the plague. 'I can't be doing with him,' muttered my grandmother, and my grandfather looked like a thief caught in the act when Schidowski dropped in for a chat.

So as might have been expected, along came Schidowski once both the police radio patrol and the *Groschenzeitung* reporter had arrived. 'An anti-Semitic assassination attempt!' he shouted. 'I knew there'd be one coming! They ran right past me, those Nazis,' he shouted, thus confusing the whole situation even further. The East European sportsmen were still standing around outside the shop, though reluctantly, because they didn't want to be involved in a criminal case, not at any price, but out of loyalty to my father they intended to do their duty as witnesses. My mother tried to get Schidowski out of the way. The easygoing police superintendent was now obliged at least to ask my father, 'Do you think that's a possibility?' and he replied at once, emphatically, 'Certainly not. Nothing but a boyish prank.' The reporter from the *Groschenzeitung* nodded and made notes. He would quote this remark, though without the context in which it was made. Next day the caption under the little picture of my father ran, 'Nothing but a boyish prank'. And the picture showed my father not in front of the broken shop window, but as a player for the national team holding a bouquet of flowers in the crook of his arm. The reporter's short account also managed to indicate, briefly, a link between the attack and the tiny anti-Vietnam demo by a couple of dozen schoolchildren and students the same day, although it was not until hours later that the demonstrators had skulked down Mariahilferstrasse, with several passers-by calling them names.

The superintendent, however, had initially thought of a very different motive: the East European sportsmen. He thought it possible that the prevalent hatred of communism in Vienna, at least on the surface of public opinion (beneath the surface everyone just went about his own business), might have led to the attack. My father was horrified by this theory. 'We're a very modest little place,' he assured the police officer. 'Nobody would know just who comes shopping here.'

'What about your son?' asked the superintendent. 'Could he have some kind of grudge against your customers?'

'Far from it,' sighed my father, flushing. 'His sympathies – oh, well, you know how it is!'

'Happens in the best families,' the superintendent consoled him. If there were no further clues, then he would file the incident away under the heading of 'youthful vandalism'. That was only too close to it for my father. 'Youthful vandalism,' he said, nodding. 'File it away. Exactly.'

'It's like a scratch on the paint of your car,' said the superintendent as he left, 'you never get to know who did it.'

A few days later, when a new pane had been fitted and the shop had its window dressing back in place, my father decided to have a little private ceremony to 'reopen' the shop. He invited the reporter from the *Groschenzeitung*, because he thought the man had 'behaved very properly'. This was the highest praise my father could give. In his eyes the propriety of the reporter's conduct lay in the fact that there was no mention anywhere of the East European sportsmen, not even of the weight-lifters and athletes who had been literally at the centre of events. 'And that would have been quite a story, even I know that much about journalism,' said my father, nodding. My brother, who with some justification thought the *Groschenzeitung* a dreadful rag, writhed at such remarks, but after the incident he had no right to protest. He was quiet and introverted as he hadn't been since he was at primary school. He even made an effort not to smoke in front of his father.

My grandmother had lent some of her press cuttings to

decorate the new shop window. So far my father had avoided any direct advertising, but he now realised that for the good of the business he would have to resort to a little personal publicity. He must give the impression that anyone was a desirable and welcome customer, not just those suspect East European sportsmen recruited by his old father at the Ostbahnhof. The *Groschenzeitung* reporter was so enchanted by my grandmother's collages that he asked Herr Schidowski if he could use his phone, and he summoned a photographer from the editorial offices.

Since my father's return, my cool and reserved grandmother had expressed her love for the son she now had back mainly by obsessively sticking newspaper cuttings into albums. She could rely on my grandfather not to miss even the smallest snippet mentioning her son. As soon as he had looked through the sports pages in the coffee-house in the morning, my grandfather would go to the nearest tobacconist and newsagent's and buy his wife the papers containing anything about their son. When my father, as quite often happened, had scored two or three goals at the weekend, he bought all the papers. Then my grandmother had the whole week to create her works of art. She always stuck cuttings containing photos in the middle of a page, placing smaller mentions and even the lists of teams printed in tiny lettering around them in a star shape. She added the date, place, opponents and results of any match in large letters, in her stern, fine handwriting, and next to this information she drew little black and white footballs in ink, depending on the number of goals my father had scored, and when a photograph was particularly exciting (my father with his eyes closed heading a ball just outside the goal mouth; my father racing full speed ahead with the ball at his feet), she surrounded it with garlands of leaves and flowers. This was the tenderest emotion she ever showed in her later years.

Of course Schidowski had to be invited to the little reopening ceremony too. It was my mother's job to watch him, and she never took her eyes off him for a second. He had brought chopped liver, egg spread and kosher slivovitz with him, for he was still trying to ingratiate himself with my family. As for his 'fanaticism', this time he had himself reasonably well in hand. 'They won't see us off,' he just muttered gloomily to himself. 'We'll see who has the last laugh.' My mother soothingly patted his arm. She couldn't stand 'the old fool', as she called him, but she was here to serve more important interests today.

Then the *Groschenzeitung* photographer arrived. The reporter posed my father in front of the little shop window so that the pages of cuttings could also be seen, narrowed his eyes and stepped back. My father smiled his shy, charming smile; he smiled and smiled until his smile froze rigid. 'Hm,' said the reporter. There was something missing. The photographer waited. 'Next generation!' Schidowski suddenly called out. 'You just wait, it's no good doing away with us, we have children to carry on the work!' My mother jumped; she had not foreseen this outburst. She quickly poured herself some more kosher slivovitz and opted out of the job of chaperone. 'Good idea,' said the reporter, hauling my brother out of the background. 'Stand here, please.' At this moment my brother had at most one second to decide between two equally unappealing options: he could create a scandal, refuse and run away, which in his present situation would probably have led to a serious long-term rift with his family, leaving him isolated and uprooted. Or he could just do nothing, let himself go along with it like a dummy, and suffer horribly all his life from knowing that a press cutting existed showing him and his father posing for the *Groschenzeitung*. 'An invaluable advertisement,' my father would always happily say later, running the tip of his tongue swiftly over his upper lip, while my brother fought wordlessly for self-control.

My brother joined the picture, placing himself at the far side of the shop window, so that he and his father had the newspaper cuttings between them. 'No, no, together, please!' cried the reporter. 'Father and son!' My father hesitantly raised one arm, my brother reluctantly placed himself under it, then my father carefully lowered his arm until it was resting very lightly on my brother's shoulder. There was a distance of one or two centimetres between their torsos, for safety's sake. 'Get a move on, he's growing so fast these days!' joked my father, acting as if he had to stand on tiptoe to put an arm around my brother. 'Very nice,' cried the reporter, 'great, super!' And to give his photographer more time, he started on a bit of idle chat. 'So what are your son's career plans?' To which my father replied, as if it were a long-standing project carefully planned in advance, 'He's going to study history. He still has a lot to learn.' An incredulous smile passed over my brother's face, mingled with just a trace of humility. At that moment the photographer pressed the shutter. Schidowski and my grandfather looked at each other and began to applaud. My mother quietly removed herself, taking the bottle of slivovitz with her. My grandmother shook her head, and went in search of somewhere to sit and massage her feet in peace. But later, of course, my brother always told this story with quite a different slant.

Idyll

In my memory, it's always summer at the Schneuzl Sports Club. My mother, in a hurry as usual, is dragging her two children down the white gravel path towards the square clubhouse building. To left and right are beds of rose bushes, lilac, and well-tended ornamental spruce trees. Every fallen petal, every yellowing leaf is immediately removed by one of the two gardeners, Dusan and Dragan, who never look you straight in the face and live with their invisible families in a dilapidated bungalow behind the indoor tennis courts.

The closer you come to the clubhouse, the more clearly can you see the dangerous, fat ladies sitting outside it at garden tables, playing poker dice. A few years and a few visits to the cinema later my sister will describe them collectively as Madame Medusa, a single multi-tongued monster. They may be playing poker dice, appearing to concentrate hard, but under their lowered lids they are keeping an eye on the gates and the long gravel path. 'My word, look at that hat!' they whisper to each other, or, 'They say he has something going with Annelies.' 'What?' the others whisper back, excitedly. 'How do you know?' But they betray themselves by mouthing words in a way that is only too visible, or sharp glances like arrows spilling from leaky quivers.

'And say good afternoon nicely, remember,' mutters my mother before she suddenly looks up with a sugary sweet smile and gushes, 'Good afternoon, Inge, hello Irene, good afternoon, ladies, good afternoon, Herr Kunz, hi there Fritzl.' My sister looks stubbornly at the ground and whispers, 'Good afternoon,' but then my mother squeezes her hand very firmly. 'Good afternoon,' bellows my little sister, and the ladies and the few men sitting there throwing dice look up, amused, and say, 'Good afternoon, dear.'

There are days when the gravel path is kilometres long. The older we get the longer it is. In retrospect even the horror of saying 'Good afternoon' nicely in childhood seems nothing compared to the visual body searches performed on adolescents, particularly girls. 'Nothing to write home about,' is the crushing verdict passed almost inaudibly on most of them. It is different only when the girl concerned is good at tennis, plays in the team and does the club credit in matches. Then it doesn't matter what she looks like. Then even awe-inspiring businessmen who aren't usually interested in anything but themselves and their secret mistresses suddenly go up to those young girls with their sturdy calves, pat them on the back and exchange a few words about the stringing of a racket, tennis balls, and the Schneuzl Sports Club's prospects of winning the championship.

Most enviable of all, we thought, were those who were pretty *and* played well. 'Now that's a smart girl,' a man who is helping out at the dice tables may say when such a marvel of nature walks down the gravel path. 'Played well on Saturday,' even the dicing monsters will admit.

Worst off are those who are 'nothing to write home about' and don't play tennis well either. There are really only three of them in the whole club, and they are my father's children. The other untalented kids simply stop coming at some point, skip children's training sessions, drop their membership and develop 'other interests', as their parents say. We hear how they ride in show-jumping events, sing in choirs, become model-railway enthusiasts. We are the only ones left. We have a reputation for being very gifted at tennis, having of course inherited a 'feeling for the ball' from our father, but we're lazy, shockingly lazy. That is the most crushing imaginable verdict. It means that we had it in our power to defend the club's reputation, to win for the club, but we failed for lack of ambition and team spirit.

My father did not share that opinion. 'Their nerve isn't up to it,' he said unsparingly of his children when anyone asked. My father thought that no talent was any use if your nerve gave way. And of course he was right. My sister got furthest of us all in tennis, on her own initiative. At twelve she was out on the court in a children's tournament, and lost dismally to a girl whose play was clearly inferior to hers. She could hardly see the ball through her tears. My father stood at the side of the court shaking his head. He did not, like other mothers or fathers, run to his child every time the players changed sides with advice, he just stood there shaking his head and watching. Only when, two or three games before the inevitable end, she flung her racket down on the red sand with a cry of rage did he stride up to her, take her by the shoulders and say, 'Not like that. You know that perfectly well.'

But apart from the iron rule that never, under any circumstances, did you misuse your sporting equipment he didn't mind anything. It was his view that you shouldn't force anyone to try to excel at a sport, and he didn't want to have children who might, for the sake of going to training camps and tournaments around the city, upset his deliberately chosen lifestyle, perfectly suited as it was to his needs.

As soon as my mother has gone down the gravel path and passed the barrier of good-afternoons presented by the dicing monsters, she hurries her children on towards the cloakrooms. On the way, walking past carefully tended flower beds, we usually meet Dr Schneuzl. He strolls up and down, lost in thought as he sucks at his pipe, and answers every 'Good afternoon, Mr Chairman' with an absently muttered 'Same'. This was his own little habit, a greeting that he had presumably coined from 'The same to you', and apart from that he really said very little. He felt humiliatingly under-employed in the Justice Ministry, and so clung to his position as chairman of the tennis club, a post that meant less and less work for him every year, but one that he guarded all the more jealously. In the end he even personally supervised the groundsmen Dragan and Dusan and, much to the disapproval of his wife, who stood on her dignity, visited the bungalow hidden behind the indoor courts now and then to see if there was anything the two Yugoslav families needed. In our childhood, we saw Dr Schneuzl as the personification of a kind of distracted kind-ness. We preserved a shy and respectful distance. If we sometimes imitated him by trying to growl 'Same' in our childish voices, we felt bad about it afterwards. 'A very decent man,' my father sometimes said thoughtfully.

My mother, dragging her two children after her, slips into the heart of the women's world here, the ladies' cloakroom. Young women with children have their lockers at the front, the part known as the mother-and-child cloakroom. Chil-dren are always standing about there naked on the long benches having their clothes changed, having sun cream rubbed into them, having their hair blow-dried and combed. My little sister too stands on the wooden bench in front of our locker, stark naked, staring between the legs of a little boy who, in a risky manoeuvre, is trying to get his own underpants off. My mother is examining a nursing bra; its owner is not happy with it and wants her opinion. 'It doesn't unfasten easily,' complains the owner of the nursing bra, and my mother nods with the air of an expert. 'Mami,' pipes my little sister suddenly. 'Look, Mami, what's that little girl got between her legs?' The 'little girl' who is really a little boy gets so hopelessly entangled in his underpants that he falls off the bench backwards and lies on the floor bawling. My sister jumps off the bench, retreats, and as usual at moments of stress gets a nosebleed. Other children join in the bawling. The flustered mothers fuss about.

Four ladies aged around fifty come into the cloakroom, rackets gracefully tucked under their arms, white pleated tennis skirts a little longer than the current fashion. Ladies like that don't take off their light jewellery even to play tennis, and touch up their lipstick after every set. With pained expressions, they try to get through the chaotic crowd of children to their own preserve. They pick their way around the little boy, who still lies screaming on the floor, and his mother, who is kneeling beside him. They move right and left to avoid the bloodstain left by my sister. She is now lying on the bench with a cold, wet towel on her neck. As soon as the last lady has reached the second cloakroom she slams the door behind her, hard.

In the ladies' cloakroom proper, which is separate from the mother-and-child part, it is cool, peaceful and clean. The noise of screaming children is muted as it comes through the door. This cloakroom is long, like a corridor with rows of lockers on the right-hand side, and the left-hand side is dominated by a long mirror. Dragan and Dusan have fitted a shelf and a seat in front of it. It looks like an extra-long choir stall with a mirror. The ladies slip into this choir stall one by one, remove their forehead bands and sweat bands, pull combs and slides out of their hair, take off their jewellery and dab their heated faces dry. Then they slip out of the choir stall again, undress somewhere out of sight, and are next seen wrapped in long towels and wearing old-rose plastic shower caps, going into the shower together. You soon can't see anything in there for the steam, and you can't hear well either because of the running water. But the showering ladies can see and hear quite enough. '. . . had a hysterectomy . . .', '. . . hormone therapy . . .', '. . . Inge cheats when she's settling up . . .', '. . . there's talk of a divorce . . .'. In the swathes of mist in the shower room no secrets are kept, and nothing escapes without comment.

If we survey everything that has ever happened at the Schneuzl Sports Club to excite the members, all stages of escalation exist side by side and can be called to mind in any order. In that, the club functions like an isolated seventeenth-century village, with the sole but crucial difference that its members don't even have to go out to work in the fields, so they have time to talk and exchange information almost uninterruptedly. For instance, when Dr Erpel left his wife – after Inge Twaroch, who had felt faint during the Ribbon Tournament and was taken to the sauna pool to cool off, heard strange sounds as she lay in the sauna, went to take a look and caught Dr Erpel in the act with a very young Göth daughter – after that Dr Erpel turned his back on the club for several years. I need hardly say that during those years the dicing ladies, and other women members too, were solicitous about 'poor Gerda Erpel', in a self-congratulatory, self-satisfied way. The Schneuzl Club members were roused to even greater indignation by the fact that Erpel, a lawyer, managed to keep custody of the couple's two sons after the divorce, but had no use and thus obviously no love for their still very small daughter. 'What a bastard that man is, what a brute,' people said when there were no children around. In the end, however, when Gerda had found a kindly widower, while Dr Erpel had long been respectably married to the Göth girl and had become a star lawyer in certain political circles, he rejoined the club, or was allowed to rejoin. He played tennis with the men who, at their wives' behest, had given Gerda Erpel a lift to the Adriatic during the Schneuzl Club's summer visit to the seaside, and gallantly greeted those ladies who only a few years ago would have thought nothing but castration good enough for him. Just before Erpel and the Göth girl rejoined the club there was a little fuss, yes, but that was all part of the ritual, which was fittingly observed. For weeks the dicing ladies told each other how they would wither Erpel with a glance the moment he showed his face. '*I* won't so much as pass the time of day with him, the beast,' announced Inge Twaroch with a steely look in her eyes, but unfortunately she wasn't on her guard, and it happened to be Dr Erpel who held the door to the clubhouse open for her when she was getting all tangled up in the straps of her tennis bag. 'Hello, Inge,' he had said to her face, which was bright red. 'Haven't seen you for a long time.' And Inge whispered, 'Hello, Franzi.'

All these stories are kept on the boil at once. And when the subject of the sexy reason for the Erpels' divorce comes up, it seems almost as deliciously sensational as back at the time when Inge came running out of the sauna screaming. When the squalid details of the divorce are enumerated, the mood becomes almost like a pogrom, with a single victim in the shape of Dr Erpel, who at present may be playing singles on Court 14 in blissful ignorance. All the same, it's possible to sit amicably in company with Erpel and the little Göth girl ('a pretty thing once, nothing to write home about now') and have what is described as a good time.

The accepted form of words was to say that you were going 'down' to the tennis club. 'Coming down tomorrow?' tennis partners, card-playing partners, mothers and the dicing monsters would ask one another at the end of a long, hot day at the Schneuzl Club, when they were all sitting peaceably at the tables outside the clubhouse, drinking white wine spritzers. The evenings were mild, the old trees murmured in the wind, the flowers were fragrant, now and then a Dragan or a Dusan scurried through the twilight tidying up, the last incorrigible card-players still sat in the stuffy clubhouse shouting at each other, children were allowed to run around a little longer, and members who had to say that for some reason they couldn't come down the next day did so with great regret.

On a normal day my mother was the first to go down, although in the early years of her marriage she had hated the Schneuzl Club. She couldn't play tennis, she couldn't play poker dice, and for a long time she couldn't win recognition from the dicing ladies. She was just 'the second wife', to be treated in a very offhand way, even though the first wife had hardly been known at all at the club. But that was their way – 'it was a school of hard knocks,' as my mother always said later with a certain pride. As a young woman she had wanted her husband to go on outings with her and the children at weekends, walking in the woods, climbing mountains – 'Am I a deer?' my father used to say, quoting my grandfather's rhetorical question, and he shook his head, revolted by the mere idea. While we children were small my father, as he put it, 'went half-way' to meet my mother's wishes with one or at the most two expeditions a year to Baden. Once there he raced around the park with his children, they were able to feed a pet donkey, and then they all met Fredi Hals and his wife at a nearby local wine bar which also served huge platters of roast chicken. That was the condition on which he came. Walking just for the sake of walking was anathema to my father; he walked to work up an appetite for the chicken. 'And you're supposed to be a sportsman!' my mother was still grumbling years later, when they had long since given up the visits to Baden, but she still felt sore about the outings she had missed. 'Yes, a sportsman,' my father snapped back, 'not a hiker.'

So finally my mother learned to play tennis. She never did learn to play dice, but after a sauna bath was built at the Schneuzl Club she became a devotee of saunas, and as her two children were born in the baby-boom years she soon made friends with other young mothers.

She had no alternative, for my father would sooner have parted from her than from his friends and the entire lifestyle of the Schneuzl Club. He played cards day in, day out with Bela and Hansi, Hupfi, Fritzl and Dr Quack; he played tennis and football with his old sporting friends, known under the collective name of 'The Spastic Bunch'. They were all former professional footballers who, once their active careers were over, had decided to join a club together and learn tennis. They included two team goalies, several players for the national team, and one man who had first played in it and was then its manager. At first, so the tale goes, they just watched for a while. Then they borrowed rackets, 'ran on', as stepping on to a Schneuzl Sports Club court is known to this day, and simply started playing. At first they were still trying to hit balls back with their knees, their chests or their feet, but soon they could all manage to send that little white ball over the net and back again with their tennis rackets. Their game probably looked very odd at that stage, and even later it had a certain unusual, self-taught style, hence their nickname. A proper tennis player, one who had learned the game as it should be played and knew how to raise his arm and follow the stroke through when he served, is said to have asked, frowning as he watched what was going on, 'What sort of play is that? They look like spastics.' That was the general tone of the Schneuzl Club.

My father loved the club and the company there for that very reason. There was always, as he used to say, something going on. Over cards they had no compunction in saying that their opponents 'hadn't a clue', were 'total idiots' or 'queer as a coot'; playing tennis they told each other they were 'disabled' or 'amputees'. Among my father's friends there were two or three well known for telling jokes (he had no talent at all for telling jokes himself), but what they liked best was devising their own catchphrases and anecdotes. For a while, if anyone smelled anything strange, it was usual to shout, 'I smell gas.' This one was thought up by Fredi Hals, who had soon followed my father and joined the tennis club as an associate member at a reduced fee, because he didn't play tennis at all.

It was Herr Bodo's fault. Among the many unpopular 'kibitzers' who looked on at card games and brought good or bad luck, or so the superstitious players thought, Herr Bodo was the least popular of all. He was sick and already to some extent mentally confused, but he was part of the furnishing of the clubhouse, and for some time he had been unable to keep himself from breaking wind. One day, when it got too much for Fredi Hals, over whose shoulder Herr Bodo liked to look, Fredi jumped up crying, 'I smell gas!' After a moment's alarm, the clubhouse rocked with laughter. Good old Fredi! I smell gas! What a laugh.

After that the newcomer Hals was accepted, even though he couldn't play anything but cards. People liked the bad taste of his jokes. He won similar laughter once in winter, when he was arguing vociferously with Hupfi Göth the calendar millionaire, notorious for his passion for fresh air. Hupfi always felt too hot, presumably because of his high blood pressure, and he also hated strong smells, whether they came from the restaurant kitchen or were the kind so unfortunately emanating from Herr Bodo. 'So then one day Hupfi throws the window open for the umpteenth time, with the temperature below freezing,' my father told the tale in a strained voice, only just managing to suppress his own mirth, 'and Fredi jumps up shouting: oh no, that Nazi will be the death of me!' My father could roar with laughter so much at this story that he never once noticed the looks my stony-faced uncle and brother were giving him.

One day Dr Schneuzl leased his huge plot of land on the Prater to the city of Vienna, and that left the way open for a coup. Suddenly civic subsidies, tiny as they were, were flowing in for the separate 'sections', the tennis section, the football section, the hockey section – money that came from the proverbial taxpayer and was now to be used for his benefit. The way was clear for a democratic revolution. Logically enough, the first person it devoured was Dr Schneuzl.

While the land still belonged to him, he had met the expenses for necessary repairs and improvements as he thought best, paying them out of the members' fees. The membership of the Schneuzl Sports Club, which was nominally independent itself from the owner of the land, did have an elected committee, but it consisted of my father and three of the others in the Spastic Bunch, and it gave Dr Schneuzl a free hand. In years when there was plenty of money Schneuzl had more tennis courts laid out by Dragan and Dusan, in other years he economised, for instance on trophies for the club tournament, or on redecorating the cloakrooms in early summer. After the agreement with the city of Vienna came to light, a couple of 'clever-clogs', as my father bitterly put it, had decided that he must be made to stop acting like the lord of the manor which in effect he had always been. The would-be revolutionaries called an extraordinary general meeting of the members, something unheard of. My parents came home that evening with expressions more suited to a funeral, showered, changed, and went 'down to the club' again for the meeting. They never did that normally, not even when they were going out to the cinema or to an evening party; instead they would plan ahead, take the clothes they were going to wear later down to the club with them, and set off straight from its premises, to avoid wasting even half an hour 'out in the fresh air'.

On the day of Schneuzl's fall it was different. By coming home and then going out again, my parents placed a kind of *cordon sanitaire* between the usual life of the club and the threat to it that evening. Open strife between the members was in glaring contradiction to anything usual at the club.

Afterwards, accounts of the meeting differed so much that fundamentally the whole thing remained a secret between those present. My father, so my mother said, had actually shouted, something that no one but his card partners could ever have imagined before. But the other side, all of them men about ten years younger than my father and the rest of the Spastic Bunch, wanted to make their influence felt at long last, and they carried the day. My brother and my cousins saw the revolution at the tennis club as an expression of the general readiness for change of the early seventies, but my father always dismissed that idea out of hand. 'We're not political at the club.'

Right at the end of the turbulent meeting, my father called for Dr Schneuzl to be made honorary chairman for life. That, he said, was the least they could do. But Dr Schneuzl had already slipped out of the clubhouse through a back door; everyone wondered later how he had managed it. My father had won much applause for his proposal from the majority, who really thought that everything ought to be left as it was, but 'hadn't opened their great gobs', as my father said angrily next day. Open conflict was conducted almost exclusively between my father and the rebels: a lawyer, an architect, a financial adviser and a doctor. In the end the old committee was voted out and the new one, consisting of those four men, took office. From that day on, however, Dr Schneuzl never set foot on his own land again, and his muttered 'Same' soon sank into the mythical treasure-chest of a golden past.

A flock of mothers and children is leaving the changing rooms and marching off to the sunbathing area. Deckchairs are fetched from a little wooden hut, and are always put up in the same places. Dr Quack's large family, complete with granny, are at the front near the spruce trees. The crazy artist with her two fair-haired children, who can scream at a pitch shrill enough to break glass, are at the back near the chestnut trees. We always sit among the young birch trees in the middle, my sister in a pink pram with a sunshade. New members whom no one yet knows are well advised to start by sitting away from the rest of us, behind the deckchair hut, the sand-box and the swings. And everyone sits there reading first the *Groschenzeitung* and then the *Kurier*. Only the artist never reads the paper, but she is known to be peculiar. Her brightly coloured clothes with their uneven hems regularly attract avalanches of comment, and not just from the dicing monsters.

Later, the women visit one another's islands of deckchairs while the children play behind them. 'Hedi is pregnant again,' my mother whispers to Dr Quack's wife. 'My word,' chuckles that lady, 'she'll get even podgier!'

'She says she has to eat for two now,' giggles my mother.

'As a matter of fact, she's eating for four,' snaps Granny Quack from her upholstered lounger. 'She eats for two when she's not pregnant.'

The longer the mothers sit on the grass, the greater is the danger that at some point they'll remember their children. It always ends with the children being told to fetch their rackets and knock up against the wall. 'It's children's practice day tomorrow, don't forget,' is another remark guaranteed to put the children to flight. First they all play in the sand-box like good kids, they go on the swings and slides. Then, once the mothers are deep in conversation, they make off unobtrusively, one by one. The land on which the Schneuzl Club lies covers several hectares, and the tennis courts, with the park and the flower beds that so captivate all visitors, are only the smaller part of it. There is a football pitch, surrounded by now dilapidated stands, left over from the pre-war golden age, when an uncle of Dr Schneuzl was a great patron of football in Vienna and the Schneuzl Sports Club team was a power to be reckoned with in the First Division. Underneath the stands are gloomy vaults where the tools formerly used to tend the ground still lie. Perhaps there were once changing rooms and showers there too, who knows? Now it is all dark and locked away, but of course there's a secret place where you can get in, or at least into a small room on one side of the stands. The children test their courage there in the twilight. Karli Quack wins two schillings by swallowing a worm. One day the children discover a half-dead sparrow, which can't be saved despite collective attempts to nurse it back to health. Now and then a rat scurries past. Children swear to be blood brothers down there, until one child gets a septic finger from a dirty drawing-pin. Sitting on the rusty roller, Bruno Frehlinger once allows three girls to push his foreskin up and gape at it. But when Bruno wants something in exchange, the girls run away, and they are not nice to Bruno for a while after that.

Behind the football pitch with its stands lie enchanted fields on which the children absolutely must not set foot. They are too far away. The children have to be within calling distance. In the evening, when the mothers want to take their children to the showers, they go over to the football field, now overgrown by weeds, and scale the stands closest to the clubhouse. Then they call their children, drawing out the vowel sounds of the names, which echo back from the oval of the football pitch. Anyone in the forbidden fields can't hear the mothers and is due for punishment. That way the children develop a sense of time, and are back on the running-track around the football pitch at the right moment. When the mothers appear on the horizon they often see their children jumping up and down on the thick yellow high-jump mat left there after some long-forgotten athletics event.

At the far end of the fields, behind tangled undergrowth, is a high fence, the boundary of the gigantic Schneuzl site. On the other side trams drive by, bells ringing, on their way to the terminus in the middle of the Prater. The children throw stones at the trams until the police turn up. It is easy to retreat like lightning into the bushes and run over the fields to the ruinous football stadium. By the time the police reach the front entrance of the club, have gained admission to the clubhouse and questioned the parents about any children who might have been involved, all the stone-throwers are standing on Court 20 like little lambs, doing what their parents are always earnestly urging them to do: practising with their cut-down rackets and the two drums full of old balls.

When the children walk along beside the fence they scratch their faces, arms and legs on the bushes, but they get to know a world outside that is always changing. On one side, the boundary of the Schneuzl park is marked by a well-tended footpath leading to the Prater. People are always walking their dogs there, right behind the deckchairs and the sand-box, while strange children cycle or roller-skate. The club side of the fence has little to offer, if we leave aside the time when my sister and her daredevil girlfriend once picked bunches of flowers and sold them through the fence for a few groschen to people walking to the Prater, until their greatly embarrassed mothers put a stop to it. The most interesting part of the fence is the long side at the back, beyond the football pitch and the forbidden fields. For a little way, as I said, the tram follows the fence, but then there is a sharp curve. The rest is the outer part of the Prater, wild and mysterious. You can see strange trees, bushes and meadows; sometimes there are men playing football in the distance or training large dogs. Over there, in the most inaccessible and remote part of the club grounds, a hole in the fence is found one day. From then on the children are fascinated by it. They know that leaving the grounds of the tennis club is strictly forbidden, particularly when they aren't supposed to be in that part of the grounds at all, 'and no one can hear us if something bad happens either,' says timid little Petra, who knows her mother's warning off by heart, although she ignores it. The children play near the hole in the fence for days on end, but they stay inside the grounds. One day Bruno Frehlinger suddenly gets to his feet, goes over to the fence and begins enlarging the hole. 'Are you daft?' asks Karli Quack. 'We can get through that anyway!' And the two of them squeeze through the hole, with everyone else admiring them in silence. Then Verena, the wildest of the girls, who is always saying she'd rather be a boy, follows. Looking a bit lost, the three stand on the other side of the fence, not sure what to do next. 'Come on,' Bruno Frehlinger finally tells the others, and then he and Karli and Verena disappear among the trees and don't come back. The rest of the children wait until twilight falls. Then, hesitantly, they go back to the football pitch and wait on the high-jump mat, feeling uneasy, until they are called back. When they reach their mothers little Petra is crying. 'Karli and Bruno have gone,' she sobs, 'and Verena too.' The other children stare at the ground. The mothers don't seem to notice. 'Nonsense,' says Petra's mother impatiently. 'They've already showered and dressed, all three of them, unlike you.'

And she is right. The runaways are sitting at their parents' tables in the garden outside the clubhouse, smirking, except for Verena, who has a large sticking-plaster on her left knee, and skin all brown with iodine around it. 'Serves you right,' my sister whispers as we push past them to the cloakrooms to shower.

The hole is soon found, all the same. Little Petra is responsible, because she tells her mother about the man who sometimes stands on the other side of the fence. 'He opens his coat and he has a stick in between his legs,' she says, and then all hell breaks loose at the Schneuzl Sports Club. Mothers are screeching for the police. Men want to go out there, armed. Grown-ups interrogate the children one by one, firing questions at them. After a while Dr Schneuzl somehow manages to get the situation under control. He mutters this and that, and the members calm themselves. Then he sits down, sighing, at a baize-covered card table and questions the children all together, obviously to reduce the number of different versions to a minimum. For instance, Karli Quack is telling Simone, 'You were never there at all.' Simone is a show-off who prefers playing with her lace-edged doll's pram in the sunbathing area, but now she wants to have given a detailed description of the monster. Asked about his hair colour, the children settle for brown, although some of them said black at first. Schneuzl can't find out much about height; they all just say 'ordinary height'. The only useful description comes from little Petra. She babbles something about a 'brown man', putting her hand to her face. And strictly speaking, she was the only one who actually saw the stick in between his legs, although two other children confirm that he opened his coat, but they were too far away to see any more. Whether the man was inside or outside the fence can't be decided. The big boys say definitely outside, little Petra, in the arms of her hysterical mother, howls, 'He was ever so close to me.' 'How could he have got in?' asks Dr Schneuzl. The children say nothing and look at the ground. 'Well?' asks Schneuzl. 'There's a hole in the fence,' Bruno finally admits, thus causing more consternation among the parental bystanders, 'but he wouldn't fit through it.'

There is a visit to the scene of the crime. Most of the members marching through the tall grass of the fields beyond the football stadium in their tennis clothes are in this part of the club for the first time. Dr Schneuzl, who has burrs sticking to his trousers right up to the knee, gets Bruno to explain everything. 'I don't believe it!' whispers Dr Quack's wife when she sees the hole. Dr Schneuzl summons Dragan and Dusan to mend the fence at once. The two of them arrive in their blue work trousers, carrying a large roll of green wire. 'Like that! Like that!' cried little Petra suddenly, pointing to Dragan's moustache. The other children laugh and shake their heads. 'He isn't wearing a coat,' says my sister scornfully. She doesn't like Petra, because my mother is always telling her 'how nicely Petra says good afternoon, unlike you'. Dragan stands there staring at the ground. He always stares at the ground, but at this moment it doesn't look good. Some of the grown-ups get a dangerous expression on their faces. 'Let me point out that no harm has come to anyone,' Dr Schneuzl reminds them. 'Not yet,' hisses one mother. The concept of trauma is still unknown at this time.

The fence is soon mended. The parents keep a close eye on their children for a few days. They have to stay in the boring sunbathing area, and are even escorted to Court 20 for children's practice, because Court 20 is some way off. The ladies playing dice in front of the clubhouse agree that, although they have been acquainted with the groundsmen for years, they really know nothing about them. 'Keeping themselves to themselves,' they murmur as they shake the dice, 'why can't they speak German yet?' Like many of the others, my father thinks Dragan should be fired, 'just to be on the safe side,' as he says. 'There are plenty of other workers from the East around.' My brother, who usually takes refuge alone in a huge old tree when he's at the Schneuzl Club, and reads there for hours, thinks this attitude is 'totally unfair'.

'Innocent until proved guilty,' he proclaims, adding that a worker from the East is a human being too. My father just shakes his head. 'Wait till you have children of your own,' he says, and my brother groans. The Dragan problem can't be solved just yet, since unfortunately Dr Schneuzl is 'deaf in both ears on the subject', as his wife says; she is one of the dice-playing ladies. The expression on her face makes it perfectly clear which side she is on.

One day Dragan disappears. Later it is learnt from the embittered Dr Schneuzl, who looked into the matter, that he and his family moved out of the secluded bungalow overnight and left. It was the end of the month. Dragan waited until he had worked off his wages. Dr Schneuzl makes the whole club suffer for it. He does not engage a second groundsman, allegedly because he can't find anyone suitable. Dusan works incredibly hard, but it is just too much for him. Members begin spraying the grass courts themselves, for it's high summer and the sand courts look 'like the Noah desert', as Dolly Königsbee would have said. Lawyers and engineers, dentists and furriers discover that spraying a tennis court is far from simple. Dragan and Dusan held their thumbs in the jet of water to produce a fine, broad spray, but you have to know the trick of it. The distinguished members of the Schneuzl Sports Club leave puddles on the courts, and then no one can play on them for several hours. After some complaints, Dr Schneuzl tells Dusan to give all his attention to the tennis courts and leave everything else for now. So the gravel path gets untidy. Many of the women unobtrusively pick up fallen leaves and petals when they come in, but no one uses a rake. The members realise that the gravel path used to be raked several times a day. Now there are little heaps of gravel in some places, the older members could easily stumble over them, and bare patches with the earth showing through in others. Small children plump down on their nappy-clad bottoms on the gravel path and begin digging in it the way they dig in the sand-box. And no one does anything.

It stays hot for weeks, and the atmosphere is explosive. The ventilator in the clubhouse goes wrong, but Dusan can't come and repair it at once because he has two grass courts to spray first. The card players squabble even more than usual. The sand in the sand-box urgently needs to be changed, because in the middle of summer small children playing there naked step up the natural amount of soiling, but Dusan has no time to deal with it. The situation is becoming intolerable. The Ribbon Tournament will soon be due, with the barbecue in the evening by the light of Chinese lanterns, a high spot in the club year. No one can imagine it taking place this summer. Who will hang up the lanterns? Who will build the barbecue? Who will get all the courts ready in time? Under his pale straw hat, Dr Schneuzl is silent as a sphinx. Only when a few of the members timidly ask whether there is any way of finding out where Dragan has gone, perhaps through Dusan, and then apologising to him in the name of the club, does Dr Schneuzl soften. 'He's back in Split,' he murmurs in an unfriendly tone, 'too late to be sorry now.' But next day he finally produces the longed-for new groundsman, a huge dark fellow with a bushy moustache, who flashes his gold teeth, smiles at all the members when he is introduced to them, and shakes their hands. It feels like having your hand caught in a vice. Dr Schneuzl takes sadistic pleasure in introducing the newcomer to as many people as possible. He escorts him from court to court, calling, 'Come here, please, ladies and gentlemen, this is our new groundsman Branko. We're very glad to have him with us.' The dice-playing ladies and several other members giggle, whether in relief or horror it is hard to say. Next day Branko's wife, her head held high and leading two children by each hand, walks through the club grounds, and for the first time the members of the Schneuzl Sports Club see a veiled Muslim woman in the middle of Vienna.

The Ribbon Tournament works like this: all the competitors are divided up by Dr Schneuzl and my father into two groups, weak players and strong players. The strong players get blue ribbons, the weak players pink ribbons – these are the ribbons that give the tournament its name – and they tie them around their wrists, rackets or upper arms. Dr Quack's wife ties hers coquettishly in her blond hair, Werner Weis the joker ties his round his neck. Lots are drawn for the first blue and pink partners, and the pairs are sent off to the courts to play doubles. A record is kept of who began playing on which court. Then they start. They play for a quarter of an hour on each court, the end and beginning of the quarter-hours being signalled by Dr

Schneuzl blowing a trumpet. He blows it from the top of the football stands, where he can see most of the courts, and anyway his trumpet will be heard everywhere. No more than three games at the most can be played in a quarter of an hour. The couple who are leading when the trumpet is blown are considered the winners in each match and go on to the next court. The defeated pair stay where they are, but separate. The winning couple from another court come along and change partners, pink to blue, blue to pink, for the next quarter of an hour. There are as many matches as there are tennis courts in play. For instance, if forty people have put their names down for the tournament, ten courts are in play for ten quarter-hours. The winner is whoever has moved on through the most courts. If there is a draw the number of games won in all is taken into account. A child bursting with pride stands beside every court with a list, keeping the tally. The child enters the names of the couples playing and the results, and hands the list in to Dr Schneuzl at the end of the day. The Ribbon Tournament is a club event devised for the weaker players. My father and most of the Spastic Bunch never compete, but their wives do, with enthusiasm.

My mother loves the Ribbon Tournament. It provides subjects of discussion for weeks on end. Of course, she just has bad luck some years. 'So I start with Blumauer, you see,' begins one of her extensive surveys, 'with that old fool of course I lose, so I stay put, and then I get Franzi Erpel's stupid Gerda. She says she has tennis elbow. So I stay put again and I get Dr Quack, but all the same I lose on the next court against him and Hupfi's wife, because Schneuzl blows the trumpet just when there's a net cord, and it scares Inge Twaroch so much that she slips and mis-hits the ball. And then . . .' These stories are endless, but my father listens to them patiently and attentively. Once my mother had resigned herself to her fate as a member of the Schneuzl Sports Club, and the more merciful first years of her marriage were over, oddly enough the Schneuzl Club was all that linked my parents, apart from their children. My father is so genuinely interested in everything to do with tennis or the club that he even asks questions about the Ribbon Tournament. 'But surely Inge plays much better than Hupfi's wife?' he asks, for instance. 'Well, she's not on form today,' my mother dismisses the question. 'She had a breast op in the winter, it was benign but she's never been the same since.'

At the club my parents are regarded as a happy couple. They are both popular in their respective circles. Both are sociable and amusing, ready to join in the general fooling around, and they get on well with most people. They both spend a lot of time at the Schneuzl Club. No one notices that at this time they hardly ever talk to one another, have little to do with each other, and certainly do not, like many other married couples, play tennis against each other or as doubles partners. In the evenings, when the members are sitting in the quiet clubhouse garden drinking white wine spritzers, when there are barbecues and laughter, when Werner Weis, after a couple of beers too many, tells his dirty jokes, which can leave my father in particular in fits of laughter for days on end ('Is she a beginner, an expert, a weirdo? Spit, swallow, gargle!'), they often sit at different tables. They are always there, but never together. If the Schneuzl Club was like a third person whom my mother had to accept at the beginning of their marriage, it soon becomes the only place where that marriage can continue. Their life together, a comprehensive failure, dissolves painlessly in this familiar, wider context, like an aspirin in a glass of water. That is another reason why they are so keen on it. They spend all their leisure time at the club, they go to the country at weekends only when Bela or Hupfi invite them to their country cottages, which is really just the same as going 'down to the club': they play tennis and cards and then have a barbecue. And in summer my parents and a large party from the Schneuzl Club go to the seaside on the Adriatic coast.

Of course there are 'eternal enmities' at the Schneuzl Club, dramas in which the protagonists cut each other dead for years on end, but a few years later again these crises are remembered like all other stories, just as anecdotal. 'Hi there, arsehole,' Schmuel Harasi has always said when greeting Werner Weis after the successful conclusion of one such long bout of hostilities, thus letting him know that he has not forgotten their quarrel but has put it aside. The cause, of course, was politics, something that drives my father to distraction. 'There are no politics at the club and nor should there be,' is his motto, but at stormy times the others jettison the principle. Seen in this light, the storm caused by Schmuel and Werner Weis was perhaps the worst that the club ever had to weather, certainly the worst for my father, because it spread to my family. Not much actually happened, only the usual kind of thing in Vienna: Werner Weis launched into a tirade about world Jewry. To make matters worse, this was in 1986. Schmuel, an amiable businessman with dual Austrian and Israeli nationality, had already several times remarked peaceably from the next table that he 'couldn't be doing' with Herr Singer of the World Jewish Congress either. But Werner Weis, by now 'het up after his fifth beer', as my distressed father would describe it later, was not to be placated.

'I heard the CIA have inflated the numbers of Jews who were gassed out of all proportion,' said Werner, red in the face and breathing heavily, 'so maybe you could all of you make a bit less fuss about the whole thing.' Here Schmuel finally put down his cards and said, distinctly, 'You're an anti-Semite.' This was just what Werner Weis had been waiting for. 'Me, an anti-Semite?' he shouted, jumping up. 'How can I be friends with a damn fool like you, then?' He further accused Schmuel of being to blame for the whole thing himself, since it was always the Jews who didn't know where to stop, and anyway . . . Schmuel, looking around for help, saw himself surrounded only by people with their minds on something else, running their fingers through their hair, concentrating on their cards, looking at newspapers or on their way to the lavatories. Concluding from this that he was on his own, all he said out loud to my father, as he left, was, 'So how about you? What do *you* say?' My father said nothing at all. The door closed behind Schmuel. 'What does he mean?' asked the rather naïve Dr Quack. 'I've no idea,' lied my father. Then they all looked for a substitute for Schmuel, since the game had to go on.

'He's not a bad man, just a fool,' my father defended himself later to my brother, who thought someone should go straight out and lay charges against Werner Weis. 'I just don't listen to him,' said my father unhappily. 'He's a nice fellow apart from that.'

'A nice fellow?' ranted my brother. 'What do you mean, a nice fellow?' My uncle and my cousins just shook their heads. On this topic, for once, they were united, and my father was the fool.

'For instance, he always took Gerda Erpel in his car when the club went to the seaside after the divorce,' my father defended himself, 'and he often took Granny Quack to hospital for her dialysis when the Quacks weren't at home. He's a very, very helpful person.'

'The point is, what would a helpful person like that have done about you in 1938,' said my elder cousin, who tried to judge all and sundry by what they would have done in 1938.

'But we're not in 1938 now,' said my father defiantly, 'and you should all be glad of it.'

The argument finally escalated when my brother announced that he was going to report Werner Weis to the police himself, citing Schmuel Harasi as a witness. My father tried to forbid him to do any such thing, but my brother had been grown up for a long time now, and of the two of them he was much better at taking the high moral ground. My father tried pleading. He could never show his face in the club again, he said, if his son had reported a well-known member to the police. And anyway, he added, Werner Weis had once been a famous skier, and 'no one will believe you'. At this point the family front began to crumble. 'He's right about that,' my uncle discontentedly muttered. 'The authorities are all corrupt.'

'Forget it,' Aunt Ka piped up eagerly, 'after all, the Groschenzeitung says much worse about the Jews.'

'So we have rights, but we don't stand up for them in case someone objects,' said my brother sarcastically, thus at least bringing my cousins into line behind him again. The argument led to further angry shouting on all sides, with my family flinging insults like 'Stalinist!' and 'Skiver!' at each other, and was ended when my elder cousin's wife clattered the dishes disapprovingly as she served dessert.

Schmuel Harasi did not let the matter rest there, in accordance with the unwritten rules of the Schneuzl Club. Not only did he ostentatiously cut Weis dead, he reported him not to the police but to the club committee. In a well-phrased letter, he demanded disciplinary procedures against Weis and his expulsion from the club. The members of the committee writhed with discomfort. They couldn't simply ignore the letter, even if the overwhelming opinion in the club was that Harasi was going too far. After all, he often threatened to cancel his own membership. 'That might be the best solution,' whispered certain members, but only until it became known that Harasi had persuaded several others to leave with him too if he went, people who were described in the papers these days as 'our Jewish fellow citizens'. 'I'd no notion we had so many of them in the club,' grunted Werner Weis, but then his unobtrusive, gentle wife suddenly shouted at him to 'keep his big mouth shut just this once'.

Of necessity, the committee held a disciplinary meeting

and issued Werner Weis with a warning. Weis made a statutory if oddly phrased statement to the effect that he was not an 'anti-Semite in general', but had just had an argument with the 'actual person' of Schmuel Harasi over a game of cards. He would sue anyone who claimed that he, Weis, had anything in general against people whom, in his agitation, he called 'mixed citizens'. Finally he agreed to write Harasi a letter apologising for everything that he, Harasi, might have misunderstood. When he emerged from this committee meeting red in the face and sweating, he is said to have told the first person he met, 'That bastard Waldheim, it's all his fault.' As I said, after that Schmuel Harasi ignored Weis for several years, and several other people including Fredi Hals, usually a peacemaker, would not play cards with Weis. But a day came when all that was over too, and since then Schmuel has said, 'Hi there, arsehole' when they meet, and Weis answers, 'Hi there, Hebrew,' and my father is happy again.

After two peaceful hours in the sunbathing area, my mother leaves it to go and play singles with Hupfi Göth's wife. These singles matches are a mixed pleasure for my mother. Their play is of about the same standard, but all Frau Göth's movements are much more graceful, thanks to the countless hours she spends practising. My mother, on the other hand, like my father, is a self-taught tennis player. My mother is very keen to win against Frau Göth. For that very reason she often loses − 'it's the nerves,' as my father would say. My mother struggles grimly. Meanwhile Branko is cutting back the Virginia creeper on the fence of Court 5 and trying to avoid the balls that sometimes fly his way. My father is standing on the sidelines of Court 1, where important matches and club competitions take place, and annoying four of the Spastic Bunch playing doubles there. 'You'll be just about ready for the Paralympics!' The next generation of children is going about its forbidden pleasures at the far end of the fields. My sister, nearly seventeen, is sitting behind the abandoned swings with one of the many Quack sons, silently holding hands. The dicing lady who always paints her lips such a very bright red shakes the dice, throws, and cries triumphantly, 'Full house!' In the clubhouse, Bela is shouting at Hupfi, 'Queen of Spades? Are you out of your mind?' Hupfi, who has just discovered his mistake, reacts automatically with defensive aggression. 'Hold your tongue, you stupid Hun!'

At this moment Herr Bodo falls out of his chair and dies a merciful, almost soundless death. Urgent calls for a doctor go out over the loudspeaker that usually summons members to the telephone or sends orders to the groundsmen. On the court next to my mother, Dr Quack drops his racket and runs to the clubhouse. When they hear the ambulance siren as it comes down the gravel path, where no car ever drove before, most of the other tennis players make for the clubhouse too, out of concern or curiosity. There lies Herr Bodo, dead, on two little tables pushed together, while Dr Quack shakes his head regretfully. When the question of his next of kin comes up, several people look inquiringly at my mother. She has a soft spot for lost souls, and has helped Herr Bodo a couple of times when he needed medicaments or a cheap winter coat. 'I don't think there's anyone,' she says, shrugging her shoulders. 'His ex-wife died a long time ago.'

'It's at times like these that we find out what the club is good for,' my father will say later, with satisfaction. For the club members spontaneously begin collecting for Herr Bodo's funeral. My mother and Dr Quack even go to his shabby little apartment in Czerningasse a couple of days later to look for a suit to put on him. Hupfi Göth's wife volunteers to give a home to his nice little dwarf poodle. Herr Bodo looked after the dog much better than he looked after himself. It goes without saying that almost the entire Schneuzl Sports Club is assembled by the graveside on the day of the funeral. Heroically, they even postpone a club match until next day. The bow on the wreath for which everyone has subscribed is in the club colours, black-yellow-black, and announces, 'In eternal memory of Herr Bodo, our greatly valued member.' The sun is shining, the birds are singing even in the Central Cemetery, and many of the mourners hardly recognise each other, since they are used to meeting only in white tennis gear. It is regarded as a sensation that even Dr Schneuzl has come – 'He's grown older,' whisper the dicing monsters. Dr Schneuzl stands at the graveside, pipe in hand, muttering 'Same!' over and over again.

Luckily the ceremony does not take long, and soon the mourners are making for their cars, all with the same destination in view: they are going down to the club. As soon as they are back in their leisure clothes the day returns to normal, with games and jokes and sports. In the evening the children are allowed to spend a little more time out in the fields behind the swings, the members sit together at the green garden tables under the murmuring giant trees, now and then Dusan or Branko hurries through the twilight, tidying up, most people drink spritzers, and only Werner Weis is on his third beer. Someone says, 'Poor Herr Bodo. I'm sure he'd have liked to be here now.'

'He reached a good old age,' points out one of the dice-playing ladies, and another adds at once, 'And he had an easy death.'

'One can only wish to have the same,' murmurs the Medusa chorus.

Fredi Hals grinned. 'Shouldn't speak ill of the dead,' he says, 'but he didn't bring me much luck.'

Werner Weis raises his tankard and says, theatrically, 'Here's to you, Bodo, old stinker.'

'Werner, please,' says his wife.

After a while my father clears his throat and says, 'But it was a lovely fine day again.'

'Yes,' breathes my mother, dreamily. 'What a summer.'
'We have it good here,' says my father.
'It's like having our own garden,' reflects my mother.
And my father says, 'Yes, really, it's a Paradise.'

Victims and Perpetrators

Day after day, when the radio alarm went off just before seven, she woke with a start, realised where she was, and a hot wave of repugnance rolled upwards from her stomach. It was the worst moment of the day. When the wave had risen up through her throat to her mouth it disappeared, as if she could simply breathe it out, leaving behind only grey, wounded indifference. She got up. Her slippers were waiting, neatly placed beside the bed. Her quilted dressing-gown was there too. She hurried off to the kitchen without switching on the light. She opened the door to the children's room and woke them by switching on her radio at high volume another door away, in the kitchen. She began clattering about, and hoped that would do it. The children were always in bed in good time, she made sure of that, and really never ought to need waking specially. If she went carefully, she'd hardly have to say a word during the next three quarters of an hour. She hurried back and forth between kitchen and living-room, put the children's clothes out for them when she heard them in the bathroom, swerved aside from her husband in the hall, ostentatiously ignoring his 'Good morning', and switched on another radio, the one in the living-room, when being with the others became unavoidable. Luckily the kids' radio show began at twenty past seven. The children loved it. She spent breakfast mostly on her feet, making toast, spreading and cutting it, taking away yoghurts that people didn't want, bringing different ones, feeling that she had to raise the children's cups to their mouths to remind them to drink as they listened to the radio, spellbound.

A moment came when they had all left, but she was still on the go. Years ago, when one of the children had been either very small or ill, and had cried all night, she happened to mention in the morning that she was tired out. In his own characteristic manner, which she could never make out, her husband had said, why didn't she lie down for a bit of a rest in the morning, but she had taken that as a sign of suspicion, if not an actual reproof. 'You think I don't have anything else to do?' she had snapped, and after that she didn't even sit down. She tidied the children's chaotic room every day, she made the beds, she pushed the vacuum cleaner round the apartment, she polished his trophies, she washed clothes or hung them out or ironed them until it was time to go shopping. Then she cooked and laid the table, and then they all came home again. She served lunch in silence, trying to move between kitchen and living-room as often as possible to avoid being asked any questions. Only an hour later did life begin. Either it was her turn to be in the shop, where she would be free for an afternoon, free of quarrelling children and a husband who, it seemed to her, was always cracking jokes at her expense. Or she took the children down to the Schneuzl Sports Club, where a number of mothers met even in winter and took turns looking after their offspring. As soon as she was rid of the children she went out into the main road, 'to take a look round'. Wrapped up warm, scarf up to her nose, she slowly walked past the rows of shop windows. Longingly, she looked at the pullovers and shoes, the handbags and cosmetics, and in the first few years she occasionally had the courage to enter a shop and try something on, but not often. She hated the way sales staff always came straight up and asked, 'Can I help you?' She muttered her usual, 'Just looking' in such a surly tone that next minute she always felt she was suspected of shoplifting.

Sometimes she thought she looked pretty, sometimes she thought she looked ugly. She swung between the two extremes at very short intervals. Her husband's friends were always paying her compliments, but she didn't trust any of them an inch, least of all her husband. She couldn't bear to be photographed either, she always gave a little hiss and turned her face away when someone tried it. She tore up any pictures of herself very quickly, before anyone could stop her.

She had imagined that everything would be very different. If she had been asked *how* she had imagined it she wouldn't have known what to say. But she could have replied, with feeling, 'Not like this.'

When she fell in love with the man who would be her husband, she was convinced that he was the very opposite of her father. Her father was a tall, heavy, unapproachable patriarch whose love and recognition his six children tried to win with varying degrees of success. For it seemed as if only what was new ever interested him, as if he thought nothing of any repetition of it. He showered his eldest son with affection, disguised as high expectations and pressure on him to succeed, and he openly loved and indulged his eldest daughter. As for the other four, they were just there. No one really bothered much about the youngest two in particular, twin girls. They were just dragged up somehow. They were taught good manners, yes, and a close eye was kept on their virtue, the patriarch was standing for no nonsense there. But no one was interested in any talents or dreams that they might have. Too little in one way, too much in another, such was my mother's youth.

They had arrived from Pomerania, a refugee family. In the cold January days of 1945 the mother and her six children, the two youngest only three years old, somehow reached Vienna in a horse-drawn cart. The patriarch was there already, had found accommodation and work. It was lucky that his wife had made it to Vienna or all his preparations would have been for nothing. As she had in fact made it, no one asked afterwards why she had been alone with the children on that fourteen-day journey, when people were freezing to death in the ditches on both sides of the road.

He was Austrian by origin, it was always emphasised, his family had been settled in Pomerania by Maria Theresia. Not a Pole, heaven forbid, although the patriarch was bilingual and a patriot, not a national but a regional patriot, what you might call an ardent Pomeranian. The patriarch's frail-looking wife had a German name too when she met him, but her mother tongue was Polish. In her old age she could be persuaded to describe the way the border was always changing where she grew up, you never knew just where you were. When she went to school to learn to read and write, the little village finally seemed to be Polish – until the Germans marched in, but by then she was already married to the Austrian-by-origin, and had pretty well mastered the new masters' language too. But although the war had begun, at home with her children she spoke Polish.

That changed as soon as they reached Vienna. Apart from the Polish for 'please', 'thank you', and 'good day', her children, even the eldest son, had soon forgotten the language. The patriarch immediately conjured up a new domain, different from the old one and yet like it. He loved to keep house in lavish style, and his family of six children pleased him most when they stood lined up nicely in a row, attractively dressed, at the balls and parties that he generously gave at his frail but tough-minded wife's expense. He was full of big ideas for business, it was just the large figures involved that gave him trouble. He was a builder and architect, but not, unfortunately, a good businessman. When he died overnight of a stroke in his early fifties, his widow's move from their grand villa was reminiscent of her bitter flight from Pomerania.

The twin girls found themselves back with their mother in a small rented apartment. Their father was dead, and the first thing they did was to have their long hair cut off. The second thing was to refuse to go to domestic science college any more; they didn't even take the leaving exam which, it was said in Vienna, you could pass with distinction in dumplings. Both found secretarial jobs within days. When my mother entered the building in Mariahilferstrasse on the day she started work there, the first person to meet her was the company's chief clerk, a man of Polish birth called Lubomierz Kat, and the second was my father, who was one of the company's customers. They both winked at her. She reddened and looked away.

She got engaged to the Pole.

At first she had probably liked Lubo's Polish patriotism. He was always running down the communists; she had never heard so much political talk before. She thought he was very sophisticated, and admired him when he and his friends plotted a White revolution in Poland. Lubo's friends secretly admired my mother's Slav cheekbones, and for a while she stopped hating her dark hair. Luckily she had never tried to bleach it; she was either too timid or had too much natural good taste for that. At the parties where Lubo and his friends planned theoretical revolutions, my mother drank buffalo-grass vodka and boogie-woogied on the tables with Lubo. She is said to have looked like Farah Dibah at this time. Lubo taught her about the heroic history of Poland. The first rift between them came when she couldn't pronounce the names properly. When she said at home that she wanted to take private lessons in Polish, her gentle mother remarked, 'Your father would have been pleased about that.'

But the idea of learning Polish died a natural death. She went to the teacher, who was Lubo's aunt, two or three times, but she was too lazy to tackle the new letters and the rules of pronunciation. She didn't think she could do it, soon gave up, and then was ashamed of herself for failing. Later, when she was more self-confident, she told herself she just hadn't been interested enough.

Her engagement to Lubo lasted three years. It finally ended because of his 'Slav jealousy', as my father would say later, grinning. He never spoke of Lubo as anything but 'that poisonous, spiteful little Pole'. On their last holiday together in Italy, another man asked my mother to dance. She saw that Lubo was losing his temper, and she wanted to make a point. So she stood up and danced, 'not close, not cheek to cheek or anything,' as she assured us later, still indignant, just 'in a perfectly normal way'. After a few minutes the crazy, besotted Lubo stormed on to the dance floor, snatched her away from her partner, seized her, pulled her to him and bit her nose in front of everyone. She had to take an extra week's holiday because she couldn't have gone to work looking the way she did. Lubo had bitten really hard. Only now that he had attacked her capital, her beauty, could she admit to herself that he had already hit her before this incident. 'But think nothing of it, I hit him back,' she told her daughter. She sent the engagement ring back to Lubo by a third party, because she was afraid of him. She looked for a new job. For some time to come Lubo stood outside her building at weekends because he wanted to see who she was going out with. She was going out with several different men at the time, including my father. After Lubo lay in wait for them the first time and called names, my father, never a hero, told her they'd better meet in a café from now on.

My father was not a Pole and not a patriarch, he was a lady-killer. He was good-looking, witty and charming, and he bowled women over. But he wasn't easy to pin down, and even when they were going out with each other more regularly and my mother saw the envious glances of other women, she didn't realise what she was doing. She tried a flirtatious little scene. Thereupon he withdrew for weeks.

She thought she would die. Probably, as so often happens, she began pining for him just because there was a part of him that she couldn't reach. She thought it was love, silly little girl that she was at the time, but the question at stake was power.

They began going out together again, but now there was a cool, invisible wall between them. She complained, but met with no understanding. The more she wanted to discuss, analyse and plan the future, the further he retreated. Finally he said he thought they ought to split up. They were sitting in an espresso bar on the Gürtel, and she stared out; the cars were blurred, her mascara was running down her face. At first it was like being in a movie, but then she suddenly understood that this was real. She thought of next day and how it would feel when she woke up. She began begging and pleading, she collapsed. He walked her home. Her thin, tough-minded mother took delivery of her desperate child in silence, and shook hands with him when she said goodbye.

She was sick. She lay in bed and tried with all her might to die. She never managed to be proud and self-confident, to show herself and him that she didn't need him, there were several other men who were keen on her, as she never tired of saying later, she never reached that crucial liberated point. She lay in bed like a heroine in a sentimental drama and waited for him or for death. She was very, very strong, and she was very, very obstinate. After ten days he came back, pale and with a bunch of flowers. They were putting on a pointless act with each other, it sapped their strength, and the shadow of it lay over their relationship from then on.

But first it all had to swing right round. To veil over the past, their happiness and delight in each other had to be on the grand scale. Relieved as they both were, they didn't find it difficult. They had never been so much in love as in the months before the wedding. Only once, as they were waiting for the tram on the corner of Mariahilferstrasse and Babenbergerstrasse, did he suddenly announce that there was something else he had to tell her. She froze. She thought he was going to break their tacit agreement and go back to suggesting a trial separation, the idea that had been so painful to them both. But she was wrong. He murmured, without looking into her eyes, 'It's just that I was born – well, I'm what they call Mosaic.' 'What's that?' she asked, surprised and concerned again. 'Is it some kind of illness?'

Their first child came along three years after their marriage, according to plan, and then the happy phase was over. The time when they could go out as they pleased had been wonderful, very close to what she had probably once imagined 'life' would be like. At weekends she sat in some football stand, freezing and applauding him, for he was still playing, although just for fun, in second-ranking clubs. Against all expectation she enjoyed it. She was always accompanied by several admirers, his and hers, who explained the rules of the game to her, found her a cushion to sit on, and if necessary held an umbrella over her head. After the game they went to a wine bar or the Weisskopf. They had a thousand acquaintances, they laughed and celebrated, life was one big party. The best of it was that he was her husband now and no one could take him away from her. He was as charming and captivating as ever, and she basked in his glory. Even when he didn't spare her his generally popular jokes – when she was very pregnant and wearing her dark blue maternity cape he called her 'my fat French gendarme here' – she was still apparently closer than anyone to the centre of this amusing little universe. She was only briefly annoyed that he sometimes came home in dismissive, sarcastic or introverted mood, that he went to supper with his old parents once a week, was out training rather often, and would sit over the accounts for hours in the evening. At such times she thought she saw that this was real life, and she was pleased with herself and her capacity for understanding. But as soon as they went out and were with other people he was his old self again, witty and sparkling, sometimes mildly outrageous, in fact an adventurer, an entertainer. Then she looked up to him with satisfaction.

When the baby was born he was out as usual at the Weisskopf or the wine bar. She had difficulty getting hold of him on the telephone, but he was pleased, that was obvious. He came to visit next day bringing her a postcard of a hairy baby chimpanzee in a white crib. He loved the baby from the first, there was no doubt at all about that. She soon suspected that he loved the baby more than her, more than she herself loved the baby. But no wonder, he wasn't at home, he didn't change the nappies and get up in the middle of the night, he wasn't having his nipples bitten, he didn't have to cope with sickness and diarrhoea, he wasn't there when she hauled the big pram down the stairs because the time came when she just had to go shopping.

She had worked right up to the birth, not yet with him in the shop but for a firm with a great many employees, with other smart young women and susceptible young men. They all went out for a coffee now and then. She was in the book-keeping department at first, then rose to be second most senior secretary, and for the first time in her life she realised that she wasn't entirely stupid and useless.

All that was over now. She was as surprised and shocked as she could be. She spent the first winter an almost total prisoner of her home. She couldn't drive a car, and even if she could have done he wouldn't have let her. At first she had bravely made herself up, wrapped the baby and herself in thick clothes, pushed the pram through the snow, hauled it into the tram and heaved it out again – you had to change quite often at the time. That way she visited her mother and her sister a couple of times. She didn't get any sympathy there either. They were always carrying the baby around and petting her, and were pleased when she laughed. They cared only for the baby.

One day when the baby had spat out her food for the fourth time, and then pushed a jug off the table, she couldn't take it any more. She snatched the child out of her chair as if she were going to put her down on the ground, but just let her drop the last half a metre. Then she flung herself on the sofa and burst into tears. Soon after that her husband came home. She sat up, mopped her face, and watched with a stony expression as the baby, gurgling happily, crawled towards him on her fat knees.

He went on with his old lifestyle. After the shop shut he trained or went to the Schneuzl Club, in the evening he went to the wine bar or played cards with Fredi Hals in the Weisskopf until late at night. She knew the expression on her face didn't exactly sweeten his homecoming, but she also knew that he wouldn't come home any earlier even if she behaved like a young bride. He obviously didn't understand at all. He did or didn't do things just as he pleased. As he saw it, now that they were a family she had everything she needed. And she never even thought of expressing a wish for his time and affection.

At weekends, when the weather was reasonable, they went to the park in Baden, to see the icicles and the snow-covered fountain, and then he pushed the pram through the snow, let it roll down a little slope, ran along beside it and laughed when the child crowed with glee. Then they went into the roast chicken restaurant, which was the same as ever. 'How's things?' beamed my father when he had spotted Fredi Hals and his wife through the steaming bowls of chicken soup and the cohorts of potato salads. 'Everything all right?'

'You look tired, dear,' Fredi's wife told my mother, who just nodded. She enjoyed these weekends much as a prisoner enjoys going round the exercise yard.

She wouldn't let him help about the house. She wouldn't let him change the baby, she wouldn't even let him set the table. Not that he had tried very often, but he *had* tried, and he might perhaps have been capable of learning. She snatched everything away from him. She said he would only drop it, he would probably even drop the baby. For she had finally realised what her ultimate task was: to be a perfect housewife and mother. And she had to perform that task all by herself, for she would have felt even more of a failure as a lady of leisure. Expecting to live in luxury as a lady of leisure was the worst thing of all, or so she said, scoring a pitiful moral victory, talking to her friends about women who neither had children nor worked.

She would never accept a household help, not even in the good years when they could easily have afforded it. She did the cleaning herself. She did everything herself. She derived a certain bitter satisfaction from it. She was sacrificing herself. She was working her fingers to the bone. She could do no more. No one would have anything to reproach her with. She did what she thought she ought to do, acting the part of irreproachable Patient Griselda. Everything she did, in line with her self-appointed priorities, was a constant excuse for everything she simply couldn't do any more. Since she was always overburdened to the point of near-collapse, you couldn't ask anything of her, make any demands of her, burden her any further. Asking her to sit down and take a break was like an obscene insult. She withdrew in her own busy way. And no one noticed, no one brought her back from that isolation.

Her husband felt nothing but helpless respect for her frantic activity. Even decades later, although at rare moments he could confess that it had not been a perfect marriage, he would immediately follow up that painful admission by saying, 'But she was always a good mother – it was amazing what she could do.' The one member of the family who did understand in her speechless way was the child. The child was not deceived. She reacted to withdrawal by withdrawing in her own turn. She threw temper tantrums with her mother. When she cried she wouldn't let her mother comfort her. She pushed her away and kicked out at her. She wiped her kisses away with the back of her hand. Her mother explained it to herself by saying she was going through the difficult stage. 'She's having a long difficult stage, that child,' she said, but she felt injured. For sometimes the child would sit for hours on Frau Hals's lap grinning like a Cheshire cat. Sometimes she said 'Mama' to Fredi Hals's wife by mistake, and her mother almost thought it was done to spite her.

She instinctively drew her own conclusions. She wanted another child, a new beginning, she would do it again, and better this time. She didn't understand herself, she gave sensible, traditional reasons. 'I always wanted a big family, like ours at home.' Her husband was dead against it. He could see what one child had done to her. Secretly, he hoped that she wouldn't be able to have any more. 'Do you think I can't manage it?' she asked, making it sound like a threat, and claimed that two children would be easier than one, because soon they'd be playing with each other.

Although no one would have suspected it of that joker my father, the break-up of his first marriage had hurt him. He knew they had both been too young, and he hoped his son would come to no harm. After all, the little boy had everything. He compared the child's upbringing with his own in England, although he had been lucky too. He thought affectionately of Uncle Tom, and how when they parted he had insisted on giving my father his enormous darts cup, his pride and joy, the focal point of his little living-room. It had been difficult getting Uncle Tom's darts cup into his seaman's bag, and then it was almost confiscated by the Russians in Bruck an der Leitha. But they had come through, he and the darts cup, and now it stood in a glass-fronted cupboard in the living-room with his own football trophies, a bitter-sweet memento of his only real childhood.

All the same, he vaguely felt, his first marriage ought not to have ended as it did. Uncle Tom and Auntie Annie had been upset by the divorce, as he could tell from their letters. He didn't want to go through that any more. He had made up his mind on no account to marry again. The stupid thing was that his girlfriends always wanted to get married at once. He turned the idea down. There were partings in floods of tears, suicide threats, illnesses lasting weeks, he knew all about it. Sticking to his principles, he had survived such things several times in his second spell of bachelordom. What made him give way on the third or fourth occasion? Was he in love with that particular girl and her high cheekbones? Or was it a kind of exhausted collapse? My father never asked himself such questions. He took life as it came, he was evasive, you could even say craven.

He reacted to this second fiasco in his own fashion: he laughed, played and joked his way through it, taking his beautiful young wife's verbal and emotional punches almost without flinching.

Once, at one of the notorious 'gentlemen's evenings' at the club that usually went on into the small hours of the morning, Schmuel Harasi, who was on his own second marriage, spoke with unexpected frankness about his marital problems. He was slightly tipsy already, and the language of the other so-called gentlemen was on the smutty side too. In Schmuel Harasi's opinion, he said, young men had never had one crucial point made clear to them: 'It'sh a fact – once they've got kids women don't want you in their beds any more.'

'Then throw your old lady out!' cried Werner Weis, who as so often was roaring drunk.

'I went wrong twice,' replied the canny Schmuel, 'who's going to guarantee me better luck third time around?' And my father laughed until the tears came into his eyes. He was still chuckling to himself days later when he remembered this *bon mot*. And of course he made it part of his repertory of anecdotes for the family table, with no idea what he was doing.

My father would have said that he had always treated his beautiful, young, unhappy and sharp-tongued wife in the same way, i.e. in a very friendly and courteous manner. It was just that she regarded every friendly or loving remark as derision, and reacted accordingly. She was sure he knew that she was unhappy. She didn't actually say so; straight talking was the one form of communication that she didn't use to convey her unmistakable messages. But he never admitted such ideas to his mind, and tried everything he could to avert the threat of discord with ever friendlier actions and words, more and more of them. That made her feel that she really was the object of derision. This, or something like it, was the way their relationship went over decades. 'Good morning, my love, did you sleep well?' he might greet her in the morning with a Cary Grant smile. 'Never mind such nonsense,' was her reply. She had probably got up in the night three times because of the children, and he hadn't noticed at all, or so she was partly convinced, but part of her thought it was impossible, what with all the noise they made. And then asking her a question like, 'Did you sleep well?' What a joke, such impudence! The curious thing about it was that they adopted this poisoned method of communication only at home, where they were on their own. Outside, no one noticed anything. Outside, of course the two of them were always in company, in large parties, and at that time only the men did the talking in company (with the exception of Aunt Ka), while the women, if they spoke at all, talked quietly to each other. Only when my mother was slightly tipsy did she occasionally snap at him in public, and then the drink served as a welcome explanation. And whether in company or not, he laughed heartily at all her attacks on him as if they were a joke that only the two of them understood.

As the children grew up, the situation might have improved. She was not under so much pressure, and his imaginary debts to her didn't increase so rapidly. But the basic debt, the basic relationship was the same. It even became consolidated, froze solid, although with the children leaving home it could have been reduced to zero again. As I have indicated, even decades later she was still able to come up with grievances about the outings they hadn't gone on, the walks they hadn't taken, anything else she'd have liked to do. She still snatched everything out of his hands. And he wouldn't let her learn to drive. He laughed at her. He didn't admit to it, he didn't even feel it was like that. Yet he regarded her, and much less privately than would have been acceptable, as slightly lacking in the field of humour, rhetoric and quick repartee. She knew that, and never forgave him for it. A cheerful bit of wordplay that she didn't understand, something he might have to explain to her in front of everyone, could turn a whole holiday into an icy hell. So they lived side by side with each other. Divorce was unthinkable, and they never did think of it. Unthinkable, she thought. Not again, he thought. 'We're old now, you can never leave me now,' she said to him when they were both pensioners, and one wonders whether that was a plea or a triumphant statement of fact.

She would always have liked to rise higher in the world. Perhaps she just wanted to go back to the relative wealth of her youth, the villa, the balls and the cocktail parties. She knew she didn't have it in her to rise in the world of her own accord, but that wasn't the way women of her kind and of that generation thought in any case. Rising in the world depended on your husband. And she had married this good-looking, popular, intelligent man with all his connections and his talents. As she saw it, he could have done anything, anything he wanted, he could have made money, had a glittering career. But he didn't want those things. He was satisfied with himself in a way that infuriated her. The shabby little back-yard shop kept going of its own accord, it didn't make much work for him and left him enough time for his hobbies. There was enough money, life was good – 'What more could one want?' he asked, smiling. Yet he was not simply unambitious. His supposed lack of ambition was more the expression of his deep-rooted need for harmony, his terror in the face of any kind of conflict. To pursue a dazzling career would have meant outdoing others, using his elbows, being hard and mean-minded – all the things that she secretly wanted him to be. He declined. He was a team player. He stuck to his position, outside right, in his lousy little shop, with Fredi Hals as supplier. That was enough for him.

But she seemed to see the golden grapes hanging right in front of her nose. Most of her friends were more prosperous than she was, and their husbands were no cleverer or more gifted than hers. They were just more ambitious and readier to take risks. Socially, my parents' circle of friends was remarkably homogeneous. It consisted of people from the petty bourgeoisie and the working class who had worked their way up in the post-war years, and now contemplated their detached houses, their construction companies, textiles companies or car firms with satisfaction. A time came when these people of quite humble origin, though some of them became really very rich – richer than was possible later on – began taking skiing holidays in Switzerland or spending the winter in Florida. My mother was consumed by envy. When she met my father she hadn't seen much of the world, whereas he had travelled to football tournaments on every continent. There were photos showing him and his team-mates riding camels in Egypt, photos of him and the other players in bathing trunks walking around Copacabana. When he looked at those pictures my father always said, with a groan, 'Oh, Lord, I've done enough flying, quite enough for one life-time.'

And so the stage was set for the Olah affair. My mother's urge to spend did not begin, as my father said later, when Jackie Olah joined the tennis club, but that was when it became more obvious. Even before the Olahs came into her life, my mother had started buying second-hand goods and antiques, with some success. Shy as she could be about trying to buy herself a pair of shoes in city centre shops, she was good at dealing with elderly antique dealers and the foreigners in flea-markets – although once, when she saw my little sister haggling over a Smurf figurine in an Italian weekly market when we were on holiday, she laughed out loud and said, 'She must get that from her father. The Jews know how to strike a bargain.'

My father was of course dead against this sideline, particularly when my mother offered to sell the pictures and vases she had bought to their friends and acquaintances at the Schneuzl Sports Club. 'People will think we're short of money,' groaned my father, who found all this embarrassing. 'I couldn't care less what people think,' my mother snapped back, 'and I *am* short of money.' Up till then money matters between the two of them had been handled in a way that now seems antediluvian. At the beginning of the month my father gave my mother a 'not inconsiderable sum of housekeeping money', as he boasted, and she had to adjust her expenditure to it. Never mind whether it was a month when there were extra expenses for the children, new purchases for the household, or dry-cleaning bills to pay, she had to make do with that sum. She would rather have bitten her tongue off than ask for more at the end of the month, although in her view no one could manage on so little. She thought it an impertinence on his part, and her ability to make it stretch somehow seemed a wonderful achievement on hers. Here again she bottled up resentment for years, without any way of venting it. But she did learn to manage money very well, much better than him. At 'normal' times, when there were no special expenses, she would save up and use the money next month for repairs and new clothes and shoes for the children. She planned her budget for the whole year in advance. All the same, money was always tight at the end of the year, and there would be a fierce quarrel about it, usually just before Christmas.

So she began dealing in second-hand goods. At the weekend she would visit the flea-markets in and around Vienna, and with her first, cautious transactions she soon had a small bank account and was independent. She specialised in silver cutlery and old china dolls, but she bought and sold a number of other things too. Much of it was used at home for a while, until she tired of it and sold it on. She had a particular weakness for pictures, most of them ugly, dark, pretentious oil paintings which she believed had been painted over the works of old masters. But she never had that checked; it was a romantic idea of hers, the dream of becoming rich overnight. After a while, when she had finally had enough of them and their picturesque bridges, autumn flowers and deer in woodland clearings, she would change them. 'Nothing in life ever really gets any better,' said my father, grinning, when he noticed new pictures, and she would give him a sour look and reply, 'What do you know about it?'

Jackie Olah's real name was Ingeborg, but to be fashionable she called herself Jacqueline, or Jackie for short. She looked good and dressed even better, for she had money, and nothing else to do with it. At heart she was a classic lady of leisure, but because of her disarming manner and her enviable self-confidence no one had ever levelled such an accusation at her. Far from it: my mother and the other women, all mothers too, admired her to an unhealthy extent. They all wanted to be like her, so they made desperate efforts at least to keep up with her in the fashions they wore. Although Jackie never found out about it, my mother and her companions in misfortune were always exchanging useful addresses and information. One stroke of luck, for instance, the kind of thing that happened at most once a year, was the time when a boutique in the city centre suddenly went broke and had a two-day clearance sale, selling off its Paris collections at a fraction of the original price. Now and then this secret fashion society went on expeditions to the outskirts of the city, where goods that had suffered damage in transit were sold cheap in unattractive warehouses. An Italian suit with a mark on the hem of its skirt became legendary; my mother shortened it to get rid of the mark, and it drew a whistle from Jackie herself. Nor did my mother shrink from second-hand dress shops if that was the only way to get a garment by Dior or Versace. Only no one must know, least of all Jackie. In this way my mother and the others were usually one or even two seasons behind Jackie, but that was a hundred times better than wearing Kleiderbauer or Tlapa. Jackie seemed to have no idea of any of this. She was always mocking herself slightly, and that was one of the qualities that endeared her to other women. 'You look wonderful again,' they said when Jackie strolled down the gravel path. 'I can't take the credit,' she laughed, showing teeth as immaculate as the best dentist in Vienna could make them, 'I spent all morning at the beautician's.'

Her wish to emulate Jackie led to the first irregularities in my mother's budgeting. Her dolls and pictures and cutlery didn't make her enough profit to pay for all the clothes she suddenly thought she needed. So she began dipping into the housekeeping money, always persuading herself that this was really and truly the last time. Her handling of her finances went out of control. One day there was no way to avoid asking my father for extra. Since my mother went about it very aggressively, like most people when they have a guilty conscience, while my father, in his own weird way, intended to enjoy both triumphs to the full – the fact that she needed money, and was being unpleasant to him about it – their marriage really was at risk for the first time. After this quarrel they didn't speak to each other for weeks. Neither tried to make it up, but nor did they venture to talk about separating. In fact my mother was in terror that he might come up with such an idea, but that only made her more helplessly rigid than ever. All her life, she was far too obstinate to be diplomatic. He, on the other hand, was firmly convinced that he was in no way to blame for the escalation of the quarrel, and waited equally obstinately for her abject apology. It was into this very delicate phase that the Olahs' immoral offer fell.

Olah, as Jackie herself called him, was a few years younger than she was, a stocky man, not at all handsome, who always looked as if he were sweating. You could clearly see that he was a butcher's son, but with his parents' self-sacrificing support he had become a lawyer. In political discussions he could be aggressive and menacing. But he also liked to laugh out loud and slap his beautiful wife's bottom as she passed. Then she always arched her perfectly plucked eyebrows coquettishly, and all the men watching gave an inward sigh.

There was something gloomy, dissatisfied and ambitious about Olah. Yet he earned a great deal of money. Jackie already had a lot of money of her own, inherited from some French aunts. But while she pampered herself, enjoyed herself, and lived for the day, he seemed to be under great pressure. It was said that he had 'tricky clients'. Later, there was talk of the family, only too well known in Vienna, who ran the brothels in District 2 of the city. He was said to be their lawyer. He was in deep with the Leopoldstadt mafia, the rumour went, he represented people whose favourite way of solving arguments with their business partners was sending thugs in leather jackets to ring the doorbell very early in the morning. How much of that was true is not clear. It is certain that from the day when he joined the club,

Olah was almost touchingly enamoured of my father, the only person who could cheer him up.

He wanted my father's company all the time. For a while the two couples were inseparable, going out to the cinema or to eat at the Weisskopf together. Later, Olah bought expensive, hard-to-obtain tickets for football matches all over Europe, as a nice surprise for my father. Knowing that he hated accepting presents, Olah started by lying to him, making out that one of his business partners was sick, and the seat on the plane and in the stadium to watch Ajax in Amsterdam would have gone to waste otherwise. If he would come, said Olah, he'd be doing him a positive favour. My father went a couple of times, and then he began to feel awkward. As I have said, he had always had great personal problems with presents and free gifts of every kind. He would let Olah invite him to the wine bar or the Weisskopf; he had come to that compromise with himself some time ago. All his friends could afford to buy their rounds more easily than he could, and he saw that as a way of levelling out the body politic represented by his circle of acquaintances. And he always paid for one or two litres of wine, he insisted on that. But regular flights and expensive tickets for matches were too much. At first Olah felt injured, like a king whose court jester refuses to perform. Then he set Jackie on my mother: how about a Caribbean cruise at Christmas? If they came along it wouldn't be costing the Olahs anything extra. There was plenty of room on the boat they had already chartered. Barbados, Martinique, San Juan. They could pay for their own flight to Miami. To my mother, it sounded like winning the lottery. It sounded to my father like prostitution. He was dead against it, but because of their earlier quarrel communication within the marriage was still minimal. It was conducted largely through third parties, her women friends and their husbands, most of whom had already been to Miami themselves. Without saying a word, my mother succeeded in presenting my father with the following picture: he lived for the day, enjoying himself, without ambition. He had no needs of his own, and he didn't mind whether his nearest and dearest had any. He had never bothered to find out. But now that a once-in-a-lifetime opportunity to see at least a little of the world came along for his wife, who had long ago learnt to put up with his feeble attitude to the management of their existence, he was still indulging in false pride. It was just too much.

He was seasick for three weeks. When he opened his eyes in the morning he felt like throwing up at once. He lay in bed cursing his fate, annoyed with himself more than anyone else, and then began cautiously climbing out of bed. Almost every day, he hit his head on the upper bunk bed in which his wife was sleeping. At least he didn't have to see her, either when he was going to sleep or directly after waking up. Everything was going up and down. He couldn't stand it. He didn't like fruit for breakfast either, and still less did he like the way his wife praised the 'lovely fresh fruit' every day, as if she were a child hitherto kept on dry bread and water and now drunk with delight. His one triumph was his ability to eat all the seafood he liked at the other meals of the day. His wife didn't eat fish or any other seafood, and indeed she ate no game or lamb either, only beef, chicken and pork. Those had been the eating habits of her father the patriarch, and curiously enough all his six children had more or less stuck to them.

My father hated the heat, an inherited family trait. He thought remorsefully of his dour brother, who had warned him. 'The Caribbean? The South Seas?' my uncle had scoffed. 'Want to borrow my mosquito net?' He didn't like swimming either. He had learnt to swim very late as a child, and if you don't learn swimming early you never really enjoy it. So he sat in the air-conditioned saloon all day, playing cards with Olah and a couple of other guests.

'Isn't this lovely?' fluted Jackie, swanning through the room in her dazzling white swimsuit, but he just growled, 'The Schneuzl Sports Club doesn't go up and down so much.'

My father was seldom really unhappy, but when he was he was a thorough nuisance to everyone around him. He moaned and groaned. He got a crick in his neck on the funny bunk bed on one of the first nights, and after that he held it on one side like a crippled bird. At first his travelling companions thought his complaints were another of his jokes, an absurd pose, but after a while they thought they saw that he was avenging himself on all of them. None the less, Jackie kept fussing around him. She brought him cool drinks and tried to cheer him up. His own wife wasn't bothered at all. She kept as far away from him as you can on a ship; she would lie on a lounger in the bright sunlight all day, holding a glass of something sparkling and flirting with the men. She enthusiastically took part in all the expeditions on land, in comfortable shoes and with a point-and-shoot camera round her neck. She looked the image of a tourist. He hated that. Even in summer, he always wore long trousers and long-sleeved shirts; he would never have made a fool of himself in shorts and T-shirts – 'like an American,' as he used to say. The worst day was the one when she came back from an outing on shore with a necklace of shells and a brightly coloured garland of flowers slung somehow around her entire body. He turned away, went to his cabin and lay down for a while. The boat didn't rock so badly in harbour.

Olah became the real problem. He was deeply injured by his jester's ingratitude. He had brought him along for the sake of amusement, and now he had to take care not to be infected by my father's depression instead. I'm depressed too, Olah told himself, and for the first time he thought of his supposed friend in such terms as 'the old fool'.

The situation could have been defused when both of

them, Olah and my father, developed a severe protein allergy. Presumably they'd been overindulging in the seafood. Suddenly they were both covered with a red rash, and their faces swelled grotesquely. The ship's doctor gave them hefty calcium injections which laid them both low. When they came round they were side by side in Olah's spacious cabin, which of course had proper beds, even a small sitting-room and a minibar. They woke up, looked at each other and laughed. 'That was all we needed,' my father tried to joke. 'We should have seen it coming.' In this helpless but intimate situation, Olah decided to take him into the secret of his great plan. Out of friendship for my father, he had decided to buy First Vienna Football Club, which had now sunk into obscurity, and with my father's expert support lead the club back from the third division and to new heights. He thought my father would be pleased: after all, he could have bought some third-league man, and there were cheaper options too. '. . . And a manager of some kind,' said Olah, elaborating his plan, 'just for the look of the thing, but we'll make the real decisions!' My father stared at Olah. The worst of the swellings on his forehead were going down, but he still looked as if he'd just lost a boxing match. 'You're out of your mind, you're totally meschugge,' said my father at last, 'you know as much about football as I know about deep-sea diving.' This new rejection struck that lonely rough diamond Olah to the heart, but he would never have let it show. 'That's Jews for you,' he snapped straight back, in a voice sharp with dislike, 'they don't have anything, can't do anything, always think themselves wonderful all the same.'

And so their friendship came to an abrupt end. Later, when my father told the story, he made it appear that Olah had lured him aboard his 'filthy ship' just to humiliate him as a pauper. He immediately forgot what Olah had said about Jews. That didn't matter to him. First inviting him, then humiliating him, that was the shocking part of it.

Visitors

'The church,' sighed Uncle Hugo, 'the school.' Yet again he was spreading out his black and white picture postcards of a nondescript village street, and my father rolled his eyes.

'Listen, Hugo,' he began, but Hugo immediately produced another postcard, tapped it with his forefinger, and said emphatically, 'The cherry tree!'

'Which little Bertl was always climbing,' we children chanted in chorus, and Uncle Hugo laughed. 'Exactly! And where is Bertl, anyway?'

'He's very sorry,' murmured my mother, wry-mouthed, coming back from the telephone, 'but his wife isn't feeling well today.' And Uncle Hugo bent his head sadly enough to melt a heart of stone, and began putting his postcards together again.

Hugo, who had descended upon us introducing himself as my grandmother's nephew, had been waiting to see my uncle, 'dear little Bertl', of whom, he said, he had 'the happiest childhood memories'. They had climbed the cherry tree – 'He was never really athletic,' my father remarked doubtfully – they had built a tree-house, and they had been the best of friends every summer, until my father came into the world. After that Hugo's Aunt Frieda, my grandmother, unfortunately hadn't come home to the village so often in the school holidays, and later all that kind of thing was over anyway.

My uncle, who was very busy with his work and anyway

wasn't interested in anyone's company but Aunt Ka's, was sticking out against the reunion. First, he grumbled, he could scarcely even remember Hugo, and – here his hoarse voice became a little sharper – 'that lot are all Nazis.'

'Is that what you want me to tell him?' asked my father furiously, and my uncle muttered, 'Tell him anything you like.' After that my parents went very carefully, keeping civil but lying through their teeth.

For Uncle Hugo wasn't at all easy to shake off. My father's regular and agitated phone calls to his brother did no good.

'Just half an hour over a slice of guglhupf,' begged my father. 'That won't kill you!'

'No,' said my uncle implacably. 'What's more, we're expecting a visit. Cilly from Israel is coming, that will be quite enough of a strain.'

'But I'm never going to get rid of him!' wailed my father. However, my uncle knew no pity. 'Has he actually moved in with you for good?' he asked nastily. 'No? Then he'll run out of clean underwear some time.'

My mother stepped up her efforts to make it clear to Hugo that my uncle would probably be 'otherwise engaged on business' for the next few weeks. But Hugo was not giving up. At some point my mother even uttered the phrase 'going away on a business trip soon', but Uncle Hugo dug his heels in even harder. He had travelled so far and made such efforts to track our family down, he argued, he could afford to wait a little longer now. Very likely, he suggested, his visit would make a refreshing change from my uncle's crowded timetable of engagements. 'A child-hood friend,' he cried, unable to imagine that his cousin wasn't longing for the reunion as much as he was. 'Life comes full circle again!' Uncle Hugo, small, angular, with the sandy hair and bright blue eyes that had once been my grandmother's, became a problem.

Apart from that he was friendly and sociable, 'unlike

some', as my father remarked now and then. His fury with his brother was mounting day by day. But Hugo's family feeling was something new to us. As soon as he arrived this total stranger made a tremendous fuss about seeing everyone again. How delightful it was to meet members of your own family once more, and what a shame that we had lost sight of each other for so long! Later, my father claimed that Uncle Hugo had actually shed tears of joy when he jumped out of the train and practically into his arms. My father shuddered with embarrassment at such a sentimental performance. 'I'm a family man,' Uncle Hugo kept assuring us, and he loved to take children by their shoulders with a firm but affectionate hand and stare into their faces for seconds on end. 'My dear little chap,' he said, much moved, to my already grown-up brother, who twisted out of his grasp. 'My little mousie,' he said to my sister, the only one of us to show any interest in him.

For Uncle Hugo was a family historian. He carried a fat, black-bound book around with him, containing all kinds of information about a family tree with many branches going right back to the eighteenth century. And then there were the postcards: they were kept in home-made transparent envelopes as if they were in a photograph album, you could take your pick any time and deal them out in various combinations. Sometimes my sister pensively dealt out only the separate cottages which, according to Uncle Hugo, had been inhabited by our grandmother's various relations, and so in a way were former possessions of the family. Sometimes the two of them put together a topography of the little village, using the postcards, for Uncle Hugo also had a map of the area to scale. When unfolded it covered our entire dining-table. The ground plans of all the houses were entered on it, with their numbers, so my sister and Uncle Hugo arranged all the houses of which they had photographs on the cards in two rows, separated only by the imaginary main street.

My little sister and Uncle Hugo happily played villages with each other. She was his only confidante among us, he kept telling her stories about the map and the postcards, the houses and the people, and she made a fairy-tale world of her own out of it all.

'And then Josefa met Ignaz at the church dedication festival,' my sister told my mother, who was cutting her toenails for her, 'and they fell in love at once.'

'Well, well,' murmured my mother absently, 'how nice.'

'But Josefa was supposed to be marrying that man called Rosmanith, the one who would inherit the farm,' said my sister reproachfully, 'not Ignaz, because he was only a poor saddler.'

'Fancy that,' murmured my mother. 'The things that happen.'

'What's a saddler anyway?' asked my sister suddenly, and my mother lost patience. 'Someone who makes saddles and other leather things,' she groaned, 'now do keep still.'

'There were only three Czechs in our village,' my sister told my brother, 'the postman, the priest and Jiři the farm hand. But they were all very nice and behaved decently, and there were no problems at all with them.'

'What?' asked my brother. 'What on earth are you talking about?' And then my brother, who was writing his doctoral dissertation at the time, also began to take a passing interest in Uncle Hugo and his stories.

Decades later, my sister liked telling her children about the young people's camps where she had been sent several summers running. 'Was that before or after Uncle Hugo turned up?' she wondered vaguely. Anyway, the camps were in the Bucklige Welt area, on a lovely farm at the very top of a hill. You had to bring folk-dancing clothes, which meant dirndls for the girls and lederhosen for the boys, and that entailed considerable problems for my mother. In the end she bought my sister a second-hand dirndl, 'because she wants it so much,' she said. 'I had no breasts at all at the time,' giggled my sister, 'I looked really silly in a dirndl.'

Those two weeks in Lower Austria were delightful. The children came from all over Austria, even from Bavaria, and some made friends and corresponded with them for years. There were paper-chases in the woods, you had to solve puzzles about plants and animals, and the various groups competed in a treasure hunt. The treasure was a wooden box containing stickers, crests and pennants, and more post-cards showing Karlsbad and Eger, Krummau and Znaim. 'Children love a camp fire,' said my sister dreamily, so they had one every evening if the weather was good. They grilled sausages on wooden skewers, they baked potatoes in the hot ashes, and one of the young men running the camp played the guitar. Unlike her siblings, my sister always enjoyed singing and sang well; she had a fine soprano which made her a star in the school choir. 'No land so fair,' they sang at the camp where my sister had found herself, through some school friends, and 'In the deep Bohemian forest', and 'In the lovely meadowland', the kind of things you do sing by camp fires. 'I always sang "shed a deer" instead of "shed a tear",' giggled my sister, 'I only found out my mistake much later.' But she could never forget that in the first year she won the general knowledge quiz at the closing party, even though she was one of the youngest there and no one in my family thought very much of her intellectual capabilities. At summer camp, however, she knew not only the names of the main cities in both parts of Germany and all the Austrian provinces, she was the only one who could fill in place-names on a map where they were just marked with dots, and she wrote them all in without making any mistakes either. Being left-handed, she had to take care not to smudge what she had just written, so she worked clockwise from the top of the map. 'Gablonz,' she wrote, her tongue in the corner of her mouth, 'Trautenau', 'Troppau', and so on until she came up the other side and wrote 'Teplitz', 'Aussig' and 'Reichenberg'. Then she added something extra: she put in another dot and wrote 'Freudenthal' beside it. That ensured victory for her.

'So *now* you ask whether it was before or after Uncle Hugo?' mocked my brother, who couldn't bear anyone's success stories but his own.

'No need to look like that,' my sister snapped back. 'I know exactly what you think of the poor man. You make things too easy for yourself.'

After my father had demeaned himself by pleading with him in vain for days, it gave my father the greatest satisfaction when his brother, my uncle, suddenly asked a favour.

'It's Cilly,' my uncle groaned down the phone. 'Not only is she getting on my nerves, she wants to see you too.'

'Unfortunately,' pretended my father, eyes twinkling with delight, 'I'm totally exhausted with all these visits. I'm not leaving the house at the moment.'

'Then ask the old bag round to your place,' grunted my uncle. 'That way at least I'll be rid of her for a few hours.'

'Well, all right,' said my father hesitantly, for he had just had an idea which at that moment seemed to him brilliant. 'But only if you'll come too. I mean, I hardly know her.'

Cilly Haas, full name Cäcilie, was the daughter of Ilse Haas, my grandmother's oldest friend. Now that Ilse and my grandmother were both dead, it was only Cilly's persistence and energy that maintained the link with my family. She chose my uncle as her contact man. There wasn't much to it except exchanging birthday wishes, and those cards pre-printed with wording that lets you send good wishes for Chanukkah and Christmas at the same time. But when she came back from Israel she always stopped off in Vienna. Once she came when she was on a coach trip to the Black Sea; another time she had been visiting distant relations in Budapest. Later, years after these events, she would come more often, because the Germans paid for her to stay at a Black Forest spa once a year, and 'it's only a stone's throw from there,' she said.

Cilly was as talkative as she was warm-hearted. She wasn't really tactless, at least not often, but compared with my cool uncle, who always kept his distance, she certainly had the gift of the gab. She thought it was fair to ask most questions among friends, even bringing up the subject of sex and other physical matters. This often made my uncle uncomfortable. But despite her loud voice and garish appearance (for Cilly, a full-bosomed, dark-haired creature, could laugh like a drain, and the older she grew the more provocatively she dressed), he thought well of her unsentimental attitude to her own past history. He had a fellow feeling for her there.

Cilly liked to talk about men, and she knew a lot about them too. However, she had had no luck with them until quite late in life. Her first husband – 'I didn't really like him, let alone love him,' she always added, roaring with laughter and shocking most of her audience – had died in a concentration camp. The second – 'a handsome man, wonderful,' she said regretfully – soon died in the Arab-Israeli War of 1948. She was unhappily married to the third for years; everyone wondered why. Once she was in Vienna with this third husband, and the afternoon of their visit went down in family legend because my grandmother, who in her later years was as short-sighted as she was uninhibited in her behaviour, kept narrowing her eyes, nudging those sitting to right and left of her, and asking in a voice that no one could help hearing, 'Ugly as a monkey, isn't he? Ugly as a monkey! Don't you think he looks as ugly as a monkey?' The fourth husband Cilly caught was the best, as she always said, a proud former Viennese who, although he had emigrated to Palestine in 1936, still knew all the Austrian wine bar songs off by heart and could sing them in the right dialect. He was respectfully known as Herr Josef, and she still flirted with him so outrageously, even at over eighty, that everyone who saw the two of them wondered anxiously what would happen when one of them fell ill, and the façade of eternal youth was cracked beyond repair.

All her life, however, Cilly bore her first husband, 'that horrible man', a grudge, although she had hardly known him and didn't even have a photograph of him. When she had drunk a little too much vodka, she could really lose her temper. 'I should never have had to go to the camp,' she cried indignantly, flushing. 'My mother was Aryan!'

'So was mine,' my uncle tried soothing her in his lowered voice, for such scenes made him most uncomfortable, 'but we were registered Jewish.'

'So why did they have to register us Jewish, then?' cried Cilly raucously, pouring more vodka. 'First those fools our parents, then my husband!'

My uncle did not ask Cilly if she would rather have been registered Christian and baptised. It never even occurred to him, for his sole desire was to change the subject. Unfortunately his wife, Aunt Ka, was no help to him at all here. 'What exactly did your husband do?' she asked sympathetically, avid for sensation. 'He just couldn't let go of me,' said Cilly angrily, 'he had me entered on his transport list, he was in the Jewish Community administration!' That left even Aunt Ka speechless. 'Very well,' added Cilly, as soon as she could muster a little pride in her confused heart, 'so I was young and beautiful, but all the same. What an egoist!'

'Ah yes, the Jews,' said Uncle Hugo thoughtfully. 'There were some of those in Freudenthal.'

'I always thought well of them,' said Uncle Hugo, sadly. 'It wasn't right, what happened to them.' No, he had heard nothing about it at the time, Uncle Hugo assured us in my brother's hearing; he had been a child, a boy, paying only very rare visits to Freudenthal. 'And there weren't any in our village.'

'Only three Czechs,' my sister backed him up, nodding portentously. 'The priest, the postman and . . .'

'There's something I must tell you,' said Uncle Hugo suddenly, and there followed the dramatic tale of how he was miraculously cured of polio, a story that my sister already knew very well. 'No one could do anything for him,' said my sister, fascinated. 'Not the doctor, not the wise woman with the herbs, not even the priest when he came with his censer of incense.'

'They gave me up for dead,' agreed Uncle Hugo sadly. 'Then they took me to Troppau, the longest journey I'd ever been on.' And there, said my little sister, with a look on her face that anticipated the happy ending, a doctor had some medicine from Switzerland, very expensive, Hugo's parents could never have afforded it. A cure was so near, and yet so far! But then – then the doctor *gave* that poor child Hugo the medicine, just like that. 'A Jewish doctor, too,' nodded Uncle Hugo, meaningfully. 'The Jews have their contacts everywhere.'

'That doctor saved his life,' said my little sister, sighing.

Over the next few years, whenever Uncle Hugo wrote to announce his forthcoming arrival, my parents played a risky game. They wrote long letters back, enclosed the latest photos of all the children, sent greetings and warm wishes, only to add regretfully in a postscript that, as it happened, they would be on holiday at the time he was suggesting, and Bertl had a business trip planned. Uncle Hugo never visited us again, but he went on writing friendly letters from some-where in deepest Bavaria, and sometimes he even phoned on birthdays. Hugo was a loyal soul. He also took it for granted that he ought to keep us up to date with events in what he called our old home, the village that was entirely unknown to us.

At some time in the mid or late eighties, he and a few other of its former inhabitants succeeded in visiting the

village. They went in a minibus, all of them grey, elderly
men, their wives not having dared to accompany them into
the communist dictatorship. The men were afraid too, but
hid their fears with particularly forthright behaviour while
they were in their bus. Strong words were uttered, such as
'political robbery' and 'genocide', terms which in the
normal way did not easily pass Uncle Hugo's lips. But they
had to stick together in that little bus, and the only weapon
they could use to reassure themselves was forceful language.
When they drove into the village about midday everything
was deathly quiet. They were soon to find out that the
population was only half as big as it had been in their
childhood, that many houses were empty, and that a
number of them on what had once been the long main
street had been demolished. They stopped outside the
church. A few curtains twitched. As they drove to their
destination, the new VW bus had moved like some super-
natural vehicle among all the Skodas and Ladas on the road,
conspicuous and identifiable. With a Munich number plate
too. The men defiantly thrust out their chins. They got out
of the bus, stretched their legs, laughing, and began to take
photographs. Hugo went down the street and stopped
outside his parental home. It looked to him small and
shabby. The garden had run wild, and had a bright red
rotary clothes-dryer in the middle of it. Plucking up his
courage, he pressed the bell, but all remained quiet. He
looked cautiously around before trying surreptitiously to
reach a branch of the cherry tree that hung over the fence.
Uncle Hugo was a small, thin man who from a distance
resembled my uncle. It was difficult, but after a few desperate and ludicrous leaps in the air, he finally caught hold of a
twig of the cherry tree and broke it off. He hid it under his
jacket and made haste to rejoin the others, who by now had
made contact with the enemy. Men from the village had
come out of the inn and asked a few surly questions. The
one member of Hugo's group who spoke the language had

tried to communicate with them, slowly and concentrating hard. It was not exactly a help to him that his companions kept muttering in unfriendly tones, hands in their trouser pockets, eyes on the ground, like a group of defiant boys now grown old but thinking like children. Thieves. We didn't do anything wrong. It's up to them to say sorry.

Suddenly the door of the inn opened again and a woman wearing an incredibly dirty apron came out. She pushed the village men aside, apparently scolding them, took the spokesman of Hugo's group by the sleeve, which alarmed him, and said in the voice of someone used to being obeyed, 'Come!' Then she led the man down the main street and suddenly took a side turning, followed by the whole frightened group from Germany. They went down an alley with a long, low garden wall on both sides – the houses in this village typically have long, narrow gardens merging into orchards at the far end. They went along a footpath overgrown with weeds, making for the wood. On its outskirts, the woman looked briefly around, took another few steps, moved a branch aside and then, arms outflung, indicated the ground in front of her. 'There!' she said, looking expectantly at the Germans. Hundreds of stones lay there in a clearing, many broken, some intact, bricks, entire sections of wall, and some rubbish. But mainly they were gravestones. A few wrought iron crosses lay among them too, the kind of thing that lasts longest. 'Mama, Papa, yes?' asked the woman encouragingly, before turning to go. One of the party took a step or so after her, saying, 'Thank you.' The woman just nodded and then went off. The men knelt there in the wood for hours, searching among the fragments, moving them around, scraping stones up and taking photographs until it was dark. Then they ventured into the inn to eat.

For a few days my father felt sure of victory. Now that my uncle had finally agreed to bring Cilly Haas to coffee with my parents, my father seriously believed he was about to turn the tables on his brother. For of course he hadn't told him that Hugo was still in Vienna, and had been there for two weeks in all. Now and then my father, who never usually cheated anyone and always spoke up volubly in favour of 'typical English fair play', felt guilty about it, but then he swiftly reminded himself of what my uncle had said about poor Hugo without really knowing him. Fancy refusing to meet an old man again, thought my father, shaking his head. Sometimes his brother was a real mystery to him.

So my uncle, Aunt Ka and Cilly turned up. Cilly was carrying a huge bunch of flowers which she ceremoniously undid, handing the flowers around with much laughter and many cries of glee at the reunion. 'He was in nappies last time I saw him,' she trumpeted, jabbing my father in the chest with her forefinger, 'and then next moment he fell out of his pram.' Even as she was taking her coat off in the hall, stories began pouring out of her – ah, that time when she had been in Vienna with her mother, visiting Aunt Frieda as they so often did. Aunt Frieda and her mother wanted a nice quiet chat, so they sent the children out and told the three big ones to take the baby in his pram. 'And by the way,' she interrupted herself, grinning, 'the last we'd heard of it was that Aunt Frieda was pregnant and needed money.' Cilly lowered her voice. 'Send me such-and-such a sum, she wrote, I'm pregnant, and my mother sent her the money.' My father changed colour. 'So a few months later we go to Vienna, and what do we find there? We find *him*!' continued Cilly, greatly entertained, jabbing him in the chest once more. 'The two of them had used Mama's money some other way, Uncle never did have any cash to spare!'

'Well,' said my mother, 'if I could ask you to come in . . .' And she flung open the door of the living-room, where Uncle Hugo was already sitting in front of coffee and cake, with a blissful smile on his face. 'What did she want the money for, then?' asked my sister quietly, tugging Cilly's sleeve. 'You don't need to know that sort of thing yet, dear,' Cilly whispered.

'Well,' Cilly chattered on, absent-mindedly shaking hands with Uncle Hugo, 'so I was telling you how he fell out of his pram.' My uncle, who was looking as if my father had invited a group of Japanese to coffee, immediately sat down at the opposite end of the table, and merely offered his fingertips to Hugo over the coffee cups, knocking over the milk jug in the process. 'Bertl,' whispered Uncle Hugo, close to tears. 'You haven't changed a bit!'

'Pleased to meet you,' said Aunt Ka politely, at a loss to understand any of this. 'A cousin, just fancy!'

'. . . tried to haul it up the steps,' Cilly was saying, while my mother crawled around with a cloth under the table and my father stood there looking like thunder, 'but prams were such big things in those days!' She spread her arms wide, almost sending the coffee pot after the milk jug, but with great presence of mind Uncle Hugo grabbed it. 'Thank you so much,' said Cilly, giving Hugo a first, charming smile, '. . . and then it was just too heavy for us two girls, and Bertl hardly helped at all. And when we were nearly at the top, there were only two or three steps still to go,' she said, her voice expertly launching into a crescendo, 'it slipped out of our hands and fell all the way downstairs. What a racket it made! Auntie and Mama came rushing out, and we got a real hiding, at least Katzi and I did, but you . . . ,' she said, looking inquiringly at my uncle, 'no, I don't think you were punished at all.'

'I really couldn't say,' said my uncle defensively, determined to pay his brother back as vengefully as possible for setting the Hugo trap, 'but Cilly, don't you remember Hugo? He's from Engelsberg too!'

★

Uncle Hugo was not an embittered man or a revanchist. Now and then he went to the meetings of the Territorial Associations of former refugees, mainly because he liked the local costumes and the music and the old songs. He wasn't as interested in the lectures as some of the others were, but nodded agreement all the same when they said 'new progress' must be made, the matter 'must not fall into oblivion', 'demands must be made' of the Federal Government. He happily sent off the little leaflets that he had been given there to friends and acquaintances, because they were all told that everyone must help to 'raise awareness' of the subject. My father once received one of these badly photocopied little pamphlets, entitled 'What Everyone Should Know: Munich and Potsdam, Historical Facts', which he dutifully looked through without understanding a word of it, and then put away with Hugo's other letters.

When a young man turned up at his house one day asking to interview him for a 'collection of life stories', Hugo happily agreed. He devoted his whole afternoon to the young man and told him the story of his life. His wife gave them cakes and fruit-juice spritzers. They sat under a sun umbrella in the garden, and Hugo showed off his modest property, his tomato plants, his courgettes, a tiny cherry tree in a pot, and said thoughtfully, 'Life would have been different over there.' Yes, he had been in the Freudenthal camp for several weeks himself, and everyone knew that not only had two dozen men been picked out there at random on account of what was supposed to have been an assassination attempt involving a bomb, but two boys of only sixteen and seventeen had actually been shot. What they were accused of he couldn't really remember, but he thought that one of them, the younger, had once tried running away home to his mother. Later he, Hugo, had to do forced labour, digging up dead Russians from round Freudenthal Castle and re-burying them somewhere else, but he didn't like to think about that; luckily the weather had been cold. 'After that things got better for me,' Hugo said, and told the young man how he had to sort through the thousands and thousands of books brought to the castle from the abandoned houses. Important works were to be kept, most were taken to the courtyard for burning; that was his job. So there he sat for weeks with *Grimms' Fairy Tales* and Goethe, Felix Dahn and Georg Ebers, wondering what reading matter the new masters might approve of and what they would not. Finally his own transport set off for Germany. He hadn't any other stories to tell, but he was glad someone had asked for once. Mainly, he told the young man, he was sorry that his family were now scattered over half Europe. His own brothers and sisters and all his father's sisters and their children – they'd all gone, they were all somewhere else. 'I'm a family man really,' he said, childless though he was, and he looked sadly at the ground.

A little later Uncle Hugo was stunned to receive a letter from my brother for the first and only time. My brother informed him briefly that he had read Hugo's 'eyewitness account' in an anthology of radical right-wing writings which, in the same publication, denied the Holocaust and claimed that happy people had been well paid for their work in the concentration camps. 'I thought it would interest you,' wrote my brother, and Uncle Hugo was in despair, because he didn't know what to do now. 'Please tell me the exact title of this work and the publishers' address,' he wrote back to my brother by return of post, but he never had a reply.

'*To není pravda*,' cried Cilly enthusiastically, '*je to pravda?*' That is not true . . . is it true? Uncle Hugo smiled awkwardly. 'Yes,' he said hesitantly, 'but I'm afraid I don't really know.'

'Then I'm sure you must have known my mama's

family,' said Cilly vivaciously, while Hugo was reaching for his postcards. 'Ilse Haas, née Heppner, from Engelsberg?'

'Ah, there were a great many Heppners,' explained Hugo with the confidence of an expert again. 'Look, we have one in our own family tree.' And he unfolded the impressive family tree that he himself had drawn up, while my mother quickly pushed the cakes out of the way. In the year 1751, Uncle Hugo now informed his audience, one Apollonia Heppner had married an ancestor of his father and my grandmother; they were his great-great-great-grandparents, so to speak. 'How many greats was that exactly?' asked my little sister, but no one was listening to her.

'Impressive,' said Aunt Ka.

'Bosom friends, and almost related too!' cried Cilly, much moved, and she nodded vigorously when my mother offered everyone kosher slivovitz.

'Of course I recognised the jeweller's shop in Freudenthal,' said Uncle Hugo, smiling, 'a lovely place.'

'Yes, wasn't it?' said Cilly happily, reaching for the postcards of the little village. 'The school,' she cried, 'the church! Have you been back there?'

'Tell him what became of your shop!' my uncle told her, rudely interrupting, as nosy Aunt Ka tried to snatch a glimpse of the postcards that Cilly had spread out on the table.

'No, they won't give me a visa,' Uncle Hugo sadly explained to Cilly, 'even though it's my dearest wish.'

'Forget it,' muttered Cilly. 'Those two years after the war were enough for me. I never want to go back again in my life.'

'What did become of your shop?' Aunt Ka asked, as in duty bound. Her husband had kicked her under the table.

'Confiscated by the communists,' murmured Cilly. 'That red rabble!'

'That's not what I mean,' said my uncle angrily. 'I mean before that.'

'Why, before that,' Cilly said, surprised, 'Mama was allowed to go on running it while Papa and I were in the concentration camp. And she had to get divorced.'

'Concentration camp,' said Uncle Hugo, troubled. 'So you too . . . ah, those were terrible times.'

Here my uncle signalled to Aunt Ka that he wanted to leave at once.

'But listen, then you must have known . . .' And Cilly began reeling off the names of all kinds of friends they might have in common, for her memory of Engelsberg was drawn only from occasional visits to her grandparents. Uncle Hugo nodded eagerly and threw names back at Cilly, as if they were juggling balls in the air. Cilly's cheeks were bright red, and she was obviously concentrating hard. They put their heads together over the map of the area and the village, and Hugo explained in detail which Heppners had once lived in which houses.

My uncle rose abruptly. 'I don't feel well,' he announced, and you could see that he didn't.

'You work too hard, Bertl,' said Uncle Hugo, concerned, but my uncle was already out of the door. Aunt Ka collected her things and cast an apologetic glance around her. 'But my family tree!' Uncle Hugo suddenly remembered. 'I wanted to add things to my family tree!'

Aunt Ka turned. 'Why, isn't it finished yet?' she asked in surprise.

'For instance, when did you marry Bertl, dear lady?' asked Uncle Hugo, snatching a paper napkin off the table. Aunt Ka told him, not without a sentimental smile. She also gave Uncle Hugo her date of birth, and even the dates of birth of my uncle's sons by his first marriage, my cousins. 'You'll have to ask him about the date of his first wedding,' said Aunt Ka, coyly, 'I just can't remember.' Uncle Hugo hurried into the hall, where my uncle was already standing in his hat and coat. 'And what about Katzi?' Uncle Hugo pleaded. 'When did she die?' My uncle and my father looked at each other. 'We don't really know for certain,' said my father at last, 'some time at the end of 1941.'

'And when was her wedding?' said Uncle Hugo, firing off his next question, because it was obvious to him that this one could well be the last.

'No idea,' growled my uncle. 'I wasn't there.'

'On the eleventh of May 1938 in Prague,' Cilly suddenly said quietly. Nothing had been heard from her for quite a while. 'It was a Wednesday.' My mother helped Cilly into her coat, and only then did she realise that she was crying. 'I was her witness,' said Cilly, passing both hands over her face. 'I have the wedding photo at home in Tel Aviv.' Uncle Hugo stood in the living-room doorway holding the paper napkin against the door frame and noting down all the dates. My uncle didn't deign to give him another glance, and left. Cilly and Aunt Ka hurried after him, after thanking my mother for the lovely coffee party. 'Write to me some time, laddie,' said Cilly to my totally overtaxed father, jabbed him in the chest one last time, and then they were gone.

'Once upon a time, when Hitler came to Freudenthal,' began my brother in the tones of someone telling a fairytale, 'little Hugo from Engelsberg jumped straight on his bike and cycled off to see the Führer, pedalling away for all he was worth.'

'My goodness, how old was he then?' asked my sister stridently.

When they had both passed the mid-life mark my sister and my brother did not get on with each other. They had different versions of almost all the family stories that had gone down in our tradition like an unalterable cultural inheritance during my father's and uncle's lifetime. They couldn't agree on anything, and indeed they were fundamentally different in character. My brother liked to say that his sister automatically thought too lightly of everything that he took too seriously. She, on the other hand, claimed that he made impossible demands, couldn't forgive or draw distinctions, and when she wanted to be really unpleasant she said that the Stalinist influence of the Marxists, Trotskyites and Maoists whose doctrines he had once followed still showed through. She was not particularly familiar with those groups and their ideas, but she considered them to be absolute evil. Here she had obviously developed my father's vague feelings into a philosophy of life.

After the death of the parental generation, it wasn't long before contact between my two siblings broke off almost entirely. But the few times they did meet one another on family occasions, the conversation would inevitably come round at some point to Uncle Hugo, who seemed to be at the root of the discord between them.

My brother calculated. 'Fourteen or fifteen,' he said slowly. 'So young, and a double-dyed Nazi already.'

'That's just blaming someone for other people's mistakes,' said my sister, looking at him as scornfully as she could. 'When I was fifteen or sixteen I went to the stadium to see the Pope.'

'You don't mean that seriously, do you?' asked my brother, with a menacing undertone.

'Yes, I do,' said my sister challengingly. 'Michael Jackson, the Pope, Hitler in the nineteen-thirties – it's all the same to children. They want to see a star.'

'What do you think about that?' said my brother, turning indignantly to my younger cousin. 'Manipulating the past!'

'Oh, do stop it, you two!' groaned my cousin, while my sister got up to go and see to the children.

'And that lovely family tree,' my brother called after her. 'The one you liked to copy out as a child so much! Where do you think Uncle Hugo got it from?'

Role Play

One day my brother turned up with an expression on his face promising sensational news, and announced that we weren't Jewish after all.

'What do you mean?' asked my father, confused. 'So why did I emigrate, then?'

My uncle just shook his head.

Both my cousins shrugged, for they had an idea what he was getting at and knew it didn't affect them.

My sister was relieved. Only recently she had told my father that her boyfriend, Dr Quack's son, thought she had a Jewish nose. She had not got around to explaining that her boyfriend meant it as a compliment and she had taken it the same way, for my father had immediately fallen into a rage. As my father never fell into a rage, and indeed hardly ever even reproved, scolded or punished his children, leaving their upbringing entirely to their respective mothers, this was a very interesting and somewhat alarming phenomenon.

'What kind of rot does the stupid boy think he's talking?' shouted my father, beside himself with fury. 'The lad's never seen a live Jew!'

'Yes, he has,' retorted my sister, who although intimidated was ready to stand up for her first love. 'He's seen you!'

My father wasn't listening. He ranted and roared and denied outright that there could be anything Jewish in itself about his children, or at least anything identifiable. 'Look at

Schacherl,' shouted my father, dragging into the argument a school friend of my sister's who had played the part of a little Jewish girl in a prize-winning film about the Holocaust years before. 'Schacherl looks Jewish enough for seven!'

'Schacherl comes from the Mühlviertel district and so do both her parents,' said my sister doggedly. She seemed, although she would never admit it later, slightly disappointed. For despite his ranting she still thought my father an expert on the subject of all things Jewish, the only one available too, and at the time she would have rather liked to think she had a pretty Jewish nose.

But then my brother appeared, and with his dramatic introductory announcement undermined the last of her certainties.

'It's like this,' he began, determined to make his story as exciting as possible, 'the whole thing goes back practically to Abraham.' At the time my brother was in the middle of his Jewish phase, as my uncle mockingly said. My uncle himself was known to be dead against all religions and spiritual affairs in general. To know what a Jew is, in his view, you hardly needed 'private coaching in how to keep the Sabbath', as he put it.

My brother, who on the one hand craved a thorough knowledge of such subjects, because he found it increasingly awkward to be unable to tell Yom Kippur from Rosh Hashana, but on the other hand knew his family well enough to be slightly embarrassed by that craving, had first claimed a purely scholarly reason for taking these private lessons: the study of Popelnik that he planned to complete demanded a trip to Israel. And for that, and for work that he hoped to do among the archives there, he would like at least some grasp of the basic linguistic and religious concepts . . . so he said, and in one way it was probably true.

At my elder cousin's recommendation, my brother took private lessons with Birn Franzberger's wife. Birn was my elder cousin's best friend, although the two of them didn't really agree on anything except their basic allegiance to a kind of humanism that Birn thought particularly Jewish, while my brother saw it in political terms – 'two Jews, you get three opinions,' as Birn always used to say.

In line with his parents' expectations, my elder cousin had tried to be a Jewish communist as long as he could. That meant coming out on the side of the Arabs at the time of the Six Days' War, when he was rising twenty. The Communist Party of Austria was pro-Arab, and so too was my cousin.

'Just as well I didn't know you then,' sighed Birn later, when the conversation came round to the subject, 'or I'd have murdered you.' Birn, the son of Jews from Eastern Europe who had ended up in Vienna by sheer chance in the post-war chaos, had tried emigrating to Israel several times, but he always came back again because, although he would never have admitted it, it was too hot for him there. Deep inside him he was ashamed of that. Of course he had been in Israel during the Six Days' War and had risked his life, although, as he confessed to my cousin, he would forbid his own son to do any such thing today.

Anyway, my cousin, that good communist, stuck to the pro-Arab, anti-Israeli side for over ten years. But when he was supposed to be throwing eggs and tomatoes at the Israeli ambassador during the thirtieth anniversary celebrations for the founding of the state of Israel, he deserted his post at the Messepalast on a sudden impulse. Stationed in the Messepalast that day, he saw some old Viennese ladies running away in hysterics because they thought what his comrades were doing was an attack by the PLO. And then he couldn't go on with it. He went away, head bent, hands deep in his coat pockets, and as soon as he was far enough off to feel he was unobserved, he took his few eggs and tomatoes out and disposed of them in a litter bin.

'That was when I understood what a Hitler Jew is,' he

always said later, with a defiant expression. 'You try hard, but there's a point when they get so anti-Semitic that you just have to be Jewish again.'

This remark ritually acted as the starting signal for a bitter argument with Birn. Whenever my cousin began talking about 'modern Hitler Jews', which was just another term for what Birn called, in derogatory tones, 'Jews who think like their opponents', Birn got extremely worked up. He thought that after 1945 at the latest you had to decide about being Jewish for yourself. Just defining yourself in terms of your forebears' persecution was not enough. Anyone who wanted to be a Jew today had to do a minimum to ensure that the Jewish tradition was passed on. But that was just the point that enraged my cousin, who held precisely the opposite opinion. Since 1945, he thought, there were clearly more Jews than just those who organised themselves into the Jewish Community and went to synagogue.

'You could stop being a Jew before the Shoah – you can't any more,' he shouted at Birn, 'and that's a burden too!' First my cousin was a communist and thus automatically godless, but then, when he wasn't a communist any more, he didn't join the Jewish Community because his children, unlike him, would not be accepted into it without question.

'Get your children to learn a few things,' Birn always shouted back. 'You can't make it that easy for yourself.'

Then my cousin started complaining of the senile old rabbis who still stuck to the principle of matrilineal descent, totally outdated since the invention of paternity tests. Here at least Birn and my cousin agreed, so their quarrel always ended with a reconciliation and usually a joke too.

After the question of communism had solved itself for him, my now rootless cousin joined one of the Jewish groups that were springing up out of the ground at the beginning of the eighties. These groups were looking for a Jewish identity outside religion, and were mainly made up of disillusioned ex-communists and the rebellious scions of devout Orthodox families. My cousin once took my brother with him. But now came the first really difficult test of my cousin's new awareness of Jewish identity, for Anny Kennich, who made her apartment available for the meetings of the group, unceremoniously threw my brother out.

From then on, though feeling guilty about it, my cousin persuaded himself that she was acting out of some kind of exaggerated feminist feeling, because my brother had been accused of being a male chauvinist after an unhappy love affair, and girl students who were complete strangers to him might sometimes still spit in front of his feet.

But my brother, for his part, was so shocked by Anny Kennich's real reason, stridently expressed, that he buried himself even deeper in his studies of Popelnik, until he had enough material to shake the whole Republic of Austria. He tried to put Anny Kennich's reason out of his mind, but unfortunately his Popelnik studies, together with the course in Hebrew which appeared to be a necessary part of them, led him straight back to it one or two years later, when he was on the point of publishing his conclusions. My poor brother had completed his education as a historian, but in the middle of his triumph he came back to the original problem again. Like the hedgehog in the fable, Anny Kennich seemed to be lurking round every corner.

My brother had come upon Popelnik at the very beginning of his studies, when he was still in the middle of his communist phase. In his course on 'An Introduction to the Study of History', the lecturer wanted to discuss the problems of oral transmission. The students were asked to find, bring along and present to the class some oral source next week. My brother almost forgot.

For at the beginning of his university studies, my brother felt free of everything: free of family constraints and those boring afternoons spent in the shop in the company of my now ancient grandparents and the ever-changing sportsmen from Eastern Europe, in whom he ostentatiously took no interest. At first the family had been very proud of him and let him do whatever he liked. 'He's a student,' my grandfather told everyone he met, 'my grandson will be a doctor.' In fact my brother spent most of his time at Trotskyite discussion groups, writing pamphlets and having earnest political conversations with pretty girls, trying to recruit them to the cause. He gave little thought to his studies themselves; he knew he'd master them somehow or other.

On the evening before the next class, he remembered his homework. We were visiting Fredi Hals, we had polished off all Auntie Hals's beef roulades, which in Vienna were considered world-famous, and Fredi was just asking if anyone would like some more 'bottled fruit', as he always called fruit compote, the usual dessert of the seventies, when my brother suddenly whispered, 'Oh, shit,' and attracted reproving glances.

'Oral sources?' inquired Fredi. 'Oh, I can give you oral sources.' And when he had rummaged around for a while in the dusty cases where he obviously also kept his foreign currencies – in the middle of his rummaging he pressed several thick wads of forints briefly into my brother's hand, saying, 'Hold those a moment!' – he gave him a few yellowed pages of the transcript of a witness statement put on record just after the war by the Haganah paramilitaries. So next day my brother held forth in class about a woman called Chaya Bendel, born in Minsk, what she had suffered in the various camps, and in particular about an SS man known as '*děcko*', 'child', because he looked so young and innocent.

'Useless for historical purposes,' my brother commented, proud of his lack of emotion, 'too vague, too general.' It wasn't even certain, he said, whether it would be worth while investigating the identity of '*děcko*', although according to her statement Frau Bendel, who by now was probably untraceable if not dead, thought she remembered that his real name was Popelnik and he was either Bavarian or Austrian.

After my brother, a girl who had interviewed her grandmother spoke. She played an audio-cassette in broad Viennese dialect, beginning, 'Ah, what a pretty young servant girl I was back then, I was real smart too,' and everyone laughed because the old lady gave such a comic account of the funeral of Emperor Franz Josef. This girl's success with her harmless old granny from the Weinviertel district annoyed my brother. His sense of being trumped was probably his reason for coming back again and again over the next few weeks to that '*děcko*' whom no one at the university seemed to want to hear about. 'They just wanted all that old imperial-and-royal nostalgic stuff,' complained my brother. 'What a poor sort of country we are.' And that, probably, was the start of my brother's interest in Felix Popelnik, President of the Austrian Skiing Association. It went on for years.

When my brother had learnt enough to equip him for his trip to Israel, Birn Franzberger and his wife invited my whole family to their home for supper on a Friday evening. Surprisingly, my father agreed to go. In the past he would have nothing to do with such things, and when Jews came on the TV screen, for instance swaying back and forth in front of the Wailing Wall, he just stared with his jaw dropping, and if he caught himself staring quickly left the room. However, at the time when my brother was radicalising his quest for meaning through taking Hebrew lessons and fanatically investigating the Popelnik case, he managed to infect my father. My brother never seems to have noticed that himself, for he registered only their misunderstandings, what he saw as my father's constant failure to appreciate him, the way that they talked without really communicating, all the misery of their complex relationship. Yet now that my brother sometimes gave or lent him books, made my father take him to the synagogue – 'after all, you're a member of the Jewish Community!' urged my brother, who didn't like to venture in on his own – nostalgia suddenly blossomed in my ageing father, who was past the middle of his life, and found a shamefaced look back more rewarding than the view ahead. My father had read newspapers rather than books all his life, but one day he read Joseph Roth's *Job* and was deeply moved by it. 'I come from there too,' my father said of Mendel Singer, that poverty-stricken, narrow-minded, non-sporting and humourless small-town Jew, and he almost had tears in his baby-blue eyes. His children and nephews roared with laughter and told him it was the onset of senility. For that very reason, however, he was happy to go along to the Franzbergers, as a seeker who was trying not to be too curious.

When we reached the Franzbergers' my brother was already waiting in the doorway. 'Don't ring,' he said in conspiratorial tones, 'even the electric doorbell mustn't work today.' Birn, who was standing behind him, laughed. 'He'll be one of the Orthodox yet,' he mocked, tugging at my brother's belt, where the door keys to his apartment were dangling. 'You're not supposed to carry anything on the Sabbath,' chuckled Birn, 'but only the really devout take it to the lengths of wearing a belt like that.'

After that it was an infuriatingly long time before my brother, chasing around the Franzbergers' festively lit apartment like an excited schoolboy, found his kippah. As a little boy he had been given one – by Aunt Gustl, of all people – embroidered with edelweiss and gentians, and his mother had only recently found it again. He was now infatuated by this kippah with its Alpine themes.

He pressed a large guest kippah into my father's hand. The seam stood out from it slightly, and partly because of that it looked like a stranded spaceship from a distant galaxy on my father's head. On the usual occasions such as visits to

Israel, wreath-layings and Holocaust memorial days, all the non-Jewish politicians of our time wore their kippahs more naturally and gracefully than my father, who when he put it on always looked like a Jewish schoolboy got up in Jewish schoolboy costume against his will.

The candles were lit, Birn pronounced the blessing, and Birn's small son also had something to say and do. My brother's expression showed what an effort he was making first to take careful note of all this, and second to feel emotional. He kept looking at my father as if wishing for a spark of his own enthusiasm to pass to him too. For this was their native land, their truth, this was their point of origin, wasn't it? My father was lost in thought, grave and intent. Before he did anything, sat down, drank or picked up his fork, he made sure that he wasn't the first. He looked like a newcomer entering the inner sanctum of a secret society for the first time, and terrified of doing something wrong. When I think of my father today, I always see two contrasting images of him: the outrageously good-looking, carefree young man being carried from the football field on the shoulders of enthusiastic fans, and this rather embarrassed, ageing man with the recalcitrant kippah on his head, trying to understand what the Sabbath is all about.

The Franzbergers did their best to be relaxed, helpful and hospitable, but the evening simply could not shake off the character of a folklore spectacle. Birn, of course, felt it too. In the hope of getting everyone to loosen up, he began talking about all the things the Orthodox did in Israel to satisfy the Sabbath prohibitions. How they put stickers over the lights in their refrigerators the day before, so that the light 'wouldn't begin to work' when they opened the fridge door. And how, on the Sabbath itself, they opened the fridge only when the motor was actually running, so as not to be guilty of setting it off. How there were Sabbath lifts in all the hotels that went up and down automatically, stopping on all floors, because anything 'that works anyway' was allowed. My father shook his head in amazement. Finally, when Birn's son was telling us how the Orthodox Jews even tore off the day's ration of loo paper on the eve of the Sabbath, my brother had had enough. He was the one who spoiled the pious atmosphere.

'Okay, so some observe the Sabbath in one way and some in another,' he protested, 'but why do you always have to make a joke of it?'

'I only wanted to explain that it's different from the Catholics, who have just one Pope and just one truth,' smiled Birn, but my brother felt that this was a personal attack.

'How can I help it if he had me baptised?' he shouted, pointing to his father.

'What, me?' asked my father in horror, raising his hands defensively. 'It was your mother who . . .' But at this point Frau Franzberger came in. She handed my brother a Hebrew text which he began to read, stumbling over the words. When he had finished, he translated the contents for us, explained the tradition and meaning behind the text, and received lavish praise from the Franzbergers. So our first Sabbath eve ended peacefully and in an atmosphere of erudition.

We couldn't be Jews, my brother finally explained, raising his voice, because our grandmother had not been Jewish, and for Jews only your mother counts. We weren't even half-Jewish, because our father wasn't. He had learnt these rules from Frau Franzberger, and now that he came to think of it, that was exactly why he had been thrown out of the Jewish group to which my elder cousin had tried taking him a few years ago.

'Yes, picture the scene!' smiled my younger cousin, who loved this story, although he had it only from hearsay. 'There stood Anny Kennich at the door, in all seriousness distinguishing between the various ex-communists by Halacha criteria.'

'It was really all because of women's lib,' my elder cousin mildly objected. He still felt ashamed of letting my brother go but staying on himself.

'We really ought to throw you two out now,' snapped my brother, 'because discussion between half-Jews and quarter-Jews is supposed to be confidential too.' My cousins were amused, for unlike the three of us they were of impeccable Jewish descent through their English mother. At around the time when his brother was turning away from the communists, my younger cousin had even joined the Jewish Community, married an Israeli woman, and now lived a more devoutly Jewish life than anyone in my family since our great-grandfather.

'I was Jewish enough for the Nazis,' my father feebly defended himself.

'The Nuremberg Laws and the Halacha are not the same thing,' said my brother despairingly.

'You don't say!' mocked my uncle. 'How amazing!'

'You do have problems, don't you?' said my sister, picking up her pink shoulder-bag and going off, probably to neck with Dr Quack's son in the cinema.

My uncle did not conceal the way this subject got on his own nerves. 'Your theory would make Nandl Königsbee more Jewish than me,' he scoffed, for as always he saw the wider implications while other people were still entangled in their feelings. 'Nandl was definitely a Nazi, though, I don't need any religious guidelines to tell me that.'

'But how do *you* explain it all to yourself?' asked my confused father.

'I don't need to explain anything to myself, I know who I am,' my uncle self-confidently assured him.

That wasn't good enough for my father. He had just been making his first diffident attempts to explore something that was obviously a part of him more closely. As secretly and unobtrusively as possible, he had got hold of books about Auschwitz and Mauthausen, the Nuremberg Trials and the

Third Reich; he had found the name of his stout, black-clad grandmother, whom he hardly remembered, in the Theresienstadt Memorial Book; and he suddenly felt full of pride because, unlike his brother, he had never left the Jewish Community, even though all he had ever done so far was to pay his membership subscription. So was he supposed to accept that now he finally had enough time and courage to study something he had concealed as well as he could all his life, it wasn't really the truth after all?

My father decided to do something about it. He bestirred himself. He made inquiries. He put on his checked hat – once past fifty, my father affected hats with ridiculous patterns and bought them in sizes much too small for him, so that they were always worn too far on top of his head – and he went to the Jewish Community offices in Seitenstettengasse. He patiently went through all the security procedures, humbly told a suspicious Israeli behind bulletproof glass what he wanted, emptied his pockets, showed his ID, let them X-ray him, and finally found himself down in the basement with the registers.

'Good day,' he said, out of force of habit, to the empty room.

'Yes?' a little woman who suddenly popped up behind the counter replied, with every sign of suspicion.

'I phoned,' said my father courteously, 'because I'd like to know if I'm Jewish.'

'Oh, it's you,' said the stern little woman, and became friendlier. 'Yes, I've just found your details.'

She went to fetch a huge old register and opened it in front of my father. She showed him the line with the handwritten register of his birth, along with the day of his circumcision and the names of the witnesses present – 'Kind of like godparents, were they?' asked my father, and the woman sighed, but then nodded. My father looked at this entry for a long time, and the woman gave him plenty of time. There was nothing there but his dates, no 'provisionally' or 'yet to be approved by the rabbi', or whatever my anxious father may have imagined.

'To think of these old books still being here!' he marvelled.

'What would you expect?' replied the woman sharply. 'The Nazis took very good care of them.' In the end the little woman even fetched my father a coffee, and then he sat there with her for another half an hour, shy and fascinated, with his checked hat on his knees. She looked up my uncle's date of birth and Katzi's. They had all three been entered in those stout volumes. When my father finally and in some trepidation came out with the Halacha difficulty, she just waved it impatiently away.

'The fact is,' she told my father, and she couldn't have made him happier, 'that made no difference at all at the time.'

'So if my father said back then, my children are Jews and will be registered, that was it,' my relieved father told us afterwards. 'They weren't so strict about it in those days.' My brother understood at once. *After* the catastrophe was different from *before* the catastrophe – 'That's only logical,' he cried, striking his brow. 'And then, soon after 1945, Israel was founded and people needed qualifications to immigrate, they had to have rules.'

The result was that my father was a Jew, there was no doubt of it, and that was all that mattered. The woman at the Community office had said so, my father was properly registered everywhere, so there was no more to be said. My brother and my father managed to go on skating on this thin ice, but they always had a guilty conscience about it.

For one contradiction remained. These days Christians too seemed to know all about the rules of descent laid down in the Halacha, and depending on the result of their genealogical inquiries would be either respectful or patronising, which induced both of them to start disowning my grandmother's origins.

In line with their different characters, one of them did so almost imperceptibly, in little details, while the approach of the other was active and extrovert. All my father really did was to stop replying to Uncle Hugo's Christmas cards, although such a discourtesy went against the grain. He justified it at the time by saying that Uncle Hugo's 'propaganda', as he suddenly began calling those pathetic pamphlets about the little village of Engelsberg, was getting him down.

My brother, on the other hand, began systematically placing his family history in a larger context. He shifted the emphasis of his work. As a historian, he had so far concentrated mainly on religious schisms of the past, the Cathars, the Baptists, the Calvinists, and was considered an expert on the late Middle Ages and the early modern period. Now he published an essay entitled 'Underground. Jews in Vienna, 1941–1945' in a journal devoted to modern history, and added, 'In memory of my grandfather', letting the general public assume that my grandfather had survived the entire war in hiding.

And the very next thing he did was to explode the Popelnik bombshell which, as he probably guessed, would not only divert his own attention from his complex family history very effectively, but would silence the Anny Kennichs of this world for a long time to come.

The essay 'Like Felix from the Ashes?', published in three instalments in what was regarded as a left-wing news magazine, split Austria to an extent never known before. It was the prelude to the Waldheim affair, and today not a few think that only Popelnik made Waldheim possible a year and a half later. Without Popelnik and the alarming amount of popular indignation felt against my brother, there might never have been so much media pressure on Waldheim or what, from the Austrian angle, was so much transparent interest in his wartime record. For if Popelnik had been guilty, if some flaw had stained even his character, then at least he should not be the only one. Such was the paradoxical logic of a nation feeling humiliated all over again as it was brought to bear on Waldheim a little later.

Felix Popelnik was a kind of folk hero. He was respectfully known as 'the sports Czar', and when he became President of the Skiing Association he radically reformed the system to foster new talent. Popelnik thought up the idea of ski schools and got it politically implemented, he sought for and found sponsors, he introduced the *Groschenzeitung* Sports Aid organisation and Stiegl Beer Stipends for children from poor families, and his particular hobbyhorse was winter sports for the disabled. He travelled to winter sports resorts, accompanied by the media, which he handled brilliantly, and during the season he attended some event or other almost every day: a young people's competition, a slalom race for eight-year-old girls in Saalbach, a downhill race for fifteen-year-old boys in Sankt Anton, a two-day skiing and tobogganing event for the schools of the Gastein Valley. 'Let's concentrate on what we do best,' he told the cameras, smiling, 'skiing, ski-jumping, cross-country skiing, tobogganing, ice-skating, rock-climbing,' and the Austrians hung on his every word.

The results proved him right. A tide of medals and Olympic victories washed over the winter sportsmen and women of Austria, and the popularity of all kinds of winter sports reached great heights. At that time, when Annemarie Moser-Pröll and Franz Klammer were racing from victory to victory, there was hardly a child in the country whose ambition was not to be a downhill skier. Popelnik even got the Austrians to wax enthusiastic about tobogganing.

But Popelnik had more to offer than the success of his skiers and ski-jumpers, who themselves never tired of suggesting that they owed it all to 'our President'. He was more than a skilful and successful sports manager. When Kreisky's star was sinking because, old, sick and bad-tempered as he was, he seemed to think nothing but the Palestinian question was of any importance, Popelnik rose to become a new and more accessible symbol of integration. Sport was less complex and alarming but far more profitable than politics, and Popelnik was extremely good at presenting sport as a microcosm of true greatness. 'A good sportsman is healthy, strong and fair – why aren't we all sportsmen and women?' Popelnik's credo could be reduced to this principle.

And so wherever Popelnik went he emphasised the value of the movement, he urged the Austrians to eat a healthy diet, he recalled long-forgotten natural remedies. Popelnik and his chubby-cheeked wife were everywhere, in the newspapers, on television, at sporting events and benefits, at cookery exhibitions and health check-ups for those who were already well. Then Popelnik's daughter opened a health farm where the cooking, training and treatments were all in line with his ideas. Soon the 'enormous popularity', as Popelnik modestly confessed to the papers, of this health farm meant that there had to be a mail-order business. The Austrians ordered Popelnik herb mixtures and Popelnik compresses, they cooked out of *Popelnik's Big Book of Natural Recipes*, and got into condition with *Keep Fit with Felix*. When an economics magazine published an article trying to investigate the 'Popelnik Empire' in depth, its editor was fired a few weeks later, allegedly for chronic lack of imagination.

At the end of the seventies voices were raised calling for Popelnik to enter politics. A questionnaire showed that after the Chancellor and Franz Klammer, Popelnik was the best-known Austrian of all. But Popelnik kept a low profile. It was said that he had excellent relations with both political parties and didn't want to upset anyone. So he went on patting small children encouragingly on the head when they won their first medals, he was the first to leap over the barrier and congratulate Annemarie Moser-Pröll when she won a gold medal at Lake Placid, and his comment when a blind man from Vorarlberg broke the downhill world record for the blind went down in history. 'Today Schorsch has shown us that a man can do anything,' he said with tears in his eyes. 'He doesn't even need to be able to see his goal.'

When the famous Felix Popelnik, not yet sixty-five, fell off a home exercise machine at his own health farm and died two days later after a heart attack, Austrians from the Bregenzer Wald to the Hungarian border mourned him, and the country was in shock. The Austrian Postal Service was the first to react, issuing a special stamp which sold out within a few days. The bereaved Skiing Association roused itself to offer a large sum of prize money for an annual Felix Popelnik Memorial Race, and then sank into months of depressed inactivity.

And of all people, it was this Felix Popelnik, this undisputed benefactor, practically canonised after his death, whom my brother unmasked as a war criminal. At this point most Austrians had forgotten that there had ever been a war at all, let alone that crimes had been committed in it. A few historians had written various essays trying to explode the myth that Austria was 'Hitler's first victim', yes, but they were disparagingly described as 'lefties' and punished by being ignored.

Then along came my brother. The trouble he had taken to prove that this Popelnik, on the first-hand evidence of Chaya Bendel and several other survivors, was one and the same as the sports Czar had been enormous, although he still lacked one final piece of evidence to clinch the case. But the chain of clues was overwhelming, even though, or perhaps because, all Popelnik's personal papers from this period were missing. The name of the SS man whom my brother identified in German and American archives and who had served at Theresienstadt and Buchenwald was Friedrich, but a stray bomb had fallen towards the end of the war in Felix

Popelnik's home town, destroying all the records of those born from 1915 to 1922. The family initially claimed that Friedrich was an elder half-brother, and anyway, someone who had worked so hard for the disabled could hardly have been a Nazi, could he? Unfortunately the Popelnik family couldn't manage to come up with so much as a photograph of the half-brother, who had gone missing in Russia, they said, but soon they weren't saying anything at all, and instead were referring all journalists to their lawyers.

Be that as it may, historians now consider that the Popelnik case has been proved, and it is sometimes compared to the affair of Dr Hans Schneider, academic and SS officer, who in 1945 adopted a new identity as Hans Schwerte and married his own 'widow'. Like the German folklorist and scholar, Popelnik seems to have expended a vast amount of energy on drawing a veil over his career, and like Schneider alias Schwerte he almost succeeded. But unlike Schneider alias Schwerte he was already dead when he was unmasked and could not, as Waldheim later did, discredit himself by the attitudes he adopted. In the first flush of indignation there were even some who blamed Popelnik's death on my brother. Yet my brother had never tried to meet or interview Popelnik, as the circles in which the Popelnik family moved claimed for a while that he did. My brother was a historian, not a journalist, and he firmly believed that written sources could speak, even sources no longer in existence.

The Popelnik affair made my father feel that the bottom had almost dropped out of his world. When 'Like Felix from the Ashes?' was published, and the storm had broken over us and the rest of the country, he often asked himself despairingly why he hadn't taken more interest in my brother's work earlier. Kindly, rather absent-minded man that he was, with his craving for harmony, he seriously thought that he could have prevented some of the fuss if he'd only known about it in time. As things were, however, the whole business was 'unfortunate', as my father put it. He was inclined to confuse the affair itself with his own state of mind. He would have agreed, gritting his teeth, that anyone was free to do research, and historians had a duty to investigate all the complex aspects of a case and describe them as they were. But did his own son have to conjure up such a nightmare?

If 'Dr Popelnik', as my father always scrupulously called the late sportsman, in line with Austrian custom, if Dr Popelnik was proved to have been that concentration camp thug, well, then and only then, in his opinion, could such a 'witch-hunt' and 'trial by media' be in some way justified, 'not that I can ever approve of it in a democracy.' But as things were? Assumptions, hints, clues, no more, and then all the international fuss, with Austria suddenly misrepresented as a Nazi country. 'And who should know about that if not me?'

'You're always so lenient to such people,' my uncle complained.

'But you don't have to . . . to . . . ,' said my father, struggling for words.

'You don't have to do what?' asked my uncle, interested.

'. . . bring it all out like that,' my father finally managed to say. 'Why does my son of all people have to be an agitator?'

'Why?' asked my uncle. 'Look at yourself, why don't you?' But then my father felt injured, although he muttered that he just didn't understand anything any more.

My father never talked about what he had to endure at the tennis club, the centre of his life, during the weeks which have gone down in the post-war history of the country as those of the Popelnik affair, but it is obvious that he suffered severely. At first far more members of the club ostentatiously cut him dead than there were members who warned him that a family may be held jointly responsible for the actions of one of its number. He probably survived the affair only because he himself was such a great sportsman, and ultimately that was what mattered.

His specific suffering was never properly understood by the rest of the family. In some respects my father, the former national footballer, was the one who had ventured out of more esoteric areas and into 'the real Austria', and so it all touched him particularly closely. My brother mingled with historians and intellectuals, my cousins moved in the circles of their mainly Jewish friends and business partners, and so did my uncle, although he didn't really mix with anyone much, but stayed at home with Aunt Ka and the dog, brooding. Only my father – of his own free will, but what difference does that make? – had moved in a world of car dealers and fashion retailers, builders, businessmen who leased petrol stations, diary salesmen, professional jokers, top sportsmen, and others whose education was only on the average side. From that vantage point, the situation in politically turbulent times looked very different, less theoretical, earthier. Of all my family, my father seemed the least afraid. While the Austrian press was methodically seeking out Jews to ask them whether the perceptible rise in anti-Semitism made them think of emigrating to Israel, while my cousins, with the light of battle in their eyes, informed such questioners that they were Austrians whether the Nazis liked it or not, while my brother had sensibly disappeared from view after the publication of his essay and stayed out of reach of the media for some time, my father did not even ignore the questions.

My brother had dealt himself a new hand of cards with this first major publication. He might be abused, threatened, and drawn into years of legal proceedings, but he was also admired and respected for his courage. 'It was about time,' my younger cousin said jubilantly, 'for someone to shift modern history from the cultural pages to the sports pages!'

'The only part of the paper anyone really reads in this country,' agreed my elder cousin.

Anny Kennich was one of the first to kiss and hug my brother when she met him in the coffee-house, and she favoured him with a monologue in which the key terms were 'at long last', 'mendacious country', and 'about time too'.

The conservative press set whole research teams to work to undermine his Popelnik theories, but these special commando units merely subverted the intention by coming up with yet more evidence that my brother was right. The *Groschenzeitung,* as might have been expected, was in its element, and made the 'brutal pillorying' of the Popelnik family front-page news for days. It claimed that for weeks Popelnik's grandchildren dared not go to school, and even quoted my brother as saying, 'I didn't want that.' My brother went straight to a lawyer, because he had never spoken to the *Groschenzeitung* at all, but the lawyer advised him to ignore it. A denial would certainly make it sound as if my brother had actively wanted to torment the innocent grandchildren.

After a few stirring weeks and much international reporting, the first waves died down, and then interdisciplinary retrospective studies began. An Austrian psychiatrist called on the country to think less about the accusations themselves than the aggressive and defensive reaction to them. A brain specialist came up with an old study of his own, according to which Austrians remember and forget in quite a different way from 'the citizens of comparable neighbouring states' – he had tested the memory for numbers and faces of a thousand people in each of the countries of Austria, Switzerland and Liechtenstein. It was a few months before the first historians spoke up, claiming that the accusations against Popelnik had been known for a long time. 'Historical writing that just concentrates on individuals,' they muttered, implying that to understand history properly you had to see it all in the much wider context. Although my brother was under enormous public pressure, it was only criticism by his colleagues that annoyed him, and he wrote a polemical article about a series of well-known Nazi criminals and their 'outstanding love of children and animals, confirmed at length after the event by all who knew them'. That had been really unnecessary, complained those who had been only envious before but could raise no real objection to my brother's work, and they added reproachfully that 'now, but only now' he had really gone too far.

Some time had to pass before it was clear what would be left after the Popelnik Affair. My brother had triumphantly succeeded in his aim of demystifying the sports Czar. He had certainly encouraged a new way of looking at 'the recent past', as the newspapers euphemistically liked to put it, and now the Waldheim election was already breaking over the country.

Yet the Popelnik Affair also turned against its creator. The name of Popelnik would be linked to my brother's for ever, as if they were twins. To this day, my brother is regarded in Austria as 'the Popelnik hunter', the historian who 'started the Popelnik Affair', or depending on your point of view the man 'who did untold harm to Austrian skiing'. My brother had ruined Felix Popelnik's reputation, but rather unexpectedly it worked the other way round as well. That first biographical study of my brother's, extensively researched and scrupulously written, cast an almost impenetrable shadow over his later work, because the name of his first subject became his own nickname. To avoid featuring in every political argument of the day as 'the high-profile historian who fouled his own nest', as the media so often approvingly described him, and to avoid being constantly asked for his comments, my brother even went abroad to work for a while, but it was no good: none of his later writings attracted nearly as much attention as 'Like Felix from the Ashes?'.

When my brother realised that, he moved away from contemporary history and, with another surprising change of direction, specialised in the history of the Sephardic Jews. Today, he critically remarked in an interview, the rich history of Judaism was almost entirely obliterated by the Holocaust, and he would happily leave the fashion for modem history to younger and less controversial historians 'for the sake of the cause'.

To his father, he challengingly represented this step of his as a filial act. 'If I go on studying the Nazis you'll never enjoy life any more,' he infuriatingly told my father, who simply shrugged. No one in my family had even known just who the Sephardic Jews were before.

In the course of his Sephardic studies, my brother came upon a banker of our own name who had founded a bank in Alexandria in a past century. It was only a short step to the jocular supposition that this banker must be an ancestor of ours. From now on the members of my family kept enthusiastically imagining how we might walk into this bank, which apparently was still in existence, and draw out money – we could amazingly but truthfully just sign the withdrawal slip with the bank's own name! We laughed heartily at the idea of being impoverished descendants of an Oriental banker, until my elder cousin's wife, an intellectual from north Germany with a mischievous mind, pointed out that this phenomenon had been understood ever since Freud: it was the farmer's boy who is convinced that he's an aristocrat's illegitimate son. 'Inflated fantasies of grand origins,' she said, beaming all over her face. 'Indulged in by people with a low sense of their own worth.' My elder cousin shook his head sadly and called his wife a spoilsport.

But my brother was not impressed, and went on dreaming his way into the wide-ranging and colourful history of the Jews, moving further and further away from people like Anny Kennich, who were in no position to see anything except in a narrow, personal sense. He wrote a slim textbook on *The Sephardic Jews – Their History and Culture*, which is regarded to this day as a standard work because it is so easy to understand and interestingly written, while still being a serious work of scholarship.

And only very seldom did he let his vulnerable point show, the point which had started him off on all this. Once, at a congress, a colleague who was then studying the latest ethnic expulsions in Europe, and was regarded with deep suspicion by other historians, spoke to him about it. Of course he might have misunderstood something, this colleague made haste to assure my brother when he saw his dark expression. 'My grandmother?' said my brother, annoyed, 'no, no, they only said so to protect themselves! My grandmother was really Jewish!'

Long-Term Consequences

My brother's decision to join the self-help group that called itself 'Half-Jews 2000' was determined by the information that you could choose a pseudonym and keep your real identity secret. The woman who ran the group, a Reform Jewish psychologist, said that identity was much more than a name, so they would refrain from using their real names in the group. The members, she added, smiling happily, would particularly enjoy being able to call themselves anything they thought suitable, or that had a certain meaning for them. My brother immediately felt he was in Paradise, except for a little nagging anxiety at the back of his mind that the whole thing could turn out to be a bad joke, a trap concealing a hidden camera.

My brother had become rather paranoid in his middle years. When his wife made cautious remarks about the possibility of professional treatment for certain mental tensions, he rejected the idea indignantly as an attempt to subject him to psychiatry, but the idea of 'Half-Jews 2000' immediately appealed to him. He represented it to himself and his wife as pure curiosity, born of the hope that he might find inspiration for his work.

The name that my brother chose for the group was Rubber. When he was asked to introduce himself briefly, he explained that as a child his father could play bridge before he could talk, his father's first word had not been 'Mama' or 'Papa', but 'rubber'. Your first word was rather like your first child, he went on, especially for someone like him who worked with language and history. He was very pleased with these remarks. The other participants looked fixedly at him. And 'Rubber', he added, sounded a little like 'Rabbi' too, so he would like to be called Rubber here. 'Pleased to meet you, Rubber,' the others murmured in chorus.

At this time my brother was regularly meeting my uncle for lunch. He had begun making these dates for my father's sake, because it was an unobtrusive way of supporting my uncle. My brother soon found that he enjoyed the meetings and kept on with them for his own reasons. For so long as certain persons who struck sparks off my uncle (his brother my father, his elder son) were not present, so long as he wasn't playing the role he had adopted all his life in front of a full house of the family, my uncle was a good listener and interesting company.

They always ate fish at one of the fish restaurants on the outskirts of the Naschmarkt. They usually discussed politics, almost never the family, and here they had a good understanding between them. Both had quick-fire phrases like 'what a scandal' and 'could only happen in Austria' ready to hand, but at the same time they competed in assuring one another that they felt composure, indeed boredom in contemplating such events, for what else could be expected in this country? At this point my uncle would always mention how in the first months after the war he hadn't for the life of him been able to find any Nazis in Vienna, and my brother laughed bitterly, because he thought that anecdote so extremely typical.

The fish restaurant was also the only place where my brother spoke openly about the 'Half-Jews 2000' group. And my uncle showed an interest in it. My brother did not seem to be speaking of a serious attempt at therapy, for my uncle despised therapy as a 'placebo for people who feel sorry for themselves', but of a kind of ethnological journey of discovery. He particularly liked the case of a young

Tyrolean woman. She called herself Nanny-Goat in the group; she came from a remote mountain village and had discovered by chance, only after the death of both her parents, that her mother had been born Jewish. My uncle and my brother, grinning, discussed the fact that theoretically Nanny-Goat could have gone straight to the Jewish Community office in Seitenstettengasse at any time and had herself registered there without much expense. But Nanny-Goat had to struggle with her extremely anti-Semitic atmosphere upbringing. As a child, both fascinated and horrified, she had accompanied her grandmother on pilgrimage to the church festival commemorating little Anderl of Rinn, allegedly murdered by Jews back in the Middle Ages, and simply couldn't accept this new aspect of her family history. She felt 'dirty', and with a blush described how as children they had never spoken of 'Jews', but of 'Christ's murderers', and now she was punished by turning out to be a Jew herself. My brother was afraid that Nanny-Goat was on the verge of a nervous breakdown, and hoped she would soon leave the group and get more substantial help. He told my uncle that to the best of his knowledge Nanny-Goat was the only person who could talk, chain-smoke, and bite her fingernails at the same time. My brother said he felt sorry for her, with all her cranky ways, for sometimes she would choke on her cigarette smoke and spit out bits of fingernail as she coughed, while smoke poured out of her nose and her eyes were streaming. Must be a pitiful sight, my uncle surmised, unable to suppress a chuckle, and my brother agreed that it was. Then they called the waiter to pay, for my brother had to get back to the university, and my uncle didn't want to leave Aunt Ka alone too long. She was already very ill at this time.

My uncle, who had begun by guarding his fortune carefully, almost avariciously, squandered it within less than two years. To this day we don't know what started him off, although his sons, paradoxically, think it was his constant fear of poverty that robbed him of his money. Or the other way around: fear of poverty had kept him working like a madman and made him lie awake at night, but he lost it when he lost the money too. My little uncle, who was still there somewhere inside my grown-up uncle, had hysterically insisted that he would never have to beg again, never need to ask for credit again, never be dependent on anti-Semitic corner-shop proprietors and bakers again, but as an adult he had failed in his aim, just as his father, my grandfather, had failed decades before. Or perhaps it was all just chance.

My cousins, the only ones to know a few details about it, thought that my uncle had been unable to cope with the late and entirely unexpected success in business of his first wife, the little Englishwoman who, only recently a housewife and mother, had suddenly begun negotiating secret deals between Israel and the Eastern bloc, and they made her rich. At the time, according to my cousins, and out of wounded vanity (for he had a low opinion of the intellectual abilities of both his wives, and indeed doubted whether they had any) my uncle had snapped up a paper and packaging factory from under the little Englishwoman's nose. It later went bankrupt, and that was the beginning of his economic decline. For my uncle, who had lost a lot of money with that company but not everything, had been so panic-stricken, they thought, that in his attempts to recoup his losses he made mistake after mistake. Whether it was really the loss of the packaging firm that sent him so badly off course, no one knows, but it is certain that his considerable fortune was squandered in a fatal series of bad investments, firms that went bust, and unfortunate stock market transactions, just as if he were gambling in the casino. It was typical of him to keep his dire straits to himself. He told neither Fredi Hals nor his sons about it, although he should have realised long ago that his two boys had made something of themselves – one was a gifted businessman, the other a dedicated economic journalist.

When he sold the BMW, my uncle told Aunt Ka that they were too old for such a showy car, and anyway it was just standing around in the wickedly expensive garage. It was all the same to Aunt Ka, who couldn't drive a car herself. Some time he must have asked her to give notice to the cleaning lady, and soon after that not to send washing to the laundry. It seems unlikely that Aunt Ka asked questions or worried. Aunt Ka accepted what her husband did without comment, and showed no sign of anything wrong throughout this period. She was, as I have said, a cheerful and optimistic person as long as her dog was in good health.

But my uncle had changed. Although he had been rather silent and introverted all his life, his manners had always been perfect. There was the way that ashtray of his didn't smell of ash. Suddenly, however, he seemed to lose all control over himself for a while, and by the time my family found out why it was too late. He acted strangely, he was under pressure, every little thing made him fly off the handle. He was always phoning, even in the evening when he was invited to supper, even in restaurants. He would look at the time, then fish out a note of phone numbers with long, unknown dialling codes, and hurry to the telephone. Two or three times he shouted angrily down it so loud that the whole restaurant fell silent, and once a waiter went over and asked him to keep his voice down. Afterwards he verbally chastised the waiter in such an embarrassing way that no one in my family would admit to remembering the incident later, or so they all ingenuously claimed. But I remember very clearly that after we had said goodbye to each other out in the street, my father went back into the restaurant on some excuse and gave the waiter a large tip. Perhaps it was hush money. The waiter had threatened to complain of my uncle to the police when, in a rage, he grabbed the man by the lapels of his jacket and shook him. My uncle was banned from that restaurant in future, and had already been banned from several others in Vienna.

Since it has always been considered very bad form in my family to pry, meddle or offer help unasked, all of which would come into the category of 'showing off', we tried to overlook the obvious changes in my uncle as far as possible. At this time it was particularly difficult to organise a family get-together, because suddenly everyone had so little spare time.

My cousins finally found out the whole story from their mother. The little Englishwoman shook her head helplessly, and explained that she had urged him to have nothing to do with the packaging factory, but he had thought that was just pretence, and accused her of wanting it for herself. Later my elder cousin thought it odd that this packaging factory had originally played a minor part in his mother's business, and wondered how his father had come by the information in the first place.

His mother had been exporting Israeli oranges to the Eastern bloc for some time, a form of trade that officially didn't exist at all because the Warsaw Pact states had declared an embargo on Israel. But the communists wanted those delicious oranges all the same. So my divorced aunt, the little Englishwoman, got this secret trade going on her own initiative. She was probably just the right combination of Jewish, communist, and citizen of a neutral state, as her new passport made her. Anyway, she regularly drove her car on her own from Vienna to Hamburg, boarded unassuming freighter ships, and checked that the fruits really had arrived without any Jaffa stickers on them. Only then were the cargos unloaded. A single crate of fruit with give-away Jaffa stickers in the Eastern bloc would have put an end to the entire orange business. But the little Englishwoman checked carefully and was very discreet in other respects. Payment was not in cash but in goods: bicycles, lathes, printing presses. The countries that wanted the oranges insisted on payment in kind for political reasons, for as they said in the inscrutable Czech, Bulgarian and East German foreign trading firms with whom she worked, 'no money goes to Israel.' The little Englishwoman developed her skill in selling on these products fast and at a profit, until she had earned enough to order another ship carrying oranges.

The packaging firm came into it entirely by chance, when she had to find a market for a few hundred Czech bicycles. She found an Israeli bicycle importer who was a fanatical lover of his own wares. She drove him to Prague, and soon her head was buzzing with all the facts about bicycles that he regaled her with during the journey. Where the bells and the wheels had to be made. How you got certain parts from Taiwan, because they were cheapest there at the time. How the two most important manufacturers in America were at daggers drawn and would presumably both end up defunct. Somewhere in Germany a major supplier had closed down, a disaster! Rubber for the tyres came from there and there alone, or it wasn't worth the money. Air resistance. Whole series of measurements. The little Englishwoman was getting glum. She couldn't even ride a bike herself. Would the Czech bicycles satisfy her customer? She had no idea. You don't have to know everything, she used to say later, you just have to know who to ask. Her husband had seldom given her any answers in the few years of their marriage. First he was in Burma for two years, then he was bad-tempered and hardly home at all, then he was gone. Even then, when he was still with the bank, she had taken an interest in his business and asked about it. But he had just muttered impatiently and glanced coolly at her standing there: two small children at her apron strings, and she'd put on weight too.

The Czech bicycles, she was relieved to hear from her customer when they reached the works in Prague, were easily the best in the world after West German bikes. And the price-to-performance ratio made them the best value anywhere, the Israeli said approvingly. He would take them all, and if there were any more available he'd take those too. He'd like to see all Israel riding Czech bicycles, he said, laughing, but obviously that was out of the question. The little Englishwoman nodded knowledgeably and thought of the Jaffa orange stickers. There was only one change the bicycle expert wanted: the packaging was too bulky. It would take up too much space, he'd be squandering money on transport costs. The little Englishwoman nodded. On the way back, she said, they could stop off in the Weinviertel district where there was a packaging factory near the border. That was how the factory came into it.

Later my cousin suspected that his father had, as it were, been spying on his mother. It couldn't have escaped his notice that her financial conditions had improved greatly – you could tell even from the clothes her sons wore. He was still having lunch with them once a week at a restaurant in the city centre. The little Englishwoman had not asked for anything when they divorced except alimony for the boys. So she lived in a very modest way for the first few years. Decades later her sons, now grown up, would tell her that pride can sometimes be downright idiotic, but then she would always smile and say well, she had got her revenge.

My elder cousin assumed that his father, my uncle, must have noticed his first wife's quiet success story, although he usually took no interest in anything that was not directly concerned with his own affairs. Reluctantly, my elder cousin found that he had to suppose the motive for what followed was pure greed. As if his mother were Croesus in person, and his father wanted only a crumb from her table for everything he touched to turn to gold. The little Englishwoman assured her son that she had warned his father. No one knew how long the bicycle trade between Prague and Haifa would last, and only while it did would the packaging factory do well. 'Look at the place,' she had told her ex-husband. 'Apart from the bicycle packaging they're almost on the breadline.' But he wouldn't listen, the little Englishwoman told my cousin, he always had to know better. Perhaps she had felt a touch of malicious triumph and so had not advised him against his project more forcefully, she finally admitted; perhaps she had secretly hoped he might suffer a loss, she said, looking unhappy. Oh, come on, my cousin had groaned in reply to that, would she please stop feeling responsible for everything?

At first, and this was the worst of it, the factory made good, almost improbable profits. The bicycle trade went on longer than my divorced aunt would ever have thought possible, and other orders were coming in too. It was like a fairy-tale. For no obvious reason, my uncle bought a tar distillery near the packaging factory, and even extended the factory itself. These were his first solo business ventures, made without the backing of Hals & Co. He obviously had his own business empire hovering before his eyes – it must have been as exciting as an addiction. He was like a gambler who believes he has found a system to win at roulette, and against all the odds keeps staking high sums on the same colour: red, red and red again. Paper, tar, paper again. It worked all right for a while, but then the whole construction collapsed. The Austrian paper industry was going through what is euphemistically called structural adjustment, and many small firms failed. Why he had ever bought the clapped-out tar distillery in the first place was something that no one could understand later. 'It was like a hobby, a fancy of his own,' said my younger cousin thoughtfully. 'How can anyone fancy tar?' asked my elder cousin, shaking his head.

My uncle didn't stand a chance. All the same, he tried bribing leading figures in the Czech Foreign Trade Office. He wanted to crank up the trade in bicycles and oranges again, just for the sake of his paper and packaging factory. He was moving in very delicate areas here, and none of it did any good. He frantically tried doing business with what was left. There was nothing to be done about the factory sites in the Weinviertel, within view of the Iron Curtain and its barbed wire and watch-towers. At first the choice of this area with its weak infrastructure had guaranteed low expenditure on wages; now the land proved practically unsaleable. He had to lease it for peanuts to a large farmer. There was nothing else he could do. When my uncle was looking for a buyer for the machinery, Fredi Hals gave him the name of a firm in black Africa that might be interested. However, as my uncle hadn't told Fredi Hals the truth about his situation, Fredi failed to issue a warning. The interested party in black Africa was a con artist ('typical', as my uncle would always say later, starting up the usual embittered family discussion of racism), and my uncle lost even more money. So one thing led to another, and his little empire collapsed.

But none of this came out until Aunt Ka rang the little Englishwoman and asked to see her. Outside the all-inclusive harmony of our family gatherings, this was rather unusual. The little Englishwoman fixed to meet Aunt Ka during business hours in her impressive office; that was the maximum humiliation of which she was capable. Aunt Ka turned up, ladylike as ever, but with her glance fixed on the floor. She quietly asked the little Englishwoman for a loan. The little Englishwoman sat behind her big desk and in friendly tones asked how much. Aunt Ka whispered an enormous figure. Then all was quiet. Even the dachshund, who was wearing his summer cape, kept quiet. The sun shone into the room, the trams ran by ringing their bells below the windows, and the little Englishwoman decided to make this moment last as long as possible. All she could see in front of her was Aunt Ka's hat. At last Aunt Ka looked up with a panic-stricken expression on her face. Then the little Englishwoman rose to her feet, saying, 'Let's see how much I have here,' and filled Aunt Ka's handbag with wad after wad of banknotes. When she had finished, and Aunt Ka asked quietly where she should sign, the little English-woman said, still in friendly tones, 'I think we can both of us remember the amount.'

That was how the little Englishwoman, whose loan, incidentally, was paid off in instalments over many years down to the last groschen, finally made her peace with her ex-husband and fashionably dressed Aunt Ka. And that was how it all came to light. When his sons tried to salvage something from the ruins, it turned out that my uncle had already thrown away more money than he was worth. He had mortgaged the bungalow on the Danube–Oder Canal so heavily that even its sale brought no relief. Furthermore, bungalows on the Danube–Oder Canal were not so fash-ionable now, and you didn't get much for them. My younger cousin shouldered the sad duty of helping Aunt Ka to hold a private flea-market. They sat in the bungalow all one afternoon, letting the embarrassed neighbours have the furnishings at ridiculous prices. With a sleepwalker's smile fixed on her lips, for which my cousin couldn't help admiring her, Aunt Ka sold everything for a song: her tea-set, her silver cake-slices, her crystal vases, the contents of her wine cellar. Only when one buyer began digging up the rosebushes did she burst into tears. But otherwise, my family always said later, she behaved with improbable courage. It was thought much to her credit that she was now doing the laundry herself, and could buy her clothes from the Schöps store at best.

'What's the matter with that?' asked my sister, puzzled. 'We've bought things from Schöps too!'

'But she wasn't used to it,' my mother pointed out. 'It was a huge adjustment for her to make.'

'Other women would have run away from the whole thing,' even my father said, nodding, although usually he had little good to say of his second sister-in-law.

'Where would she have run to,' laughed my sister, once again missing the point, 'with that fat dog?'

Fredi Hals had to dispense with my uncle's services. It was unavoidable, for my uncle's reputation in trade was ruined, and a couple of intemperate scenes with banks and business partners had helped to finish it off. 'It breaks my heart,' wailed Fredi. 'Don't let it worry you,' said my uncle drily. Now that it was all over he had recovered his usual impassivity, as if nothing had happened. My younger cousin managed to find him a modest post as a book-keeper with a business friend of his. As a book-keeper, my uncle was ideal. He was meticulous down to the third decimal point, and since it wasn't his own money he was once again as cautious as he had been in trading for Hals & Co., as attentive as he had been at the sewing-machine in Dean Street.

But the whole story of how he lost his fortune was taboo after that. For a while he didn't even mention the Danube–Oder Canal. The framed colour photo that used to hang in their front room in Vienna was quietly removed by Aunt Ka and disappeared for ever. It had been a rare picture, because we were all together in it and all of us almost happy: victorious in Austria, my uncle stood in front of his own property, the bungalow in summer, brown skin, yellow rubber dinghy, my old grandparents, my uncle with Aunt Ka, my two cousins, my brother, my sister, the dachshund and me. Later it was possible to mention 'those days by the Danube–Oder Canal' again, for after a while my uncle seemed to believe he had sold the bungalow with its garden going down to the water for reasons of good sense, not in disgrace and shame.

At the meetings of 'Half-Jews 2000' the members didn't always talk about themselves, their inner conflicts and where they belonged – should they convert or just come to terms with the facts? There were meetings when the participants discussed the politics of the day, Israel, the questionnaires applying for compensation that many of them helped their parents to fill in, the internal business of the Jewish community. At the time when my brother joined the group, there was a certain amount of fuss about the *mikwe*, the ritual bath, which converts were forbidden to use. Some of the 'half-Jews' had been studying for months in preparation for converting. They were the ones with Jewish fathers. My brother knew from his own experience that people with definitely Jewish names generally had a harder time of it. They sounded like Jews because they bore their fathers' names, they were publicly regarded as Jews because of their names and they felt like Jews, but among Jews themselves they were not regarded as Jews because they didn't have Jewish mothers. Meanwhile the others, who had Jewish mothers and could have joined the Jewish Community without much difficulty, usually had entirely non-Jewish native Austrian names like Zembacher, Hochleitner or Niederreiter, and if things got 'too tough for them', as Nanny-Goat put it, they could always keep their heads down and remain anonymous.

A certain Christl Herschkowitz, whose name in the group was Lea and who had a Jewish father, was the first to convert seriously. She learned Hebrew and took instruction from a rabbi in London for more than a year, flying over to see him several times. 'You need money to convert,' muttered the oldest participant once, a silent man from Leopoldstadt. 'Where there's Jews there's money,' a few others immediately wisecracked, and then they laughed, for it sometimes helped them emotionally to parody the classic anti-Semite. When it came to the point for Lea, and only a visit to the Jewish baths separated her from what she longed for, she was not allowed to use the *mikwe*. It was so long since there had been any converts in Vienna that the rabbis wouldn't take responsibility for the legitimacy of her conversion. Few of the half-Jews could understand how the rabbis felt. Since most of them hardly knew their way around the complicated rites and regulations, and indeed felt threatened by them, the majority assumed the idea to be that Lea might 'desecrate' the Viennese *mikwe*. The atmosphere in the 'Half-Jews 2000' group was explosive. Some members wept. A few were angry and called for a demonstration in Seitenstettengasse. Others thought that would just make the half-Jews look ridiculous. And there were some who humbly accepted every humiliation and warned, timidly, of the dangers of escalation, because such discord would only attract the attention of anti-Semites and the *Groschenzeitung*. They quarrelled with the pro-demo camp over whether this was a 'conflict within Judaism' to be averted, or whether the Community office was being intentionally provocative, so as to antagonise the half-Jews and keep them at arm's length. So there was bitter argument this way and that until a phone call came from the Jewish Community saying that Lea could have her ritual bath in Budapest. The 'Half-Jews 2000' decided to make it a group outing in her honour. Lea was as excited as a little girl.

What with all these complications, which happened to be reaching their peak when my brother joined the group, he had plenty of opportunity to get used to it all before he came out with his individual story and the reason that had led him to join 'Half-Jews 2000'.

It was ultimately because of Canada. He had suffered other setbacks before that, experiences that left him furious and baffled. Being thrown out by Anny Kennich was only the first in a whole series. But Canada was the last straw. After Canada he knew he must clear the whole thing up for himself. His reason for going to Canada had been a large congress on the Sephardic tradition. My brother suffered quite badly from fear of flying, and in the normal way would never have accepted an invitation from so far away. But when the international scholars studying the Sephardic tradition decided to meet in Canada, he had just begun investigating the story of the aunt he had never met.

The state of information about her within the family was shockingly scanty. When he asked his father about her, the only answer was a muttered, 'Died during the war . . . pneumonia or a car accident . . . in Toronto, I think.' When he asked his uncle, he had been told, 'TB . . . no, definitely not Toronto, something beginning with W, Windsor or Waterloo.' Finally he had turned to the little Englishwoman. She had never met Katzi herself, but just after the war she had heard a little about her from my grandfather, and she mentioned an unhappy marriage, rich parents-in-law, and 'some kind of lung disease'. But at least the little Englishwoman came up with an address for Katzi's parents-in-law in Toronto. It was from an address book that she had used only up to 1950, so it was no more than a clue, an indication, somewhere to begin.

My brother thought his father and his uncle hard-hearted, cold and indifferent. He called to mind the common experiences of the so-called second generation. Those children of Holocaust survivors who he knew generally suffered from having grown up with so many of the dead sitting around the table with them. Except that with our family, characteristically, as it seemed to my brother, it was the other way around. Our family had lost relations in the war and was still covering up their loss with silence. I'm not sure if he had heard about my grandfather's strict orders for no one ever to mention Katzi's name again. But if I know my brother, he wouldn't have let this strange prohibition pass unchallenged. So he began his researches. He soon found out that there were few records of her in the Austrian archives. 'Office worker', 'of the Mosaic faith', said her last registration form, and 'leaving from Prague'. He had known all that already. So he had to go to Canada.

A stout colleague met him at Toronto airport, 'Jewish nose squared,' my brother would tell the Half-Jews group later, wrinkling his own, 'and gay too.' His stout colleague was amiable, forthcoming, and extremely well prepared. In the taxi he asked politely if anything new had been discovered about Popelnik, and whether my brother would like to take part in a radio programme that he, the stout man, presented. The subject this week was, 'Living as a Jew in Germany Today'. My brother agreed, although strictly speaking he didn't quite qualify on either count. Over here, however, it all looked the same, he joked, and the stout man roared with laughter. Yes, geography wasn't the strong point of the North Americans, he said. My brother felt at ease. The stout man seemed to respect him a great deal, he would look after him and organise everything, my brother could use him for his own purposes. His name was Herbert, but everyone called him Herb. My brother noticed that Herb had special status among the historians at the university which was holding the congress. He was a historian too, but also a journalist, and the value of anyone whom he interviewed and invited on to his programme seemed to be automatically enhanced. My brother felt flattered that Herb was paying him so much attention, introducing him to the others, preferring him to the rest of them. On the second evening, he told him Katzi's story. Herb was fascinated. A secret, a personal link between my brother and Ontario! And Katzi's husband had been called Herbert, just like him. What had become of her husband? Perhaps he was still alive! Herb promised to look into it thoroughly, and he called the National Archives. Within a day my brother had Katzi's death certificate in his hands, containing more information about her than anyone else in his family had ever discovered. It gave as the cause of death, in black and white, 'Tuberculosis of the lungs', adding, 'Profession: housewife', and it told him where she was buried and her last address.

Herb promised more, spoke of the immigration office and the register of companies, but some distinguished scholars from Spain and Israel had arrived, so he couldn't devote himself entirely to my brother any more. My brother had intended to hire a car and drive to Windsor, but now he didn't feel like doing it without Herb. He persuaded himself that he had duties at the conference on Sephardism. Finally he called my uncle. 'From Canada?' asked my uncle. 'Are you totally meschugge? Do you know what it costs?' But my brother claimed to be calling at the university's expense, and asked about Katzi's parents-in-law. What kind of people had they been? What did they do? My uncle hesitated, sharply describing this phone call as 'a piece of detection rather late in the day'. He said he had never met Katzi's parents-in-law himself; all he knew was that up to 1938 they'd had a business of some kind but he couldn't remember exactly what it was, maybe something to do with paper, or it could have been chemicals. My brother thanked him and hung up. He sat in his hotel room looking at the Toronto skyline and wondering why he was suddenly so moved by an unknown, long-dead woman, aunt or no aunt. For he was moved to tears. He thought how only one remark could ever really be got out of his father and his uncle: 'She was a beauty.' He believed it with his heart, but not with his mind. She was so beautiful because she had died so young. She was so beautiful because she was so unknown. Once again he wished he could set off and visit her grave, see what her husband Herbert had put on it, 'Katzi' or her real name, the one that nobody ever used. Instead, he really had to change his clothes now or he'd be late for his own lecture.

'But I'm digressing,' he told the 'Half-Jews 2000', who were patiently listening to him. 'The problem isn't Katzi, it's that man Herb.'

Only on the last evening was Herb available to him again. He'd had so much to do, he apologised, all those distinguished professors kept wanting something extra, and he sighed in a conspiratorial manner. My brother laughed and was happy. He had felt a little lost without Herb. When Herb invited him to what was said to be the best Korean restaurant in Toronto, my brother eagerly accepted. That was his last evening salvaged – 'Or so I thought,' he growled, looking grim. 'I mean, fair enough, this Herb had found me a whole lot of material,' said my brother, 'but . . .'

'About Katzi?' asked Nanny-Goat excitedly, chewing at her forefinger.

No, Herb had found out mainly about Katzi's parents-in-law, the B.s, Jewish industrialists from Vienna. Somewhere or other he had tracked down some correspondence between old B., Katzi's father-in-law, and the Austrian authorities ten years after the war. Old B., so the correspondence revealed, suffered from cirrhosis of the kidneys, was bedridden and unable to work; his son Herbert, who was to have taken over the business, had been dead for many years, following his Katzi to the grave very soon, perforation of the appendix – 'Oh, what a tragedy,' sighed Nanny-Goat.

Old B. wrote all these letters, and even hired a Viennese lawyer, first because he wanted to have the apartment building he had owned in Döbling back, and second he was applying for an Austrian pension as a wartime victim, since his poor state of health and his long-term inability to work were due not least to his several months of imprisonment in Dachau. 'The whole spectrum,' sighed my brother, 'we've seen it all before.' The Austrians had come up with a thousand reasons why they could comply with neither request. They needed an official medical certificate from the independent examining doctor at the Austrian Embassy, address enclosed, and as for the expense of the certificate, 'you would have to meet the cost yourself, should the occasion arise.' 'Should the occasion arise,' said my brother derisively, 'they were hoping old B. wouldn't be in any state to do it.' In the end the apartment building was returned, but it proved to have been leased out permanently and cost as much in expenses for its upkeep as the rent it brought in. Around 1957 the letters became more urgent.

There is a sworn declaration by B.'s wife, Katzi's mother-in-law, about her husband's state of health, adding that all their savings were exhausted. There is a sworn declaration from a Canadian lawyer, representing B.'s Canadian firm and confirming that because of his client's inability to work it was on the brink of bankruptcy. He insists that support for his client 'from any source whatsoever should be forthcoming immediately', for as the B.s' German-speaking family doctor also explained in writing, 'no improvement in his health is to be expected and prognosis is poor'. Both of old B.'s companies, obviously a chemicals firm which distilled tar and a small paper factory in the country, had already passed into the hands of third and fourth owners, and anyone taking them away from the present owners would be penalising not whoever aryanised them in the first place but an innocent party. However, B. didn't want those firms back anyway, or at least there is nothing to that effect in the files. His experience with the apartment building seems to have been enough for him. Old B., on his deathbed, was asking for cash, presumably mainly to provide for his wife. Finally B. received one payment of fifteen thousand schillings and another of thirty thousand schillings from the Austrian state, and then he died. 'Enough to break your heart,' said my brother, 'even though those people are complete strangers to me, it was appalling.'

'Still, he lived his natural life out,' objected the eldest of the Half-Jews group, the taciturn man from Leopoldstadt, who had lost a large part of his family in the Holocaust but now, by the standards of the Halacha, apparently wasn't Jewish at all. No one knew anything much about him. He had come mainly to listen, he had said on his first evening, and that was all right by the 'Half-Jews 2000'.

'I have to tell you something,' Herb had suddenly and portentously whispered in the Korean restaurant, and then, in the style of a secret agent, he had revealed that Herbert B., Katzi's husband, was strictly speaking only half-Jewish because his mother, Frau B. ('Would you believe it?'), had been a Sudeten German. Herb looked triumphantly at my brother. That was quite something, wasn't it? Yes, my brother had hesitantly said, it was indeed quite something. The same old story, my brother had murmured, more to himself than to Herb, and as if in a trance had begun to talk about our grandmother, who against her entire family's wishes had married an unreliable Viennese Jew and later saved his life simply by staying with him, although no one appreciated it now because they all wished she had been Jewish too, which would have made matters much easier for her grandchildren. If she had been Jewish herself, both my brother's grandparents would certainly have perished, which would have meant more blood and violence in the family history but also much more clarity about their identity. It's a strange world, murmured my brother, looking up and seeing, as he later said, the face of Herb, that Canadian Zampano, in the act of changing from an expression of horrified amazement to one of civil disdain. Herb immediately looked down, applied himself assiduously to his food, and without thinking allowed himself to say, 'Oh, then you're only a quarter Jewish!'

My brother had been fool enough to preserve his composure, he told the Half-Jews, and he once told the same tale to my uncle as they ate their fish lunch: instead of getting up and leaving he had explained, loftily, that the situation before the war was quite different from the situation today, that back then no one asked a Jewish 'head of the household', as they put it in those days, what his wife's religion was, for at the time Jews were self-confident and in possession of all their civil rights, there had been no need for any rabbinical law to . . . his father had emigrated as a small child, in danger of his life, because he would undoubtedly . . .

'Sure,' Herb had said with his mouth full and a non-committal smile, 'sure, I understand.'

Only a quarter Jewish. 'Some Jews are bound to be idiots,' said my uncle casually in the Naschmarkt.

'What a racist!' hissed Nanny-Goat, meaning Herb.

'Let's not be anti-Semitic,' murmured the gloomy soul from Leopoldstadt, meaning Nanny-Goat, whether ironically or not.

'And that's why I'm here,' my brother finished, clearing his throat and turning up the palms of his hands in embarrassment.

'Where else?' said the group leader with her delighted smile. 'Well done, Rubber.'

The Heiress

Sandy walked down the gravel path towards the car park, swinging her shoulder-bag, walking with a stride that in spite of the short skirts she usually wore was rather too long, too virile. They had all three called 'See you!' and 'Till tomorrow!', and waved in an affected manner, as they always did. The affected wave had originally been meant ironically, but now they had been waving at each other that way so long, they'd soon have to take it seriously.

Under half-opened lids, my sister watched her go. Max, my sister's husband, used to call it her 'bored bedroom look', and he used to pinch her somewhere when she looked like that, but he had stopped doing that some time ago. Angie, who was sitting next to her languidly putting the dice back in their container, followed the direction of her eyes. 'I think she goes to the solarium too often,' she said.

'Oh, well,' said my sister, 'she does have a bit of cellulitis, but that's not just because of the solarium.'

Since they could think of nothing better to do, she and Angie ordered a glass of strawberry punch. 'My old man will get upset again,' said my sister, and Angie made a face and said, 'Forget it.' Then they sat there in silence, watching the last tennis players coming off the courts, sweating profusely or less profusely on their way to the cloakrooms. Some Miroslav – or was it Hussein? – began slackening the nets on the courts, and the other, Hussein or Miroslav, brought along a fan-shaped rake to rake the gravel.

'Where are the kids?' Angie finally asked.

'My big girl's on a week in the country with the school party,' said my sister, taking off her sandals and rubbing her feet against each other. Her toenails needed repainting, somehow the nail varnish always chipped when you were wearing tennis shoes, it was a mystery to her why. 'My little girl's at home with a friend.'

'There's Willy Plavacek grinning again,' said Angie, beckoning to the waiter with two outstretched fingers.

'The hell with him,' murmured my sister, and looked away. She would be eternally sorry she'd told Angie anything about it. Angie was obviously keeping mum, but when it was just the two of them together she was always making some remark like that. It was over a year ago, just five minutes in the sauna, my sister made a face, and if she'd only kept her mouth shut, instead of being stupid and frightened enough to tell Angie all, then she probably wouldn't even remember it now, it would be almost as if it had never happened. It would have been better to tell Sandy, but it was too late for that. If they both knew they'd discuss it with each other, and just discussing it would make them feel it wasn't so secret any more. And then the dam would break. That was clear as day to her. The waiter put two glasses down in front of them. It was her firm intention never again to spend five minutes doing anything with Willy Plavacek or any other man that could make her vulnerable to blackmail, but if she did she was damn sure she'd keep her mouth shut afterwards.

'How's our accounts?' she asked, leaning forward.

'Same as usual,' said Angie, pushing the slip of paper over to her. 'Sandy owes each of us a few euros.' Angie finally took off her sunglasses, which had looked a little ridiculous in the twilight. 'Not enough to buy anything,' she said, grinning.

'Herr Klaus, would you bring us the *Groschenzeitung*,

please?' called my sister suddenly, because she had thought of something.

'Been betting again?' asked Angie, but my sister didn't answer. 'Oh, all right, I'll be on my way too,' said Angie, her feelings injured, and rose to her feet.

'See you tomorrow,' said my sister, without looking up as she leafed through the paper. She breathed a sigh of relief. That eighteen-year-old Spanish girl had reached the final. It had looked very unlikely – but she'd done it. And my sister had picked the winners of the men's semi-finals correctly too. About 150 euros, she estimated, feeling proud of herself; the odds against the young Spanish girl had been high. She ordered another glass of punch and began rummaging in her handbag. It was a long business. As usual, she felt cross about her huge handbag, a habit of hers first inherited from her mother, and second dating from when the children were still small and she always had to carry dummies and baby wipes around in her bag, and later on bottles of juice, plasters and Barbie clothes. Finally she found her mobile. 'Guess what?' she tapped in. 'Spaniard won. You want to trust me more!' Then she sent the message to her father, her favourite betting partner. He was back in hospital, but the first day he went in she had had a receiver for the foreign sports channels installed. It cost a lot, and Max had been annoyed. 'Why grudge him the pleasure?' she had muttered, but Max had said she was doing it at least as much for herself, so that her betting circle wouldn't suffer. She had furiously denied it, he's old and ill, she had snapped, what else does he have left? But here and now in the twilight, with her second glass of punch in front of her, she smiled and admitted that Max was right.

'Hello, darling,' said her mother suddenly behind her, putting a hand on her shoulder. 'Will you give me a lift part of the way in the car?'

'I'm not leaving just yet,' said my sister unforthcomingly, 'I want to go in the sauna again.'

'Love to the girls, then,' said her mother, carefully walking down the gravel path towards the exit. She's well preserved, thought my sister lazily, watching her go. If it hadn't been for the accident she might still have years of playing tennis ahead of her, she thought; even old ladies of ninety still play here, and she shook her head over such bad luck. Her mother, that swift walker, who had never learnt to drive because she was too scared, had been standing between two parked cars, about to cross the road, when one of the parked cars jerked forward and crushed both her knees. A young woman driver, 'a novice who had only just passed her test', as the *Groschenzeitung* put it, hadn't put her foot on the clutch or made sure the car was in neutral as she started it. Just bad luck. My mother's beautiful legs, thought my sister, her own legs and her sister's could never compete with them, neither daughter's legs could hold a candle to their mother's. Legs holding candles, the old man would like that idea, thought my sister. But he's in hospital feeling sorry for himself.

By now it was nearly dark. The lilac had a heavy perfume. She hated lilac. One of the old ladies here used a lilac-scented perfume and sprayed it all over the changing room. She was a silly cow, that old lady with her wonky hip. She uses all that perfume so no one will smell the beer on her breath, my sister always said nastily to her girlfriends, but you only have to look at her face to know, you don't have to smell her breath at all. The woman with the wonky hip was always bright red in the face, a nightmare. People like that don't belong in Hietzing, thought my sister. But she was too lazy to find another club. She knew everyone here, most of them since her childhood, and all that green space was something special in Vienna, she had to agree with her mother there. Not just a tennis club, a wonderful park. And a feast for the eyes, she sometimes said, the eyes can take their fill too, and she didn't notice that she already sounded exactly like her mother.

She slowly stood up, said, 'My husband will pay to-morrow' to Herr Klaus, who gave her a little bow, and went off to the cloakrooms. She felt wonderful, and noticed that people were looking at her. In her twenties she had been terrified of ageing, and at the same time youth didn't actually seem to be flying by. Then she was the first of her girlfriends to get pregnant, which still surprised her today. She often thought how fast you declined, even if no one noticed yet, even if, on the contrary, you looked as if you were in your prime. She took an almost unnatural interest in those years when you were already beginning to decay, although your outward appearance still seemed to be fine; she took an interest in all the little aches and pains which she used to regard as the mark of senior citizens, the kind who neglected themselves, of course. After her second baby she had had her haemorrhoids removed, which was almost worse than the episiotomy with her first child. Her gums seemed to be constantly inflamed for some time, and bled easily. She had had problems for some time with a slipped disc, a tendency inherited from her father. Last time her cervical vertebra was X-rayed the orthopaedist had mentioned in passing that she had the beginnings of arthrosis of the jaw, and she was mute with shame and surprise. And a year ago she had dandruff, not the kind that sheds but a different sort that stuck to her scalp in white scales, and she found it only by chance. She still felt sick when she thought that her hairdresser might have been the first to notice. Luckily she had discovered it herself. She didn't tell anyone, and washed her hair with evil-smelling shampoo for weeks. There was no problem about washing her hair at home for a while instead of at the club; even her girlfriends weren't as beady-eyed as all that. And Max was a typical man anyway, and would never have noticed a new little bottle in their chaotic bathroom. When she was drunk my sister sometimes said she could leave condoms lying around at home, Max wouldn't catch on, and Angie and Sandy always squealed with laughter. But ever since that dandruff, she had regularly taken a close look at her friends' heads, and after the sauna sometimes even offered to blow-dry their hair at the back in her secret search for revenge. Thirty years ago, when she was still a child, she had once heard her mother say that finding your first white pubic hair was the worst moment of all. She was still undefeated on that front, but who knew how long it would last? Who knew why Angie always had all her body hair removed by the beautician, and didn't even keep that little triangle? Angie had been tinting the hair on her head for years, as those who start out naturally black often do.

She ran straight into the arms of Willy Plavacek. 'Hello there, pretty lady,' he said flatteringly, and twinkled at her a little too conspicuously. 'May I offer you a glass of punch?'

'That's kind of you, but not today,' said my sister evasively, looking somewhere else, anywhere but into his grinning, good-looking, disgustingly self-satisfied face. 'Scared of what the posh folk of Hietzing will say? Well, we'll see!' he said straight out, and left her standing there. She thought at first she couldn't have heard correctly, and when she realised that she had it took her breath away for a moment. All she could hear was Hussein's rake in the background. In the changing rooms, she quickly fetched the things she was going to take home to wash, and then went to sit on the terrace again. By now it was almost entirely dark there. Herr Klaus hurried to put candles in glass containers on her table and five others. They looked romantic. The trees were rustling and the lilac stank to high heaven. She spent some time rummaging around in her handbag again, and called Max. All she reached was his mailbox. 'Hi, it's me,' she began, but then ended the call.

Herr Klaus brought her another glass of punch – 'From Herr Plavacek,' he said. 'Tell him thanks,' my sister replied feebly, not daring to refuse the drink. She looked at her mobile, panic-stricken, and then tapped in another number.

'Hi,' she said cheerfully to her father, 'how are you today, everything fine?'

'Well,' said her father hesitantly, 'things could be better.'

'Don't start complaining,' she reproved him, 'you get the best food in all Vienna there! Did you watch a good match?'

'Oh yes,' he said, getting livelier, 'guess what, Real . . .'

'Don't tell me,' cried my sister, 'I've been recording it at home!'

'How about you?' asked her father. 'How are the children?'

'They're good girls,' said my sister, 'they send their love.'

'And Max?' asked my father. 'What's he doing?'

'What do you expect?' grumbled my sister. 'He's at work.'

'Well, someone has to bring home the bacon, the way you get through money!' chuckled her father. 'Yes, sure,' said my sister, too lazy to feel insulted. 'Been playing?' asked her father.

'Yes,' she said, 'doubles with Angie, Sandy and Monika, Monika and I were partners, six-three, six-four, six-three.'

'My word,' said her father, surprised, 'you won that easily?'

'Yes,' she said, 'Sandy has tennis elbow. Hey,' she said, about to end the call, 'what's your tip for Wednesday, Bayern against Inter?'

'Difficult,' said her father, 'the game's wide open. What's yours?'

'Three nil to Inter,' she said, sure of herself. 'I can smell it.'

'You're crazy,' he said, laughing, 'but with your kind of luck . . .' Then she promised him to look in next day, and rang off.

When she was in the car at last she didn't go the usual way home. She drove over the bridge, well into District 3, and by the time she admitted to herself that she was looking for her mother she had found her. There she went, walking terribly slowly and keeping close to the walls of the buildings, but with her head held high. My sister let the window purr its way down and called in her cheekiest Viennese tone, 'Here we go, then, transport for the disabled!'

'Jesus, did you ever scare me!' said her mother crossly, but she thankfully made her way to the car. Back at home her mother made her a thick open sandwich, the way she always used to. 'Open to anything and everything she likes to put on them,' was how her father had always described her mother's open sandwiches; as children they had always thought that funny. This time there was no gherkin. 'What, no gherkin?' grumbled my sister. 'I can't eat that!'

'I ran out,' said her mother apologetically, and my sister murmured, 'I don't believe it!' with the mock-indignation she had affected for so long that you almost had to take it seriously.

Then the two of them sat there by the open window in silence. 'Where's Max?' asked her mother at last.

'Never at home,' complained my sister, 'works day and night.'

'That's men for you,' said her mother, making a face. 'But they want to be looked after when they get old.'

'Papa's pretty sprightly,' objected my sister.

'I don't know,' said her mother, 'the doctors are being kind of funny about his condition.'

'Because of his artificial hip?' asked my sister.

'There's something or other on his lung,' said her mother, 'they don't know what it is.'

'Oh, no!' cried my sister, and burst into tears.

'What's the matter?' asked her mother, painfully embarrassed. 'There's nothing certain yet.'

'Does he know?' asked my sister, between her sobs.

'Of course not,' said her mother, 'he gets upset enough as it is.'

When she left, her mother pressed a bottle of red wine on

her, 'for when you're home,' and a large, rather dusty package. 'It's a rug,' she explained, shrugging. 'Apparently very valuable, it was Aunt Gustl's.'

'Aunt Gustl?' asked my sister. 'Was that the funny old lady with the tights?'

'Yes,' groaned her mother. 'Just don't remind me of it.'

'So where did it suddenly come from?' asked my sister.

'I was clearing up,' said her mother, 'I must have forgotten about it. But,' she said, becoming more animated, 'it really is supposed to be worth something, and with your old furniture . . .'

'Let's hope it doesn't have the moth in it,' said my sister, wrinkling her nose as she tentatively poked the package with a finger.

Everything was quiet in the apartment. There were no lights on. She put the package of rug down in the hall with the dozens of pairs of shoes and went into the kitchen, where she found a note from her younger daughter saying that she was sleeping over with her friend who had really been supposed to sleep over with them. She called Max, but only got his mailbox. She opened her mother's bottle of red wine, after critically examining the label, and sat on the kitchen balcony. Hietzing smelled of lilac too.

One of the contradictions in her life was that everyone thought she couldn't have caught a better husband than Max, but she might never have married Max if she hadn't been pregnant. She had admitted that to herself only for the last few years, and only when she was alone and everything else was rather out of joint anyway. As a young girl she had been a princess, her father's last child. He was more of a grandfather than a father to her, or at least so her half-brother once said, but he always had such weird opinions. She had become a princess at the Schneuzl Sports Club when she suddenly began playing tennis again at the age of eighteen, not in the First League, admittedly, but for the club, which was proud to be represented in most leagues and at most tournaments, and had once even had a pair of players who were world champions in the veteran doubles, her father and one of the others in the Spastic Bunch, over ten years ago when they were approaching seventy.

In favour of Max were his good looks and his status representing the club in the men's team, but most of all the fact that he was much desired by the tennis-playing young ladies from the day he first appeared. But he seemed to be shy, and turned down all invitations and barely veiled amorous approaches. My sister didn't seem to have noticed him at first. She, whose beauty was now generally praised – even the dice-playing monsters allowed that she was a 'smart girl' – liked to appear haughtily indifferent. She thought herself that there was someone very special waiting for her, a kind of fairy-tale prince for the pampered princess. On looks alone, Max fitted this scheme of things perfectly. After a few weeks the two of them were suddenly a couple, and no outsider could say afterwards when and how it had come about. There were broken hearts at the tennis club and two fifteen-year-old girls swore eternal vengeance on my sister. But all the others leaned back, sighing, and believed they'd seen it coming from the first, it was like a happy ending right at the beginning of the film. No one felt sorry for Dr Quack's unassuming, freckled son, the boy-friend of my sister's youth, who suddenly had to clear his things out of their student room. He should have known he wasn't good enough.

When she became pregnant three years later they married at once. Max's family, well-heeled industrialists in Viennese society, were conservative about such things. They were so fixated on etiquette, good manners, and the values of the cultured and educated classes that even my sister began to feel like a nonconformist after a while. At the family villa in Döbling she played her part almost perfectly, but at home she mocked her mother-in-law and her subscription to the

Josefstadt theatre, her sister-in-law's silk scarves, and her father-in-law's Christian charity associations. At first she had been almost afraid of this father-in-law, whom she sometimes called the top prig to Angie and Sandy. He had always been friendly and courteous to her, but she had sensed a certain reserve. Max once surmised it was because of her Jewish half-brother and his radical political views, whereupon my sister, next time she visited Döbling, explained unasked that she was hardly even in touch with her half-brother. But soon she was indifferent to that and indeed everything else, and in fact sometimes liked standing up to her husband's family on unimportant little matters. Once, when she had taken one of the children to her in-laws, the newspaper that she sometimes read at the time had fallen out of her bag. Her father-in-law, who gallantly picked it up for her, had taken a look at it, seen the shoe-box-shaped memorial in the picture, and made a face. 'Now they're giving us another blot on the landscape, that construction in the Judenplatz,' he had said, and although she had never been to the Judenplatz she replied, 'I rather like it myself.' After a short pause he said, 'You're right, we had to commemorate the Jews,' and for a moment she was almost proud of herself for her easy victory.

Just as she was about to go to bed she heard a sound at the door. She quietly went back to the dark kitchen balcony and sat down. She heard Max coming in and moving through the apartment without putting a light on. She tried to guess what he was doing. He would take his shoes off and curse quietly when he stumbled over other shoes; the hall floor was covered with them. Then he would go into the living-room in his socks and watch some kind of stock exchange news with the door closed. After that he would put his head into the girls' rooms, and very likely be surprised to see just their empty beds. He had probably forgotten that the elder girl had gone off with the school party for a week in the country again, although she had put on her usual hysterical show at breakfast – 'Papa-I'm-going-to-miss-you-so-much' – something my sister hated more than almost anything else. My sister felt that her elder daughter was watching and evaluating her almost improperly, so with that child she was always alternating between great severity and indulgence, which didn't help. The younger girl had been easier from the first, but she too sometimes did just as she wanted. In a few years they'll have left home, thought my sister, and she knew that however much the girls got on her nerves at times, she was afraid of the prospect.

Inwardly, she awarded herself points for all the things her husband did that she had correctly predicted. After scoring four easy points, there was a pause. Max had been in the living-room, not long enough, she thought, to look at the stock exchange prices, but she gave herself the point all the same. One point for each of the girls' rooms, but that was cheating a little, for Max would never look in on only one of the children, 'your sleeping angels', as my sister sometimes derisively thought, for in the first hectic years he had seen them mainly when they were asleep, or so she always said, holding it against him. At the moment she couldn't hear anything else. She went through all the possibilities. Eight points if he finally went to the fridge to get himself a beer, she had never understood how anyone could drink beer before going to bed, or indeed how anyone could drink beer at all. She suddenly remembered his look on their honeymoon; they'd gone only to Carinthia because she didn't dare travel further in her condition – she had been slightly hysterical right through her pregnancy, Max had even remarked to a friend that it was getting him down. Unfortunately she had heard him say so, and her rage had been immense. Anyway, on their honeymoon in Carinthia Max had tried to kiss her after drinking beer, and she had twisted her mouth and turned her face away. He looked at her in a way that was both baffled and furious, and she had thought in surprise, well, well, there was more in him than she'd known, or at least more than all she thought she knew already. Over the next few days she had been almost excessively nice to him, and then, as if idly, began trying to get him to tell her about his previous girlfriends, but he wasn't about to tell her anything new, apart from having snogged with a girl from school on his skiing course. When they first got together he hadn't been a virgin, all the same, she already knew that grotesque story of the Germans in Greece which reached its climax in the discovery that sand and skin rendered vulnerable by sunburn were a very painful combination, and he assured her that there hadn't been anything more to it.

My sister wondered what her chances were over the beer. If he came home so late and she hadn't been able to get in touch with him for so long, he ought really to give up the idea and come straight to bed, for the sake of peace. On the other hand she had made it her principle to bet against the odds; she was bold in her betting. So she bet on the beer, although personally she hoped he wouldn't have any more. The difference between gambling and life. She tried to imagine his reaction when he found that she wasn't in bed. Perhaps he wouldn't even notice? In the first part of their marriage she had trained him to be very careful if he was coming to bed late, for while she was pregnant she had trouble with disturbed sleep, and particularly with being woken and then being unable to get to sleep again for a long time. So was it possible he would slip into bed so cautiously, with his face turned away, that he wouldn't notice her absence at all? To be honest, she didn't really know what he was like coming to bed these days, for she was almost always asleep by then, the result of her alcohol intake, which happened preferably but not exclusively in the evening. She had the feeling that it helped her to sleep. She resolved, for the umpteenth time, to have a few alcohol-free days.

She heard Max coming out of the bathroom and held her breath. However, he didn't go into the bedroom, but back to one of the girls' rooms. My sister hurried to the kitchen doorway and looked out. She heard murmuring. He seemed to be telephoning – at this time of night? She hurried into her elder daughter's room and peered in. There he was, sitting on the bed, a dark outline in front of the lighter shape of the window, with a brightly lit mobile held to his ear. Confused, she went back to her point of departure. She poured herself a little more red wine. She wondered whether this unexpected turn of events made a difference to all the rest of the points she had calculated in advance, or had she already lost her bet against herself?

The kitchen light came on. She jumped. 'Goodness, how you startled me,' she lied. 'Oh, there you are,' said Max, opening the fridge and taking out a beer. Six out of eight points, decided my sister generously, not bad. 'How was your day?' she asked. 'Same as usual,' said Max, 'that new client is a nightmare.'

'The bank?' asked my sister.

'The insurance firm,' said Max. 'Where's the little one?'

'Sleeping over with that girl Philippa,' said my sister.

'Philippa,' said Max. 'What a name. How about you?'

'My brother and sister are coming tomorrow,' said my sister, wry-mouthed. 'Both of them, because of our father.'

'Oh God,' said Max, 'so that clever couple will be in town. Not going to stay with us, are they?'

'Yes,' said my sister, shrugging apologetically. 'But that means we'll be left in peace for a few years then.'

'You're the specialist in that,' said Max.

'How do you mean?' asked my sister.

'Forget it,' said Max. 'So when do they arrive?'

'They're going up to see the old man first, then they'll come on here,' said my sister. 'I really couldn't unload them on Mama, not at this time.'

'I suppose,' said Max, looking directly at her for the first time, 'you'll be cooking the usual?'

'If you don't like it,' said my sister, 'we can send out for something.'

'Oh, I just love chicken with cashew nuts,' said Max, his face expressionless. 'Sixteen years ago I'd never have thought I'd get to be so fond of chicken with cashew nuts.'

'I'll order something from Rumpel, you sod,' said my sister.

'Now, now, keep calm, dear lady,' cried Max, 'I beg you most humbly to cook chicken with cashew nuts.'

My sister turned the right-hand corner of her mouth down in a way Max knew so well that he could never have interpreted it as just one thing. That wry mouth meant not only, as outsiders might have thought, pure, prim scorn, it also told those in the know: I'm not sure what to do now, I'm all confused, I'll act indignant for safety's sake. Max knew that very well, but he would never have given his knowledge away, for it was clear to him that if it ever came to the crunch, such secretly amassed knowledge of her was his only chance.

'Come on,' he said soothingly, putting a hand on her forearm. She shook it off violently, but it did seem to calm her down. 'You've always had something against my brother and sister,' she snapped.

Max laughed. 'Only for love of you.'

'Who were you phoning just now?' she asked, looking at him challengingly.

'I was listening to my mailbox,' he said. 'Sorry my phone was turned off so long.'

'Liar,' she said.

'You'd like that, wouldn't you?' he said equably, and stood up. 'I'm going to bed now.'

'Good night, sleep tight,' she called, feeling cross again, and hated herself because her desire for a quarrel, in which she had to persist all the same, seemed to have barred the way to bed for her. Now where was she going to sleep? On the sofa, dramatically? She had a last sip of red wine, and all of a sudden she didn't mind any more. She decided to act as if nothing had happened and go and sleep in the bed that was rightfully hers. Years ago she had lost the ability to indulge in the furious, pointless rage that would have kept such an argument going into the small hours; she had always felt, vaguely, that this breathtaking rage was wasted on Max. Now she had surrendered to circumstances, and she had to say those circumstances were not the worst possible. She had always lacked the strength to make drastic changes. She couldn't stand her everyday life, she had dreamed of something different, but she didn't have any courage either, so everything went on as it was. That was life. It could have turned out worse. Now she just hoped she would fall asleep quickly, before Max came out of the bathroom. To go to sleep quickly and have no dreams would be the best thing. And my sister's modest wishes were always granted.

Looking Back

Although it was far from certain whether he ought to fly, I gave my father a present of a trip to England. We had several appointments at the hospital in Lainz, where they checked his general state of health. Finally, as he said with a grin, they gave him the all-clear. He was a little proud that the medical director had said, 'You can thank God you were a sportsman,' nodding with some slight hesitation. My father was old, but he didn't look as if there was anything wrong with him. He refused to take his walking stick. He thought walking sticks looked ridiculous. He could never understand, he said, why his father had carried a stick for so long, and he for one wasn't going to. 'You feel like an old man with a stick,' he said reproachfully, although he had long ago passed average life expectancy in Austria, which itself was high on an international scale. Instead he got out of the taxi clinging to a canvas seaman's bag which he refused to give up. He would let no one else carry it, and he didn't say what was in it. 'That bag is coming to England with me,' he said, and so it did.

Once in London, he immediately wanted to go to a certain store near Piccadilly Circus where he had always bought 'wonderful shirts' when he came back before to visit Uncle Tom and Auntie Annie. He emerged from the Tube, looked briefly around, and then hurried straight off in a certain direction. He didn't move very fast, but for a man in his state of health he was running, glancing back over his shoulder now and then to make sure his child was following. Suddenly he stopped and looked up, unable to take in the fact that the 'best and finest gentleman's outfitters in London' had become an H & M store on several floors. He stood there shaking his head, put right off his stroke. 'When did you last go shopping here?' I cautiously asked, and he thought about it. 'Wait a minute,' he said, using his fingers to help him count, and I realised that what he was counting were the decades. 'Oh well,' he said at last, 'I don't really need anything.'

We went to Stopsley. A man called Harry, a kind of stepnephew of Uncle Tom's, had said he would pick us up and drive us around in his car. 'To think he's still alive,' said my father, as the train slowly moved through the suburbs of London. 'He must be younger than you,' I retorted. 'Thanks, very kind of you,' snapped my father, and I asked, 'What's the matter with that? It's true!'

When we got off the train in Luton my father whispered to me, in sudden panic, 'I've no idea what he looks like,' and I pressed his arm reassuringly. Apart from us, only a few other people had got out, and there was a pear-shaped man waving. He wore the kind of glasses that used to be called 'Rex specs' in Vienna, after the thick glass of the bottoms of Rex preserving jars. And here came Harry limping towards us, shouting, 'Sunny! I knew you at once!' Laughing, my father shook hands, clapped him on the shoulder, and cried, 'Harry! You haven't changed a bit!' I could tell from the corners of his mouth what satisfaction this twofold lie gave him.

As we were driving down a long street in Luton, Harry pointed out of the window to left and right and said, 'Not a white face in sight these days,' then glanced at me in the rear-view mirror and added, 'I don't want to sound racist, but it's really getting to be too much.' My father, sitting in front, nodded sympathetically and looked at the dark children, the dark men, and the Indian and Arab shops with their mysterious inscriptions past which we were driving. I thought it best to keep quiet. On this point, as my father saw it, he could only win. 'Would you want it to look like this at home?' he would have said calmly, and I would have involved myself in forceful protests about settlement policies that failed to meet their targets, and poor policies on minorities that took no interest in those ethnic groups. I would have claimed, without mustering any good arguments, that it could be different, that it didn't always have to end with ghettos, and by then his ironic nod alone would have driven me to white-hot fury.

We had some tough arguments behind us. At the end of 1986 I had moved away from home because I couldn't bear to think that my father had voted for Waldheim. 'He's not a criminal!' shouted my father. 'He's a liar!' I shouted, my brother shouted, my cousins and my uncle shouted, and even the gentle little Englishwoman was roused to anger. 'It's not fair,' cried my father, who minded about fairness more than anything, 'and anyway you lot won over Popelnik.'

So I moved out. I had put the sticker with the line crossing out Waldheim's profile on the door of my room, and my father had said he didn't have to tolerate political statements of that kind in his own apartment. It was bad enough, he said, that he obviously had to put up with the horrible oil paintings that my mother bought at auction and hung in the living-room in ever-changing combinations, but an anti-Waldheim poster, no, definitely not. I packed my things, and it was not an amicable farewell. After the first disturbed night in my brother's student room, which he had lent me in a spirit of solidarity, I wandered around the cold winter streets in a district that I didn't know, looking for a supermarket where I could buy breakfast. I was in such a rage that I dared not ask anyone, and I went back to the silent, strange room tearful and hungry. It has to be this way, I defiantly told myself, and thought of home, which at that moment seemed to me like a refuge, even though my mother would be serving breakfast there with her usual stony expression, even though my jubilant sister had already commandeered my room before the last packing cases were out of it. Always banging her head against the wall, they used to say about me then, and if they really wanted to annoy me they added, 'Just like Granny Frieda, heartless and stubborn.' And then they would nod and laugh.

Some time later my sister told me that our father had forbidden her to go out with an American fellow student, just because he was black, and sure enough I kicked up a fuss. I didn't realise that if my sister had been genuinely interested in the American she would have ignored my father's decree, for in my early twenties I felt most myself in the role of prickly moralist protecting relationships threatened by society. Without batting an eyelash, my father did not deny it when I tackled him, but actually confirmed it. In his experience, he said, nothing but problems ever came of mixed marriages. Quite true, I spat, and even betrayed my own righteous views in order to make the next, wounding point, quite true, and for proof of it, I said, he need only look at his own marriage. Then he threw me out.

I was still worried about such views of my father's years later. At first, in my youthful self-righteousness and moved by the monstrous charges, I called them 'pure racism'; later, almost excusing them, 'stupid prejudices'. Finally I stopped mentioning these views to third parties at all, because there comes a time when if you can't understand something you'd better keep quiet about it. My brother was the only one in whom I confided, for we liked to talk about our father and the puzzle he presented.

'It's still a mystery to me,' I said at a coffee-house table when my father was already in the hospital that he was never to leave again. 'With a history like that behind him!' I had just, agitated and indignant as ever, been telling the story of the 'black student affair', as we called it for short, for the hundredth time, and my brother kept giving me comforting cigarettes. I had started smoking again when my father went into hospital. My father himself, that rabid non-smoker, couldn't see it or smell it, because we had already been to see him that day; he was shut up there, and I had been trying for weeks to drive a bargain with the gods, using a ridiculous little magic trick: I would smoke only until he came out of hospital and then I'd stop at once. My brother scratched his ear at length, and through the clouds of smoke that we were both puffing out I suddenly had the impression that I was sitting opposite my grandfather. It was just the same little movement.

'You know what Uncle Bertl once said to me?' my brother finally asked, smiling. 'Uncle Bertl once said some Jews are bound to be idiots too!' I looked at him for a moment, shocked, and then we both began to laugh out loud and couldn't stop for a long time, and at such moments I loved my brother dearly, crazy and unpredictable as he usually was.

In the last ten years our political conflicts with our father had almost entirely ceased. When we were all together, my cousins and their grown-up children, my brother, his wife and I, we no longer asked him to sign petitions against keeping the small children of Afghan asylum-seekers in custody, because we knew by now that he would refuse. 'The Interior Minister must have his reasons,' he would say, 'I'm sure the Interior Minister wouldn't do anything illegal.' So for our own sakes we spared ourselves the insanity which a discussion with him would automatically have set off. Nor did we contradict him when he launched into his usual anti-Haider tirade. 'Who are these people who vote for him? It's a crying shame!' Now that he was older and more anxious, we stopped pointing out that the identity of the prime minister of Carinthia was irrelevant from a global or even just European viewpoint, for we realised that his sense of living in the middle of an Austrian disaster brought about by Haider protected him from other, greater fears at a time when bombs were going off everywhere and synagogues were burning again.

We completed the entire Stopsley programme as planned, stage by stage. First Harry drove us to the little street where my father had grown up. I took the photo in which my father is standing beside the street sign saying 'Chiltern Road' and smiling, Uncle Tom and Auntie Annie had lived with the three children right at the end of this narrow, shabby street full of low-built terraced houses, in the last cottage of all, which was almost covered by honeysuckle and elder. Behind it, even sixty years later, lay flat, undeveloped land. 'A small place, eh?' said my father, and seemed to be proud of it himself. 'We kept the rabbits over there,' he said, pointing. 'How I hated those rabbits!'

As we passed what had once been the Dog and Duck my father saw, with displeasure, that it was now part of a chain and was called the Rat and Parrot. 'Rat and Parrot,' he said crossly. 'Idiotic name!'

'There are hardly any independent pubs now,' said Harry, and my father, shaking his head, said, 'And there was I thinking that at least would never change in England!'

Later, we stood on the edge of a football field with goalposts standing crooked, the paint flaking off them. Now I could see for myself, remarked my father, that there were football pitches on every street corner in England, and I could have ended the sentence in chorus with him, but I refrained: 'And at home they wonder why there's no new talent coming along.' The shabby football pitch lay deserted in the sun. I tried to picture my little father with his thin legs running around in every free minute he had, and not hearing much about the war. I couldn't imagine it very clearly. My father was whispering to Harry behind my back. I thought he probably needed to go to the lavatory.

We went into the Rat and Parrot. For my father's sake I've always liked English pubs, those dark, greasy caverns, and I can't tell the difference in quality between chains and independent pubs, but my father said I had no idea about it at all. We sat in the noise and the smoke, which my father could tolerate only in a pub, and Harry said he would never forget the junior final in the year forty-five, 'when you scored that wonderful goal,' he added, and my father thought. 'Oh yes, in Luton,' he suddenly remembered, and he smiled; it had been his first match in a real football stadium, with stands, paying spectators and everything. 'It wasn't a particularly good match,' he told Harry, but Harry didn't agree. 'We won!' 'Yes, we won,' said my father thoughtfully. The score had been one-all, and the Luton Colts couldn't seem to do anything, the whole game was a series of useless rushes and equally useless counter-attacks, until a quarter of an hour before the end my father had got the ball, and in his position of outside right he was able to move forward with it. Another player had moved into the middle of the pitch just outside the goal mouth. 'You take these decisions in a split second,' said my father, who had seen that the goalkeeper and defenders were expecting him to centre and were beginning to mark the player in the middle, while the goalkeeper was coming a step or so out of goal. Then my father shot at an angle and scored, a risky move. 'But the best of it is,' said my father, suddenly looking really happy, 'I shot exactly the same goal again later, in a much more important match.' It was against Happel and Zeman, the two Austrian miracle players for Rapid, who had even had special stamps showing them printed by the Austrian Football League a few years ago. He had shot the same goal playing against Happel and Zeman – it was a sensation at the time. 'You were "head and shoulders above all the rest",' quoted Harry admiringly; he still remembered the newspaper report almost sixty-five years later. 'Head and shoulders above all the rest?' repeated my father in English, grinning. 'And now here I am, a cripple,' he said to me in German.

Harry was afraid my father would find the walk to the cemetery too much for him. We couldn't take the car right in, he explained to me, we'd have to go quite a way on foot. He suggested finding an excuse to miss out the cemetery, saying there wasn't much to see there anyway. He tried to persuade me while my father was in the lavatory for the third time. I was against dropping the idea; the cemetery seemed to be a central part of this trip for my father, and anyway he was much better on his feet than he looked. 'We'll take our time,' I told Harry, 'we're in no hurry.'

'Shouldn't we go and see the school?' asked Harry, whose concern, paradoxically, made him hope that my father would soon feel tired. The school might be a good idea, he said.

'Harry thinks we might visit your old school,' I suggested to my father when he came back, suddenly wanting to show Harry where he was wrong. My father was not a cripple, and even if he liked to joke about it he had more stamina than I did. When he travelled he suddenly seemed to summon up all his strength, and then I suppose he would rest and recover when he was home again. I remembered, with alarm, his visit to Berlin a few years earlier, when he wanted to go on foot, in blazing heat, from a Holocaust memorial to the next notable Jewish sight.

'This isn't Vienna,' I tried to explain, showing him the city street map and the distance between that memorial and the synagogue. 'Nonsense,' said my father, 'it's only a stone's throw away. But if you're tired we can have a coffee,' he added, looking mischievously at me, and I teased him back. 'I just don't want you having a stroke here so far from home.' That only made him laugh. 'I'm not dying among these Germans,' he said, 'don't you worry.'

'You never used to like walking,' I pointed out later, breathless from visiting many other places to do with the Holocaust and the Nazis, but he had the last word.

'I'm seeing the sights,' he said triumphantly, 'not just walking aimlessly through the woods. Am I a deer?'

My father thought visiting the school was a good idea. On the way Harry kept apologising for not asking about a visit in advance, but he didn't know any of the teaching staff now. My father didn't mind about that. He pressed the bell and when the intercom came on explained cheerfully that he had been to school here – 'let's see, seventy years ago?' – and he would like to see his old classroom. When the electrically operated door opened, a secretary stared at us in surprise. My father began on his 'seventy years ago' explanation again, but she interrupted him, ran off, and came back with the headmaster. He asked us into his study, and while we drank tea he rapidly assembled a small recorder. He put a microphone in the lapel of my father's jacket and positively begged him to tell his life story to the schoolchildren, 'if it isn't too painful for you.'

'Painful?' said my father. 'Why would it be painful?'

The headmaster was an eager young man who had obviously only just caught the local and regional history conservation bug, and thought this was his lucky day. And so it was that my father, with his checked hat in his hands and the microphone on his lapel, suddenly featured as an eyewitness to history in front of a class of primary school-children wearing dark green uniforms. With a grave expression, he told them how many Jews there had been in Vienna before the war, and how few were left after it. The teacher wrote both numbers on the board, but the first number and the difference between the two seemed too great for the children to grasp. 'And where did they go?' asked a puzzled little girl. The teacher apologised: they hadn't yet reached the persecution of the Jews, they'd be getting to that next year. My father, who had obviously thought, from hearsay, that being an eyewitness to history was meant to be a mournful business, immediately adjusted his ideas, and speaking much more in line with his own nature and his experiences told them about the fun he had had here, the football games, his kind foster-parents and their home where he had grown up. He mentioned his favourite English dish, Christmas pudding, which unfortunately was unknown in Austria. He said that he had found saying goodbye to England very difficult, because he could hardly remember his real parents any more.

'Was it difficult for you to learn English?' asked the children, and my father replied that what he remembered most was how difficult it was to learn German again later, because he had entirely forgotten the language. The children were amazed. 'Did you recognise your parents?' one little girl asked, and then fired off the next question at once, 'And didn't they understand what you were saying?' My father thought. He couldn't quite remember, he said hesitantly, but he had an idea that his brother had recognised him at the station – his brother, by the way, had fought in the British army. 'Just think of that,' said my father gratefully to the children, 'after a while they let him fight in your army.'

'And I think he recognised me at once,' said my father. The little girl was still looking inquiringly at him. 'Yes, that's how it must have been, because they came straight towards me.'

Before the girl could repeat her second question, the headmaster asked a small black boy to show their guest the history corner. The child took my father's hand – 'a dear little boy he was,' my father would say later – led him to the back of the classroom, where there was a display board with photographs of German air squadrons in the clear sky, ruined buildings in London and the bombed city of

Coventry, and delivered a little lecture in his piping voice. Then my father told them about the only night of bombing that he had been through in London. He had obviously gone to the city a second time to meet his brother and sister, but he had arrived too late. They had both left, his sister for Canada, his brother for the internment camp. So he had spent the night with a Jewish tailor who had employed his brother. And that particular night had seen one of the worst bombing raids of all on London. 'I still remember the smell of the gas masks,' said my father, and the children nodded knowingly. Then the little boy handed him one of the two gas masks hanging on the board as historical exhibits, and took down the other himself. They looked at each other for a moment, and then they both put their gas masks on. The boy held my father's hand again, and they turned together to face the class, one small person and one taller person with insect faces, one all in dark green, the other carrying a checked hat. The children laughed and clapped. The teacher was delighted. 'Please take a picture for me,' he whispered to me, but I had been taking photograph after photograph for some time already, because I didn't know how else to hide my emotion.

The cemetery he had been looking forward to seeing so much was a bitter disappointment to my father. It was a wonderful day, yes, the flowers were in bloom, the birds were singing, and you could hardly imagine anywhere more like Paradise than this park, particularly in the industrial area around Luton. Masters of the traditional English art of horticulture had done all they could, they had laid out paths and pools of water, and topiary hedges, but for my father the visit was disastrous. At first, with his usual happy and indeed enthusiastic approach, he had been well on the way to thinking that everything without distinction was very interesting, everything was fine. He walked slowly on purpose, he seemed to be enjoying spinning it out, he kept asking me to take more photos, he insisted, with a mysterious smile, on carrying his seaman's bag, and he often stopped to admire one of the artificial pools of water, or crack a joke about the ducks. For some reason my father seemed to find ducks comical. Otherwise he hardly noticed animals, and he hated the budgies my mother had taken to breeding with the wholehearted eccentricity of a woman whose children have long ago left home. But he liked ducks, including Walt Disney ducks. When we were children he passed judgement on our friends according to whether they pronounced 'Donald Duck' correctly or said 'dook', with a German U sound. If they said it like that, I am sorry to admit, he would shake his head scornfully.

Of course he told Harry, on this occasion, the hoary old tale of the duck in Hyde Park which he thought he had seen diving when he was a little boy. 'It's had its head down in the water an awfully long time,' he told Uncle Tom, full of admiration for the duck, until other people noticed too, and there was no denying that although the duck was drifting on the surface of the pond it was indeed dead, its head and neck below the surface as if looking for something. The duck had died during its last dive, a wonderful death. My father concluded this story with his usual wish to die quickly and suddenly himself, preferably in his sleep. As always, I was against the idea. I thought nothing in life should be so sudden, that both the dying person and his family would need a chance to come to terms, to prepare, to say goodbye.

'That's too sad for me,' said my father, making a face. I objected that hardly anyone, himself included, went to bed at night with all his conflicts resolved, all accounts settled, all his fields cultivated, so to speak.

'Suppose you've quarrelled with someone and you want to say you're sorry for it next day,' I said, wondering as usual why I let myself in for these unrealistic and absurd mind games, 'and that's the very night when you . . .'

'I don't quarrel that badly with anyone,' my father interrupted me, 'and if I'm dead he'll forgive me anyway.'

'What do you mean, forgive?' I asked, observing with annoyance yet again how I couldn't shut up, how my father and his friendly, childlike persistence could always provoke me into hopeless arguments. 'He might even be thinking your death was his fault!'

'Well, in case you have yourself or your brother in mind,' said my father, grinning at me, 'I can assure you here and now that I won't reproach you afterwards.'

'Here we are,' said Harry, pointing to a stone bench standing among some rose-beds. 'Where?' asked my father excitedly, taking the seaman's bag off his shoulder. 'Here,' said Harry, with an expansive gesture towards a picturesque group of trees. 'But where's their grave?' asked my father, baffled. Harry explained that this area was called a Garden of Remembrance, you could have your ashes scattered here, and that was what Uncle Tom and Auntie Annie wanted. Strictly speaking, it was what Auntie Annie wanted, because she had outlived Uncle Tom. She had kept the urn with Tom's ashes in it on the mantelpiece at home in Chiltern Road during her lifetime, and then, after her death, her ashes had been mixed with his and they were scattered here in a little ceremony.

'But why on earth did she do a thing like that?' asked my father, looking thunderstruck. The mad idea occurred to me that he might have a stroke on the spot, and I started wondering what red tape I would then have to battle with in order to take someone who had actually died in a cemetery back to another country. I suppressed an urge to laugh, and felt guilty for having such thoughts in view of the alarming picture that my old father suddenly presented. Harry said he had often talked to Annie about it; she thought that graves that no one ever visited were so sad, and since she and Tom had had no children of their own, the expense of a grave seemed unnecessary. And she had loved roses so much, Harry went on, but my father didn't seem to be listening to him any longer. At the words 'no children of their own', a painful expression had come over his face. And now he was looking around for help. 'You mean there's nothing saying that . . .' He cleared his throat. 'Saying that they were scattered here? No name, no plaque? Even in the concentration camps they have rooms now where . . .'

'Oh yes, yes,' cried Harry, who was looking as uncomfortable as I felt. 'There's a memorial room with a book where . . .'

'Let's go and see it,' said my father.

But the memorial room did not improve matters. There was indeed a fat, gilded book in a glass case, with the names of all the 'scattered people', as my father called them from now on, entered in it by a calligrapher, each on the day of his or her death. The page was turned in the morning every day by the cemetery staff, to show the page for today's date. 'Polly Greenwood,' read my father, baffled. 'William S. Bulldog . . .'

'They died one in March and one in April,' whispered Harry. 'I can look up the exact dates at home.'

'You mean no one will open this case up for me now and show me the pages?' asked my father, with the energy draining out of him.

'I'm afraid not,' said Harry.

We quarrelled all the way back, but in German so as not to hurt Harry's feelings. My father thought a funeral like that was barbaric, and I made out that I didn't know why he was so upset.

'A rose garden is a beautiful place,' I said. 'It's different.'

'I mean, different from that ugly gravestone you put up to

our grandparents,' I said reproachfully, but there was no persuading my father.

'I had to buy that ugly gravestone myself because my clever brother Bertl had gone broke at the time,' he said crossly. 'Do you know what a proper gravestone costs?'

'No idea,' I said. 'I think wooden crosses look good too.'

'We couldn't have put a cross on Grandpa's grave,' said my father furiously.

'People need a place where they can go to visit,' he added crossly, and I said, 'But we did go to the rose garden.'

'You're bent on misunderstanding me,' said my father, 'I might just as well have gone to look at the ducks in Hyde Park, I was there once with Uncle Tom too.'

'We can go and look at the ducks in Hyde Park to-morrow,' I suggested, and he said wearily, 'Maybe.'

After a few more steps he began again. 'And I brought the cup all the way here from Europe. For nothing!' My father always said 'Europe' when he wanted to distinguish England from the Continent. I said I doubted whether we would have been able to leave a huge darts trophy on a grave in an ordinary cemetery, just like that.

'And why not, may I ask?' said my father sharply. 'Artificial flowers and candles in plastic containers, yes, but not a beautiful cup like that?'

'We don't have to fight about it,' I said, trying to mollify him. 'I mean, the question doesn't arise now.'

'Oh yes, it does,' cried my father. 'We need somewhere to leave the cup!'

I thought hard, but with the best will in the world I couldn't come up with any ideas. And I couldn't concentrate properly because I was in a temper. My father was so selfish and illogical! Where his own death was concerned, he wanted to get it over with as quickly and painlessly as possible, never mind the shock to his bereaved family, which would include me. But when it came to visiting his foster-parents' grave he was posthumously denying them their right to make up their own minds. He wanted a place where he could grieve, full stop. And now I had to think of something to do with Uncle Tom's darts cup. Really, it was like being in the kindergarten.

Still, I should have known. I should have known that I would soon be reproaching myself, because then it would be too late, and I wouldn't even have tried. I put it down to the unaccustomed nicotine that I kept waking up at night now and imagined myself talking to a member of the cemetery staff in Stopsley. At first this faceless man was unforthcoming and stubborn, but when I had controlled myself and told him the whole story calmly he softened up, and in the end he agreed to display the cup prominently in the memorial room, and even to get the calligrapher to write a little plaque: 'In Memoriam Thomas Cook, beloved foster-father of little Sunny who came to England in 1938 as a refugee from Nazi Germany . . .' Here at the latest, when I didn't know how the memorial text should go on, I realised that I was dreaming with my eyes open, that I was about to lose my father, and I was afraid of it.

On the other hand I could have remembered that my father's moods of annoyance and unhappiness seldom lasted long. That evening, when we were back in our London hotel, he was able to call my mother and tell her about our lovely day in Stopsley. 'Guess what, they had their ashes scattered in a park,' he said in a chatty tone. 'People do things differently here.' I wasn't very good at laughing at myself for my attitude to my father, but at that moment I managed it, at least after the event. I went into the bathroom to laugh there. It was no use, all my attempts to smooth-talk him into understanding the point of the Garden of Remembrance had been totally superfluous, for he was a master of smooth-talking himself, 'a past master', as he liked to put it when he thought he was really good at something. 'I'm a past master in four disciplines,' was one of his favourite and even slightly lewd sayings, 'football, playing cards, tennis, and you can guess the fourth for yourselves.'

For me the best moment of our trip was when the smiling officials of Arsenal Football Club hurried to meet my father, surrounded him, shook his hand and clapped him on the back, and when the club photographer took pictures of this lively event with as much interest as if he were standing on the edge of the football field with the Arsenal forwards making for the goal mouth. Perfect thinking ahead, I congratulated myself. One of my friends in London knew someone, who in turn knew someone else who was a nephew of one of the Arsenal officials, and in this convoluted way, which really was typically Austrian, it had been possible to awaken interest in an ancient letter that my father had received over sixty years before. Let's not be under any illusions, however; the letter alone would hardly have been enough to attract such interest. Just anyone with an old letter like that would hardly have made it to the VIP lounge, to have his photograph taken and be given a glass of wine, but the link between the letter and the story of a former refugee child saved by the English opened all doors.

The letter hadn't in fact reached him in Stopsley, but had to be sent on to him in Austria at the time when my grandfather was grimly trying to get him a job as a car mechanic or a lathe operator, and it must have seemed to my father like a message from his lost Paradise. Arsenal of London, the football club which, even in his old age, my father followed more enthusiastically than any other, had said in writing that it would like to recruit 'the young Austrian boy' for its junior team. A man who was a fatalist and pessimist, as my father was not, might have seen this letter as the first of a long series of strokes of bad luck which had put obstacles in the way of an even more glorious sporting career for him. First he had to go back to Austria instead of joining Arsenal. Then he did play at top level in

Austria, but in his time there were more good players than you found there later, so he was only one among many. During the World Cup of 1954 in Switzerland, when Austria reached the sensational and historically unique heights of third place, he was in hospital for months because of his lung, which must have looked like Katzi's lung thirteen years earlier, with the life-saving difference that penicillin had now been discovered. He had been in the national squad, and that World Cup might have been the springboard to an international career. But he was suffering from tuberculosis, fighting for his life and health instead of the World Cup. Finally, my father might even have lamented being born too early. 'Thirty, forty years later and I could have been a multi-millionaire,' he sometimes used to say, thinking of the gigantic incomes of modern footballers. He didn't mean the word 'multi-millionaire' literally; to him, it stood for just having plenty of money, which he never did. But even when he said something like that he was not complaining, just stating a fact. He was unemotional and professional enough to know that he had lacked the physical strength to be a really outstanding player. There was no disputing his extraordinary talent, his feel for the ball. But he was always a little too thin, too slight. In the circumstances, he may well have thought to himself, he had fulfilled his maximum potential.

So he just smiled shyly when we visited Arsenal, thanked them courteously for the free ticket, and wasn't nervous until one Arsenal official wanted to borrow the photo my father had brought with him to prove his credentials, and print it in the club's newsletter. It was one of the pictures showing him in the Austrian national strip, holding the bouquet of flowers in the crook of his arm, just before the whistle went for the start of the match against Hungary. 'It's the original,' he whispered, hanging on to it with both hands. 'Of course,' said the PR man, letting go of the photo, 'I quite understand.' Then they had all suddenly disappeared, and we went to our seats. 'Do you think he's angry about that photo?' asked my father uncertainly. I was speechless. 'He's a clumsy idiot,' I said at last, and my father reproved me. 'You're always so aggressive!'

'I shall be eternally sorry I didn't go with you,' said my brother, lighting a cigarette from the stub of its predecessor, because in my clumsy way I had used up all the matches. 'Oh, it wasn't much,' I consoled him. 'A small English town, a rose garden, a football match.' I thought of the cobblestones in Stopsley after a brief shower of rain, when the sun shone on the wet road in front of the tiny terraced houses, and my father, standing beside me, said with good humour, 'The weather's still the same.' When I wanted to take a photo he posed so clumsily that there was always a branch of the elder bush in front of his chest. He stepped to one side, stumbled, caught hold of the honeysuckle and tore a piece off. We both laughed, and I told him that if he stood there he'd be hiding the house number. 'The elder bush, then,' said my father, and made his way back to it. Finally he went right behind the elder, spread its branches with his hands and peered through them with a mischievous expression. 'The old star's childhood haunts have long been overgrown,' he announced, imitating the tone of a TV newsreader, 'but the few remains will be conserved by a team of archaeologists from London University and saved for posterity.'

I thought of the kitsch lamp my father had bought me in a London flea-market, because we both liked it and we were sure that everyone else we knew would think it hideous. Even as we were wondering how to get the unwieldy thing home with us, I had realised that that lamp would be with me longer than my father, and would always remind me of him later. But who'd have thought it would be so soon? Now I had stolen a march on my brother in having all these memories, and the photos weren't any use to him. However, I would never let him know that. 'Look,' I said, 'it's only like computer data bringing up subjective associations.' My brother looked inquiringly at me. 'Our father's childhood in England,' I tried to explain. 'It meant nothing to us for ages, and now he's old we're collecting photos of the place, but what good will that do?'

'I don't know,' said my brother. 'Cousin One thinks we become less and less of a family the more we try to construct one out of stories and anecdotes.'

'He's a fine one to talk,' I mocked, and with an apologetic expression I took another cigarette, although the smoking was making me feel ill. 'Years ago Cousin One made dozens of tape-recordings of his English granny.'

'Is that so?' asked my brother, surprised. 'I never knew!'

'And he knew it was the last time,' I told my brother later, because we liked trying to make a kind of hero out of our father to each other, even if it was a hero of the Parsifal kind. I told him about our journey back from Stopsley. Harry had taken us to Luton Station, and as we were all waiting on the platform he suddenly brought out another old photo of the Boys' Club. My father seemed to remember hardly any of the faces, but Harry put names to them all. One had died in a car accident in his mid-twenties. My father looked shocked. Another died of cancer last year, a third was still alive, but had senile dementia. But these boys, Charlie, Gerry, Willie, Dinkie, Joe and Phil, all still lived in Stopsley and were in the best of health.

'Next time you come, when I have more time to plan ahead,' said friendly, helpful Harry, shaking hands vigorously with my father, 'I'll round them all up! That'll be fun!'

'Yes, that'll be fun,' agreed my father, smiling and looking at the train coming in. 'We definitely must do it!'

As soon as we were in the train he said drily and without a trace of regret, 'Well, that will have been the last time.' Then my father opened the window, waved to Harry again and shouted, 'See you soon!'

The End

In retrospect, I feel as if the end came out of a clear blue sky, but we can't agree even about that. My younger cousin, the only one of the family whom I still see every few years, mainly to talk about that end once we've exchanged all our news of children and grandchildren, my younger cousin thinks that given the characters and all the circumstances, we could have seen the end coming. It was only a matter of time, he claims, turning up the palms of his hands, before our minefield of a family history would explode and blow what ought really to have held it together to smithereens. Moreover, did I realise that, absurdly enough, certain conflicting parties who were well known to me saw confirmation of their views in that crisis? But I don't want to hear what he says about that. 'Oh, stop going on about their characters, and for goodness' sake shut up about the family history,' I protest angrily, although I sense that he is right, and he consoles me, grinning, by pointing out that it might have happened much sooner too. 'And then we'd have been the poorer by a number of amusing evenings,' he adds, and I always wonder how much of it he means seriously.

Yet it began just as usual. The evening before, I'd concluded weeks of negotiating over the dates with all concerned, and I am glad they realised, anyway, that without my patient efforts these meetings would have lapsed a long time ago. But for my 'family mania', as they called it with the usual touch of irony, we too would have been a family that meets only at funerals, for we now lived too far apart even for weddings and round-number birthdays.

That was not because the others didn't like seeing each other, or didn't enjoy these rare family evenings as much as I did, it was just that my cousins and my brother were caught up in a complicated network of pride and blame. When someone had issued the invitations for a family gathering, then it was someone else's turn next time, but as my younger cousin and my brother either felt a pressing desire to see the family several times in succession, or went months without communicating, simply forgot the dates agreed and were thus very unpredictable, my elder cousin felt almost permanently insulted, and would say he had no time to come. 'I'm never inviting him again,' said my brother. 'If the family means nothing to them, what do I care?' said my elder cousin, and my younger cousin said, 'This is all ridiculous, I've had enough of both of them.' The only one who, within these neurotic relationships, was not taken seriously and thus enjoyed neutrality was me. So for many years I had been organising regular family gatherings at long intervals apart, to which everyone else graciously agreed to come after I had been begging them for weeks.

By way of recompense they laughed at me. 'Her father all over again,' mocked my elder cousin, 'she thinks being physically present is the same as belonging together.' And then everyone laughed and nodded. 'Well, what else is it?' I used to say, unmoved, knowing I was right, although they all flapped their right hands just as my grandfather apparently always did in dismissing an idea.

So it began as usual, and until the explosion it had been fine. The family was getting larger and larger and younger and younger. My two cousins' grown-up daughters had said they would cook and serve the meal. My son, who even as a child had been strikingly gentle and sociable ('He'd make a useless sportsman,' my old father had once remarked critically, sending me into a furious temper which made him laugh mischievously in his own turn), was looking after the small children who were crawling and toddling everywhere, my two cousins' first grandchildren, who were little Jews and little Protestants, for in the third post-Holocaust generation a clear choice of religion had become immensely important again, even if that meant we produced two different kinds of Austrian outsiders. My cousins, their wives and their sons-in-law, my brother and my sister-in-law sat harmoniously around the table; we smoked and drank, and during this preliminary skirmishing those in the know could already see the men warming up and getting into position as they vied with each other in making witty remarks and cracking jokes, while the women commented by sceptically raising their eyebrows, shaking their heads or laughing ironically.

The talk was about politics and Austria, about Israel and international football, and I was patiently waiting for it to move on to what for me, from childhood, had been the main business of these family gatherings, the inevitable part of the programme that my elder cousin's wife had baptised years ago as 'Em-Em', 'manic mythologising'. When it began, when the old family stories were brought out for the thousandth time, mulled over and reinterpreted, the women who had married into the family fled theatrically to the kitchen for a while, saying they didn't want to hear any more about England, Burma, football, films, the Weisskopf, crafty Aunt Gustl and her son who stole some kind of sticky pudding. But they soon came back, for although they would never have admitted it they had come round to liking the polyphonic firework display of point-scoring, the endless series of 'genuine Dollyisms', all the cosiness of this family blanket of stories in which we pleasurably wrapped ourselves, because it anchored our brief meeting in the past, putting down a short but sturdy root.

And in particular it kept the dead alive. My father had known that when, eyes twinkling, he had expressed a wish to be at the centre of such stories 'some day later', as his father my grandfather was. At the time he said it my brother had just been giving an unforgettable performance, re-enacting my grandfather's part in the hijacking of East European sportsmen at the Südbahnhof. We were all quite tipsy, and it was rather late, and then my brother suddenly fetched an umbrella from the hall and ran round the dining-table with it, jabbing the tip of the umbrella towards the ceiling again and again and calling out, 'Cheap, cheap, come along,' following it up with something incomprehensible that was presumably meant to be Czech and Hungarian, crying, 'Best goods, best prices, forints, zlotys, dinars all accepted.' So my brother ran round the table, jabbing the umbrella in the air as he reached virtual business cards up to virtual train windows, and we laughed and shouted and put our hands in front of our hot faces, until my brother got the umbrella entangled in the chandelier and the light went out. And it was into this brief, shocked silence that my old father said he hoped such stories would be told of him 'some day later', stories like those we were now telling about poor Grandpa, who'd certainly be glad to think we still appreciated his qualities as a salesman.

My father didn't need to wish for that specially. As the weight shifts, and the generations almost imperceptibly pass the baton on to each other, it was quite natural for my children and my cousins' children to begin telling stories about the famous footballer. They gave their children and their friends accounts of his brilliant combination of passes, his centring of the ball and his wonderful goals as vividly as if they had been there, and the story became more and more exotic because football was hardly important in Austria at all any more. The heroic deeds recounted by his grand-children, at a time when for over a decade the Austrian national team hadn't taken part in any international competitive footballing event, sounded to them as extraordinary as the fact that my grandparents had once spoken the languages of the places over the border sounded to me as a child – places beyond the barbed wire, only half an hour from Vienna, where in my childish imagination darkness and crime prevailed.

Among themselves, this new and now grown-up generation of grandchildren also talked about the trade with the Eastern bloc, the shipments of oranges organised by their grandmother, the brave little Englishwoman, who in my cousins' daughters' imagination began to feature as a master spy, a cross between Mata Hari and Greta Garbo.

To this day I like the oldest stories best. They are the most adaptable and promising, because their true nucleus lies so vanishingly far back in time that almost anything is permissible. My brother and my older cousin were equally talented, for instance, in picturing Aunt Gustl's malice, trying to mimic her sparkling gaze, and describing in detail the many cruel ways in which she had tormented first her father the devout Jew, then poor Dolly the amiable but dim bank manager. 'Pater semper imperfectus,' chuckled my brother. 'Ultimately everything else is of primary importance,' chuckled my elder cousin. But strictly speaking the witty passages were just the interlude among more serious discussions. These circled around the unknown, theories were constructed, surmises expressed, and the more agitated the conversation became the less any clarity became possible. Had the grandparents ever thought of getting out of the country? Had they, like so many others, been lulled into a sense of security for too long? Had my grandfather really helped to build the Danube–Oder Canal during his forced labour, the waterway beside which we all spent such lovely summers later, while he sat quietly under a sun umbrella, always in long trousers and a suit jacket? What had really happened to the rug, the 'one valuable item', the loss of which my grandmother had constantly lamented in the days before her death? For a while my brother the historian tried to find out more about our grandfather. There must be records, said my elder cousin accusingly. But the first records my brother found were those of our grandfather's early jail sentences, and so he soon stopped looking any further. He had always been more interested in heroic tales, so he turned his attention back to the Alexandrian banker and his family, from which, as he discovered, several Jewish scholars of note had come over the centuries. Just once I heretically asked what that had to do with us, but then he accused me of being too small-minded to appreciate great, rounded poetic and historic truths, while my two mischievous cousins concurred, murmuring, 'Granny Frieda all over again.'

On one such evening I found out that my uncle, that frail, silent chain-smoker, was once said to have attacked a Nazi and thrashed him with an umbrella in a football stadium. 'He was no coward,' conceded my elder cousin, who usually still continued in grim opposition to his father, even though my uncle was long dead, but still, fathers and mothers as they exist in their children's minds should not be confused with the people they really were. 'It was at a game against Rapid,' said my brother appreciatively, lighting a cigarette. 'The Rapid team were always the worst anti-Semites.'

'And the Austria was thought of as a Jewish club,' said my elder cousin. 'I saw that all the time as a child.'

'How exactly did they let people know it?' asked my son incredulously, for he had grown up in Germany, where customs were entirely different in this respect.

'Well, every time one of the Austria team got the ball

they shouted, "Jewish swine, Jewish swine" at him,' said my brother, nodding portentously.

'I don't believe it!' cried my son, shocked, and looked pleadingly at me.

'Well, not all of them,' I had to admit, 'but some did. I remember that too.'

'And there were no Jews at all playing in the whole of the country,' remarked my elder cousin. 'Uncle Sunny was probably the last.'

'Yes, but he was still playing when my father beat up the anti-Semite,' said my younger cousin. My elder cousin vehemently denied it. The incident had taken place at the beginning of the seventies at the earliest, but Uncle Sunny stopped playing in the mid-sixties, he said, so the brawl had been much later. 'Was either of you there, and if not where did you hear about it?' I asked, but no one was listening to me. 'Never mind that – how does the story go?' cried my brother, and my sister-in-law shook her head ironically, murmuring, 'Typical.' My elder cousin's wife, the dry north German woman, gave my sister-in-law a signal and jerked her chin in the direction of the door. My sister-in-law hesitantly shrugged, but couldn't bring herself to go into the kitchen, for this was a new story. Instead, she bent down and picked up a child who was crawling around under the table.

'Calling it a brawl is going too far,' pointed out my younger cousin. 'Well, almost a brawl,' cried my elder cousin. 'Who knows what might have happened?'

'It was a case of class warfare, if you ask me,' said my younger cousin.

'Aha, he's letting the Marxist in him loose,' teased my brother, laughing. 'No, I didn't mean it like that,' murmured my younger cousin, but then I brought my fist down on the table and shouted, 'Will you let him finish?'

'All right, Granny Frieda,' said my brother. 'Carry on, then, Cousin Two!'

So my younger cousin said there had been a fat, drunken fan holding a huge beer can in the row in front of him, and he kept muttering something about the Jewish swine that Hitler had forgotten – I watched with alarm as my son turned pale, and wondered whether we really had to unload old stories like that on young people – and then my uncle, who generally wore a suit and tie even in the stadium, suddenly said out loud that the fan had better shut up or he'd get it in the neck. 'Get it in the neck?' I said, irritated, 'Uncle Bertl never said a thing like that!' But no one was taking any notice of me. So the proletarian, my younger cousin went on, ignoring the 'Oh, please!' uttered by my brother – it was better not to use that word in front of him, for 'proletarian' originally meant just a worker, as he had told me when I was only fifteen and deeply ashamed of how little I knew of political and etymological sensibilities – so the proletarian had just turned round briefly and kept babbling, 'Shut your gob.' A few minutes later one of the Austria team reached the edge of the penalty area with the ball and was going to take a shot at goal, but instead he fell in a tangle of defenders and lay there. The referee blew his whistle and hesitated. He went over to consult the linesman, and at that moment the spectator in front of my uncle went spare. He jumped up, shouting, 'Faking it! Jewish swine! Faking it! War profiteers!' while frantically waving his beer can, which had long been empty, and then, so my cousins said, my uncle picked up his umbrella and brought it down with all his might on the drunk's shoulders, once, twice, three times, until someone grabbed his arm and stewards dragged the drunk away. He could still be heard bellowing in the tunnels. For a few seconds after that the whole stadium held its breath, because a penalty was given, thus preventing further escalation of the trouble between my uncle and the drunk's friends who were still there. Everyone was staring at the field, where Robert Sara put the ball safely

344

away in the left-hand corner. After the penalty a few more dark looks from the front row went my uncle's way, but he stared back with eyes narrowed and chin jutting, to show that he would strike again without fear or favour at the next anti-Semitic remark. 'It reminds me how Grandpa slapped Nandl's face in the middle of the war,' sighed my brother comfortably, and I cried enthusiastically, 'Tell us!' although I could have recited the story along with him, and although of course it hadn't happened in the middle of the war but before the Anschluss, which makes a certain historical difference. But I really had to stop being so self-opinionated.

So everything seemed to be pursuing its normal course. In between the individual stories, when we filled our glasses, helped ourselves to food, and talked idly, I was wondering which story I should dig up, one that hadn't been told for a long time, or whether there was some detail known only to me, a detail that I could add to the Em-Em process and thus earn merit in the family. Recently I had been particularly interested in Aunt Gustl. Very little research had been done into exactly what she got up to during the war: did she stay passive just out of fear, or was it her convictions that made her refuse to help my grandparents? In the course of time-consuming research into the archives, and thanks only to some amazing coincidences, I had found out that there were several German nationals and Austrian fascists in kindly Dolly Königsberger's family. One of Dolly's uncles had even played a very suspicious part in the burning of the Palace of Justice in 1927. All this raised several questions for me. How had Aunt Gustl managed to marry into such a family in the first place? And what did her membership of that family mean later? Did she have to lie low during the Nazi period and make great efforts to hide her origins, or did the name Königsberger, on the contrary, lend her a certain power? The letter in which she informed my grandparents of Katzi's death had been sent from the Salzkammergut. Had she fled to her friend Baroness O. there in real need, or had she chosen the Salzkammergut simply because she could live more comfortably there in difficult times? I was so deep in these thoughts that I almost missed the outbreak of family hostilities.

'. . . a pious prig from the Waldviertel,' I heard my elder cousin saying, 'every Sunday at High Mass, and you looked like a gilded angel.'

My brother was white with rage. 'When you're a child,' he spat, 'your parents can do what they like to you. You weren't proud of having to mourn all day with your mother on the anniversary of Stalin's death either!'

'I'm still not proud of it,' said my cousin, apparently casually, 'but I don't act as if I knew nothing about it.'

'What's going on?' I whispered to my second cousin. 'Territorial disputes,' he whispered back, grinning. 'Who's the better Jew?' I didn't understand a word of it.

Suddenly the pair of them had started in on the Vietnam War. My elder cousin claimed that my brother owed him his entire political education. 'Back in Kitzbühel, remember?' he said. 'Where Two broke his toe?' That was where he had first told my brother what was really going on in Vietnam and elsewhere, because at the time my brother had still shared his father's cosily naïve, pro-American, dyed-in-the-wool conservative view of the world.

'But apart from that you were always happy to borrow from my father,' cried my brother, red-faced, 'apart from his view of the world he was always a great guy to you!'

That was true. For a time it seemed as if my cousin and my brother would happily have swapped fathers. They did agree that their fathers were total failures as such, but they often quarrelled over which was the worse father, a competition in which each of them naturally saw his own parent as the victor. My brother always spoke highly of my uncle's grasp of politics, his intelligence and wide reading, while my cousin was full of praise for my father's wit and charm, and his enjoyment of life, by comparison with his own gloomy, cool father, who was always buried in his work. The way they stuck together like brothers in the curious atmosphere of the annual skiing holiday with their fathers and their fathers' second wives, while on the other hand each had to try holding up his uncle as a good example and a sympathetic figure, seems to me now both consistent and unfortunate, but that evening everything was happening much too fast for anyone to have a chance to point out these subtleties.

'You're both renegades in your own way,' said my younger cousin equably, reaching for a bottle of wine. 'Maintaining your self-images makes you creative in one way, unhappy in another.'

'So what makes *you* so cool?' said my brother, venomously, and my elder cousin joined forces with him. 'He did everything properly, right up to choosing a wife.' For a moment I was relieved, because the anger of both now seemed to be turning against a third party, and luckily my younger cousin's Israeli wife was out of the room just then changing her circumcised grandson's nappy. But I ought to have known that my younger cousin would never have got involved as a strategic lightning conductor, since he didn't fancy telling white lies to maintain a delicate state of affairs. He was much fonder of seeing things take their natural course, maybe knocking the first domino down and then sitting back to watch with interest. My younger cousin, Cousin Two, as we had called him for some years, was provokingly well-balanced. I had often wondered how he managed to keep so entirely out of all family quarrels, ignoring all the difficult problems of our identity and where we belonged, but it was probably simple enough: there was no other part available for him to play. That made him, as it were, a more thoughtful – and more Jewish – version of my father, a good-tempered, skilful businessman who moved through life like a fish in water, immune to higher questions about Being and Becoming, the inheritance of his ancestors or his own legacy.

'I think it's unhealthy to deny a part of your own background,' Two went on, but my elder cousin immediately interrupted him again. 'Not just unhealthy, most of all it's dishonest.'

My brother was shaken. 'Are you trying to get at me or what?' he asked, and I begged, 'Oh, do stop it!' but as usual no one was listening to me. So I decided to join in.

'I had to say my prayers too as a child,' I shouted, stamping my foot, 'just like him! Every evening, in front of the picture of my guardian angel!'

I did succeed just for a moment. They stared at me as if I had gone mad, and judging by what was thought proper behaviour in our family they had a point there. Then my younger cousin began laughing. The corners of my elder cousin's mouth were already twitching, only my brother's strangely smooth face puzzled me. 'I lie down and close my eyes,' I snarled, in the hope of holding their attention a little longer and thus letting the bad feeling between them evaporate; I imagined being Robert Sara and taking all the time in the world, because no one would start fighting until I had shot my goal – 'Let me rest until sunrise!' I tried not to look in the direction of my son, who had been made to go to ethics classes, although he would have been more interested in religious instruction.

To this day I am surprised that up to that moment I had entirely forgotten my own childhood prayer. Indeed, I had always said that my mother left us entirely alone in the matter of religion, despite her own Polish Catholic background. And now that I wanted to support my brother these scraps of memory suddenly surfaced, memories of candles and incense, of my little Polish grandmother, of murmuring in Polish and my picture of a guardian angel, and a little golden cross that I had worn around my neck, and finally, as briefly as a flash of lightning, I remembered an icy, scornful glance from my other grandmother, Granny Frieda. How old had I been? Why had it all stopped, rather suddenly, I assumed, otherwise I probably wouldn't have forgotten it for so long? 'So how does it go on?' asked Two, with his infuriatingly cheerful expression. 'It doesn't sound like a prayer.'

'Now I lay me down to sleep – I pray to the Lord my soul to keep,' my brother coolly replied for me. 'You can find it in any book of nursery rhymes!'

Although he is the last of my family that I still see, I shall never forgive my younger cousin for not dropping the whole thing at this point. After all, I had almost succeeded in saving the day with my tasteless Catholic striptease act. But now Two wanted to know all about it, and perhaps I am wrong about him and he isn't as provokingly laid-back as the rest of us always thought, but obsessive about getting everything cleared up instead. For with a malicious smile he began wondering how we half-siblings would have felt about each other if one of our mothers had been Jewish. With some reason, he said that our good and affectionate relationship, despite all our fights, was the result not least of the fact that we were that precarious mixture, the children of a Jewish father and a Christian mother. At the same time, he added, no one had to look too closely at the question of whether Sunny, Bertl and Katzi had been really Jewish themselves; that made no difference. For once, it could be taken for granted in this particular thought experiment. Moreover, he added, right at the end, in the hospital ward, Uncle Sunny had told him that he suspected he hadn't really needed to emigrate as a child at all, because of his Aryan mother, but he mentioned that just in passing.

After this the discussion finally exploded. I can't get all the shouting, arguments and hostilities that followed into any kind of order, and in sheer self-protection I've forgotten a lot of it. Today, I can distinguish, with difficulty, only certain individual groups of subjects which were bitterly disputed, in particular two. For the sake of simplicity I'll call one historical and the other topical. My brother and I had always agreed on the historical part, our assessment of the religious identity of our father and our uncle, and we had probably also suspected all along that our cousins, who could rest easy in the knowledge that their mother was Jewish beyond any doubt, did not share our opinion. It was just that until that day we had carefully avoided the subject. Now, however, it was all out in the open, and belligerent arguments pursued the most absurd lines of reasoning. While my brother and I, relying only on the little lady who had been in charge of the registers in the Jewish Community office thirty years earlier, insisted that the Halacha ruling on Jewish descent had become a strictly enforced distinction, a demarcation line again only after the Shoah, my cousins laughed at us because they said we were basing our claim on a vanishingly small period of local rabbinical *laissez-faire* and wanted to make a law of it. My brother happily held forth at length on whether the Viennese Jewish community of the twenties had perhaps been more liberal than elsewhere, but I insisted, with all the strength of desperation, on what seemed to me irrefutable: the fact that the two children had been sent out of the country, and returned to find their parents now strangers to them and broke, and then there was our grandfather's dog-tag, his 'sauced labour', his mother's transportation to Theresienstadt; wasn't that enough to give the little family a clear identity as Jews in 1947 when my father came back, wasn't it enough to class them with the victims of persecution? But then one of our two cousins, and perhaps even my brother too, said that yet again I was confusing individual identity with the facts about religious affiliation, and then I may have turned angrily on my brother and asked if he was going to stab me in the back now, whereupon one of my two cousins said that Uncle Sunny for one had never felt he was either a Jew or a victim or both, and then it could be that Two asked, with his mischievous look, why on earth we were insisting on being Jewish, and then I am sure my brother shouted that we were not insisting on anything, whereas Two, on the other hand, was carrying on like someone personally implementing the Nuremberg race laws, and so it went round and round, back and forth, with no solution, no way out.

When we came to the subject of present circumstances the fronts were drawn a little differently. Two and I could agree more easily on conceding that communities make rules which have to be kept. My younger cousin, who with his Jewish mother and Israeli wife was undoubtedly a respected member of the Jewish Community of Vienna, was of course keen on rules because they gave him personal security. I, on the other hand, had always been very sceptical about affiliation to any particular confession; it wasn't important to me, it left me cold. For that very reason, however, I could share Two's opinion: anyone who wanted to belong to one should surely be able to bend the rules, so if you felt confessional Judaism was important to you, why not convert, become a Jew, learn, pray, and sway your torso back and forth for the good of your soul? My brother and my elder cousin, on the other hand, would not at any price accept that the wisdom of Jewry should not modernise itself by also guaranteeing admission to people whose fathers had been obviously Jewish. The Halacha ruling that a Jew was someone whose mother had been Jewish just meant that a

Jew must be descended from at least one Jew, that one of his or her parents must be a Jew – so my elder cousin argued for about the hundredth time, as if the rest of us were a rabbinical court and he had to convince us. Since for six thousand years it had been possible to be sure only of the maternal line, up to now, understandably enough, attention had concentrated on the mothers. 'But now we have genetic paternity tests and the matrilineal principle is out of date,' my elder cousin shouted at his brother, because he was annoyed to think that his daughters had not been able to join the Jewish religious community just like that, with the result that one of them had married a nephew twice removed of her mother's, thus reinforcing the north German Protestant element in the family out of pure contrariness, as her father my cousin now thought; he had never particularly liked that son-in-law.

My brother, on the other hand, had obviously still not got over being thrown out by Anny Kennich almost three decades ago, or at least he reverted to the subject again and again, always describing 'certain people' as racists, which yet again sent Cousin One off the deep end. Cousin One thought he should remind him of the reasons for which they had both once left the Marxists. 'Describing Jews as racists always has something revanchist about it,' cried my elder cousin, 'so it's anti-Semitic in the pure sense of the word!'

'Your father had more sense than you,' spat my brother back, 'he knew that some Jews are idiots!'

'He was right there,' said Two, grinning, 'and Anny Kennich was certainly among them.'

'Although she defended your Halacha law so valiantly!' said Cousin One corrosively, but that was just a side-swipe, and his brother ignored it.

Meanwhile all the others, the wives, my cousins' daughters and their sons-in-law, had heard all this going on and came in, and they assembled around the fighting cocks in two groups, trying to calm things down. It was no use. My brother and my elder cousin kept freeing themselves from the soothing murmurs of the peacemakers to shout new accusations at each other. It finally boiled down mainly to whether my brother must bear some of the responsibility for being regarded by the Austrian public, ever since the Popelnik Affair, as what the newspapers always liked to call 'a provocative Jewish historian', which in fact he was not, at least in the opinion of both my cousins.

'The Jews don't know how they got into this,' teased Cousin Two, smacking his lips slightly, 'but you might at least have asked if we wanted someone stirring things up first!'

'Arrogating a Jewish identity!' cried Cousin One. 'Very good publicity, though!'

I was amazed to realise how much offence and anger my elder cousin must have been bottling up all these years. I had long suspected Cousin One of being very envious of my brother and seeing himself as a scholar and historian *manqué*. Now and then my elder cousin had published short articles on historical subjects in the economics journal on which he worked, and my brother, who undoubtedly suffered from a sense of rivalry, had made occasional remarks about them which my over-sensitive cousin liked to misunderstand as patronising. But was that a good enough reason to attack him like this now?

My brother, on the other hand, was a very special case. I had firmly believed that there was an unwritten law within the family to accept him as he was – 'You always treated him like a prince, you always let him off the hook,' Two would tell me, and I would be so indignant that I hardly knew what to say. In a certain way Two was right. I did think my brother a kind of artist, an expert in the art of living. The whole business of his courageous exposure of Popelnik, which had brought him as much hatred as recognition, as much prominence as professional disadvantage, still seems to me the basic pattern of his life. And ultimately, doesn't it say more about the Austrian public than about him that someone fouling his own nest is always supposed to be a Jew? Yes, he liked to be challenging and provocative, he liked to be the accuser, to present himself as someone who discovers and casts light on the facts, but at the same time he had always been extremely sensitive, and reacted to opposition with positive hysteria because he mistook it for the withdrawal of love. I sometimes think that right inside he is still the little boy who so much wanted to play football and win his father's approval, but whose feet, unfortunately, were far too big. Two once roared with laughter when I put this theory to him. I was indulging in the most superficial kind of psychologising, he said, and everyone has to work to improve himself instead of spending his whole life thinking that he is the victim of some kind of childish injustice.

But secretly I think, all the same, that you can't lump everything together. My brother was the way he was, sometimes pretentious, sometimes crazy, but after all he has achieved not just wide influence but remarkable academic success. And I don't mean just Popelnik, necessary and salutary as I think the scandal was for the Austrian popular mind. No, I think his early studies of heretical schisms are the most important of all his historical works, and they are still waiting to be properly appreciated and then seen in a wider context, indeed the widest possible political and philosophical light. Few things are really as topical today as my brother's 'Thoughts on the Uses of Heresy'.

Who would seriously dispute that to create intellectual masterpieces you need a certain amount of insanity, a tendency to show off plus an inferiority complex, an element of posturing, exaggeration, desperation? And who should know better than I do, mere observer that I always was, the perfect successor to Granny Frieda, noticing and scrutinising everything, but without an ounce of inspiration of my own? At least, aren't all artists and intellectuals making a spectacle of themselves in a certain way? Some more so than others . . . I can just hear Two saying, 'People who don't make much of a spectacle of themselves are what we call normal.' Why won't Two's voice shut up inside my head?

For that, ultimately, was the reason why I couldn't do anything on that fateful evening: I took up no clear position because I have two souls in my breast, and that's not all, I still let both of them have their say, and didn't throttle one long ago. That's always been my problem, really. When I was still a child, listening to my loquacious family, I had one great wish: I wanted to have an opinion of my own. Truthfully, that's what I wished for. Having my own opinion seemed the opposite of what I knew around the family table, which was dominated by myths and stories, aphorisms and *aperçus*, my grandfather still grumbling away in the afterlife and his all-powerful life history, all-powerful because it was incomplete. But in this family, where facts were often uncertain, where everything was whole and true only if you could make it into a story with a punch-line, I was obviously never going to succeed. And so I wavered that evening, I wasn't in any position either to take sides or to mediate, either of which would probably have been better than my muddled indifference. Was my brother really 'an imaginary Jew, an academic lame duck', as my elder cousin finally spat at the height of his diatribe, just before my brother rose to his feet and walked out? Was my elder cousin a 'renegade who feels he's a rabbi' as my brother shouted? And what part was my younger cousin playing while he just sat there smiling most of the time, as if this unnecessary and damaging family quarrel provided him personally with great entertainment?

I don't know. There's been a good deal I haven't really

understood since then. All I know is that when no one could stop my brother leaving, the rest of us went on sitting there and suddenly began talking about the whole concept of the family, courteously, in muted tones and with circumspection, as if we could undo what had been done that way. I too pretended I had no reason to ask my cousins a few uncomfortable questions about the aggressive stance they had just taken, the absurd and hurtful boundaries they had set, passing right through the family, I too sat there with a friendly expression listening to my elder cousin saying that to him 'the family' had always meant the other side of it, his communist English granny and the little Englishwoman's brothers and sisters. There in Willesden, among immigrants from all over the world, he had felt at home, not in the stuffy, dark Augarten apartment to which they were taken several times a week as children because there was no one else to look after them. Two didn't see it in quite such a negative light. Indeed, he said he had enjoyed playing chess with our grandfather. Yes, it was true that Granny Frieda was always scolding the children and calling them to order, but he didn't mind. 'Sad?' he asked in surprise, looking straight at his brother with an expression that I thought was the first genuine one that evening. 'Oppressive?' No, he hadn't felt sad and oppressed in the stuffy Augarten apartment. He would like to remind his brother, he said, how much fun they had with Grandpa, who regularly made derogatory remarks about 'old shitface', a name that as children they thought wonderfully vivid and shocking. 'Sometimes he took all three of us to the coffee-house,' Two reminded his brother, meaning all the old man's three grandsons, including my brother, who was the youngest, 'and then we had a strawberry soda and pretended to be playing bridge with Grandpa.'

'Granny Frieda was cold and unapproachable,' my elder cousin obstinately insisted, 'and she passed it straight on to our father.'

'Leave Grandpa out of it,' one of my elder cousin's daughters suddenly spoke up, meaning her own grandfather, my uncle. Ever since she was little, she said, she'd been listening to people saying what a bad father and cold-hearted man her Grandpa had been. She didn't think so at all, she added, while a glimmer of pride appeared in the face of her mother the dry north German; to her and her sisters he had been the kindest, most loving grandfather imaginable. She couldn't help wondering what was his two sons' problem, and she meant in particular her father, who seemed to have been taking it out on *his* father all his life. 'And Uncle is the same,' she said, pointing to the door through which my deeply insulted brother had left some time before. 'Exactly,' her cousin suddenly joined in, one of Two's daughters, and I had the distinct impression that a brand-new, different, peaceful and less exciting story was beginning, 'exactly,' she said, 'you're all obsessed with the past.' We had forgotten to live our own lives, she went on – while her uncle tried to smile arrogantly at this emotional declaration – because we were desperately looking for directions and guidance, political and ideological guidelines from the past. 'So just what is our so-called family history?' she rhetorically asked, reaching gracefully for her glass and draining it; our family history, she said, consisted of nothing but well-polished anecdotes on one hand and glaring great gaps on the other. 'It doesn't amount to anything coherent,' she said, putting her glass down, 'it's just silly talk.' Then she got up and went out, because one of her children had started howling in the other room. 'Ah, well, youth always has to be right even when it isn't,' said Two, stretching his legs, while Cousin One began on a final injured counterblast. There was a vast difference, insisted Cousin One, between just hearing about an icy, emotionally absent father and knowing him yourself. 'Oh, do be quiet,' said his wife, laughing, 'you haven't the faintest idea what they mean.'

And so it all ended. It was painful for those present and incomprehensible to everyone else. A family quarrel, that was all, an inability to resolve conflicts, obviously inherent in the first post-war generation. 'You don't know where he is either?' my husband will ask me every year round about the time of my brother's birthday, when the newspapers once again publish speculations on where exactly and for how much longer 'Austria's only historian of international standing' has gone to write his great work – for since he disappeared somewhere in South America, and only occasionally publishes essays in English-language journals, public opinion has of course adopted him as its favourite son. 'Why don't we meet again some time?' I'll keep asking Two on the phone when I'm thanking him for his annual Christ-nukkah card, and he will reply non-committally, 'Good idea, let's call each other soon and get together.'

'I saw Two's daughter on TV,' my son will tell me when he's home on holiday from working for the aid organisation in Israel. 'I think it was the elder one. What's her name again?'

Many years ago, when my brother and my elder cousin were still close, like brothers, like companions in misfortune, they sometimes used to say of each other, 'Your best friends are the friends you'd have chosen for yourself if they didn't happen to be related to you already!' And then they would roar with laughter and clap each other on the shoulder, they smoked and drank, invented new Dollyisms, which of course from the moment of their invention were served up by all present as originals, and told themselves and us stories. Your best friends and worst enemies usually do 'happen to be related to you already'. As long as my father, my mother, my uncle, Aunt Ka and the little Englishwoman were alive, they personified all the contradictions and inconsistencies of our family, they were evidence of everything that's possible, as long as they lived we children could be best friends and members of the same family too. But once that generation was dead, we sad successors to them struggled for explanations that no one before us had needed. And my amusing family has to end here, and so does the whole delightful Em-Em business of myths and mythologising.

Obituary

On the day of my grandfather's cremation the weather was changeable. Clouds were chasing over the Central Cemetery, with the sky vaulted high above them. The sun kept coming through, flickering, but its light looked wrong, too bright, like false gold. It was still warm, but near the ground there was a smell of November, damp and musty, although the year wasn't nearly as far advanced as that yet.

When my father and my uncle came to fetch her, my grandmother was already 'awake'. For months she had withdrawn further and further into a depressive, apathetic state, which many people thought was senile dementia. In this condition, when she was 'asleep' you couldn't make contact with her and she didn't seem to recognise anyone. But when she was 'awake' she was fully aware of everything, and explosive outbursts were possible at any time. She informed her sons, at the apartment door, that she would spit at Gustl if Gustl ventured to come, she would push her into the grave or murder her outright, that old shitface, if she dared do any such thing. My uncle walked past her in silence to the window and stared out at the narrow grey yard, twirling his car keys around his finger. My father ventured to point out to his mother that she was wearing shoes that didn't match. To ensure that they left soon, he decided not to intervene when my grandmother began stuffing old letters into her handbag, blinking back a few tears. Most of what she was muttering couldn't be made out, apart from several furious curses. Perhaps my grand-mother, in the hope of settling accounts with Aunt Gustl, actually cursed her as a 'snake in wolf's clothing' for the first time that day, who knows for sure?

Of course Aunt Gustl did come; she was never going to pass up an opportunity to make an entrance. She was still at home standing in front of the mirror, trying on several dark hats, with and without veils. She had already decided to wear the big garnet brooch, and her granite-grey stockings with the back seams might have been glued on. She opened the window to get a rough idea of the temperature outside. Down below a tram hurried past, ringing its bell, and the overhead wires hummed. She saw the racing clouds, shook her head, and was about to close the window when she saw her son. He was coming along Porzellangasse, as usual too slowly, just dawdling, she thought, as if he had no honest business to do. Nor did he. At this time Nandl Königsberger was at liberty again, freed only a few weeks ago, not that it really bothered his mother. She hadn't spoken to her errant child for years, and had lost all interest in the perils he ran. But she was making an exception for today. She had phoned him and imperiously demanded his presence; he must go to her brother's funeral at her side. Children are status symbols at family gatherings, and all she had was this one, not very bright child. When he turned up she inspected him in an unfriendly way. He didn't look very good, rather dough-faced, and he'd put on weight. His clothing was hopeless. He couldn't go like that, she decided, and felt his sleeve with scorn. From somewhere or other she produced one of good old Dolly's suits; she seemed to have kept everything. Its cut was not entirely up to date, but the fabric was expensive and looked like new. Nandl put it on and was childishly surprised to find that he could fit into his father's clothes. In his blurred memory his father was a giant, a good-humoured, massive giant standing between him and the sunlight. And now he was wearing Dolly's made-to-measure suit, which even Karli and Joschi would have envied him back in those carefree days.

When the doorbell rang he was ready to open it. His dangerous little mother was still powdering her nose. Outside the door stood Baroness O., Aunt Gustl's faithful shadow. What the link was between them no one knew, but they always stuck together, different as they were, at least outwardly. Like many female members of her class, thin Baroness O. always had a heavy suntan, which at her age made her look rather like an American Indian. Her obsessive maintenance of that tan – rumour said she was tanned all over – was in striking contrast to her total absence of any make-up, for women like her want to look like merry, wholesome country children all their lives. Unlike Aunt Gustl, who was generous with the spectacle of her physical charms while they lasted, the Baroness favoured striped, high-necked blouses and flat ballerina shoes with bows on the instep, which in contrast to Aunt Gustl's low necks and slit skirts were a style that could be worn even at nearly eighty. Aunt Gustl came out of the bathroom with her mouth painted cherry-red, and offered the Baroness her cheek. 'Well, what do you think of him?' she ironically asked, indicating Nandl with her chin. 'Delightful!' murmured the Baroness, with a sly smile. Then they called a taxi.

Hals & Co. stopped work on the stroke of nine. They had worked for an hour and a half as if it were a perfectly normal day, but at nine Fredi entered the business premises, coming from his breakfast at the Weisskopf, and had only to look around him with a portentous expression for his employees to end their phone conversations, stop writing their business letters, put the files back on the shelves and get ready. At his own expense Fredi Hals had put a large death announcement in the *Groschenzeitung*, in the family's name and, as representing 'all his friends', in his own. And so for Fredi Hals there could be no question but that his entire firm would pay a last tribute to his old friend. He had simply dismissed the objection that urgent long-distance calls from Asia came in at that time of day, and unforeseen emergencies might call for action of some kind. My uncle had suggested leaving a capable assistant behind, but Fredi wouldn't hear of it. Where my uncle was cool reason, Fredi was an emotional genius. Asia would just have to wait this morning. And all Vienna would see that he, Fredi Hals, knew what was right and proper when a good friend had died.

He and all his employees took the tram. Hals & Co. filled almost an entire tramcar, but dark-clad men are not a rarity in the Number 71. Fredi Hals's wife and adolescent son had come straight to the business premises so that they could all arrive at the Central Cemetery together. Three of the employees were carrying an enormous wreath. Its ribbon bow said, with affecting brevity, 'Goodbye! Fredi, Aniko and the firm'.

Fredi Hals himself reacted irrationally in emotionally distressing situations. He had indignantly rejected the idea of ordering the wreath from a flower shop to be delivered direct to the cemetery in the usual way. He wanted to see what he was paying for, he bellowed, and he personally would make sure that there was no chance of the wreath's failing to arrive at the right time. Such things had happened before, he had thundered, and even if everyone was sorry afterwards that wasn't good enough for him. So his chauffeur, his accountant and his chief clerk carefully carried the wreath, lifted it into the Number 71 tram, and held it upright in the centre aisle.

Frau Erna the chiropodist had seen the notice in the *Groschenzeitung*. She passed a difficult few days wrestling with herself: should she go or should she not? She was afraid of meeting my grandmother, although they didn't know each other personally at all. From various intemperate remarks made by my grandfather, she had gathered that my grandmother thought chiropody was 'just throwing money away'. But my grandfather thought well-tended feet were an essential mark of the gentleman; a man of the world should be clean and well-groomed in every respect, he had told Frau Erna, winking, and not just where it showed. It was a long time now since my grandfather had come to her for a pedicure, but Frau Erna still clearly remembered those conversations. For decades she had humbly revered and idolised my grandfather, although she thought herself unutterably beneath him. There was she, the stout country girl with a tendency to blush, and there was he, the elegant gentleman who looked like the screen heroes in the cinema, with the difference that he was not cool, grave or soulful, but amusing and easy-going, and he, according to his bold remarks, could see right through her – seeing exactly what, she didn't want to know. Now and then he had his bad times, as she knew, having been acquainted with him for decades, but after she had seen him sitting in the Café Johann Strauss in the middle of that very bad time, she felt better about him. If he can sit in the Café Johann Strauss, she had thought, he can't be in quite such a bad way as many others.

So with just one long break, they had gone through life together, my grandfather and Frau Erna, meeting every few weeks for his pedicure. He had always praised her abilities to the skies, and was still thanking her years later for the way she had once removed his septic toenail. She had protested modestly that anyone could remove a toenail, but no, he had cried, that toenail was a real emergency. Who knew what would have become of him if she hadn't removed it? Frau Erna never quite believed him. However, as he always came back, she had soon begun to suppose that the toenail he made such a fuss about was a clue, a code for something that he didn't want to say straight out, or couldn't say, but which unfortunately she didn't entirely understand. However, her heart always beat so fast when he mentioned the toenail that it became important to her too. Later, when they were both old and the dreams of youth were muted and almost ridiculous, Frau Erna sometimes ventured to be a little flirtatious. Like an old fellow conspirator, she allowed herself to whisper, 'Well, and do you sometimes think of that bad toenail you once had?' But by then my grandfather didn't want to be reminded of it any more, he changed the subject, gave a melancholy smile and said, 'Oh, Frau Erna! How can I remember separate occasions when you're such an artist with people's feet?'

So now he was dead, now it was finally over, and she wanted to do what was proper, to pay him a last tribute, but how in the world could she offer condolences to the widow, how could she face her, a woman she didn't know but whom she imagined as queenly, and whom she had envied more than any other woman in the world for so long? Frau Erna, retired chiropodist, mulled over the question, and after finally deciding the evening before the funeral that she wouldn't on any account go, no, it wasn't right, she was not one of the family and would only make a fool of herself, she watched herself next morning putting on her dark coat and skirt, getting out the hat she had already worn for both her parents and all her brothers and sisters, even finding matching gloves, she watched herself with bated breath from outside, and then she set out, and her split ego left her no room at all for doubts.

The former caretaker of the grey building near the Augarten had arrived so early that he thought at first he had got the wrong day. Undecided, he shifted from foot to foot and looked at the stormy sky. Was it going to rain? That wouldn't matter much, for the main business would take place in the crematorium. He tried to send a few thoughts the dead man's way, because that was the thing to do. Pull yourself together, you and your memories. The dear departed had always been in a hurry, such a hurry that the former caretaker was more than once afraid he would slip and fall on the freshly cleaned stairs. Luckily it never happened, but the gentleman did have some falls, at least two of them in the war, though who knew if those were really just accidents? The former caretaker hadn't been there, he'd been in Spain. Ah yes, Spain . . . and afterwards the gentleman walked with a stick, always fast, tripping along with small steps. Then his son became a footballer when it was all over, he remembered that very well. A talented lad. He could speak perfect English too, he'd been over in England during the whole thing. The caretaker had liked the father, who always tipped him. Yet they had nothing themselves after the war, but who had anything then?

The former caretaker was suddenly addressed by an old man whose question showed that he had the right day after all. So they waited together, looking at each other with goodwill. How had he known him, the old man asked at last, and the former caretaker didn't tell the exact truth when he said they had lived in the same building for a while. He had always felt uncomfortable about being just a caretaker, so he offered the information, unasked, that until he retired he had owned a shop selling knives and scissors in Löwengasse. Oh, in Löwengasse, cried the old man, delighted, he himself had come into the world in Adams-gasse and grew up there, he knew just where the knife shop had been situated later. But he had never needed knives, he added a little apologetically, that was why the two of them met only now on this sad occasion. Yes, very sad, repeated the former caretaker, asking in his own turn about the old man's link to the dear departed, and he too was pretending just a little when he said they'd had a professional relationship, but that was so long ago that it didn't really count

any more. However, the caretaker, who himself distinguished clearly between highly regarded ways of earning a
living and those that you had to embellish a bit, went on
asking questions. So had he been a commercial traveller too,
maybe in the coffee trade? No, no, confessed the old man,
smiling thoughtfully, it was before that, much harder work,
and not entirely voluntary either, you know how it was.
'Ah,' cried the relieved caretaker, understanding perfectly
now. 'I was in Spain then.' But at this moment the employees of the firm of Hals & Co. arrived with the wreath and
several other mourners, and the two of them began wondering who the new arrivals were, and were soon separated
from each other.

The boss of Arabia Coffee came with his wife, and many of
the mourners noted that he, not she, was wearing mink. It
was only a mink collar, not an entire mink coat, but the
collar alone was so large that some of the mourners instinctively shook their heads. My father would say later that there
was really no need for the man to make such an improper
show of his wealth, particularly as it had been acquired by
the labour of people like his own father who were industri-
ous and loyal, even if stupid in this respect. But Herr Arabia
was not at all injured by such considerations. On the contrary, he seemed to be glowing with self-satisfaction for
having condescended to come to the funeral of an insignificant commercial traveller pensioned off ages ago, but my
grandfather had not been just any little representative, as
Herr Arabia assured my grandmother in a booming voice,
but a really valuable employee, perhaps the most valuable
employee ever to work for him. He had been ready to do
anything, Herr Arabia said appreciatively, while my father
looked pained, he hadn't even thought himself too good
to change the tubes in the Arabia Coffee neon sign ads;
now that was what he called commitment. You didn't
get employees like that these days, boomed Herr Arabia,

basking in the importance he was so generously sprinkling around; today's reps knew more about their rights than their duties. Here my father agreed, he agreed effusively, he nodded vigorously as he agreed, but no one picked up on his sarcasm. However, there was nothing else he could have done in that context, my father often thought later, and he wondered time and again if he didn't sometimes overdo the civility and general thoughtfulness.

It was only to be expected that Dr Schneuzl would put in an appearance, however hard it was for him. His break with his life's work of the Schneuzl Sports Club was only a few years in the past, and since that extraordinary general meeting from which he had slunk away like a criminal while the members were still discussing his fate, he hadn't seen any of his adversaries of the time. His life had been emptied of meaning at a stroke, and it had taken him some time to find out how to fill it again as best he might. At first he just sat at home for weeks under pressure from his wife, who was pestering him, and whose spineless opinion it was that enough grass had grown over the whole business by now. As honorary president for life, she said, he could just go down there again, act as if nothing had happened, and play tennis and cards as before. Oh yes, he asked sarcastically, and was he to get the architect Hinterstodl to let him play, was he to point out to the lawyer Wewerka when a court was not well tended or the gravel path had not been raked? No, he wasn't going to make even more of a fool of himself, sighed Dr Schneuzl, and when his wife would give him no peace he looked for occupation away from home. He had been regularly taking his old mother to play bridge in the Prückl for some time, and sometimes he played himself if one of the elderly players failed to appear without advance notice. And there at the card table he had heard of my grandfather's death, for Dr Schneuzl had never in his life read the *Groschenzeitung*.

Hard as it was for him, Dr Schneuzl would have come anyway, for he had known and valued my grandfather, but he would have done it even more for my father's sake, for ultimately, Dr Schneuzl secretly thought, you go to a funeral more for the living than for the dead. In spite of his deeply Catholic and conservative origins, Dr Schneuzl was really a free-thinker who had his doubts, although only very secret doubts, about some of the lines drawn by society. To outward appearance, he moved within the reliable and fixed framework in which he had grown up, for to leave it intentionally, he knew, would have meant being destroyed by the forces that would be released. So Dr Schneuzl stayed within it, and no one would ever know that he had come to the funeral entirely of his own accord, out of friendship for my father, hard as it was for him. However, and this was enough of a reason for his appearance to satisfy the members of the Schneuzl Sports Club, Dr Schneuzl had to escort his parents. His mother used to play bridge with my grand-parents, and my grandfather had known his father, Coun-cillor Schneuzl, for ever, although no one but the two of them now knew how. Councillor Schneuzl was in his wheelchair, and his wife wasn't very good on her feet any more either, so everyone assumed, seeing Dr Schneuzl pushing his father's wheelchair and supporting his mother, that he had come in the capacity of their son. It was only for that reason that he was venturing out of his self-imposed exile, thought those members of the Schneuzl Sports Club who were still proud of having recently ushered new and more modern ways into the club, even if by main force. But they were wrong: Dr Schneuzl would have come entirely of his own accord, even without his parents.

To my father's considerable displeasure, my brother had brought some student friends with him. They stood about over to one side smoking, tall young men wearing shabby coats from the flea-market. My father described those coats as 'smelly horse-blankets'. They all looked grim, grim and challenging, but fortunately they kept their mouths shut. It was quite enough for my father to see them smoking all the time, before, after, and almost during the committal ceremony in the crematorium, but they just managed to stop themselves in time. The young men with my brother were in a certain way, a way unknown to my father and all the more difficult to understand, the avant-garde, they were ten years too early for it but, as with an avalanche, you get a few snowflakes falling first and only much later does the entire slope come down. The young men who were studying with my brother had come because they wanted to be there when a victim of the Nazis was carried to his grave, a victim who of course had never been atoned for, and indeed was hardly recognised as a victim. It was even possible that a few old Nazis from the tennis club might come along, my proud and wrathful brother had told them, for his father had never feared contact with such people. The young men found that very interesting; many of them may well have had Nazi grandfathers themselves, but of course they had long ago broken with them and the generations had nothing in common. However, they could not imagine that even Jews might be in contact with old Nazis, as my brother claimed. These were the years when the whole thing was fermenting but was still far below the threshold of public perception. Suspected criminals were being cleared all the time by a prejudiced, indifferent, or at best overworked legal system, but there wasn't a word about that in the *Groschenzeitung*. There were many acquittals in Austria, and little attention was paid to it. My brother was already working on the Popelnik case, but no one knew about that yet. Another young man, who stood around smoking, would soon try to uncover the involvement in euthanasia of a highly regarded psychiatrist who had acted as an expert witness in the courts, but at first he simply triggered a libel suit that went on for years. For that was typical of the late seventies: one step forward and two steps back. This method of movement changed only much later into progress in the right direction.

So there stood the angry young men, smoking and bringing my father into disrepute, as he saw it, and when Werner Weis, Herr Bodo and Hupfi Göth turned up with a large group of Schneuzl Sports Club members, my brother actually began whispering and pointing at them without even attempting to conceal it.

Vickerl Weisskopf was nearly late. He had given himself a vodka quite early in the morning, he gave Fredi Hals one too, and then they both embarked on mournful lamentations. In the end he had drunk three little vodkas before nine, so the whole morning was in a muddle. Then Vickerl in person had prepared large platters of egg salad and chopped liver; the chef wasn't allowed to do it on a day like this, for no one could season such dishes quite like Vickerl. The mourners were coming back to the Weisskopf, of course, my father had reserved the whole of the room known as the Red Saloon. That was what my grandfather had wanted, and that was what they would do.

Finally it was so late that Vickerl hurried out of the restaurant still wearing his white apron, with red and yellow stains splashed all over it. When he reached the corner and noticed he ran back, and so he must just have missed his tram, for when he finally got to the tram stop it was an infuriating quarter of an hour before another one came along. That tram would take him only to Schwarzenbergplatz, where he had to wait again. It was drizzling slightly when he finally came through the gate and made for the crematorium, and there was no one left outside. He pushed the heavy crematorium door open and saw it all from behind. Dark-clad backs, the nearest to him being the least interesting, the people who were sitting in the back rows. Right in front of him a woman he didn't know turned round. She looked pink-cheeked and friendly, although she narrowed her eyes as if she were on her guard. Her face was bright against the gloomy background, bright and reassuring. Vickerl wondered whether this could be one of my grandfather's former mistresses. Having known his friend longer than almost anyone else, he had expected to see several elderly ladies. But this one didn't seem fashionable enough. The old bags in question, Vickerl noticed, were sitting much closer to the front, all side by side in a pew like Yiddish lady choristers. They had turned up as a group of my grandfather's bridge partners, and carefully kept from one another those other little secrets that most of them had shared with him at some time.

Vickerl peered at them. From behind, he saw a hat that must belong to Fuchsi. One of Fuchsi's idiosyncrasies was that she nearly always lost at cards but never liked paying her gambling debts. It had always been her habit to put off settling them by paying the older ones first, but never those incurred that day. Somehow she seemed to hope that she would have to pay less in total that way, but no one could say whether that was true, because soon people didn't know where they were with her. She had been a beauty in her youth, but that was far more than half a century ago. Vickerl Weisskopf, who suddenly noticed as he scratched his nose that his hands smelled of egg and chicken liver, was carried away by his memories. What fun they'd had before the war! And what a scandal the affair between my grandfather and Fuchsi had been! Back then Vickerl had thought my grandmother would throw him out, but you didn't do that kind of thing in those days. Instead, my grandmother had won the day in her cool, taciturn manner by getting pregnant again. Admirable calculation, thought Vickerl Weisskopf, but in a way she had always been the stronger of the two. First Fuchsi wanted to kill herself, then she went to Switzerland for a few years. And that had saved her life, thought Vickerl, amazed because this was the first time it had occurred to him. Fuchsi had survived because when it all started she was already in Switzerland. And afterwards they'd all played bridge together again as if nothing had happened.

There was quite a disturbance in the row of former bridge partners. Fuchsi kept shaking her head, muttering, 'Oh no, no, no,' and nervously patted her hat time and again to make sure it was on straight. Her friends to left and right of her didn't know where to look. They kneaded their hand-kerchiefs, they shuffled their feet, they scratched every-where they could reach, even under their skirts, they twitched each other's clothing, they talked under their breath and hoped it would soon be over. Even Aunt Gustl, sitting at the very end of the same row, joined in the uneasy muttering, whispering and rustling, and Baroness O. faith-fully copied her.

For the fact that my grandfather had chosen to be cre-mated was sacrilege. Jews must not let themselves be cremated, my father had told us children, it was one of the few times when the word 'Jew' was spoken out loud in our childhood. Christians ought not to be doing so either, my mother had added, shaking her own head disapprovingly.

My grandfather, however, had insisted on it, old, sick, grumpy, tired and stubborn as he was, and the one person to back him up, of all people, was my grandmother. 'Into the fire and then it's done with,' she had sometimes murmured, waving her hand in the dismissive way that she usually reserved for my grandfather. And she had made it emphat-ically clear that she wanted the same for herself. 'A small grave and little expense,' my grandfather had said on the few occasions when he deigned to give a reason. Apart from that they didn't talk much any more. They sat in their musty apartment near the Augarten and waited for it to be over. They were not an attractive sight any more. They both felt that they had grown too old, older than was right and

373

proper. 'Survived back then, waiting for ever now,' my grandfather is reported to have said once, but this remark was regarded by most of my family as a cynical invention attributed sometimes to my brother, sometimes to my younger cousin.

All efforts to get them to move to a retirement home were thwarted by their joint and insuperable obstinacy. There was a good residential home in Laufbergergasse, and it wouldn't be far for them to go from there to the Meierei to play cards. My father and Aunt Ka had been to see it several times, they'd secretly put my grandparents down for it, and finally a two-roomed apartment there fell vacant, 'a nice little place with a view,' my father said. But at some point the secret so carefully kept by my father and Aunt Ka – and the snag was its secrecy – had of course come out. My father and Aunt Ka had hoped that once the plan to move them was far enough advanced my grandparents would resign themselves to their fate out of sheer apathy, but they had been mistaken. In fact the two old people had simply been waiting to find some reason for refusing to go on moral rather than practical grounds. A doorstep could be removed, the lighting improved, the beds changed round. But there was no getting away from the fact that the Catholic welfare organisation ran the home. My grand-mother threatened to throw herself 'out of a top floor window into a font of holy water' on the very first day; my grandfather, on the other hand, kept calm. 'Live with the Christians?' he asked, as if amazed at the idea, and even laughed a little before making his typical dismissive gesture. 'The Christians? Oh, go on with you!'

When someone finally suggested the Jewish residential home for the elderly, he was beside himself with fury in his own turn. 'What, live with that devout lot who talk about Theresienstadt all day?' he said indignantly. 'We're staying here!' My grandmother entirely agreed with him, as she very seldom did in her last years. She got quite enough of *them* playing bridge with them, she muttered, and the family gave up the attempt.

If less pressure had been put on them to go into a home, they would never have thought of the cremation idea, said my younger cousin reproachfully later. It was painful to him that he couldn't bring a rabbi to our grandfather's grave. But there it was, and the family and their friends had to accept it, even if it was difficult for many of them, including the delegation of bridge-playing ladies who had been his life-long friends. What Aunt Gustl had against cremation remains a mystery. My father claimed that converts are always the worst, more papal than the Pope. Long ago, when Gustl converted, said my father, cremation had been forbidden to Catholics just as it was to Jews. The fact that cremation was now permitted, and had been for several years, said my father, who had clearly looked into the subject, for he had never been noted as an expert on funerary customs before, is rejected by many Catholics as a new fashion. 'They insist on tradition,' said my father, with a malicious laugh. 'Would you expect Gustl of all people to be a reformer?'

For obvious reasons, Vickerl Weisskopf had to be the first to leave. He cast an exploratory glance at the line of people that had formed in front of my grandmother, and decided to put off expressing his condolences until later. He thought that once she had drunk a small vodka and had a few egg and chicken-liver sandwiches in front of her, he could find a more compassionate moment than here and now, when she was standing unsteadily outside the crematorium, looking as if she wasn't quite sure what all these people wanted. The sun had come out from behind the clouds a few minutes ago and was shining right in her face. That can't be comfortable, thought Vickerl Weisskopf, who noticed such things, she probably couldn't even see who was standing in front of her talking to her. He would bend down and whisper the usual things into her ear later, in the Red Saloon. There, he could put his hand on her arm, murmur something soothing and pour her another drink, that would be personal and attentive. He just had to get back. He couldn't rely on his staff, but he had always been too good-humoured to fire anyone. He knew the Red Saloon wouldn't yet be ready as he wanted it, or if it was then his waiters had been neglecting the first lunch-time guests. He wasn't sure if he had tasted the last dish of egg salad or not in all the haste of his departure. He quickly left the Central Cemetery, and this time the Number 71 tram came at once. When he was in it he thought sadly of my grandfather, who would certainly have liked to be there too, because he had always loved sitting in the Weisskopf in the morning with chopped liver, chopped egg and a small coffee with a drop of milk in front of him, although it had been a constant source of conflict between them that Vickerl brewed Santora coffee, not Arabia brand. Perhaps I ought to change after all, thought Vickerl Weisskopf, and for a moment tears came to his eyes, but then he remembered the boss of Arabia Coffee with his mink collar, the kind a gay might wear, and he quickly dismissed the idea again.

My brother and his friends were not sure what to do next. They shifted from foot to foot, smoked and waited. My father had gone briefly up to them, but did not deign to look at the friends and spoke only to my brother himself. He hoped my brother knew that a table had been reserved in the Weisskopf, my father reminded him, and he owed it to his grandmother to be there.

'Can I bring them along?' asked my brother, who was always civil and never insolent when talking to his father, and he indicated his friends. My father cast a brief glance at the herd of horse-blankets and said, 'Do as you think right.' And so now none of them knew what to do. On the one hand, their convictions demanded that they should never sit at a table with 'old Nazis' – and that was what they took certain members of the Schneuzl Sports Club to be, while there were some who were obviously too young for that, so could only be neo-Nazis at the most. On the other hand, right-thinking people should assert themselves and stay on, in order to be in the majority. They were curious, too. And then again, the occasion might offer an opportunity for indignant contradiction if there was stupid talk, as my brother hoped rather than assumed there would be.

While my father went back to his mother, who was still standing there in the sun, looking lost and shaking hands, my brother said casually, 'He looks very like my grandfather.'

His friends stared at my father.

'When he's really old he'll be the image of him,' said my brother.

'And in other ways?' asked one of his friends.

'In other ways?' repeated my brother. 'My grandfather? Communist Party member, always renewed his membership right from the summer of forty-five until last month.'

But back in the tram the conversation reverted to football: could my brother remember this or that game of his father's, had he been there, who was selected for the team, what about other details? And there was no more talk about my grandfather. As usual my brother was slightly annoyed that the talk was all about football, but on the other hand some reflected glory was cast on him, as my father's son and their informant, for unfortunately he really knew hardly anything about my grandfather and what had actually happened to him in the war.

The old Schneuzls insisted on going to the Weisskopf. They didn't have much else to do. 'It's right and proper,' old Frau Schneuzl murmured calmly, and the Councillor mentioned that from all he heard the Weisskopf had no steps or difficult thresholds, so his wheelchair could easily get around in it.

What the Councillor kept to himself was that he had been waiting for decades to get into the legendary Weisskopf, said to be a haunt of left-wingers, as well as a place to which artists resorted, a hotbed of crazy ideas and theories. In his youth in the twenties Councillor Schneuzl had spent a few months in Paris, and although at the time he had come home totally confused, not to say shocked, and had rapidly taken refuge in the career preordained for him as a lawyer in the service of the state, he was soon thinking of those days nostalgically.

A little like Paris, that was how he had always imagined the Weisskopf, a restaurant full of chain-smoking emigrants and half-naked women. In his days practising as a lawyer the restaurant had several times swum into his ken, but not for any really dreadful crimes, as he now remembered, although he had once seen it far more sternly, it was more just the peccadilloes of young men operating on the borders of legality, harmless Viennese would-be Capones. With his position and his origins, of course it had been impossible for him simply to walk into the Weisskopf for a cup of tea out of curiosity – well, think of it, in this city everyone knows everyone else. But now that he was an old man in a wheelchair, no one could really think ill of him for going to the wake of a distant acquaintance, and strictly speaking most of those who *would* once have thought ill of him had gone on ahead long ago anyway, and were now with the Lord.

Their son Dr Schneuzl was far from enthusiastic. In well-chosen words, he reminded his parents how shamefully he had been driven out of the Schneuzl Sports Club, and how some of his adversaries of that time were now certainly on their way to the Weisskopf too. He didn't want to go, he began, but he was interrupted by the displeased shaking of heads. His parents had always thought that managing a tennis club was no proper occupation for their son. For a long time they had hoped he would take up the trumpet again, or throw himself into working for charities, the kind of thing that was usual in their circles. Finally they had accepted the tennis club as an eccentricity, but when their son left it because of some trouble with recalcitrant sportsmen they were very pleased. They considerately kept that from him, and civilly expressed their regret. But now they didn't want to hear any more about it. 'You're not hiding from . . . from some kind of tennis players, are you, Kurt?' asked the Councillor, annoyed, and left all the despicable epithets appropriate to those tennis players hovering unspoken in the air. And his wife, who usually protected her highly-strung son from his father, also thought that there was no question about it. Which deserved to come first, those proletarians or proper behaviour to the family of the deceased? 'One does not acknowledge such people,' she informed her son, referring to his enemies. 'One passes a friendly greeting and looks straight through them.' That decided it. Dr Schneuzl was put out, but refrained from any rejoinder. However, as he hailed a taxi, he was wondering whether this was an opportunity to learn something about pride and appearing invulnerable. He had long experience of making himself look on the bright side.

Aunt Ka acquitted herself heroically in making sure that the boss of Arabia Coffee was not invited to the wake. It had been no secret from the mink-clad boss that after the simple ceremony, which came to its climax when the small casket was lowered into the ground amidst a few Oohs and Aahs from the bridge-playing ladies, the occasion was to end on such a note, for several people had been told the way and given an address. The mink-clad boss and his wife were still waiting to offer my grandmother their condolences, but it would soon be their turn, and then my father, wry-faced, would tell them the address and issue a polite invitation. And then it would be too late. Aunt Ka knew her brother-in-law. She could tell from looking at them exactly what he and his brother, her husband, thought of the boss of Arabia Coffee, but those two would never manage to keep him away from the Weisskopf. They would say afterwards, shrugging, that it had been nice of him to come, after all, he'd earned a vodka and an egg sandwich. But if someone else could prevent it they'd be thankful, as Aunt Ka knew. Since she was the only member of the family who had a gift for performing uncomfortable and embarrassing tasks, Aunt Ka took a deep breath, went up to the Arabia couple and embarked on a long monologue in a high-pitched voice, opening her eyes very wide, pursing her lips, and several times apologising as she patted their forearms with her fingertips. Drawing on the basic concepts of 'only close family and friends', as well as 'limited seating, a great many elderly people', Aunt Ka in her inimitable way constructed long and involved sentences, and no one could resist her downcast and apologetic expression, not even the Arabias. 'Of course,' boomed the husband, and his wife twittered along with him, of course they had never for a moment thought of intruding on the family circle, as it happened they had an urgent appointment on the other side of town anyway, they ought to have been on their way in the car by now; they were already looking around in panic, they finally shook my grandmother's hand, and then fled in their new Mercedes.

They said nothing all the way down Simmering high street. Then the boss muttered something about 'poor organisation' and 'should have hired a larger restaurant', it was no way to behave. His wife nodded. The deceased hadn't been very well organised himself, the boss continued, always chasing about from coffee-house to coffee-house, wasting time because he never went the sensible way to the nearest, first to Wipplingerstrasse, then to Josefstadt, then back into the city, no normal person would have done it that way. If he was reprimanded he had always contended that there was method in his madness, there was a certain

380

right time for every coffee-house, he used to claim, as if it made any difference whether they ordered coffee and paper napkins early in the morning or at midday. Poor organisation probably ran in the family, added the boss, still thirsting for vengeance, that was why none of them had ever amounted to much. Even a talent for football wasn't enough for a man's whole life, after all. 'He knew how to sell things, though,' added the boss, softening again, 'the Jews are good at that.' The boss's wife replied that she fancied they had been asked not to come to the Weisskopf out of consideration for themselves. After all, one knew what kind of a restaurant it was, and they would probably have been dreadfully bored among all those moribund mourners. 'The daughter-in-law meant well,' said the boss's wife firmly, 'she knew a wake like that is not what we're used to.' Her husband thought it very likely. Suddenly in a better temper, he suggested taking his wife to the Belvedere for a glass of champagne. 'I mean, what else are we to do with the day, darling?' he boomed, stepping on the gas.

'Are you going to the Weisskopf too?' the unknown old man asked Frau Erna's back. It was still shaking, although she had offered her condolences without stammering. She turned and looked at him aghast, her face covered with red blotches. She murmured something about not knowing the family circle so very well, and the old man, whom no one knew at all, nodded. 'I'm not going either,' he said, 'these things are always so sad at first, and then it all rings so hollow when everyone gets drunk and merry.' Frau Erna looked at him again, less nervously this time, more surprised. Then she smiled, although she still had tears in her eyes and blotches on her cheeks.

'I pedicured his feet,' she said at last, as if in explanation, but really as a way of thanking him, because she felt he had spoken to her in such a kind, friendly way. But the old man misunderstood. 'Now, for the funeral, you mean?' he asked.

'Oh goodness, no, no,' cried Frau Erna, with a horrified laugh. 'No, in the old days!'

Then the old man laughed too and smoothed over the embarrassing misunderstanding with ease, for which Frau Erna admired him very much, and he said yes, he'd always been elegant and well-groomed, you could say he thought almost too much of his appearance. Oh, very elegant, Frau Erna agreed eagerly, so elegant and such an educated man, a real gentleman. He had dropped out of sight for a while during the war, he had only once been to her in the war, for a septic toenail. Frau Erna's country accent became thicker as she talked, because she was still all upset, and because since retiring she hadn't paid so much attention to her elocution. He knew about that too, said the old man, yes, a bad foot at the end of forty-four. 'Something fell on it,' said the man slowly, as he remembered, and then it was inflamed.

'Oh, have you known him all that time?' asked Frau Erna happily, and the old man nodded. By now they had reached the Number 71 tram stop, where some of the other guests were already waiting. The old man nodded to the former caretaker and Fredi Hals, but did not join them. Nor did Frau Erna, who was now glancing shyly at the others. 'Do you know about his illness?' she finally whispered timidly. 'Did he suffer?'

'I'm sorry,' said the old man, shaking his head, 'it's ages since I was last in touch with him.'

When the tram came they both got in and sat side by side at the back. To outward appearance it now looked as if they had come together. Frau Erna was relieved, immensely relieved, for the situation could have been difficult on the way back too. This way, however, everything seemed to have gone smoothly. She allowed herself to feel a little proud now, and cast a cautious glance at her companion. 'He often came to see me after the war, with his boy,' the old man was saying, staring thoughtfully into the distance.

'Came out to see me in Kagran. I had a lot of fruit and vegetables out there in the old days.'

'Oh, he brought the boy to see me once, so he did,' said Frau Erna, laughing, 'oh, dear me, were his feet all bruised!' The old man looked at her again, smiled and said, 'No wonder, a footballer, and what a footballer too!' So they went together as far as Schwarzenbergplatz. Here the old man plucked up his courage and asked if he could offer the lady a coffee, not in the Schwarzenberg itself, but he knew a really nice espresso bar quite close . . . Frau Erna nodded, quite surprised at herself, and then she threw all her reservations overboard and said jokingly, 'But only if they brew Arabia brand there!' And she smiled all over her face like a young girl.

The former caretaker stayed close to Fredi Hals. He had been impressed by the majestic way in which Fredi walked into the crematorium at the head of his employees, preceded only by the men carrying the wreath. However, as soon as the wreath was in position, and he had adjusted the bow himself, Fredi was on his way around the hall, here bending down with concern in his face to the widow, then telling off his adolescent son under his breath for swinging his legs, there shepherding his employees into their pews in an order of precedence visible only to himself. After the ceremony it was the same: Fredi was everywhere. The former caretaker, who had known him back then, thought he understood that Fredi was taking the burden off the family, was organising and arranging everything so that they could grieve in peace. He felt respect and admiration, so at a suitable moment he went up and introduced himself. 'Why, of course!' cried Fredi. 'I remember you!' The former caretaker flinched slightly and doubtfully bowed his head. Would Fredi Hals be tactless enough to utter the word 'caretaker'? 'I remember you,' cried Fredi again, shaking his hand vigorously, and suddenly winking as hard as if he had something wrong with his eyes. 'Didn't you once have that knife shop in Löwengasse?'

That was Fredi Hals; he knew everything and everyone. And so the former caretaker kept close to Fredi on the way to the Weisskopf. He sat just behind him on the tram. In the middle of a conversation with his wife, Fredi suddenly turned and bombarded him with the surprising information that he, the caretaker, had done a great deal of good back when my grandfather's talented son didn't want to be a motor mechanic. The caretaker was all confused. He didn't really know, he stammered, but he couldn't imagine that he would have been consulted over such a matter at all . . . 'Oh, go on with you, what do you mean, consulted?' cried Fredi impatiently, flapping both hands. 'You said what needed saying: Yids don't make good motor mechanics!' The caretaker was at a loss, but he didn't contradict Fredi any more. First, it was difficult to get a word in edgeways with Fredi anyhow, and second, he wasn't going to destroy the good reputation he obviously enjoyed here, though heaven knew why, not unless he had to. So he let himself be carried along in the wake of kind, energetic, quirky Fredi Hals, who was soon treating him like one of his large crowd of friends. And so the former caretaker sat in the Red Saloon of the Weisskopf among all those people; he was even sitting right next to a councillor's wife, drinking vodka, trying the chicken liver and feeling good. He was hardly bothered that the son, the former footballer, obviously didn't recognise him. 'Although I often helped him out with his German words,' he told the Councillor's wife beside him; he was already slightly tipsy. 'Why, at first he didn't even know the word for a rubbish bin!'

Aunt Gustl was almost forcibly sent home. My father and my uncle, as if they had drawn self-assurance from Aunt Ka's victory over the Arabias, took her arms, one each side of her. Like a black beetle pinned down by its thin little arms and legs, the otherwise dumpling-shaped Aunt Gustl wriggled between the two of them, and was carried a few steps further on.

'You have to understand, Auntie,' said my father with all the emphasis of which he was capable, 'this is more than she can stand.'

'Do it for her,' commanded my uncle, so sarcastic that he almost bit his tongue off. 'Do it for her sake, please.'

'She's very ill and confused,' said my father, hating himself for the lie. 'You saw that she doesn't know what's going on any more.'

'And then she sometimes gets aggressive,' threatened my uncle, 'and it really would be better not to provoke her.'

They couldn't put it more clearly, civility forbade, and anyway they had never known anything in detail. Aunt Gustl sobbed like an enraged crocodile. 'My brother,' she wailed, 'my only brother.' Later, my father said that at that moment he felt like saying, 'You might have thought of that earlier!' and then my uncle always grumbled discontentedly, 'If only you *had* said so!'

'I'll find your son and he'll take you home,' my father said instead, looking inquiringly at my uncle, who nodded, in confirmation that he still had a tight hold on Gustl's arm. My father let go, went up to Nandl, drew him a couple of paces away from the skinny Baroness, whose eyes were almost popping out of her head with curiosity, and spoke to him softly. Nandl just nodded mechanically. It would later be claimed in my family that he had looked 'rather diminished' for the first time that day. Finally my father clapped him on the shoulder, reinforcing his remarks, and said with assumed jollity, 'And how's life otherwise, Nandl? Everything fine?' Nandl just nodded, muttered something and then led his mother away. She was sobbing and weeping, and only too well aware of the pitying glances of the other mourners. Poor woman, they would all be thinking, so Aunt Gustl hoped, the only one of his sisters still alive. That wasn't quite true, Gustl was just the only one present; the other four had scattered all over the world long ago and had never come back again. Poor woman, everyone would be thinking, her brother dead and her sister-in-law too confused to recognise her any more. It must be terrible, people would be thinking, or so Aunt Gustl hoped, terrible when the only person anywhere near so close to him, the one with whom you could have mourned your loss, the only person to have known him anywhere near as long as a sister, is already totally senile. What a scene, recapitulated Aunt Gustl as she hid behind a huge handkerchief in the taxi, and she could almost have chortled. Instead, she sniffed noisily, and when the Baroness, who had climbed into the dark back of the car with her, laid a hand on her thigh she pushed it off. 'What do you know about it?' she hissed, and the Baroness flinched away.

Towards the end of the ceremony Aunt Gustl had already been surreptitiously looking around, for in her opinion she ought to be one of the first to condole with the widow because of her close relationship. Where will they stand, she wondered, as the dreadful machinery under the coffin began to hum as a sign that it was about to swallow up my grandfather. Probably outside, thought Aunt Gustl, for the hall with its rows of seats and narrow central aisle wasn't a suitable place. She stood up. Thereupon everyone else stood up too, as if it were the right course of action when the coffin sinks out of sight, although there are no hard and fast rules for these new-fangled things. As the last bars of music died away she watched out of the corner of her eye as her nephews helped their mother, the widow, carefully out of her seat and led her towards the exit. All the mourners courteously stayed put, heads bent, and let my grandmother take her time. Five seconds less courteously than all the rest, Aunt Gustl set foot in the central aisle. However, she was not the first to get outside, since those who had been sitting further back automatically had the advantage. She had to stand in line, although a vulgar-looking woman with a bright red face did move aside at once to let her go first. But only that one woman, no one else made way for her. Gustl had a gap of half a minute to bridge, and half a minute can be a long time. She hid behind her huge handkerchief and made muffled sounds. When it was her turn at last, she let the handkerchief drop, looked up as if startled, spread her arms wide, and in a voice which perfectly mingled the strident and the hollow, as she herself thought, in that wonderful tearful, grieving voice she uttered a single word. 'Frieda!'

My grandmother flinched in horror. She raised her handbag in both hands like a shield to protect her, took a long step backwards, and called pitifully for her sons. My father and my uncle supported her, one at each elbow. Aunt Gustl took another step towards her, my grandmother raised the handbag yet higher until it was level with her breast, and retreated again.

'Who is she?' she snapped, looking from one son to the other. 'Who's this person?'

'It's Gustl, Aunt Gustl,' whispered my father, embarrassed, while my uncle stood still, almost smiling. 'Your sister-in-law, Father's sister, Gustl.'

'I don't know her,' stated my grandmother firmly, and narrowed her eyes. 'I don't know her, never saw her in my life. Make her go away! Shalom!'

First Aunt Gustl froze where she stood, then she slowly lowered her outspread arms. For a historic moment, she herself didn't know what to do next. Finally she retreated two steps to the left, moved to my father's side, took his forearm and said, with concern, 'I'm so sorry.' My father awkwardly pressed her hand, and then she walked around him and my grandmother, keeping her distance, approached my uncle from the other side, said the same to him, and added in a whisper, 'I had no idea it was so bad!' Finally she stepped aside and waited for everyone to set out for the Weisskopf. When she was banned from the party, however, like a naughty child being sent home, when she had to go without the vodka, egg, chopped chicken liver and all the company, she gave vent to her fury in shrill and steady howling. And for my grandfather that was surely the high point of his funeral.

Back in the car it seemed to my grandmother that the cemetery would never come to an end. They drove and drove, and outside the car the long wall moved on and on, broken only now and then by brief patches of colour, stalls selling flowers and wreaths. My grandmother knew that rather than seeing it. She had cataracts, and the whole world was hidden behind a veil of grey. She felt comfortable with that grey partition between her and the world, she had always liked to keep her distance. She could tell that the sun was shining. The air smelled of autumn already, but the light coming in to her from outside was still summery light, almost glaring. She was exhausted, as if she had something very difficult behind her, but just at the moment she didn't want to think what it might have been. At the same time she felt content, more content than she had been for a long time. Outside the wall still went on and on, as if all Vienna were one huge cemetery. The thought made her giggle. She had got into the habit of giggling only at the very end of her life, it was about the last thing she ever learned to do. She had always despised giggling girls. Her cousins, those sturdy, big-bosomed dirndl-wearing girls, had giggled all the time, morning and evening alike, and that was one of the things that had shown her she was quite different. She had gone to Freudenthal and learned how to use a typewriter and do accounts and take dictation, so as to rise in the world as far as possible. And then they didn't giggle any more when she left the village on her sophisticated fiancé's arm, their little pink mouths had dropped open. While she merely perceived the light from outside now, and paid no more attention to the cemetery wall, she saw inside her a brief, bright picture of the landscape through which she had travelled then with her fiancé, the wide Moravian fields, a few low hills, she was leaving it all for ever when she went away, away from the village and the farmers and her giggling cousins. Because they had wanted her fiancé for themselves, those silly lambs, they had joined forcefully in the outcry of the true believers, the lamentations of her aunts and her mother, who had swiftly changed her mind when she got the first pictures of Katzi, her first grandchild, in those lovely little dresses with the expensive ribbons.

It wasn't always easy with him, she thought, her mind dwelling on her husband, she wasn't quite sure why she was thinking about that, for she had already forgotten that a few days ago she wrote 'R. died' in her pocket diary from the savings bank, underlining it twice and adding an exclamation mark. For the day before, the diary had said 'Meierei – bridge', and for the day after it said, 'Bridge – Meierei, F. owes 15 schillings'. Just that one day said, 'R. died'! It wasn't always easy with him, he was wild, and he wasn't a faithful husband, but as for those said to be faithful husbands, well, she wouldn't have wanted them if they were handed to her on a plate. She thought of Councillor Schneuzl, he was one of them, Catholic through and through, bigoted and boring, although her husband thought highly of him. He had probably provided help some time a thousand years ago, her husband had always needed help, he had done very little by himself. But he was a good father, he hadn't put himself to much trouble but he'd loved the children, yes, he had. 'He didn't put himself to much trouble,' said my grandmother reproachfully to my father, who was sitting beside her, and my father said, 'Yes, that's right, Mother.'

She looked at her hands. They were covered with the liver spots of old age, ugly. A person ought not to grow so old. She wore her wedding ring on her left hand, which was unusual, but she had always worn it there because you ruin any ring on your right hand doing housework. And she'd never taken off her wedding ring, not in fifty-nine years. They sometimes took it off her in hospital, using soap and water, it stuck so fast, but otherwise she always wore it. I'm sure he didn't always wear his, she thought, making a peevish face, no doubt he made himself out a bachelor to his little girlfriends. Never mind. On her right hand, on special occasions, she wore a ring with a smooth, square, black stone in it. It had an ornate gold setting, reddish gold, slightly reminiscent of a tiny wrought-iron garden fence. Golden curlicues, very old-fashioned, she thought. He had given it to her right at the start, even before they were married, and she had thought it showy at the time. Now, in among the wrinkles and the liver spots, it looks good, she thought, takes your mind off them. She had grown into that showy ring. He wanted to impress me, she thought, wanted me to think he was rolling in money. And I'm afraid I did, at first, but that's not why I took him. I took him because he was so amusing. And he was amusing too, at least at first. She sighed. My father asked, 'Everything all right, Mother?'

'He could be very amusing, your father could,' she said. My father nodded reassuringly.

'Even when life wasn't amusing at all,' she said reproachfully. She thought of the black Persian lamb coat that he had given her to atone for one of his little indiscretions. Was it because of Fuchsi? Fuchsi, she thought, wrinkling her brow, if only his women had at least shown some style. I didn't have that fur coat long either, thought my grandmother, annoyed. She tried to think what had become of it. Probably went missing during the war. She thought again. Did I give it to Katzi? For Canada? No, she had one of her own, a present from that fat show-off Herbert. She thought some more. Something else stolen by Gustl? Oh, excuse *me*, she thought sarcastically, not stolen, of course, just taken away for safe keeping, and then unfortunately she forgot it had ever been handed over to her. She thought again. The car stopped. When the car door opened, a shower of sunlight fell on her. A hand descended from above, her younger son's hand. She took it and let him haul her up into the light, groaning. Then she remembered the fate of the magnificent Persian lamb coat, and she giggled. 'Do you know something?' she asked Vickerl Weisskopf, who was standing on the pavement next to my father. 'My son's birth was a precipitate delivery.'